WITHDRAWN

## About the Book

The sun's rays parch Juma as she leads her all male family toward the main village. Nothing and no one will stop her from becoming the chieftess' apprentice. So she ignores the heat. Everything will be better near the lake. But the fields that should sprout green by now lie bare, with precious soil cracked and dry. Even the lake, thought to be everlasting, dwindles.

Juma discovers that heat daemon Mubuntu is out of control and that the rain goddess is still sleeping. But only Netinu, the chieftess' son, believes her, and he seems more interested in courting her than in the welfare of the tribe.

With her dreams going up in flames, Juma prepares to battle the daemon and wake the goddess – and maybe, in the process, prove herself worthy of becoming chieftess.

## About the Author

Ever since she was born, Katharina Gerlach had her head in the clouds. She and her three younger brothers grew up in the middle of a forest in the heart of the Luneburgian Heather. After romping through the forest with imagination as her guide, the tomboy learned to read and disappeared into magical adventures, past times or eerie fairytale woods.

She never returned to Earth for long, although she managed to successfully finish training as a landscape gardener, study forestry and gain a PhD. But then, she discovered her vocation: storytelling and realized she'd have to write to make her dream of sharing her stories with others come true.

Katharina loves to write Fantasy, Science Fiction and Historical Novels for all age groups. At present, she is writing at her next project in a small house near Hildesheim, Germany, where she lives with her husband, three children and a dog.

Mehr Informationen:                    http://de.KatharinaGerlach.com

# Juma's Rain

## A Fantasy Romance Novel
### set in Stone Age Africa

*For Jane Juma, my Word Vision Goddaughter.*
*Thank you for lending me your name.*

# Katharina Gerlach

**Juma's Rain**
published by the Independent Bookworm, USA und D
This book is also available as eBook. It has been published in English and in German.
If you find any typos or formatting problems in this eBook, please contact the publisher (www.IndependentBookworm.de).

© 2015, all rights remain with the author
© 2015, cover art by Katharina Kolata
© 2015, title firegod by Hendry Iwanaga, Indonesien
© 2016, title model by BeautyStockPhoto, Shutterstock
© 2015, title backgrounds from Pixabay.com
© 2015, Paragraph divider by Katharina Kolata
copy-editor: Ethan James Clarke
printed On-Demand Publishing LLC, 100 Enterprise Way, Suite A200, Scotts Valley, CA 95066, USA, www.createspace.com

ISBN-13 978-3-95681-049-7

More Information on the Homepage:
http://www.IndependentBookworm.de

For my family:
Without you, I would have failed.

For Holly Lisle:
Without you, I would have remained ignorant.

For my dear readers:
Without you there'd be no reason to write.

# TABLE OF CONTENTS

## 1

THE SUN HAD BARELY RISEN above the horizon and the air already shimmered in the heat. Juma adjusted the kikoi on her shoulder. The long woven cloth, useful as a coat or a cover or a skirt, was the only protection from the sky's merciless glare as she walked single-file with her family through the red dust. The fabric rubbed on her sweaty body, and she was glad that she only wore a loincloth beneath it.

"Can't we go faster?" she asked her father. As the only woman of the family, it was her right to take the lead. However, her father knew the way much better, so she had allowed him to take her place. It was a little embarrassing, but getting lost would have been worse. "We'll need ages at this pace." She suspected that it wasn't decent to show her impatience like this, but she had waited wishfully for this day. It marked the beginning of her training, and no one was better suited to become the chieftess's apprentice. Her heart sang. Soon, she would be more than the-girl-from-the-family-with-the-male-mother.

"If we go faster, we'll never make it." The voice of Tolobe, her eldest brother, carried from the back of the line. "We'd tire too soon."

Know-it-all, Juma thought, but refrained from scolding him for the unbidden answer. She didn't want to fight today; her happiness wouldn't allow it. Therefore, she trotted silently after her father.

Soon it became evident that her brother had been right. When they finally left the plains behind and walked through gently rolling hills, her throat was parched. The pebble in her mouth helped to keep her mouth moist which made the thirst bearable, although she grew thirstier with every step she took. The heat burned her feet through the sandals' soles. Stolidly she forced herself to put one foot in front of the other.

Hours passed as they walked through the yellow, withered grass in silence. Juma missed the usual green, and she also couldn't spot any animals. Rain was long overdue. In the distance, the holy mountain kissed the bright blue sky, but not even a tiny cloud hovered above it.

They reached the first fields. Juma recognized wheat, yam and black-eyed peas, but the crops were sparse and paltry compared to last year. If the rain didn't come soon, the tribe would find it hard to make ends meet this year. And the sun was still burning relentlessly from the sky even though evening wasn't far. Juma struggled now to match her father's steady pace. Red dust clung to the dark skin of his calves. How much longer was it anyway?

"Vanamate be praised, we're nearly there," Tolobe said. They were the first words spoken since his objection in the morning.

Her father didn't acknowledge his statement, but soon, the dusty path widened and merged with others. Families arrived from many directions, all headed toward the village. Their colorful clothes made a nice contrast with the dried earth. Children pointed excitedly at the herds of goats and sheep. The families merged, turning single streams of people into a river of color.

Not her family, though — they were warriors through and through.

Juma pressed her lips together. If only Mother had lived to lead us here.

As they walked up the last hill before the village, Juma pushed back a strand of her long, black curls and straightened. Dignity, she thought. After all, her mother had been the last chieftess's eldest daughter and should have been chieftess herself.

Juma bumped into her father, who had stopped at the hill's summit. She suppressed a shout of surprise. A gentle decline would take them to the plateau where the village's thatched adobe huts huddled around the oval Central Hall.

"I expect you don't want us to stay." Juma's father pulled his plain brown kikoi closer and pointed to the wide open gates in the fence of prickly bushes that surrounded the village and kept it safe from lions and other dangers.

"Hey, I want to see a couple of my friends." Lomba, Juma's second brother, stepped past her, but her father stopped him with a strong arm. His dark eyes looked stern but gentle.

"It's Juma's choice, and we have to accept her wishes. You can visit another time."

Lomba's mouth snapped shut, and he looked at Juma. Silently, she considered the situation, wishing she had done so before they left home. But her desire to start training had blinded her to this question. Of all the tribe's people, her family lived the farthest north. They had left home before the stars faded, and now the sun hung already low. If they left now, her family would have to travel all night. She knew just how much Lomba hated to walk that much. She lowered her head.

"I'm sure the villagers will welcome you."

A tiny smile tugged at the corners of her father's mouth as he turned toward the gates. Four inhabitants greeted the arriving travelers with millet beer, bread, and salt. Juma spat her pebble into her hand and popped it back in after she had swallowed the traditional welcome food.

"Will your family stay for the ceremony?" the fattest woman of the welcome committee asked Juma.

Juma nodded.

"You will have to share the guest hut with others. Too many will stay." The woman turned to Juma's father, who towered over her. She pointed to an oval hut close to the prickly thornbush fence. "Since you're without a wife, you may accompany your daughter to the trainee center."

"Isn't it exciting?" An unknown girl dug her elbow into Juma's ribs. Her short curly hair bounced around her face as if alive. "Two more years, and we'll be initiated. What will you train for?" Her generous lips curved into a wide smile.

Juma shrugged. The others would find out early enough that she intended to become the next chieftess, a place that should have been her mother's by right.

The girl didn't seem to mind Juma's silence. She grabbed her arm.

"I would love to become a herder. I love animals." She chatted on as she dragged Juma toward a building that was hardly more than a roof on stilts.

Juma frowned. What did the girl want with her? Why did she pull her along to the open house? It took her a while to realize that it must be the training center. All girls entered it without their families. Everywhere girls hugged their mothers. Juma would have loved to do the same. She bit back tears. There was no use crying over something that couldn't be changed. She glanced over her shoulder. Lomba was already talking to a broad-shouldered young man, but her father and Tolobe still followed her.

The girl at her side glanced back too, and moved her head closer to Juma's.

"Do you see that gorgeous young man behind us?" She giggled. "I wouldn't mind having him as a husband. Do you think we'll see him during the ceremony?"

"He's a warrior!" Juma's voice held all the contempt for her brother's choice of work she could muster.

The girl's voice dropped to a whisper. "My family would be shocked at first, but I'm sure that my parents would get used to the idea." She half turned and smiled at Tolobe.

His dark skin turned even darker. Juma had never seen her elder brother this embarrassed. His gaze fixed on Juma. He cleared his throat, placed his right hand over his heart, and bowed.

"Fare thee well, dear sister," he said, then turned and walked away as fast as he could.

The girl sighed and watched him go. "I didn't know he was your brother."

Strangely enough, Juma liked this girl who had pushed herself onto her. So, her comment turned out a lot friendlier than the situation demanded.

"We're here for training, not match-making." Juma turned back to the training center where thirty or forty girls milled around.

Reluctantly, the girl followed her example. "Wow, so many trainees!" Her eyes widened. "We'll be lost without friends. What luck that we already found each other."

She wants us to be friends? With only brothers around, Juma didn't have much experience with friends. She smiled tentatively, hoping to do the right thing.

The girl smiled back. "By the way, I'm Sundera."

"Juma. Jumatoa Botango." For a fleeting moment, Juma feared her heart would escape with the words, but aside from a slight wobble in her voice, nothing happened. Her first ever friend.

Sundera cocked her head. "That Botango?"

Juma didn't have to answer. Her cousin Kandra marched toward her, and her heart plummeted.

Towering over the girls that followed her, Kandra wore a multitude of necklaces, and her skirt was red. It must have taken ages to collect the tiny bugs needed for the color. Juma felt a pang of jealousy. She would have loved a skirt like that.

"Cousin, dearest." Kandra offered Juma the palm of her hand in the traditional greeting for low-caste tribe members. "Where is your mother? Oh, I forgot." A smile marred the otherwise perfect features of her face. "What will you train for? Warrior?"

The greeting hurt, but Juma had expected as much. During the few visits in her childhood, Kandra and she never got along. She clenched her teeth and walked past the chieftess's daughter with barely a nod as a greeting. If Mother hadn't followed Father to the tribe's north border, she'd be chieftess, and I'd be the one wearing expensive clothing.

"Her mother chose a warrior." Kandra's voice held nothing but contempt, and the girls surrounding her giggled. Juma's ears smarted, but she didn't know what to say. Of course she loved her father, but he was a man and—even worse—an ex-warrior. And her brothers were warriors too. Why couldn't they at least be hunters? Had the witch determined their talent like she did for the girls? She knew so little of the men's traditions.

Sundera's voice sounded stern. "A warrior is just as needed as the men taking care of the fields or the animals. You should be ashamed of yourself for making your own cousin feel miserable."

Kandra's jaw dropped. "Do you even know who you are talking to?"

"To a girl who's extremely rude to a family member." Sundera didn't step down.

Why is she taking my side? Juma wondered. She doesn't even know me. And Kandra outranks her enough to make life miserable for her. She marveled at Sundera's courage, especially since anger was written all over Kandra's face. Still, her cousin kept her temper and put her hand apologetically on Juma's shoulder.

"I am sorry, little one. I didn't mean to upset you. Take my heartfelt apology."

Juma looked up to see if she meant those words.

Kandra pointed to the only man in the crowd surrounding the training center, Juma's father. "Don't you want to pay your respect to the head of your family? I thought your mother taught you how to behave."

Juma gasped. Kandra was asking too much, and she knew it. The smug smile had returned. But Kandra's words and tone had been friendly and concerned. If Juma refused to follow traditions, she could forget about becoming chieftess even before training started. But traditionally, I would pay my respect to my mother, not to a man. Burning with shame, Juma walked back to where her father stood. He raised his eyebrows but didn't say a word when she put her arms around him.

"Thank you, dear father, for bringing me here." Juma hoped that her voice didn't give away the anger she felt. She was the niece of Chieftess Jakombe, she could follow embarrassing traditions without giving away her feelings.

The voices around her and her father died down. The eyes of the people burned holes in her bare back.

Her father patted her shoulder and kissed her hair like a mother would have done. It felt good despite the murmur of the people around them.

"It has been my pleasure to assist you. Step into your new life untroubled," he said.

So, he knew the ritual. For a second, Juma wondered how much about women's traditions her mother had taught him before she went with the gods. She let go and returned to Sundera without looking back, fighting the urge to throttle Kandra. Behind her, all the people seemed to talk at once. Juma could make out a few comments.

"Single parent, I assume." The voice sounded apologetic.

"The chieftess's brother-in-law," someone else said.

"Still… hugging a man in public…" The voice dripped with disdain.

Juma pressed her lips together and tried to ignore the sparkle in Kandra's eyes.

The other girls had already changed the subject. This time, they talked about the kind of husband they would choose when the time came. Thankful for their short attention span, Juma suppressed her embarrassment. She let their voices fade out and looked around to find out what she needed to do next.

Below her feet, the earth trembled ever so slightly, as if something had disturbed the Nameless' sleep. Juma looked around to see if anyone but her noticed. The crowd's chatter mixed with the bleating of the sheep and goats that were kept near the village's edge and there wasn't a single chicken or dog around. Had they felt the god shift too? People around her seemed unconcerned. When the earth didn't tremble again, Juma shook off her worry and concentrated on a woman with a wooden board who sorted through the trainees like a seed selector through grain.

"Why were you so embarrassed when you hugged your father? He seemed to enjoy it. Don't you like him?" Sundera took her arm again and pulled her toward the sorting woman.

"He's a man. Didn't you hear the comments?" Juma wondered why Sundera didn't seem to mind walking with a girl from an all-male family.

"My father's a man too. And if he'd take on a woman's duty upon the death of my mother, I'd love him even more."

"Well spoken," the sorting woman said. She looked at Juma and cocked her head. "You must be Jakombe's niece. You've got your mother's face. I'm Mama Lubeda." She opened her arms and pulled Juma into a bear hug against her wide chest. "Your mother was my best friend. I was delighted when I got word you'd come."

Juma fought for air, and Mama Lubeda let her go. "If anything is amiss, just let me know. I've put you in the biggest hut." Her gaze fell on Sundera. "I assume you'll want to go with her, right?"

Sundera nodded.

"There are two free beds on the left beside the door." Mama Lubeda smiled at them, patted Juma's shoulder, and turned to the next girl.

Juma and Sundera left the crowd of girls in search of their hut. It was easy to find. When they entered, they let their eyes adjust to the twilight inside. The round room was small and no fire burned in the central fireplace. A half-circle of benches stood close to the wall with three pegs over each bench. Obviously, these were the beds. Juma wondered how one would sleep on a raised platform. What if she fell out in her sleep? But she hung her bundle on a peg and laid her kikoi neatly folded on the bed to claim it.

Sundera had dropped her stuff in an untidy heap on the second bed. Now she stood at the door, waiting. "I just hope someone will snore."

"Why that?" Juma joined her.

"It would help me not to get homesick. My mother snores."

For the first time since her arrival, Juma laughed.

Juma had not visited the village much, but it was evident that Sundera had been here often. She dragged her new friend around, explained everything, and introduced her to everyone she knew. The sun dropped behind the horizon shortly after they left the hut, and it got darker by the minute.

An hour later, when Juma's head swirled with names, faces, and advice from countless people, she noticed that most people had left the village through the lakeside gate in the thornbush fence to a place where a bonfire burned.

"Let's get our kikois," Sundera said. "The ceremony will start any minute now, and it might get cold later."

They ran to their hut where they had left their colorful woolen capes. Their roommates had returned too. They took one look at Juma and ran off giggling. Juma's heart sank. After the relaxing time with her new friend, she had started to look forward to training. Well, she would have to get used to it. A chieftess probably didn't have many friends anyway. Wordlessly, she slung the kikoi around her shoulders and walked through the lakeside gate in the prickly thornbush fence as regally as she could with Sundera at her side.

Together, they followed the well-trodden path that led down to the lake, keeping the holy mountain's silhouette on their left. At a safe distance from the lake's reed belt, the bonfire's flames reached for the sky, the tribe members' dark shadows against the red glow.

It must have been a lot of work to gather so much dead wood and carry it here from the other side of the village, Juma thought.

Sundera nudged her to the right, where a small group of new trainees huddled beside Mama Lubeda. Juma wondered what they wanted to train for. When they joined the group, she realized that none of her roommates were there. Neither was Kandra. Then she remembered that Kandra was nearly a year older than her. Maybe the others were from the same age-group.

Soft drumming made her nerves vibrate. Like heartbeats. The thumping rang through the night, calling the new trainees, their families, and any other visitor or tribe member.

**2**

*A* RED SHAPE FLICKERED BEHIND the growing crowd. Juma shook her head. She must have misjudged the distance. Surely, it had been a spark from the fire.

A low voice joined the drum, singing about birth and death, new beginnings and endings, fire and water. Juma closed her eyes and allowed her body to swing with the rhythm. The air was cool and carried the scent of water and greenery over from the distant lake. Once in a while, she felt Sundera's sweaty upper arm bump into hers, but she didn't open her eyes until the music ended.

The chieftess stood beside the fire with her arms raised to the sky. Her words got lost in the thundering of the drum, but Mama Lubeda's voice reached Juma's ear.

"She'll call us any minute now. Get in line."

Juma watched Mama Lubeda arrange the new trainees in pairs. She placed Juma and Sundera at the front of the group. The drum fell silent.

"Let us now welcome the future of our tribe," the chieftess said. "Rest assured, dear mothers. Mama Lubeda will take great care of them, as she did with countless other trainees."

A couple of people clapped their hands as the line of trainees began to move. More and more fell in. Juma felt like a piece of jewelry, displayed for all to admire but worthless in itself. Why did she have to be at the front? Sundera had to pull her or she would have retreated. A voice in the back of her mind reminded her that she'd better get used to this kind of attention if she wanted to become the next chieftess. She straightened herself and held her head higher.

Still, her heart bled. She had hoped for a friendlier welcome from her relatives. Her aunt, the chieftess, hadn't even bothered to greet her in private before the ceremony.

A man elbowed his way to the front of the crowd. His skin was lighter than any Juma had ever seen, a little like the pale wood of the Koto tree. The most stunning feature about him was his hair. It was bright red. Juma couldn't take her eyes off the man. He fascinated her in a morbid way. She had the feeling his soul might be as dark as his skin was light. Before she had to turn her head to watch him, he was gone; winked out like the flame of a candle. Juma frowned.

"Did you see the red-haired man just now?" she asked.

"Red hair? No one's got red hair." Sundera shook her head. "Better concentrate on the ceremony." She bowed deeply to the chieftess. Juma followed her example as fast as she could. Warm hands touched her shoulders and pulled slightly. She straightened.

"Welcome, trainee Botango." The chieftess pursed her lips and winked. That was so like her aunt. Consoled, Juma winked back and walked to a bench where Mama Lubeda already waited.

"Welcome trainee Jandeba." The chieftess pulled up Sundera and nodded to her. Then she went to the next trainee. She greeted every single one by name, nodded and moved on. Juma let her gaze wander the crowd. Standing right beside her brother, the red-haired man was there again. Or was he? This man's skin was charcoal black, darker even than that of her father. He couldn't possibly be the same man, could he? But it was equally impossible that there were two men with hair the color of fire. She nudged Sundera.

"Do you see him?" She indicated the direction with a small nod, since she didn't want to draw the man's attention.

A smile spread over Sundera's face. "Thanks for pointing him out to me. I thought you'd disapprove."

"Disapprove?" Juma's eyebrows shot up.

"Of my crush on your brother."

Juma's jaw fell. Sundera fancied her brother? Was that the reason she wanted to be her friend? Then she remembered that Sundera had followed her before Tolobe had shown up. She sighed with relief. So what about the attraction? She didn't mind.

Sundera pointed at the chieftess. "Look, she's done."

Juma looked for the man again, but he had vanished once more. Now, had Sundera seen him or not? Her reaction hadn't been very helpful. What about Tolobe? Had he noticed the man? Juma looked at her brother, whose gaze was fixed on Sundera.

Juma shook her head. It seemed they were both love-stricken. What a start. The girl that was first-place contender for a best friend was falling in love with her brother. That couldn't possibly work out.

The chieftess stepped back, and a shriveled old crone walked toward the fire. She supported herself on a stick adorned with feathers, teeth, and dried herbs that identified her as the village witch. Despite her age, her teeth shone white in her face as she smiled at the girls.

Juma bent forward. She'd never seen the witch before.

"I am sorry to keep you from the feast a little longer, but this is more than the usual welcome ceremony." The old woman spoke with a raspy voice. "Every year, Vanamate, Mother of the Tribes and Keeper of the Water, gets tired and goes to sleep. For one moon or two, she rests from her arduous work encircled by a ring of fire to allow her plants to withdraw. For one moon or two, Mubuntu, the Lord of Fire, plays tricks on her children. We do not complain; we do not call for her, she needs her rest, and so do the plants.

"But this year is different. Never in my life, and it has been a long and blessed one, has Vanamate rested for six months. So, sing with me the old call for help. I cannot do it alone." The old woman raised her stick.

The drum set in, and the witch sang the first notes of a song Juma had never heard. The elders joined the song immediately; the younger people took a while longer. Juma concentrated on the melody. It was haunting and reminded her of a lonely child's cry. She merged her voice with the others, allowing the song to lift her heart. Somewhere at the periphery of her vision, she saw the red-haired man move unnoticed through the crowd, closer to the fire.

The air began to tingle and pressed in on her. A wave of music carried her upwards, and the world around her glowed in unearthly colors. Juma stared in disbelief as the ground vanished below. She didn't dare to stop singing. The voices of her tribe still filled her ears. Am I having a vision? She expected her heart to race but it thumped in the steady rhythm of the drums while she floated toward the sky. A line, as thin as a woolen thread, reached from her belly to the world below her. The bonfire was barely more than a flicker of light in the distance when she reached a ring of fire. A beautiful woman sat inside, crying softly in her sleep. Her tears evaporated before they managed to seep through the low flames.

Awed, Juma stared at the goddess Vanamate. Why was she still asleep? Tentatively, she reached over to touch the goddess. She didn't wake, but Juma's fingers got wet.

Then the drum stopped, and with it the song. Juma was back with her tribe beside the bonfire. She blinked and tried to adjust to the sudden change. Her eyes settled on the village witch who lay like a felled tree on the ground in front of the fire. The red-haired man stood near her. His hands glowed like coals as he reached for a young man close by. The young man collapsed, jerking and twitching. Juma's jaw dropped when she realized who the red-haired stranger must be.

"Mubuntu," she whispered.

"Netinuuuuuuuu!" the chieftess's wailed through the silence from the side of the circle. She came running and knelt beside the young man on the ground. The red-haired stranger crouched opposite her and pressed his pale fingers against the young man's chest, watching his legs twitch. The heat-dæmon looked up and grinned but didn't take his hand off the young man. The twitching of the legs became worse, the chieftess's wailing louder.

Without thinking about it, Juma pushed through the people in front of her and rushed at Mubuntu. She reached for him, and a handful of water flew from her fingers, hissing on the heat-dæmon's skin as it evaporated. Where had that come from? The man howled in pain and vanished.

The rest of the water splashed into the young man's face. He spluttered and licked the wetness from his lips. Then he opened his eyes and looked at Juma.

"Who are you?" His voice sounded sore, but now that his face had lost the painful expression, he was the most handsome man Juma had ever seen.

"Thank Vanamate, you're better." The chieftess pulled him up and hugged him.

Juma retreated and no one took any notice. Everybody was busy hustling around the witch and the chieftess's son. Juma stared at her hands. Had she really chased the heat dæmon away? With water from an imaginary visit to the sky? The traces of wetness on her fingers suggested this. *How did I manage to get Vanamate's tears from my vision into reality? Or was it more than a vision? In that case, I must really have been with Vanamate. Why doesn't she wake and leave her circle of fire to bring rain to the world?* Lost in thought, Juma walked back to the hut she would live in from now on. She didn't feel like celebrating any more.

The next morning, the chieftess walked into the hut just as the girls washed and dressed. Juma was still trying to cope with the fact that she had seen two gods. She didn't notice her aunt until she felt her hands on her shoulders.

"Thank you for helping Netinu. I told Mama Lubeda that you can skip field work and join the water-bearers right away as a reward."

Juma was dumbstruck. Jakombe had noticed? And now, she considered carrying water a reward? For that, Juma could have stayed at home. She opened her mouth to protest, but the chieftess was faster.

"You don't need to thank me, dear. Come and visit us soon, will you?" Without waiting for an answer, she turned and walked away. Open-mouthed, Juma looked at Sundera.

Her friend sighed. "Lucky you. I'll have to weed and water plants, while you get to cool your feet in the lake."

"Don't they examine us to see what we're good at?" Juma asked.

One of the older girls shrugged and said, "Mama Lubeda will talk to each of you in turn. Until then, you'll do the work you've been assigned to do. Apprenticeship is no bed of Muuti flowers." She slung her kikoi over her shoulder and walked out of the hut followed by her friends. Sundera and Juma looked at each other.

"I guess this will be everyday life now." Sundera grabbed her kikoi and hooked her arm into Juma's. Together they left the hut in search of Mama Lubeda.

After breakfast, the families of the new trainees said their farewells. Juma was glad her father had decided to leave earlier. Surely Kandra would have embarrassed her again had he still been there. Juma took a pail and a grass ring, and followed a group of older girls to the lake. They walked a narrow path through bushes and grass as tall as Juma.

"Careful, there are vipers in the grass." One of the girls smiled at Juma.

Another girl frowned. "Don't talk to her."

"Why not?" the first girl asked.

"Kandra says she's too much like a boy. No wonder, her whole family is male. Did you see her hug her father?" The girls giggled.

A pang of pain shot through Juma's heart. She had expected Kandra to cause trouble, but it still hurt. After all, it wasn't her fault that her siblings weren't female. She pressed her lips together, kept her gaze on the path ahead of her, and tried to ignore the girls' whispering and giggling.

Finally, the bushes ended at one of the few places where the water could be reached without climbing down the high bank. There were two more slopes like this, a wider one on the other side of the lake where wildebeests, zebras, elephants and the occasional lion quenched their thirst, and a smaller one a little to their right where the herders took the flocks to drink twice a day.

Juma looked around. Where was the water? Her jaw fell open. Where once little waves had lapped at the sand, caked and cracked mud spread to either side. The water had retreated so far back, she could hardly make out the sun's sparkling reflections. The other girls seemed used to the view. They marched on toward the thin sliver of glittering wetness. Juma had to run to catch up.

Her neck tingled as if someone was watching her, but she couldn't see anyone no matter how much she looked around. On the other side of the lake, a couple of tired zebras scuffled back into the shade of the bushes that grew in great numbers at the top of the steep cliffs.

But even the plants' leaves drooped in the heat. Maybe she felt itchy because she was walking on the lake bed. Juma wondered where all the water had gone. There was no river leading into the lake or out. No one knew where the water came from or where it went. The lake had been a gift from the gods. It had always been there. Didn't anyone worry about this? She looked at the girls who gossiped, giggled, and sang while walking. Well, they obviously didn't.

On the new shoreline, the girls filled their pails with water, set their grass rings on their heads and the pail on top. Carefully, Juma balanced her load and walked back to the village, wondering what would happen to the tribe when the water in the lake was all gone.

The whole morning, Juma carried water from the river to the fields on the other side of the village, pondering and worrying. The line of girls dissolved as they distributed the wealth from their pails. Soon, Juma walked to and fro on her own.

For the last few trips before midday, heat waves danced on the horizon, blurring everything. Juma's feet were numb. Sweat ran into her eyes and made her blink. She was glad to reach the shade of the bushes.

A viper hissed right at her feet, and Juma jumped back with a small yell of surprise. Water sloshed over the rim of her pail and soaked her back. Luckily, the viper slithered away without attacking. Juma closed her eyes and breathed deeply several times to calm her racing heart. Then she returned to the lake and refilled her pail. When she reached the place where the snake had been, the chieftess's son leaned against a small tree. Netinu — Juma reminded herself. His name is Netinu.

It was an awkward situation. Being alone with a man would get her punished, but having the son of the chieftess search her out would mark her for years. Hopefully no one saw them.

He touched his forehead with his hand and bowed, waiting for her permission to speak. Juma didn't know if she had the right to grant it. Ruled by Mubuntu and giving in to their violent traits far too easily, men were inferior to women, but Netinu was the chieftess's son. With Juma's low rank, they should be on par. But she longed to send him away before the other girls returned. When the silence became unbearable, she swallowed to moisten her throat. "Why are you here?"

"I have come to express my gratitude." He lifted his gaze, and Juma's knees grew weak. Why did he have to be so handsome? The blood in her ears roared so loud, she missed his next words. Only when he held out his hands did she realize he had asked for permission to help her.

"Leave me alone." She shook her head as best she could with the heavy water pail on it. Steadying it with one hand, she set out toward the village again. "You shouldn't have come. The elders wouldn't approve."

"Pah. They won't catch me." Netinu easily kept up with her since the path was wide enough for two. "I am glad I came, but you'd better not tell Mother." The look in his eyes pleaded with her.

She nodded. Somehow, a big, throbbing lump had formed in her throat, making it impossible to talk. Angry with the reactions of her body, she held herself even straighter and hoped Netinu would soon lose interest. It'd be bothersome if someone saw them together.

"I am really glad I managed to get you alone. Kandra wouldn't approve one bit." His smile soothed the worry his words caused.

Juma realized that he mostly had come to annoy Kandra. Somehow that made it even harder to cope with his interest. Sweat gathered on her upper lip.

"Sometimes I wish I were a girl, just to annoy my sister." His low laugh vibrated through Juma's bones. She shivered. What was happening to her?

"By the way, I'm very grateful that you saved me. No one had the sense to give me water." Netinu traced her upper arm with one finger in the accepted gesture of gratitude. It sent shivers of pleasure through Juma's entire body, and her heart began to race again. How could she tell him that it hadn't been water but Vanamate's tears, when she felt as weak as a newborn? And should she tell him? No. it would be better to keep it a secret.

Netinu cocked his head and eyed her with a sparkle in his eyes. "I must have had heat-stroke. The witch is still out."

Safe terrain. Juma seized the chance to change the subject. "Will she recover?"

"Mother thinks so. The witch has suffered more from the heat than the rest of the villagers. Maybe it's because she's so old. Kandra is sitting with her, cooling her forehead with a wet cloth." He grinned. "So, will you join me for the midday meal?"

Juma shook her head. How dare he suggest this? She wouldn't survive a full meal with him without becoming the target for gossip for weeks to come. And maybe her heart would give out before the meal was over.

"Thank you, but I've already promised my friend Sundera to join her." Juma hoped Sundera wouldn't prove her a liar. She'd been with Kandra's pals the whole morning. Maybe she had changed her mind about friendship. But for now, it helped to get rid of Netinu. Through the bushes, Juma saw the ashes of last night's welcome fire. She stopped.

"I'd rather walk the rest of the way alone." A valid excuse flashed through her mind. "I don't want someone to tell Kandra where you have been. She'd take it out on both of us."

"You're right." Reluctantly, Netinu left. Only when he had reached the first hut did Juma follow him. She took her water to the cooking area, put her pail and ring away, and joined the other trainees for the midday meal.

As they sat with their bowls around the big pot of stew Mama Lubeda had received from the cooks for her charges, Kandra stretched her legs and whispered with her friends.

"Have you seen her farewell yesterday? With that sort of mother, she's a warrior's training away from becoming a man."

Several girls laughed, and all of them stared at Juma. She pretended she hadn't heard and prepared herself for a more direct attack. She didn't have to wait long. Kandra turned to her and smiled, but her eyes burned like black coals.

"Have you decided what you will train for? Or will you elope with a warrior like your mother did?"

"Leave my mother out of this." Juma set her bowl aside.

"Well, it wasn't my mother who let a man decide her future." Kandra's smile was smug. Juma longed to shove it right back into her face, but that was male behavior and would make life even more difficult than it already was. She needed a retort, something that would tell Kandra she wouldn't bear her mocking. But it needed to sound polite. An image flashed through her mind's eye—Chieftess Jakombe wailing at the side of her twitching son. Juma's eyes narrowed as she turned to Kandra.

"Are you so unfriendly with me because your mother favors your brother?" She smiled, hoping it would look benevolent.

Kandra's mouth fell open. She stood and stared at Juma. The mocking in her eyes was gone, replaced by hate. Juma shivered despite the heat.

"Come on girls, we've got a treat for you this afternoon." Clapping her hands, Mama Lubeda stepped into the circle as if she hadn't noticed the unnatural quiet. "The Council meets today, and you've been chosen as witnesses."

Sundera sighed, grabbed Juma's arm and pulled her in line. "Thank Vanamate, Mama Lubeda came. I thought Kandra would kill you there and then," she whispered.

Juma didn't answer. She still had goosebumps on her arms.

Mama Lubeda led them to the Hall of Council, the big, oval hut in the middle of the village Juma had seen from afar. The wall consisted of woven mats that had been rolled up to allow light and air. The members of Council sat in a half-circle with the chieftess's throne in the middle. Kandra chose the place right opposite her mother's throne.

For a second, Juma had thought about claiming this place of honor for herself, but decided against it. She could still do that when the choosing ceremony had confirmed her as the chieftess's apprentice. Silently, she selected a place as far away from Kandra as she could get.

When everybody sat, the chieftess walked in. She wore her ceremonial garb: a crown of wheat, a necklace clay beads, a skirt of rushes and fur, and the red cloak of leadership. In her left hand, she held an ornately carved herder's staff. She sat on her throne and opened the meeting with the traditional words.

"Wisdom we seek, peace we shape. Welcome, Wise at Heart."

No one said a word. The quietness seeped into Juma's bones and her muscles relaxed. Sundera seemed alert, waiting for something to happen. Kandra and some other girls fidgeted. Finally, the eldest member of Council stood up.

"The drought is hard on us and on the herds. The witch has been begging for rain, but Vanamate has not heard." She sat down again.

Another member of Council stood up. "Even when more or less the whole tribe called, our song didn't reach Vanamate's ear. What can we do?"

"Why won't she hear us?" another member asked. "We tried every song, every prayer, and every dance that worked in the past. Do you think Vanamate abandoned us?"

The chieftess shook her head. "She made us, how can she forget about us?"

"But Mubuntu is getting stronger by the day. The water in the lake is so low, it will not last another month. Our animals will die, our children suffer thirst." The youngest member of Council, who nursed a baby, didn't hide her agitation. "We need to do something."

"I sent spies to the lands of our neighboring tribes," Chieftess Jakombe said. "They suffer from the drought too. None of their witches has been able to contact Vanamate either."

An energetic middle-aged woman in the dress of a herder got up. "If Vanamate doesn't help us to defeat Mubuntu, we'll have to fight him ourselves. Our herds are parched, and so are we. We need rain."

The woman nursing her baby said, "We should fetch the witch. She might know a way."

A couple of trainees were sent to fetch her. The old woman took her time. When she arrived, Juma was shocked by her frailty. Her arms and legs were thin as the twigs they used for cooking. The witch was dressed in a brown tunic adorned with red stitching that hung to her knees. Juma had never seen a dress like this. Also, the old woman wore leather garments that covered her feet entirely. The top was rimmed with fur. What a strange notion to wrap up your feet, Juma thought.

The witch walked to the middle of the circle and bowed to the Council.

Chieftess Jakombe touched her left shoulder. "Do you know what happened to Vanamate?"

The witch straightened. Her joints popped. "I have been searching near and far, in our world and in the realm beyond, but I can find neither her nor her sister, Monnatoba." She raised her arms. "All I see are Earth Spirits and Air Sprites bowing to Mubuntu."

"Is the Nameless still asleep?" the eldest asked.

"As he should be." The witch bowed. "But yesterday, he stirred in his sleep. I am sure a tribe in a distant land has felt him turn."

The members of Council exchanged worried looks, and Juma felt her hands grow cold. If the Nameless woke, the end of the world was near.

## 3

"WHAT CAN WE DO?" ASKED the mother and moved her baby to the other breast.

Chieftess Jakombe pointed her staff at the witch. "What would you need to fight Mubuntu?"

Everybody looked at the witch. >From her place at the side, Juma saw the old woman pale before she bowed again.

"To fight him, we need to call him to earth and bind him to a temporary body. That will be very dangerous to all involved."

The young mother spoke again. "Can't we sacrifice a lamb or two to appease him?"

"No chieftess has ever sacrificed to a male god before, and I'll not be the one to start." Chieftess Jakombe stared at the young woman until she blushed.

One of the elders said, "You know it worked once, Jakombe."

"We need other options."

"We have to take emergency measures," the herder said. "I suggest rationing water. No one knows how much longer the lake will sustain us. I will take half the herd to the Endless Well. There is little food, but at least water won't be a problem."

Juma perked her ears at the mention of her home. She wanted to tell the herder how hard grass would be to come by, but she didn't dare to speak up. She wasn't a member of Council.

As if the eldest had read her mind, she turned to the chieftess. "This is a time of need. Why don't we hear suggestions of the young? Sometimes wisdom can be found in unexpected places."

The room fell quiet. Chieftess Jakombe looked at every single member of Council in turn. Each considered the question; each nodded. Finally, the chieftess turned to the girls in the semicircle before her.

"Does any of you have a suggestion that might help?"

Kandra fidgeted some more, but remained silent. Juma considered options. Should she tell the Council about the burning man she could see? Maybe not. Kandra would only use it to tease her again. But she had a different idea. Slowly, she raised her hand. The chieftess nodded to her.

Juma cleared her throat. "Can't we send ambassadors to our neighbors? Maybe, if all the witches come together, they will be able to find Vanamate."

Another hand went up, another nod from the chieftess. "What about the river people? I've heard the river is fed from high up in the mountains where it rains every day even when Vanamate sleeps. Maybe they'll allow us to spend some time on their land?"

Kandra's hand went up hesitantly, but Juma could tell she was playacting. Her smile was way too smug. When her cousin got permission to talk, she got up and bowed.

"Dearest mother, you would not be the first to offer a sacrifice to the fire god. I just remembered something you taught me a while back. Do you remember the one male chief the tribe once had?"

"I told you, no one talks about this dark chapter of our history."

"Yet, he averted a drought by sacrificing his son to Mubuntu." Kandra cocked her head. "I'm not suggesting we should follow his example. But why are you so averse to sacrificing a lamb or goatling, like it has been suggested?"

"We will not sacrifice to the Father of Conflict." Chieftess Jakombe stayed firm.

"What if all other options fail?" Kandra didn't give up.

Jakombe frowned at her but addressed all the girls. "Now get back to your duties while the Council and I will ponder your suggestions."

Quietly, the girls scrambled to their feet and filed out of the shade the Hall of Council provided. Juma fell in line with her fellow water-bearers and went back to work. Would the Council use the girls' suggestions? It'd be so nice to see a messenger carrying his Baobab crown to the witch of a neighboring tribe. It'd show that her ideas were worth considering. Juma daydreamed about her soon-to-be training while she carried the water to where it was needed the most.

On her third trip back from the cooking area, a man with a crown of Baobab leaves passed her. So the Council really did take her advice. Juma's heart danced with joy. Her first successful step toward becoming chieftess. The rest of the afternoon, she had to force herself not to skip and jump, or she would have spilled the precious water.

After the evening meal, Mama Lubeda took her arm and pulled her aside. "I want you and Sundera to come with me. The others don't need to know." She looked around, but none of the girls took notice. "Meet me at the gate at sundown."

Sundera watched her leave. "It's a test. I'm sure it's one." Her eyes sparkled with excitement. "What do you think we'll be asked to do?"

Juma shrugged. They'd find out in time. She just hoped Kandra wasn't there. "We'd better make up a story for the girls," she said.

"You're right." Sundera walked toward their hut. "We could tell them that we'll go for a walk. Or maybe I should hint at a meeting with a secret suitor." She giggled.

Just as the last sliver of the sun vanished behind the horizon, Juma and Sundera arrived at the gate. Mama Lubeda already waited for them. They settled beside her. A little later, Kandra and her best friend approached. When Kandra's lips tightened, Juma sighed inwardly. Would she ever be able to make peace with her cousin?

Mama Lubeda opened the gate just wide enough to let the girls slip through.

"Walk toward the moon," she said. "And don't linger. They're waiting for you." Without explaining who "they" were, she closed the gate behind them ensuring the tribe's safety in the ring of prickly thornbushes.

The four girls walked through the night. Kandra stomped ahead. Her friend had problems keeping up, so she finally joined Juma and Sundera. They tried to walk silently. A lot of wild animals prowled the night and it wasn't wise to be noisy. Juma's heart beat like a drum and her hands grew sweaty.

After a while, she took Sundera's free arm wordlessly. Everything looked so different bathed in the moon's silvery light. Shrubs looked like earth sprites, the grasslands like a silver sea. Even the trail they traveled seemed magically changed. Without the sun's relentless burning, it was a pleasant walk.

Soon after the giant stone that marked the path's summit, it widened into an oval of hard-packed earth. Three dark figures were waiting for them in the center; one was definitely Kandra. Juma's heartbeat quickened. Could this be the famous war-arena, the place where warriors of conflicting tribes met to fight until one side won? What if Kandra had arranged this to fight with her? Would she stoop so low as to use male rituals? But no. Mama Lubeda wouldn't have played along. She clearly liked Juma.

There were darker patches on the ground. Could that be blood? She sidled closer to Sundera, and noticed that Kandra's friend did the same. Juma squinted to get a better look at the two women at Kandra's side. One was most definitely the witch, the other the chieftess.

"Don't dawdle. Fetch firewood," Chieftess Jakombe said. "All of you," she added when Kandra didn't move. The girls spread out and collected what they could find. Juma wondered why they hadn't brought wood from the village. That would have been easier.

The village witch answered her question as if she could read her mind. "For what we will attempt, we can only use material from this place. Hurry up, we haven't got much time, and we don't need much wood."

When they returned with their twigs and branches, the witch laid a mat the size of a person to the side. She had woven it from the long, dried stems of the grass surrounding them. With practiced fingers, she prepared a fire. Then she made the girls sit by her side and handed a calabash around. The drink inside was bitter and left a sickening aftertaste on Juma's tongue. She suppressed her disgust and passed the gourd to the next girl. When everybody had taken a sip, the witch put it away.

"I will call Mubuntu and try to force him into this world to bind him. The potion you just drank will enable you to witness what goes on in both realms," the witch said. "But you will be firmly rooted in your bodies. I will be the only one who will leave hers for a while. That is the reason why you are here. You will protect my body from harm. Each of you will sit where I put you, and no matter what, you will not leave." She looked around, and her gentle eyes exuded a stony determination. "If you fail to protect me, I will die, and the whole tribe will suffer. Chieftess Jakombe will make sure you follow your orders."

"May I ask a question?" Sundera put her palms together apologetically.

The witch nodded and Sundera continued. "Why haven't you chosen older, more mature women to watch over you? Why us?"

A smile crinkled the witch's face. "This kind of magic only works for virgins. The potion I gave you is magical and will help you to see Mubuntu and me. Can we start now?"

The girls nodded in unison.

Chanting in the old language, the witch cut a rectangle with the fire at one end into the hard, cracked earth. She placed the four girls at the corners and lay down inside the rectangle. With both hands, she held the knife, resting it flat on her chest. Juma wondered why she didn't use the mat. Wouldn't it be more comfortable? The witch uttered a word that cut through Juma's thoughts, and she flinched. The fire sprang to life and burned without consuming the wood they had collected. Its glow flickered and made everything look like a dream. The witch resumed her song. When her chant ended, her breathing slowed. A foggy figure rose from the tip of the knife. It condensed into a much younger semblance of the witch and darted away.

Sundera's jaw dropped and her eyebrows rose. She stayed frozen in that position and stared after the witch. Juma suppressed a grin. She hadn't thought it possible that her new friend would ever get into a situation where she was lost for words.

"Pull yourself together. You look like an idiot," Kandra said.

Sundera twitched as she returned to reality. "Sorry, what do we do now?" She looked at the witch's body that lay without breathing. "Should we treat her like an ill person?"

"Nothing like it." The chieftess supported herself with her staff, lifted her left leg and placed the foot sideways against her right knee. "Now, we will wait."

"Why do we have to do it at night?" Sundera asked.

"That's obvious, silly." Kandra shot her an annoyed look. "At night, Mubuntu loses some of his power. He can't draw on the sun's heat, and Monnatoba will oppose him to help us find her sister."

Juma considered telling them that she had seen Vanamate but somehow it didn't feel right. The girls weren't the right people to tell. Maybe she'd have to see the witch — if the old woman survived the fight with the heat dæmon.

After what seemed like a long, long wait, a golden glow streaked across the sky followed by a dark dot. The witch and Mubuntu. The fire flared up, drawing the heat dæmon closer. How did the witch do that? The dark dot circled the dæmon's glowing form, forcing him toward the arena where her body lay and the girls waited.

Juma tore her gaze from the struggle and looked at the others. Chieftess Jakombe dutifully watched the girls. She smiled at Juma, and Juma smiled back. The closer the witch drove the dæmon, the better Juma could make out their features. She wondered what the others saw. Sundera and Kandra's friend stared open-mouthed. Even Kandra seemed engrossed. She had turned a bit to see better. The chieftess nudged Kandra and the girl returned to her original position, twisting her neck to follow the witch's struggle like the other girls did. Were they able to see Mubuntu? Or was he nothing but a blur in the air for them?

The chieftess seemed oblivious to the fight. Juma wondered why until she remembered that the chieftess hadn't had a drop of the drink. Did the witch think the chieftess couldn't stand the sight of a burning man? Somehow that didn't make sense. On the other hand, if the chieftess could see Mubuntu, it would distract her from watching the girls and any other duty the witch might have given her.

Realization dawned on Juma. Naturally, the witch hadn't given Jakombe the potion. The chieftess wasn't a virgin any more.

With a tail of flames, Mubuntu evaded the witch and headed away from the magical fire. She called a few words, spread her arms, and he swerved back in the direction she herded him. The fire threw sparks into the night, and the chieftess picked up the grass mat. Once more she nudged Kandra, who had shifted her position again.

Juma looked past her at Mubuntu, who was much closer now. Flames leaped from his body and face and tried to hurt the witch, but she evaded them. Mubuntu howled, a sound that sent icy shivers down Juma's back. She drew up her shoulders and lifted her hands to block the sound. Since none of the other girls reacted, she wondered if they had heard it at all.

The chieftess nudged her. "Sit straight."

Despite the knot in her stomach, Juma obeyed. The fire flickered higher and higher, engulfing Mubuntu as he was forced to step closer.

"He's there, isn't he?" Chieftess Jakombe asked.

Juma's throat constricted as she tried to describe Mubuntu.

"His presence is burning my skin like a hot summer sun," Sundera said.

Chieftess Jakombe hurled the mat through the air and jumped after it. With her whole body weight, she pressed the mat over the fire, trapping Mubuntu's arm underneath.

He screamed again. A man-sized flame shot from Mubuntu to the sky.

"Mother!" Kandra screamed and tried to get up.

Sundera caught her arm just in time. "Stay put! Interrupting a spell is dangerous."

Reluctantly, Kandra settled back, but her gaze never left her mother. Juma noticed that one line of the rectangle was slightly marred. Since this could break the spell, she opened her mouth to tell Kandra to redraw. Before she could utter a word, Mubuntu's flaming body dissolved, and a streak of light shot away. The witch shouted another word that made Juma's hair stand on end, but the heat-dæmon was gone.

"Elephant dung," the witch said and returned to her body. The closer she came the more she turned to fog until the tip of her knife's blade sucked her back into her body. With a sigh, she sat up and looked at the girls still sitting around her.

"So, you're back!" Chieftess Jakombe got up. Kandra's face relaxed when she noticed her mother was in no way harmed.

"Mubuntu escaped. One of the girls broke the line." The witch slumped. Juma caught her shoulders before she toppled.

"Thanks, girl." The old woman closed her eyes and breathed deeply. "Mubuntu was uncharacteristically strong tonight."

The chieftess knelt beside her. "Does that mean everything was in vain?"

The witch shrugged. "Have you looked under the mat?"

When no one moved, the witch pointed at Sundera. "Go, have a look."

Juma's friend stepped gingerly to the pile of sticks that was no longer burning and lifted the mat. The wood didn't show any sign of fire. Something white shone between the twigs. Sundera bent to pick it up. Before her hand came anywhere near it, she shrieked and stepped back hurriedly.

Chieftess Jakombe went over, moved a couple of sticks and took the white thing with two fingers. The corners of her mouth turned down and she wrinkled her nose before she held it out for all to see. It was a hand with a wrist and a little bit of the forearm. And it was as white as the hair of the tribe's eldest. The area where the arm was severed wasn't as it should be; no bones, no ligaments, no blood, just the same paleness the skin showed. Juma shivered.

"Wrap it up and take it to my hut for me." The witch held out a cloth to the girls. "I'm not strong enough to touch it right now."

None of the girls moved. Finally, Juma took the cloth and approached Jakombe. The haunted look on the chieftess's face relaxed into a tentative smile. Her relief was so evident, Juma felt even warier of Mubuntu's hand. Reluctantly, she wrapped the unnatural body part into the cloth. Even through the fabric, it was warm to the touch as if Mubuntu's fire was caught inside. As Juma tied the bundle to her belt, the witch relaxed and looked younger than before the fight.

"The spell has not been in vain," she said. "We stole a significant portion of Mubuntu's power, and he might bargain for it." She held out her arms to the girls. "Now, help me to get back to my hut. It's time to rest. Tomorrow will be another exhausting day."

Juma and Sundera took her arms and helped her along the path, while Kandra and her friend picked up the mat and dispersed the unburned twigs. Chieftess Jakombe took the lead.

The height of the moon surprised, Juma. Had they been away that long? Uneasy, she adjusted the warm bundle at her thigh. A finger slipped through the folds and connected with her skin. She jerked back and suppressed a shout. The world around her spun, and she looked at a completely different scene from an unexpected height. The unusual angle confused her a little, but then she recognized her home, the Endless Well. Below, their hut was burning. Beside it, groups of people pulled water from the big well. But instead of dousing the flames, they handed it around for everyone to drink and watered their herds. Where had all the people come from? Why weren't they putting out the fire? Juma scanned the crowds for her family. Where were her father and brothers? She searched. There, movement. Lomba was running from a couple of warriors. He limped, and a trickle of blood had dried on his face. Juma wanted to call out to him, but no sound escaped her throat. Who had hurt her brother? Why were the men chasing him?

Lomba led his followers in a war dance pattern back toward the Endless Well. After he escaped capture for the second time by speeding up, Juma realized he had only pretended to be wounded. She sighed with relief until she remembered that lapwings did the same when they tried to divert a predator's attention from their brood. Surely Lomba was trying to lead his followers away from Tolobe and her father. Where were they? Had they been hurt? Before she could look around again, the world spun once more.

The warmth of the old witch's arm hung on her arm like a leaden weight. She was back in her own body. Father. Tolobe. I need to tell Jakombe. Before she could call out to their leader, someone came running on a path that joined theirs at an angle.

"Wait!"

At first Juma thought it was Mubuntu again, but then she realized it was a different man. His features seemed awfully familiar in the silvery light of the moon. He panted and stumbled more than he ran.

"Wait for me."

Chieftess Jakombe stopped and looked toward the running man. Sundera's hand flew to her mouth.

"It's Tolobe!" Juma's whisper was much too loud, and the worry in her voice drew the attention of everyone. Except for Sundera, whose gaze was fixed on Tolobe, everybody stared at Juma until her ears burned. She was glad that the attention soon focused on her brother when he came closer, panting heavily. In the bright light of the waxing moon, a crusted cut on his shoulder resembled a black snake.

"We need help." He sank to the ground trying to catch his breath. The crust of the small cut broke and a little blood oozed out. "Father is injured."

**4**

HE CHIEFTESS'S FACE TURNED TO stone. "What happened?"

"Warriors. They drove us from our home. We were outnumbered. And they fought like madmen. I came to inform you of the incident. Lomba follows me with Father as fast as possible."

"They did what?" Jakombe stared at him, wide-eyed.

"They tried to kill us."

"But… I don't… How…?" The chieftess searched for words. "It's been many generations since a tribe attacked another one. There are traditions to solve disagreements. Who were they? Why did they attack you?"

"They came with their whole tribe and were desperate for water. If we don't act fast, they might attack the village too, for the Endless Well will not sustain a whole tribe for long." The longer Tolobe knelt before the chieftess, the calmer his breathing became.

The chieftess gritted her teeth and signaled Kandra and her friend to help Tolobe. "Take him to the guest hut and wake the healer and a couple of men."

"Of course, Mother," Kandra said. What was that? No impudent refusal? Juma wondered if Kandra was always this friendly and polite with her mother but didn't have much time to ponder the question. The witch set out toward the village again.

"They should not talk to anyone without you," the old woman advised. "We've never had a situation like this. It needs to be handled with care."

"I will not leave you. We will be an easy target if we lose you." There was a determination in the chieftess's face that surprised Juma. The witch smiled and nodded her approval. What amazed Juma even more was the worry on Kandra's face.

"Now, do as I told you, and don't talk to anyone until I return," the chieftess said to her daughter and pointed to Tolobe.

Kandra helped him to his feet, the corners of her mouth turned down with disgust, her repulsion clearly visible. Tolobe half turned and smiled in Juma's direction, but she wasn't sure if he meant her or Sundera. Blood seeped from the crust over the cut in his shoulder and dripped to the ground. He swayed a little and seemed grateful for Kandra's steadying hand.

Juma felt like hugging her brother, her strong, brave brother. He'd risked his life to gather vital information for the tribe. A true warrior. What did it matter that he was at the bottom-most rung of the social ladder? At the same time, worry clouded her vision. How badly hurt was her father? Would Lomba be able to get him to safety? A lump formed in her throat. What if her father couldn't flee fast enough any more? What if Lomba didn't escape his followers?

"Hurry up." Jakombe nudged Juma and they followed Kandra and her friend, who helped Tolobe along. Since the girls and the young warrior could walk faster than the exhausted witch, despite his injury, they were soon out of sight.

As Juma walked beside the witch, she fought an emotional whirlwind. Oh, Vanamate, what if her father died? Her hands grew cold. Sure, he was only a man, but he had been there for her ever since her mother died. She swallowed, but the pain in her heart stayed. At least Tolobe wasn't hurt, and Lomba… he had looked well enough in her vision. She blinked away a tear.

The witch patted her hand. "Don't worry. I am sure Jakombe will take good care of your family. It wouldn't do to ignore a tribe member's plight, male or female. Also, you're part of her family."

Still, Juma couldn't help worrying but tried not to let it show.

When they reached the gate, three men and a woman were waiting with the gate's guardians.

The chieftess told the woman and one man, "Take the path toward the Endless Well and help my sisterman and his son. Carry them if necessary. I want them here as soon as possible. Alive!"

The two left at a sustainable trot.

Then Jakombe sent the remaining men to the other settlements outside the village to tell all the tribe members to come to safety. "We'd better face this together."

Gently, the witch nudged Juma. "We need to talk to your brother, and then we'll have to hide the hand."

Juma and Sundera helped her to the guest hut. A healer sat beside Tolobe, who lay on his belly on a mat on the ground. His head rested on his arms, and he breathed evenly when they entered. The healer sewed the wound at his shoulder and treated it with herbs.

"He's exhausted," she said to the witch.

Sundera put her mouth close to Juma's ear and whispered, "Isn't he a marvel? Running a whole day's worth of travel in half a night."

At the same time, the healer put away her needle and said, "Also, he lost blood, and the running didn't help."

The witch nodded. "Regardless, he's got vital information for the chieftess. I'm afraid you will have to wake him. But if you wish, we can brew him a potion later that will make his strength return faster."

"That would help. Will you watch over him?" The healer stood up.

"I believe we've got someone else quite eager to do the job." The witch looked at Sundera, who blushed and lowered her gaze. She sat at Tolobe's side when the healer left.

Juma smiled. She should have known the witch would guess. It was surprising that the two young people had fallen for each other so fast. Juma wondered when they had found the time to talk and whether they were already thinking about a wedding. They'd need her permission for that. After all, she was the only woman in the family and had to approve. Of course, they might not have reached that point yet. But one look at Sundera's worried face told her she wouldn't have to wait for long.

The witch nudged Tolobe with her foot. "Wake up, young man."

She had to repeat the action a few times before Tolobe was awake enough to understand where he was. As he sat up, the chieftess walked in.

"We need to talk, Selenta." She looked at the girls in surprise. "What are you doing here?"

"He's my brother," Juma said. "I have the right to see if I can help him. And this is my brother's future wife if she consents, and if he wants her."

Sundera's eyes widened and a smile spread over her features that made her look truly beautiful. Tolobe grinned like a madman. Although he had to fight for air, he took Sundera's hand. "Thank you, Juma."

"My best wishes." The chieftess sat down on one of the bed-benches. "Unfortunately, we need to focus on something more important right now. Tolobe, sisterson, did you see which tribe took the well?"

"The river people."

"Are you sure?"

"The kikoi patterns fitted. Also, Father met their witch a few years back shortly after Mother died, and she helped him with the funeral ritual. Her face is hard to forget." Tolobe looked at the chieftess without fear or signs of discomfort, but his skin was pale and his breathing ragged. Suddenly, Juma feared for his life.

"But the river always holds water," Sundera said.

Tolobe shook his head. "I overheard someone mention that the river has dried out."

"Something terrible must have happened." Chieftess Jakombe's lips narrowed and she kept quiet for a while. When she spoke again, worry lines marked her face. "Who led the warriors at the Endless Well?"

Tolobe described a lean young woman with a crown of reeds and fishbone. Chieftess Jakombe stroked her chin. "My old friend must either be ill, or she died, and her daughter has always been a hothead. I will send a messenger to her and see what can be done." She got up. "Make yourself comfortable and recover. You did well, Tolobe Botango."

She left the hut, and Tolobe lay back. The color of his skin had a grayish tinge, and he closed his eyes with a sigh. Juma realized how much sitting up must have cost him, and her heart went out to him. Usually she felt closer to Lomba, but not tonight.

"I am awfully glad I met you out there." His voice dropped to a whisper. "I don't think I would have had enough strength left to wake someone."

Juma stayed until the healer returned. Since Sundera didn't want to leave Tolobe's side, Juma walked with the witch to her hut alone. The sun was not yet up, but many people flitted to and fro. Juma felt her eyelids droop. It had been an exhausting night.

"Put the hand in here." The witch fetched a bag woven of reeds.

Carefully not to touch the pale skin again, Juma untied the bundle from her hip and dropped it into the bag. Relieved to be rid of her burden, she turned toward her hut. Her knees felt like wax and her eyes insisted on closing every so often against her will.

Netinu stepped from his mother's hut. His face lit up when he saw Juma. Her heart tingled in her chest like the tickle on her fingers from the butterfly she had once caught. She held her breath, suppressed the feeling, and looked around. For a tiny moment in time, they were alone. Netinu didn't waste one second. "Will you allow me to seek you out on the path of the water-bearers again in the afternoon?"

Juma fought unsuccessfully to suppress a yawn before she answered. "Would you take a no for a no?"

He shook his head.

"Why are you asking then?" She stepped around him and walked on, trying not to let him see how much her knees trembled. His gaze burned on her back and made her skin tingle. She was glad to reach the hut.

Inside, she lay down, but she couldn't sleep despite her tiredness. Her father's and brother's injuries worried her too much. Combined with Netinu's open adoration, it robbed her of sleep. Why would Jakombe's son court her of all people? There had to be candidates in the village that were more promising, a girl with cattle or a talented healer. Why did he choose a girl with a man as mother? He surely didn't love her. There had to be another reason.

After much pondering, Juma still hadn't found an answer. The only thing she was sure off was that he affected her ability to function properly. What if her legs grew so weak that she fell? She should make him stop the courtship. On the other hand, he could be the one to convince Chieftess Jakombe to let her train as her successor.

Eventually Juma's tired brain shut down. With the first rays of the sun lighting the sky, her eyes closed and she fell asleep.

Juma had to concentrate not to spill the stew she had for the midday meal. Her head seemed heavier than usual in the way it kept nodding forward. Sundera sat her side, babbling away about Tolobe's recovery, but Juma's muddled brain found it hard to remember last night. Something had been wrong with her father, hadn't it?

A bunch of children ran toward a group of men carrying a stretcher. Lomba walked beside it, holding the hand of the person lying on it.

Father! Juma tried to rise but her legs refused to obey. Her mouth felt as dry as if she had traveled the whole day. A whimper escaped her. What if he died? Only then did she realize that the helpers were back surprisingly fast. Lomba must have carried their father while running. What a feat.

Sundera grabbed Juma's hands, pulled her to her feet, and pressed her kikoi into her hands. "Let's see how he is."

Struggling to stay upright, Juma followed her friend and the group with the stretcher to the healer's hut. Before they could knock at one of the wooden poles framing the doorway, Lomba came out.

"You can't go in." He shook his head. "The healer forbids it. She says the only one she'll let talk to him is Jakombe."

Juma's knees buckled and she found it really hard to stay upright. Her father's injuries must be even worse than she had thought. What if she would never talk to him again? What if he never learned of Tolobe's betrothal?

"We've got a very good healer and an extremely competent witch." Sundera put her hands on Juma's shoulders. "I am sure that between the two of them they'll heal your father."

Juma swallowed and moistened her lips, trying to say something, but Lomba beat her to it.

"I'd better see Mama Lubeda about a place to sleep tonight." He ran off, leaving Sundera to embrace and comfort Juma.

The witch parted the woven fabric that covered the door and stepped through.

"Shouldn't you be at work?" she asked.

Juma moaned. How could she work if her father lay dying?

The old woman smiled at her with understanding in her eyes. "Work has a tendency to take your mind off things," she said. "Give it a try."

Juma nodded meekly and followed Sundera to the central place. After a final hug, her friend turned toward the pens, and Juma picked up her grass ring and pail.

In the next few hours, she carried as much water as her protesting legs would allow. She filled pail upon pail and carried it to the huts and the watering channels in the fields. After her tenth trip, dizziness claimed her. She found a secluded spot in the shade of one of the bushes on the lake's shore, put the pail beside her, and relaxed.

"There you are." Netinu sank into the sand at her side. "I've been looking all over the place for you."

Juma jerked upright and looked around.

"No one's near. I checked." Netinu grinned.

"Why do you keep following me?" Annoyed, Juma closed her eyes. Maybe her heart would behave if she didn't look at him. It didn't. She felt the warmth of his body close to her arm, and her heartbeat accelerated already. At the same time, she was angry. How dare he come here to flirt with her when all she was craving was news of her father?

"Mother said that the healer has said your father will make it," Netinu said as if he'd read her mind. He smiled at her. "All he needs is rest and a lot to drink. Don't worry about him. He will not go with Monnatoba yet."

Juma stared at him, her jaw working, but no word came out. Finally she sighed and spoke, her voice nor more than a whisper. "Thank you for letting me know."

"I like you. The other girls always give me a feeling of being inadequate. They hate me for being the chieftess's son while simultaneously vying for my attention." He grinned sheepishly. "You're not like them. Sometimes you're even rude to me. You behave like a woman should when a man pesters her. That makes you attractive, you know."

"So if I treat you like the idiot you are, you will keep courting me?"

"Definitely!"

"What if I pretend I fell in love with you and swoon like some of the other girls do when they see you?" Juma opened her eyes and looked at him. His gently curved lips invited her but she refused to let her body take control.

"You won't get rid of me so easily." He bent forward. "May I kiss you?"

Juma glared at him, stood up, and reached for her pail. She had stayed too long already. If one of the other girls saw her flirting with him like this, she'd be in trouble.

"Wait. Please." He held her back.

Juma shook off his hand, rolled her eyes, and sat down again. But *only because my legs are too weak to walk.*

"I'll try to be more serious," Netinu promised. He stared at the ground for a while. "You know, when Father died, I lost my only real friend. The second I laid eyes on you, however, I knew you'd be the person who could replace him. Tell me something about yourself, so I'll get to know you better. I swear by Vanamate's wrath that I'll never let anyone know."

Juma gasped. That was a very strong vow. Now she could reveal her deepest secrets, and the goddess would protect her words. He'd never dare to break this oath.

This was the best chance to discuss why she kept seeing Mubuntu. Or had Netinu brought someone to eavesdrop? She looked around but the sand around the lake and the cracked seabed were empty, and so were the bushes behind them. She decided to trust his vow.

"Do you remember when you collapsed during the ceremony?"

"How could I forget?"

"A burning man held you down. Last night, the witch fought the same man. It was Mubuntu." Juma stared at her hands, forcing them not to fidget. Why did she see the heat dæmon when obviously no one else did? Was it a sign from the gods? Holding her breath, she waited for Netinu's reaction.

"That's weird," he said. "I didn't see a burning man, but that doesn't mean much." Before Juma could say anything else, he added, "The witch sees things all the time, and Kandra does too, at least once in a while." He put his hand on her arm. "There is much more to our world than an everyday fool like me will ever understand."

Juma closed her eyes. The skin where he touched her tingled, but it was a comforting feeling. "If only I knew whether to tell someone or not. Could it be a sign?"

Netinu pulled his knees to his chest and wrapped his arms around them. After a while, he said, "If you want to tell someone, talk to the witch. She's the only one in the village who can understand. If Kandra finds out, she'd ridicule you all the time."

"She hates me."

His head shot round, and his eyebrows rose. "I don't think it's hate, more rivalry. She picks on you because you're the only competitor with a good chance of becoming the next chieftess. After all, your mother was the eldest daughter of the last chieftess."

Juma knew better but she decided not to press the point. She got up. "I'd better get back to work."

Netinu helped her refill the pail. He carried it along the path. When he spotted Kandra at a distance, coming toward them, he hurriedly handed pail and grass ring to Juma.

"What are you doing here?" Kandra frowned at him. Juma noticed that her gaze held just as much contempt for Netinu as for her.

"If you tell anyone, I'll let everybody know that you wear Mother's regalia when she's not looking." Netinu shot his sister a warning look and walked past her toward the village.

Kandra stared after him, her face contorted with anger, before she turned back to Juma. "Are you two lovers?"

"What do you want?" Juma stared back. "You surely didn't come to help me."

"I wanted to let you know that I'm really sorry your father's hurt so bad." Kandra gave her a surprisingly genuine smile. "I'd be worried sick if it were Mother lying wounded."

Juma searched for the barb in her cousin's words but couldn't find any. Was this a peace offering?

"Give me the pail and go to your father. He insists on seeing you." Kandra held out her hands. "I wish I could tell you whether he's recovering or dying but I truly don't know, so you'd better run. It might be your last chance."

Juma's heart plummeted into Mubuntu's fire. Wordlessly she pressed pail and grass ring into Kandra's arms and raced off.

## 5

$\mathcal{S}$HE REACHED THE HEALER'S HUT out of breath. The healer allowed her in.

"Try not to talk too much. He's very weak, and will not survive if he exerts himself," she said.

Juma pressed her lips together and nodded. Twilight reigned inside the hut and made it hard to see the furniture. When her eyes had adjusted, she sat on a stool beside her father's bed and waited for him to notice her. Meanwhile, she studied his face. It looked so different, haggard and drawn. Had her mother looked like this when she died? Juma bit her lip not to cry.

After a while, her father opened his eyes. A smile eased his features.

"Glad you came." His voice sounded hoarse.

Juma took a bowl with water and helped him drink. "Please don't die," she whispered.

He frowned and lay back. "I won't. My children need me. You need me."

Although she smiled at her father, her eyes watered. Unfortunately it was Monnatoba's decision if he would live or not. She took his hands and kissed them gently. "I'm very glad to hear that."

"Will you stop hating me?" His hands pressed hers.

"I don't hate you!"

"From the day your mother died, you resented me taking her place." He smiled weakly. "I tried hard to be a good mother. It's not easy for a man."

Juma pressed her lips together. Had she really been angry with her father for not being her mother? She scanned her memories and had to admit he was right.

"I'm sorry," she said. "I didn't mean to hurt you."

Her father smiled again, but his eyes fluttered and he was barely conscious.

"We'll talk about it when you feel better." Juma fought to keep her voice steady. As gently as she could, she wiped the sweat from his forehead with a wet cloth, blinking away the tears in her eyes and struggling to smile.

Her father sighed and closed his eyes. Soon his gentle snoring showed Juma that he slept. She sat at his side until the healer sent her away for the evening meal.

Later, Juma told Sundera about her father.

"I treated him like a servant," she said in a voice barely audible to herself. "I let him down."

Her friend hugged her wordlessly. Juma stiffened at the unexpected gesture but then relaxed into the embrace. It felt good to have a friend.

"Your father is a great man. He will accept your apology," Sundera whispered in her ear. Just when she let go of her friend, the chieftess entered their hut. Kandra squeezed in after her. Juma pressed her lips together, glad that her cousin hadn't seen them hug.

"I wanted to thank you for last night's help," the chieftess said. "You are free to do what you want tomorrow morning."

Kandra's nostrils widened. Even in the receding light of the evening, Juma saw the hate in her eyes. There was no mistaking it. Netinu had it wrong.

"By the way, Mother, did you know that Juma skipped work today?"

"I would never do that!" Juma glared at Kandra. Why didn't Jakombe deal with her daughter's spite? "I rested for a few minutes when I felt dizzy from the heat."

"You smooched with Netinu. Alone!"

"I did not!" Juma clenched her fists, struggling with her anger. How she longed to slap Kandra. Breathing deeply, she forced herself to appear calm. She'd never convince the chieftess to train her if she couldn't control Mubuntu's fire.

The chieftess turned to Kandra with a stern face. "We will discuss this in private, not in front of a whole group of outsiders. Go to our hut."

Kandra pressed her lips together, straightened, and left the hut. Juma was relieved until the chieftess said, "You will visit me first thing tomorrow morning, Juma."

Juma nodded and the chieftess left. The other girls giggled and whispered. Sundera put her hand on Juma's arm.

"Let's sleep outside," she suggested.

Juma grabbed her kikoi and followed her friend. Side by side and silently they found a lonely place close to the thornbush fence that protected the village from wild animals. They wrapped themselves into their capes and stared at the stars above. They flickered like the hearth-fires of countless families. Juma enjoyed the peace she felt when looking into the night sky.

After a while, Sundera said, "Don't let Kandra's false accusations ruin your composure. The chieftess will find out you haven't done anything wrong."

"What if Netinu tells her he wants to marry me?" Juma sighed.

Sundera shook her head. "He wouldn't dare to confront his mother like that."

That didn't comfort Juma one bit. She would still have to face the chieftess tomorrow. Would she be angry or happy about Netinu's attention toward her? She didn't know. And what's more, her own body's reactions to Netinu's courting worried her. What if she fell for him? Would she throw away all her dreams to be with him like her mother did when she followed her father? She breathed in deeply. Definitely not! Or would she? She turned to Sundera.

"What is it like to be in love?"

Her friend smiled, but her gaze went out to an unseen place. "Tolobe is part of me, something I've been missing without knowing. I feel healed. Complete. It's hard to describe."

"But it happened so fast. You've only known each other for a few days. Did you use a love potion?"

Sundera giggled. "Of course not! Love is magical but that doesn't mean you can use magic to find it."

"How did you know Tolobe was the right man for you? You didn't talk much."

"We talked more than you know — in secret meetings. Also, we have many things in common, and there was a strong bond between us right from the start. I feel at ease even when we don't talk. It feels right." Sundera sighed. "You need to experience it for yourself and you will know. But you need to trust your feelings."

"And you think I don't?" Juma frowned.

"I couldn't say. I can't read your mind," Sundera said. "We'd better sleep. Last night was way too short, and you'll need your strength tomorrow."

Juma agreed and pulled her kikoi closer, but her worry kept her awake for a long time.

The next morning, Juma went to the chieftess's hut, wishing she could be somewhere else. Chieftess Jakombe, Kandra, and Netinu were having breakfast in front of the hut. The chieftess told her to sit and join them, but Juma couldn't eat. Cross-legged, she sat beside the chieftess and waited. Despite her worries, the fact that Netinu sat on the other side of the pot with porridge made her heart race. Warmth spread through her body whenever she glanced at him. Finally, the chieftess turned to her.

"I have discussed this subject with my children last night, and they already know what I expect from them." She put her hand on Juma's shoulder. "Are you in love with Netinu?"

The question made Juma squirm inside and her jaw clenched. Did she love Netinu? She thought fast to find the most diplomatic answer. There was no way she could explain her confused feelings, not with Netinu and Kandra listening. But she couldn't say no either. It might make the chieftess think she wasn't interested in becoming her successor.

"He is very attractive, but I have not yet chosen," she said. That should be vague enough and diplomatic — and it was true.

One of the messengers arrived that had been sent out. He bowed his head and waited patiently for the chieftess to notice him.

The chieftess ignored him and nodded. "You have to understand that Netinu will marry the next chieftess, unless it's Kandra. That has been the tradition ever since Vanamate created us."

"Juma's the better candidate," Netinu said. Kandra glared at him.

"That remains to be seen." Chieftess Jakombe flexed her fingers and got up. "The testing will start tomorrow or the day after, depending on how things go with the invaders. Every girl who is qualified and willing to take the burden will be taken into account. Until then, there is plenty of work. You will all help with the herds today."

Juma decided not to remind her that she was supposed to have a day off. Instead she watched her walk away with the messenger. When she got up, Kandra stood in front of her, arms akimbo.

"This isn't over yet," she said. "I will not let you steal my rightful place as chieftess."

"You heard your mother. Every talented girl has the right to try." Juma tried to push past her, but Kandra grabbed her arm and held it so tight it hurt. Juma bit her lip not to wince. She had to look strong.

"Your mother abandoned the tribe for a man." Kandra's beautiful face contorted with barely suppressed anger. "You're not worthy to wear the crown."

"Oh, come off it, Kandra. Let her go." Netinu stepped beside Juma.

Her heart began to flutter. Again. That was so annoying. Juma felt her ears grow hot. She didn't need a man to protect her, thank you.

"Stay out if it," she snapped at Netinu, cringing at the hurt in his face. She jerked her arm free from Kandra's grasp and said, "I don't think it's for you to decide who will become the next chieftess."

Head held high, she marched off toward the cattle pen.

The herders assigned three trainees to each group. Juma was glad she could go with Sundera. The leading herder, a slender woman with sad eyes, told them what needed to be done.

"We have to diminish our herds. Most of you will help to separate the strong animals from the weak ones and bring them to us; the others will dry the meat." She pointed to a low fire with wooden racks to hang up strips of meat. "My fellow herders will tell you the details."

Juma looked to the other herders who were sharpening their knives with mask-like faces. Only then did she realize what the leading herder's words meant. A mass slaughter. She shivered but followed her group.

"Why do we have to kill so many animals?" Sundera asked.

"If we don't do it, the drought will. The grass is wilting and fodder is already scarce. The stronger animals push the weak ones aside. If we don't interfere, most will starve to death." The herder pointed to the animals in front of them. Many hung their heads and waited, motionless, barely twitching an ear to chase away an impertinent fly. Some bleated when they saw the group; maybe they hoped for water or food. The herder blinked away a tear. "With the outlying settlers here, water will get even scarcer, and the animals will suffer more. If we pick the ones to die, we will at least salvage the meat. Also, the strongest will bear offspring next year."

Juma noticed flames licking at a familiar figure on a rock at the other side of the herd. Her body stiffened and her eyes grew wide. Not Mubuntu again. Why did she have to see him all the time? She wasn't anyone special. Was it possible that he knew she could see him? She didn't think so, but just to be safe, she turned her head, watching the god from the corners of her eyes. He stood with his arm stump behind his back. Had he come to gloat? Or did he have something more sinister in mind?

"What if the drought never stops?" she asked the herder.

She didn't answer for a long time. Her gaze went to the horizon, and her features sagged. Juma expected tears but they never came. Finally the herder said, "It must rain. Now, let's get to work."

The morning dragged on. Catching the weak animals wasn't too difficult since they hardly ran. It broke Juma's heart to watch them stagger and fall. After they had moved the weakest animals into a separate pen, the trainees had to lead them to the slaughter. It would be a long day since there were more than a hundred extremely weak animals. Juma swallowed at the thought of killing them all, but the lump in her throat stayed.

The trainees were told to hold the animals. Every time Juma had to hold one whose throat was cut, a gush of blood washed over her arms. Tears stung her eyes when she felt the life ebb away, and blinking didn't help. Her heart bled with the dying animals. Trying to be strong, she bit her lower lip until it was sore.

The herders killed the animals at a rapid pace. Juma thought them heartless until she noticed tears running over their faces. This was hard for them too. They had cared for the animals from the day they were born.

Soon, the ground south of the cattle pen was soaked in blood and tears. The once cracked and dry soil had become slippery and muddy. The blood's coppery sweetness clung to her nose. Surely she'd never get rid of the stench again. She was just glad no one so far had accidentally cut into the guts. The reek of rotting grass would have been even worse.

It became increasingly difficult to pick up the carcasses to carry them to the place where they were skinned and the meat prepared for drying. The cooks already had several piles of animal hide waiting for treatment. The smoke from the fires drifted into Juma's eyes and nose, giving her an excuse to cry openly.

Taking the animals to the slaughter was the nastiest work Juma had ever done, but she didn't complain. It was necessary.

>From time to time, she noticed Mubuntu watching the herds. She flinched whenever his flickering form appeared. How she hated to be able to see him. The day was bad enough without a god's malicious glee. When he pointed at one of the animals, it sank to the ground, drained of energy, calling for water. It was a death sentence.

Juma wiped at her tears and blinked, but her crying wouldn't stop. Her vision blurred, making it difficult to choose which animal to fetch next. It got hotter the longer she worked. Her tears dried out and thirst glued her lips together. Once, she asked for water, and the herder gave her a minuscule sip from her calabash.

"We have to ration it. No one knows how much longer the water from the lake will last. The water level is sinking rapidly."

Reluctantly, Juma handed the calabash back and returned to work. Clearing the dust from her eyes hurt because she didn't have any tears left. The more her eyes burned, the less she could see. She barely noticed the slight tremble of the earth, shrugging it off as a slight disturbance of the Nameless's sleep. Nothing had happened the last time, nothing would happen now. After a while—her mind and body numbed by the monotony of her task—she worked automatically, ignoring her thirst, her sorrow, and the dust.

There was Mubuntu again. His flickering body was hard to miss even with her unfocused vision. He talked to someone half hidden behind a cow.

"Thou cannot command me, little one. I do as I please." His deep voice roared like the bonfire at the welcome ceremony.

A voice, distorted by rage and the need to talk quietly, reprimanded him. "Blocking the river was stupid and might ruin our plan."

"Who needs plans? Anyway, everything goes swimm... I mean burningly. Just look at the slaughtering." Mubuntu sounded miffed.

"You want dead worshipers? The river people haven't come for a friendly chat."

Was that a person? Juma found it hard to concentrate on the words but some part of her insisted that this was important.

"I want my hand back. I don't like humans to have it even if the witch doesn't know what to do with it."

"I managed to convince a couple of Council members to insist on a sacrifice. That should restore some of your power."

The voice sounded familiar to Juma. If only she weren't so tired. She blinked several times to clear her vision, trying to ignore the pain of the grains of dust scratching her eyes. When she finally managed to produce enough tears to clear her eyes, she focused on the place where Mubuntu had been. Both he and whoever he'd been talking to had gone.

It took her muddled brain quite a while to understand the implications. If Mubuntu had really spoken with a real person, she wasn't the only one who could see him. Someone else could make him out well enough to talk to him. She wondered if she could address him too. Maybe, she could ask him to show mercy. She decided to try, but no matter how much she looked, Mubuntu didn't return.

During the hottest period of the day, everybody rested. Juma felt drained. The heat had sucked away all her strength. She had meant to visit her father again, but was too tired. I'll go tonight, when it's not this hot any more, she thought.

Beside her, two women talked.

"Do you think it will work?"

"I hope it does. Jakombe isn't sure, but many Council members are in favor of it."

Juma was wondering what they were talking about, when the Council walked past them with Jakombe in the lead. Everybody got up and followed them. In the Central Hall, the Council turned to face the gathered tribe. The oldest woman stepped forward, and the crowd fell silent.

"We, the Council, have overruled Chieftess Jakombe. Drastic times require drastic measures, but we differ on the details. For now, Jakombe has given in to our demand. There will be a sacrifice tonight. Let us all hope and pray that it will have the effect we are hoping for."

Silence greeted her words. Juma didn't know what she should think. Was this a good idea? Who was the sacrifice for? Vanamate or Mubuntu? She thought of the discussion she had overheard and suspected it was the latter.

The Council sent out several men to cut down one or two dead trees. Others were told to take the wood to the arena. Then the elders sent everybody back to work.

When Juma arrived in a group of girls at the kitchen area, one of the herders pointed to a pile of carcasses. "Carry those to the arena," she said.

"Why?"

"Isn't that obvious?" Kandra snapped as she swung an animal over her shoulder. "They're for the sacrifice tonight."

"I thought a sacrifice has to be alive." Juma wasn't entirely sure of this. For as long as she remembered, the tribe had only sacrificed plants.

Kandra just shrugged.

"None of my animals will be burned alive," the herder said. "The slaughtering was bad enough. If the Council insists on a sacrifice, this is all Mubuntu'll get."

"But… so many?" Juma stared at her, open-mouthed.

The herder nodded. "It's a waste. Even with a sacrifice, I don't believe Mubuntu will go gentle on us. I bet he's having way too much fun. No one can stop him but Vanamate."

"She left us," Kandra snapped. "Isn't that obvious?"

Juma thought of the vision she had had that first night in the village. To her, it hadn't looked like Vanamate stayed away of her own free will. If only she could think of something to help the goddess.

Silently she picked up a carcass and carried it out of the village, to the place where the witch had fought Mubuntu. A man took the dead animal from her shoulders and put it on a pyre before piling more wood on top.

"We need more wood." He bowed to her as was custom when a man wanted something from a woman. "Would you be so gracious and provide some?"

"Aren't the men going to bring a tree or two?"

"That will not be enough. A fresh carcass contains too much moisture to burn easily." The man bowed again.

Secretly relieved, Juma attended to the new task. It was much better than lugging dead animals around. She found Sundera, Netinu, and Tolobe searching for wood side by side and joined them.

They worked without speaking for a long time. Finally Sundera looked at Tolobe and said, "Do you think it will work?"

Before he could answer, Netinu said, "Kandra seems to be sure. She said there'd been precedence that Mubuntu can be placated with the right kind of sacrifice."

Sundera's gaze locked on Juma. "Let's just hope he'll be happy enough with a quarter of our herd."

"That much?" Juma understood why the herder had thought it a waste. Half the slaughtered animals were more than reasonable. Vanamate was a gentle god. She never asked for anything but a small share of their harvest. How she longed to get back Vanamate's gentle rain. Not only would it end the drought, it would also put Mubuntu back in his place, and life in the village could return to normal.

## 6

THEY WORKED UNTIL THE SKY flamed with pinks and reds for a short while before the sun dropped behind the horizon. Tired as they were, they didn't return to the village. They cleaned themselves with sand. The caked blood on Sundera's and Juma's arms rubbed off easily enough but it left a sickening smell. Juma hated how long her arms would stink now before she got a chance to wash them in what was left of the lake.

Together with Tolobe and Netinu, they sat as far from the pyre as possible. More and more people arrived wrapped in their best clothes. The kikois sprouted every color and pattern Juma knew, and most reached from the shoulders to the ankles of its bearer. Netinu took Juma's hand, and her fingers began to tingle. She pulled them away fast, but the tingling spread through her whole body. She was glad when Lomba squeezed between them.

"Guess what?" he said. "They won't allow Father to come."

"Father was very close to dying." Juma smiled.

"That's no reason to stop him from witnessing something so important." Lomba's voice rose. "He's the last chieftess's son-in-law. Doesn't that mean anything?"

Knowing her father, Juma suspected he might secretly be glad he didn't have to come. Before she could say so, Tolobe intervened.

"Shut up, Lomba."

Lomba's jaw dropped, then closed with a thud. Juma grinned. Their older brother had never before told them what to do.

The elders began beating the drums, and the hubbub around Juma silenced. Dressed in formal attire, the chieftess approached with the witch at her side. They sang the ancient song of mourning, and the crowd fell in.

Mubuntu appeared in a sitting position on top of the pyre twice the size of a man. Juma flinched and closed her eyes, but when she opened them again, he was still there. Despite the distance, she could see his grin. At least his hand hadn't grown back. He closed his eyes and swayed to the song.

Juma forced herself not to look at him. She searched the crowd for someone who could see him too. Most eyes were fixed on the chieftess and the witch, who both seemed oblivious to the god's presence. Only a handful of people looked at the fire, and Juma couldn't tell if they saw the god or not.

The witch danced around the pyre twice, while the chieftess called to the fire god for mercy. Then both took torches offered to them and started the fire in several places. They threw their torches on top of the pyre and settled down to watch the fire spread.

The flames licked at the dry wood, leaping and dancing. Mubuntu laughed. He stood up and danced too. His sculpted, naked body was calling — calling for anyone. Juma saw a glow emanating from him. It arched in ribbons of light through the night toward the people around the fire. Could that be his magic? When the light fell on her briefly, she suddenly felt an urge to touch the stiffness that stood out from his loins. She tore her gaze away from him and fought against the urge. She wouldn't succumb to that kind of spell.

Staring into the flames, the witch licked her lips and sweat ran down her forehead. Was it due to the fire, or was she fighting the same urge? The whole gathering was bathed in Mubuntu's light.

Juma noticed that several couples had slipped into the night. Lomba was gone, and so were Sundera and Tolobe. She heard moaning in the bushes behind her.

The smell of frying meat filled the air, sweet and delicious, but Mubuntu's dance drove it from her mind. Her whole body tingled, and her heart raced. Her mind went numb, and all she wanted was to touch someone. The warmth of Netinu's leg registered on her brain with delay. He was sitting so close that his thigh pressed against hers. His hand caressed her back. Heat shot through her spine to her limbs. She gasped for air. What a feeling! Her nipples grew hard.

"Do you feel the magic of this night?" Netinu's breath caressed her ear, arousing her even more. "Be my bride. Let's seal the pact."

A tiny spark of free will remained. Juma clutched it like to a lifeline. "What about your mother? She wouldn't like it at all."

"Forget about Mother." He nibbled at her ear, and his hand slipped between her knees.

A moan escaped her lips. This was wrong, no matter how much she wanted him to touch her like this. It had to be Mubuntu's spell that made her body run riot. Juma forced herself to breathe more calmly. She'd never give in to a spell. No way. Forcefully, she pushed Netinu away. After all, it wasn't as if she was in love with him. Or was she?

"What's wrong?" His eyes, big and searching, pleaded with her. "I thought you liked it."

"This isn't us. Can't you see Mubuntu dance?"

"I don't care." Netinu panted like the ram when the sheep were in heat. "I want you. Now." He bent over, pushed aside her kikoi, and sucked her nipple.

"I said stop it!" Juma shoved him away as hard as she could. She needed to make him see the truth, but what would free him from the spell? Her gaze fell on the chieftess, who seemed unaffected by Mubuntu, and she knew what to say.

"You're not in love with me. You only want to annoy your mother." The words felt like rocks tumbling out of her mouth, and they seemed to hurt Netinu as much as hurtling stones.

He paled and pressed his lips together so tight they became a thin line. Without a word, he got up, walked toward the fire, and sat beside his mother. Juma's heart went with him. Had she been wrong? Did he really care for her? She longed to talk to him, somewhere were Mubuntu's spell wouldn't distract them. A single tear rolled down her cheek. The drums and the dancing god faded from her mind. Why did his anger hurt so much? Did she care for him? The place where her heart should be felt hollow and dark. Had she fallen in love with Netinu?

The smell of burning meat disrupted her thoughts. It made her gag. The witch knelt before the flames and called out to Mubuntu with her face lifted to the stars above. The god was barely visible behind the curtain of thick, dark smoke that rose from the fire.

"Mubuntu, we beg you to stop the heat," the witch chanted. "Our gratitude will be with you for as long as our tribe exists. Take this sacrifice as a token of our goodwill."

Mubuntu's laugh rang through the night. It was melodious and sent shivers of pleasure down Juma's spine. At the same time, it chilled her bones to the marrow.

The witch's jaw dropped as Mubuntu stepped down the crumbling mountain of burning meat and wood. His skin seemed to inhale the black fumes, and he grew bigger with every step. The witch pressed her face into the ground. She can see him! He must have revealed himself to her. Juma clenched her fists. Why can she only see him if he wants her to? Why do I have to endure him all the time?

She didn't want to know the answer to that question, so she focused on the pyre and the god. The fire burned faster and hotter, and Mubuntu sucked up the smoke in no time. When only ashes were left, he stood there, high as the sky and laughed. Again his laughter tore at Juma's heart.

"Why aren't you satisfied?" The witch looked up at him. "What else do you want?"

Mubuntu's finger pointed at Netinu.

An alarmed gasp escaped the witch. "You can't have him," she said.

Mubuntu shrugged and showered her with sparks. Then he whizzed off — a streak of lightning speeding toward the horizon. Bits of ash floated in the air, and the few glowing embers that had been left of the fire died.

Open-mouthed, Juma stared after him. He wanted Netinu? Why would a god ask for a human's life? She knew all the old stories. Her mother had told them to her often before she died, but no god had ever asked for a human life before.

The witch got up and killed the last sparks with slaps of her hands. The sound of the drums died. That's when realization hit Juma. No one but her had seen the exchange between the witch and Mubuntu.

She scanned the crowd, but everybody seemed happy and relaxed. Sundera and Tolobe sat next to her again, holding hands and staring at each other. Lomba was just returning from the bushes. Grinning sheepishly, he adjusted his loincloth and sat down beside her. Fleetingly, Juma wondered who he had been with. Then she focused on the witch.

"Where's Netinu?" Lomba asked.

Juma ignored him. She stared at the chieftess's face. As the witch whispered in her ear, it lost all color. Jakombe got up and clenched her hands. She walked away without answering the witch. Still, no answer was a kind of answer in itself. Juma was sure the chieftess would never agree to Mubuntu's demand.

All around her, people got up and left. Sundera asked Juma to come, but she shook her head. She wanted to see if Mubuntu came back. When most people were gone, it was apparent that he wouldn't. Juma walked toward the village wondering why Vanamate didn't wake and end the matter. She had always been strong enough to stop her brother's antics. If she didn't intervene soon, he might even wake his terrible father, the Nameless. Juma listened and felt the ground; no trembling yet. She sighed. Let's hope that will never happen, she thought. A drought is bad enough without the ground shaking and burning stones flying through the air.

Netinu cleared his throat. "May I talk to you?"

Juma's knees turned to jelly. That bloody spell... Netinu took her silence as permission.

"You were partially right when you said I wanted to provoke someone. You just got the person wrong. You are the most likely candidate to shatter Kandra's dream. Your claim to the position of chieftess is better than hers. So, I was guilty of courting you to annoy my sister, but..." He looked at her and his dark eyes were pleading with her. "...things have changed. I really love you. Also, Mother doesn't see Kandra taking her place someday or she wouldn't insist that I marry the next chieftess. With your claim, there is no better match for me in the whole tribe. I'm sure Mother would approve if we asked her as soon as your talent is verified. May I court you openly then?"

Juma didn't know what to say. Her heart wanted to believe him but her mind was in turmoil. Becoming chieftess obviously had some side effects, but she needed to time think about whether she liked this or not. For now, she changed the subject.

"Did you see Mubuntu dancing on the pyre?"

He shook his head. Then his eyes widened.

"You saw him." His voice made it half question, half statement. "If you can see him, doesn't that make you a witch?"

"I am not a witch and I never will be." Juma closed her eyes for a short moment, and then looked at the ground. She wasn't a witch. Witches could call the gods, do magic, and help the healer. She could do nothing of the like. Seeing Mubuntu might not be normal but it didn't mean she was a witch. She was absolutely sure about that. I'd better be careful what I tell him, she thought. She wanted to believe her secret was safe with him, but she didn't dare to openly admit to her weird talent. However, she had no choice but to warn him. Although she wasn't entirely sure what she felt for him, she didn't want him to die. So she chose her words carefully. "I had the feeling that he demanded you as a sacrifice."

Netinu frowned. "Are you trying to scare me?"

A little shocked that he seemed unimpressed, Juma shook her head. Maybe he thought she'd had a bad dream. Her mouth dried out. If he chose not to believe her, there was nothing she could do about it.

"He's asking for your death." She squirmed at how pathetically pleading her voice sounded, but she didn't know what else to say.

"Even if you're right, Mother will never agree to a human sacrifice. Especially if the human is me." He walked by her side without showing any fear. His posture calmed her as much as his conviction.

Of course Jakombe would not let him come to harm. Meanwhile, all Juma could do was try to find out who was working with Mubuntu. There had been a person talking to the god. Maybe the same person had made him ask for a human sacrifice. There had to be a way to find out more. As she racked her brain for an idea, they walked in silence. Only when they neared the gate in the prickly thornbush fence did she realize how companionable it felt.

Before the guards could see them, Netinu put his hand on her arm to hold her back. Immediately, fire spread through her body.

"You haven't answered my question, Juma." He looked into her eyes, and her heart seemed stuck in her throat. "May I court you openly?"

She mustered all her strength fighting to keep her knees from trembling. "Would you leave me alone if I said so?" She was proud that her voice didn't quaver.

"I'd find it very hard to do."

Juma didn't have the strength to fight. She wanted him in her life more than she cared to admit. She just wasn't sure if she wanted him as her husband-to-be. Sighing, she said, "Do whatever you have to. Just make sure that your mother will not fault me." Without looking at him, she marched through the gate and turned toward her hut, trying to forget the warmth his touch caused.

Firelight flickered on the wall of a hut in the men's quarters, and Mubuntu's voice drifted through the air. "They refuse to let the river back into its bed. And I can't kill them with my hand missing."

Another voice answered so low that Juma didn't understand. She tiptoed nearer, emboldened by the fact that the heat dæmon's power was less dangerous at night. This was her chance to find out who was collaborating with Mubuntu. Maybe she could learn why Vanamate didn't interfere. The rushes on a roof rustled when she steadied herself against a wall. She held her breath. The flickering of Mubuntu's flames was still there, as was the murmur of his voice. Juma stepped closer.

Kandra's hand fell on her shoulder. "What are you doing here?"

Juma's brain worked fast. "I wanted to tell Father about the ceremony."

"Do that tomorrow. It's time to sleep. If I see you near the men's quarters again this time of night, I'll tell Mother." Kandra glared at her.

Juma turned reluctantly and walked toward her hut, wondering why Kandra hadn't told Jakombe right away. That would have been her style. Maybe she was visiting a lover and didn't want her mother to know. While she washed, she tried to recall where Kandra had been during the ceremony but couldn't remember. When she lay in bed, her thoughts wandered back to Netinu. Had he tried to charm her again or had he been earnest? She fell asleep before reaching a conclusion.

After breakfast, Mama Lubeda sent Sundera, Juma, and two more girls to help with the preparation of the midday meal. Scrubbing yams was dirty work, but the chatter around the fire took Juma's mind off Netinu's unwanted attention.

The day dragged on and the villagers went after their usual chores. A resigned apathy filled the hot air, but Juma didn't spot Mubuntu anywhere. She wondered what he was up to and feared the worst when a dust cloud rose over the southern hills. From the cooking area in the village center, Juma watched the cloud grow bigger for a while, and then settle.

A group of six people appeared over the hills and descended toward the village. Juma wondered how a small group like that could cause a dust cloud like the one she had noticed. Three men and three women approached the southern gate in the thornbush fence. They were smaller and stockier than the members of Juma's tribe with clothing dominated by yellow and brown. At the gate, they were made to wait, and a messenger ran to Jakombe's hut. Juma wondered what the strangers had come for, but it had to be important because Jakombe personally went to greet them. A little later, the strangers had been assigned a hut, and the head cook dumped more yams at Juma's feet. She went back to work with a sigh.

After the midday meal, Jakombe gathered the tribe in the oval Central Hall. The people stood silently with a big, open circle in the middle and a narrow passage for the strangers to walk through. Children and toddlers sat in the front, their eyes wide with anticipation. Most of them had never seen a human from another tribe before. Juma was glad that she wasn't one of the taller women who had to stand in the back. Whispering like the others, she and Sundera exchanged guesses of why the strangers had come.

"Welcome in the Lake Tribe's village," Jakombe said when the strangers approached her throne. She stood tall, dressed up with all the gold she could fit on her neck, arms, and legs. The bright red cloak flowed from her shoulders like molten stone, and her face was motionless.

The strangers tried hard to look just as impressive. They had donned golden chains and bracelets and wide scarves of a yellow material. Their nearly black skin glistened from the fat they had rubbed in it, and they were unarmed. Juma had to admit, they looked good.

"Thank you for the gentle greeting, great Jakombe of the Lake Tribe," the oldest of the women said. Slightly stooped, she supported herself on the messenger's staff. A second woman waited at her side, and three warriors stood a few steps behind her at an honorable distance, carrying bags.

"Please accept our humble gifts." The eldest waved her companions forward, and they presented their offerings. One laid a red cloak of finest fibers at Jakombe's feet. The next one took scented herbs from his bag, the woman presented a necklace made of artfully twisted strands of gold, and the last warrior pulled a small, wooden cage with a colorful bird from his bag.

Juma marveled at the display of wealth, but she wondered why a rich tribe like this had come to see them. Also, she missed the sixth figure she had seen earlier. Where was she? The answer wasn't long in coming.

The eldest bowed to Jakombe and said, "May we present to you our Princess Chunte, High Priestess and Leader of our Tribe." The gift-bearers pulled out flutes and began to play a monotonous melody that called the last member of the delegation.

A slender young woman loaded with gold and dressed in the finest, most colorful kikoi Juma had ever seen walked toward the throne. She nodded at Jakombe gracefully. When she spoke, her voice was a warm alto that made Juma wonder what she would sound like when singing.

"We come from a far-away place on the other side of the holy mountain because we have been urged to choose a royal husband by our advisors." Princess Chunte nodded toward the eldest. "Since we heard that you've got a strong and able-bodied son, we decided to pay you a visit to see if he would be suitable."

Juma's jaw dropped and an unknown hurt shot through her heart. It felt a bit as if someone had cut a slice off of it. Obviously, the rest of her tribe was just as surprised. The expectant silence had given way to agitated murmuring. Jakombe quieted the crowd with the simple gesture of peace, her hand raised with the palm facing the princess.

"We feel honored at such a request. Our son is strong and fast. He's a good hunter, and his teeth are straight and as white as the desert sand." She looked the princess over. "He is of good standing, but he cannot be had without a price."

"Our tribe has grounds of good soil where crops grow to twice the usual height. We have water aplenty coming from two rivers that pass our lands on either side. Wildebeest and zebras roam the steppes in great numbers, and of predators there are but a few."

Juma detected an undertone of annoyance in the princess's voice. She wondered why Jakombe didn't ask the guest why a princess of a rich tribe was interested in Netinu. It seemed their tribe had everything they needed. Was she only jealous of another woman courting Netinu or was there truly something strange in this proposal?

"Much as you might dislike it, I will not let my son leave," Jakombe said. "He's to be joined to the next leader of our tribe. Should you marry him, you will have to stay with us, and we will test you as a candidate for becoming the next chieftess." Jakombe's gaze bored into that of Princess Chunte. "Be aware that we evaluate the candidates carefully. Would you be prepared to live with us? Will you give up your tribe to join ours?"

"If your son is the man I'm dreaming of, I would willingly join my tribe and my lands with yours. Imagine what strength our combined tribes would have." Chunte's eyes shone. "Still, I would need to get to know your son and to learn more about your tribe before I can decide on settling here. Would you graciously allow me to stay until High Moon to see if my folks would get along with yours?"

Jakombe nodded and pointed to a vacant chair at her side where Kandra usually sat. "Be our guest and join my house. The festival of High Moon would be an appropriate time to announce any decisions made in this matter. We admire the wisdom of your course of action."

The princess sat down at the same time Jakombe did. Juma, Sundera, and the other girls slipped through the crowd to fetch the refreshments they had prepared. They handed out water and buttered bread until the last of the visitors withdrew.

## 7

*A* LOT OF WORK HAD been left undone because the welcoming of the guests had taken them much longer than anticipated. Juma, Sundera, and the other girls cleaned dishes long into the night. On the way back to their hut through the silent, moonlit village, Juma turned to Sundera.

"Do you think she'll stay for good?"

Sundera shrugged. "It depends. Maybe she'll fall in love with Netinu."

Again the unfamiliar pain sliced through Juma's heart. Why did it hurt to think of Netinu getting married to an obviously wealthy and very beautiful princess? Would the hurt continue, and would it stop when decisions were announced at High Moon festival?

Sundera didn't seem to notice her pain. "It would be a great gain if both tribes would merge. We'd be the strongest clan around."

"Why would we want to grow that big? We don't have enemies."

Sundera's smiling face grew earnest. "With the drought getting worse every day, it will only be a question of time before the tribes surrounding our territory will try to take the lake from us. We don't have many warriors because they are valued so little. If Chunte has enough talented hunters and some warriors too, they might teach our men how to fight in an emergency."

Juma fell silent. She didn't like Sundera's reasoning but had to admit she was right.

Just as they turned toward their hut's entrance, Netinu stepped from the shadows. Wordlessly he grabbed Juma's arm and pulled her into a darker patch beside a hut. He bent forward and whispered into her ear.

"I just came to let you know that I'll never, ever marry that princess. She sized me up like an animal for slaughter. She touched my private part to see if I'd be able to please her, and she looked into my mouth as if I were a slave for barter."

"There's no need to tell me." Juma freed her arm and spoke louder than necessary. Pushing him away was the hardest thing she'd done in her life. "You will not be allowed to choose your own bride, and I am not going to go against the tribe's wishes."

"I wanted to let you know that my heart belongs to you." Netinu lowered his head. "I think you'd make a much better chieftess for our tribe than Princess Chunte or my sister ever will."

Juma's insides felt raw from fighting her feelings for Netinu. He had to be off limits until Jakombe's succession was settled.

"With Kandra and the princess competing for the job, I don't think I'll have a chance anyway," she snapped.

"Don't give up before you tried." Netinu grabbed her shoulders, pulled her close, and pressed his lips on hers. Juma froze, and he vanished in the dark so fast, she couldn't stop him. Her lips still tingled when she lay in bed, and she couldn't sleep for a long time.

When she woke, she was still tired, and her feelings were just as confused as when she had gone to bed. She was glad that Sundera hadn't commented on the previous night's scene. She simply smiled whenever Juma looked in her direction.

"It's the first day of testing," one of the older girls said to Sundera. "Have you settled on a favorite work or are you leaving it up to the witch?"

The question jolted Juma from her musings. Testing day already? She washed and dressed as fast as she could hoping to be in the first batch of girls. But she had to wait.

"No food today. You'll have to fast for the testing to be effective," Mama Lubeda said to the twenty-seven girls before she sent five of them to the witch's hut.

Juma stared after them with envy and settled into her chores with a sigh. Soon, her stomach cramped and her lips chafed. She put her well-used pebble in her mouth to quench the worst of the hunger pangs and the thirst.

"Why are they letting us wait?" she said to Sundera who was helping her peel the yams. "Am I not the previous chieftess's daughter?"

"There are many girls this year and I bet the choosing takes some time. Our turn will come."

Juma knew her friend was right. Regardless of how much she despised the wait, there was nothing she could do. She might as well try to bear it with the dignity expected from a chieftess's heir.

For most of the day, she saw girls leave anxiously and return with big smiles on their faces. Whenever her stomach grumbled, she sucked harder on her pebble. Finally, it was her and Sundera's turn. They walked toward the hut with three more girls.

The hunger growled in Juma's belly like an angry lion, and the aroma of frying meat didn't help. Her mouth watered. She swallowed and tried to ignore the delicious smell.

Not far from the witch's hut, Tolobe waited. Sundera's face lit up and she hurried over, touching his arm gently. Juma followed her with a frown on her face.

"You're not allowed to be here today," she said. "It's testing day."

Tolobe nodded. "I know, but the chief hunter sent me since Chieftess Jakombe will pass here on her way back to the testing. When we were out hunting today, I noticed something strange she needs to know."

"Something strange about what?" Sundera looked up at him expectantly. Her cream-colored skin stood in nice contrast to Tolobe's much darker shade.

"The visitors brought many more people than they made us believe. This afternoon, I went with the hunters around the lake to see how the young of the wildebeest zebra herd fared. In a place between the woods and the plain, we discovered at least three hundred people with the same build and skin color as the princess's delegation. They camped in the open, had only a few belongings, and food was scarce. I noticed women, children, and elders."

"They brought the whole tribe?" Sundera frowned. "Did you find out why?"

Tolobe shook his head. "We were too busy wondering about them to really listen. And their dialect is a bit difficult to understand. But if the chieftess requests, I will go back and see what I can find out."

Juma, who had kept an eye on their surroundings, pushed him. "Jakombe is coming. Hurry. You wouldn't want her to see you with us."

"She has to be told. The chief hunter was adamant."

Sundera put her hand on his arm. "This is testing day. Find out more and see her tonight."

"You might be right." Tolobe slipped away so fast, Jakombe never saw him as she approached the witch's hut.

"Come on in, girls." She lifted the zebra skin that covered the entrance and let Juma and Sundera enter before her to join the three girls already inside.

The witch nodded at them. "Welcome, girls. Have you refrained from eating?"

When the five girls all nodded, the witch made them sit in a circle on the ground. Chieftess Jakombe stood at the door, arms folded in front of her chest.

"First, we will find out which work appeals to you most," the witch said. "After that, we will evaluate your talents. Considering all we learned, we will assign you to your training."

"I'm hungry," one of the girls complained.

"There will be plenty to eat afterwards," the chieftess said.

Juma recalled the piles of meat that were still dried on the racks or fried over open fires. She tried to shake the picture with little success.

"Drink this." The witch handed a bowl around with a foul-smelling liquid.

"What is it?" Sundera wrinkled her nose.

The witch smiled. "It doesn't taste as bad as it smells."

"What does it do?"

"It will open your mind so I can search for your heart's desire."

Holding her nose with one hand, Sundera drank her share and passed the bowl on.

The witch put on a headband with feathers, pearls, and sparkling stones, and started to burn incense. It filled the air with a tangy odor that made Juma's eyes water and her throat dry. In combination with the magical drink, her head felt as if it wasn't attached to her body any more. Although she knew it was where it belonged, the strange feeling persisted. A smile grew on her face that she couldn't suppress. She giggled as her head seemed to bob through the air without her body. It felt so strange to be only part of the whole. Where was the rest of her? She looked around, but couldn't see it despite the fact that her hands and feet tingled. What a truly strange experience, she thought and giggled some more.

"What would you love to become?" The witch directed her voice at Sundera.

"I would love to care for others. My dream is to become a herder, but the duties of a healer appeal to me too." Sundera's voice sounded so far off, Juma had to search for her to make sure she hadn't drifted through the opening in the roof that let the fire's smoke out. Her friend was already sinking to the ground, as if speaking had made her heavy again. One girl after the other answered the witch's question and sank back to the ground, growing limp as they did.

Finally, the witch turned to Juma. "What would you love to become?"

"Why am I drifting in the air like this? And where is my body?" Juma meant to answer the question but her curiosity was much stronger.

The witch smiled. "You're not floating. The feeling is only a side-effect of the herb I gave you."

"Oh." Juma pondered this. "So, my body is still there after all. Why did you give us the drink if it does this to us?"

"With it, you cannot hide your true wishes when I ask."

"Does that mean I couldn't tell a lie even if I wanted to?"

"Give it a try." The witch's teeth glowed white in the hut's semidarkness.

"I would like to become…" Juma stopped. The words 'a warrior' refused to be spoken. Strangely, it relieved her. Warrior was the last profession she wanted to train for. "I want to be the next chieftess, and I've got a good enough claim. After all, my mother would have been in Jakombe's place if she had lived long enough." Juma expected the chieftess to react, but she stood motionless at the door. A little smile played around her lips, and her gaze lay gently on Juma. Didn't she mind that her niece challenged her daughter's claims? Or couldn't she hear them like when the witch tried to catch Mubuntu?

The witch threw some herbs on the fire and the scent of spring filled the room.

All of a sudden, Juma felt the ground beneath her again. The floating sensation was over and her body had slumped. She sat up and looked around. The others sat in the circle without moving. They looked at their hands or on the ground. No one dared to speak, so Juma stayed silent as well. She closed her eyes and breathed in deeply. The air in the hut smelled of turned earth and freshly planted vegetables, of early morning rain and wet dog fur, and of Vanamate's tears falling from the sky. How did the witch do that? How can one capture the essence of spring in a few herbs? Juma opened her eyes with a new respect for the old woman.

Six totems hovered over the low fire glowing in a gentle bluish light, each representing one kind of work the girls could train for. There was a tiny spear for hunters and warriors, a bowl with bandages for healers, a pot for cooks, a crook for herders, a plough for field workers, and a red cloak for the chieftess. When all the girls had opened their eyes, the witch placed a final item in the middle of the circle of symbols—a pouch for the witch.

"Each of the fields you can choose comes with their own pleasures and duties. Hunters and warriors provide for and protect the tribe. They will be gone from their families often and give their life if needed. Healers will do their best to treat injuries and illnesses but must also witness infirmity and death. Cooks feed the tribe and will go hungry in times of need. Herders care for our animals, missing nights in their family's hut when the lion hunts or an ewe is born. Field workers plant and harvest what we need and face Mubuntu's heat every day. A chieftess leads our tribe through bad times and good times, putting her own needs aside. And a witch watches over the tribe's wellbeing with her magic, giving up her chance to marry and have a family."

Really, a witch couldn't get married? Juma suppressed a grin. Did the old woman really believe she could recruit a successor from their ranks? No one would want to train for a job that made it impossible to have children, despite the fact that everybody revered and loved the tribe's witch.

"Spread your arms and lay your hands on your knees with the palms up," the witch said.

She started a monotonous singsong that tugged at Juma's nerves. She longed to change it into a real song, but she pressed her lips together. Not everyone had her ear for music, and it was never a good idea to interrupt the witch.

The blue glow of the seven symbols intensified. When they glowed so brightly Juma could hardly look at them any more, the witch pointed at one of the girls. The symbols whirled to her and circled around her head. After a while, the pot lowered itself into her palm.

"You wanted to be a cook, and the profession chose you. You may go," Jakombe said.

The girl squealed with delight, got to her feet and hurried out of the hut.

The witch pointed to Sundera. The pot resumed its place in the glowing circle that now orbited Juma's only friend. The symbols whirled around her head for a long time.

Juma wondered. Why does it take so much longer than with the other girl? She bent forward to see better. Now and again, one of the items seemed to sink but shot back up into the circle as if they couldn't make up their minds. After what seemed like an eternity, two symbols sank into Sundera's outstretched hands. Unbelieving, Juma stared at the crook and the cloak. A candidate for chieftess training? Sundera? How could that be? The symbols must have erred.

"This is a surprise," the witch said.

Jakombe added, "Please wait outside until we finish with the other girls, since we need to discuss this."

Sundera nodded, got up, and stumbled from the hut as if in a daze. The witch directed the floating objects to the next girl.

With every selection, the circle around the fire grew smaller. It didn't take long until Juma was the last one sitting there. Anticipation made her sweat as the objects whirled around her head. As with Sundera, they circled much longer than usual. Juma thought her heart would jump from her chest, it beat so hard. After another eternity, two objects landed on her hands. She didn't dare to breathe, fearing they'd vanish. They felt cool and soft to the touch. When she finally had the courage to look at the objects, she was not surprised to see the red cloak of a chieftess's candidate on her left palm. What shook her to the bones was the pouch that had settled on her right.

"I can't be a witch," she said into the silence. "I haven't…" The words, 'a drop of magic in me,' froze on her tongue as she remembered the vision she had during the welcoming ceremony and her ability to see Mubuntu. She must have worked magic without even realizing it. Her throat went dry. She didn't want to be a witch. As a witch, she couldn't become chieftess. Her mother would be so disappointed if she gave up her dream. As a witch she wouldn't even be able to bear children who could one day claim her birthright. How could this have happened?

"Sorry, but I really can't become a witch," she repeated.

"The totems say you can." Her face an unreadable mask, the witch collected the symbols and put them into a pouch of blue leather. The minute she touched them, they stopped glowing and looked like ordinary items again.

Jakombe put a hand on Juma's shoulder. "It is your duty to sacrifice your wish of becoming chieftess to the tribe's greater good. Selenta is getting on in age. She might not be with us much longer, and we've waited years for the totems to find a replacement. Since they selected you, you've got the strength to become the next village witch. Do not disappoint us."

As gently as it was phrased, it was a direct order from the chieftess — one Juma could not ignore. Coldness spread through her, turning her heart into an icy knot.

"You could find a more talented girl next year." Her protest felt weak compared to the storm brewing in her heart.

"I've been searching ever since I passed my fifth year as the village witch," Selenta said in a low voice. "The totems always came up empty. You might be our last chance, Juma."

The half-hidden plea splintered on the icy knot in Juma's stomach. Lies! They must both be lying. Somehow Jakombe had rigged the test. She had always objected to her as a chieftess trainee because she wanted Kandra to follow in her footsteps. There was no denying the fact.

"Be gentle," the witch said to Jakombe. "Becoming the tribe's witch is hard for a girl her age. It will take time for her to adjust to the fact that she can never marry."

"Never marry?" Juma echoed. Wasn't it enough to be forced into an apprenticeship she didn't want?

"As a witch, you must stay a virgin, or your magic will pick up elements of Mubuntu's ferocity."

Juma glanced at Jakombe and thought she looked smug. She sprang to her feet, her hands clenching the folds of her loincloth. "Something must have gone wrong," she insisted.

"The ritual cannot be affected from the outside." The witch got up too. "I understand that you're upset. I felt the same many circles of the sun ago."

She tried to reach out, but Juma jerked back. She knew there was no way she could oppose Jakombe without getting banished from the tribe, but her heart was bleeding. She had to become chieftess, so her mother could be proud of her. It was her birthright, and the cloak in the ritual had confirmed it. The rebellion brewing in her heart must have been clearly visible on her face.

"There will be no further discussion." Jakombe glared at her warningly. "I order you to start training as the next village witch tonight."

Juma clenched her fists and forced herself not to talk back. Still, she wouldn't give up her goal for as long as she lived. Maybe things would change once they had called the rain. The emotions churning inside of her choked her. She stormed from the hut, ignoring Sundera's surprised call.

## 8

FIGHTING BACK THE TEARS, SHE marched through the village. This was so unfair. Why couldn't Kandra train as the next witch? Or Sundera? Or anyone else, for that matter?

Surprised, she stared at the witch's hut. She must have walked a circle without noticing. With a sigh, she forced her thoughts away from the painful subject and realized she had a much more pressing problem. Her stomach growled like an angry lion, so she turned and walked toward the eating area.

"Wait a moment." Sundera ran after her and grabbed her arm. "Why did you run away? I thought you'd wait for me."

Juma forced a smile. Luckily her friend was preoccupied and didn't notice the sadness in her eyes.

She linked arms with Juma. "I had the strangest feeling when they called me back in. Could you imagine me as a chieftess? I'm so glad they didn't force me into that training. I'll be much happier as a herder."

"So they did let you choose?"

"Sure. They said that it's rare for more than one totem to choose a person, but when it happens, the person has to do the choosing." Sundera smiled. "I'm so glad. I wouldn't be able to live with all the responsibility a chieftess faces daily."

Juma's smile was grim. They let her choose, and I wasn't allowed to. This is so unfair. It occurred to her that Jakombe had done it on purpose to push a wedge between her and Sundera to distract them. That would give Kandra an edge over her competitors. Juma decided she wouldn't allow that to happen.

"I'm glad you can do what your heart desires," she forced herself to say.

"Me too. What will you train for?" Sundera cocked her head.

"I'm the witch's new apprentice." Juma only answered reluctantly.

"Oh, wow!"

"I know. It's nothing compared to the rank of chieftess." Juma heard the bitterness in her own voice but couldn't help it.

"Who cares? The witch is held in high regard by the whole tribe. Without her, we couldn't afford to have so few warriors. Her responsibilities are as important as those of the chieftess, maybe even more so."

Juma had never thought about that before.

Sundera went on, "For me, what you do and how much people value you, is far more important. I think it's marvelous that you can become a witch. You'll be able to communicate with the gods. Imagine what you'll be able to do for the tribe." Wide-eyed, she beamed at her friend.

Juma didn't get a chance to answer.

"You must be starving, dears." Mama Lubeda took their arms and led them to the Central Hut. Wherever Juma looked, she spotted happy faces. It seemed all the girls had gotten the training they wanted except for her. She bit her tongue to keep from crying. It made eating rather difficult.

When the sun set, a little boy came running and stopped when he saw Juma and Sundera. "The witch wants you," he said to Juma and raced off again.

She remembered Jakombe's threat, and her heart grew cold. "I'd better go," she said. "The witch meant to start my training tonight." Then she remembered something else. "I haven't visited Father today. If he is awake, could you tell him I'll see him tomorrow?"

"Sure. Tolobe and I meant to look in on him anyway." Sundera put her hand on Juma's shoulder. "I bet you're going to be the best village witch ever."

Juma's heart warmed at the words, and facing the witch again didn't seem half as daunting as before.

She entered the semi-darkness of the hut a few minutes later. The old woman was sitting on a mat beside the fire and dressing a clay figurine with garlands of dried flowers.

"I didn't think I'd see you again today." She didn't look up from her work. "But truth be told, there are worse fates than becoming the village witch."

Juma didn't answer.

"I'm sure you think I would have told Jakombe if you hadn't shown up. Don't fear. I remember that it took me two months to come to terms with my talent and with the fact that I'd never hold my own child." The witch picked up a pouch with powdered herbs and rubbed some into the figurine's elaborate hairdo.

"I've been ordered to learn, so I will learn. But the minute I suspect that someone has the same amount of talent or more, I insist on another test." Juma folded her arms in front of her chest, crumpling her kikoi in the process.

"Fair enough," the witch said. "The thing is, I can't spend a lot of time on teaching you the basics the way I was taught. But the drought is getting worse every day, and I see trouble on the horizon. Until we manage to alert Vanamate to Mubuntu's games, you will have to tag along and see what you can figure out on your own." The witch looked up at her, and her dark eyes were serious. "I do not know if our tribe will survive the coming season, but if it does, and if I'm still around to teach you, I'll do my very best then."

Suddenly, Juma's anger evaporated. Her stubbornness felt foolish compared to the trouble the tribe was facing. She knelt beside the witch. "What am I supposed to do?"

"Every witch accesses magic in a different way. My way is herbs. I can talk to them, and I can make them speak for me," the old woman said. "We will have to gather enough magical energy to send our prayer to Vanamate with force. It would be helpful if you could sing with me, since she likes music, and I'm not very good at it."

The witch started a song Juma had never heard, moving her hands through the air in front of her as if guiding something invisible to her chest. The movements and the words of the song were easy enough to copy, but Juma couldn't make head or tail of the melody. In the end, she invented her own, trying to fit it to the witch's unmelodious mumbling as best she could.

Pressure built up around them, and the hair on Juma's arms rose. A strange glow began to gather on her chest. The herbs the witch dumped into the fire burned in black clouds and forced water from Juma's eyes. Her head felt light as if it was about to float away again. This can't be healthy, she thought, but kept on chanting and gathering magical energy. She glanced at the witch whose chest glowed like a star. With a swipe of her hands, the old woman pushed the glowing energy toward the sky, calling out loud a short prayer. Juma copied her gesture and her words.

"Vanamate we call for you."

"Vanamate, we cry for your help."

"Vanamate please come and bring us rain."

The glowing pressure on her chest vanished and ripped the words from her mouth. She thought she could see both careen through a small opening in the ceiling toward the sky, but she wasn't sure. Hopefully that will wake Vanamate.

The witch's song came to an end, and a glow appeared in the dark cloud the burning herbs had created. Pictures appeared in the glow, and Juma shivered. Blood and dust filled the vision as people were fighting. The picture shifted to two shady figures facing savage animals whose burning furs alighted even stone. The flames licked up, leaving the picture of a beautiful woman. The dark of her skin glistened in the light of countless flames flickering around her. Her eyes were closed, but tears welled out nonetheless. They evaporated in the heat, and tiny clouds of steam blurred the vision again. The smoke dissipated and the vision was over.

The witch closed her eyes and leaned back. A tear ran over her cheek again. "If only Vanamate would send rain," she whispered. "I don't know what else to do."

"She's still sitting in her ring of fire," Juma said. "Didn't you see?"

"See?" The witch opened her eyes. "You saw something?"

Juma described the vision she had. The witch's eyes grew bigger with every word.

"I never saw a thing," she exclaimed. "The women of our tribe haven't had a true vision in many generations. You must be very talented indeed, especially since you had to make my magic work for you. Let us determine what your vision means."

They readily agreed that the fighting could mean war with another tribe. With the dwindling water supplies, it was more than likely that one tribe or another would try to force access to the lake. War was a problem that the tribe hadn't faced in generations. It was something Chieftess Jakombe would have to handle.

Neither the witch nor Juma could make head or tail of the burning animals, but the crying woman in the circle of fire was definitely Vanamate. The old stories said she sat in a fiery ring for three months every year so Mother Earth could warm up again.

"Why doesn't she wake and come out of her protective circle?" Juma wondered.

"Maybe she's sleeping too deeply this time and our songs don't reach her ear," the witch said. "Or Mubuntu did something."

"Do you think he holds his sister captive?"

"It comes to mind. His is the element of fire, and he uses it freely these days." The witch sighed. "The longer the heat lasts, the stronger he will get."

Juma wondered what the heat dæmon was up to. "What reason does he have to capture Vanamate? I know he likes to play tricks on everyone, but would he harm his sister?"

"I do not know. He's never done this before as far as I know," the witch said.

Juma knew that the witch knew a lot more than the average villager. So why was Mubuntu playing tricks on Vanamate? Or wasn't he? Would they be able to wake the goddess? What would they need to do? She pondered the questions.

Finally, the witch said, "It's late. Go back to your hut and rest. I will think of something we can try tomorrow."

Juma walked through the night, enjoying the cool breeze. It was still warm enough so she didn't need to pull her kikoi tighter, but it was cool enough to soothe her burning cheeks. Surprised, she realized she had enjoyed the old witch's company and the magic they had wrought together. It had been more interesting than she had expected. Could Sundera be right? Was it more important to do something she liked than to gain high social status? She thought of the contempt in Kandra's eyes whenever she looked at Juma's father and shook her head. She would never allow anyone to look at her that way, and with a high rank, no one would dare.

A flicker of light in the reed field near the lake caught her attention. Who would start a fire in the reeds in this drought? Such carelessness. Juma hurried toward the flickering light. When she drew nearer, she heard someone sing a prayer. She slowed down, not wanting to disturb whoever was praying. Still, the fire was dangerous, so she walked closer, set on dowsing the flames as soon as the prayer was over.

In a little clearing in the reeds, Princess Chunte had erected a small shrine of dry wood with a clay figurine on top. She had taken off her kikoi and laid it out in front of the shrine to kneel on it. The flames of two small fires lit her naked body and made her skin glow from within. She lifted her hands to the sky and sang.

"Mubuntu, most desirable of all gods, thank you for saving us from the Nameless's rage."

Tolobe was right, Juma thought. The princess's native tongue was similar enough to their language but pronounced in a way that made it hard to understand. The song went on.

"Mubuntu, I pray to thee, come to me in your glory and strength, so I might participate in your power, to rule and guide my people in your honor."

Juma gasped when Mubuntu appeared out of thin air on the shrine. He was naked too, and his manhood stood proud and erect. Muscles played under his skin which was as pale as the rising moon. He would have been perfect if it weren't for the hand he had lost to the witch. The clay figurine crumpled under his feet as he stepped down to the kneeling woman. He pulled her up, and his lips closed on hers. Drawing her close, he moved between her legs, laughing when she flinched.

"It's a small price to pay for the power I'm giving you," he said.

Princess Chunte forced a smile.

"Your glory is no burden to bear, as long as I get my heart's desire."

With his strong arms, he lifted her onto his lap, moving with strong thrusts, his greed and pleasure showing plainly. Juma cringed at the pain she saw in Chunte's face.

A bolt of lightning shot from Mubuntu into Chunte. It filled her, lit her from within like a lantern. She screamed, and her pain cut through Juma like a knife.

Mubuntu pulled away from Chunte and set her down. Instantly, the hurt expression was gone, replaced by elation.

Juma felt the strength of the magic he had passed to her and shivered. The princess was dangerous. If she allowed Mubuntu to claim a husband's rights to gain power, what would she do to Netinu or the clan when she got what she wanted? Juma walked backwards slowly.

"We are not alone." Mubuntu's head flew up, and he looked in her direction as if he could see her perfectly clear. "Someone is listening."

"Kill him," Chunte said.

"You know I can't harm humans unless they're mine."

"Then catch him, and I'll kill him."

"Your wish is my command." Mubuntu rose.

The color of his skin turned to the darkest shade of ebony. It was a strange sight seeing someone change the color of their skin. Juma tried to run and hide, but her knees trembled so much, she couldn't even walk. Disregarding dignity, she sank to the ground and crawled. The soil felt wet on her fingers, and she knew she was leaving a clear trail. But Mubuntu was a god, not a hunter. Hopefully, he wouldn't find it.

A hand closed over her mouth, and a strong arm pulled her into a thicket. Juma struggled to get free until she recognized the familiar smell. She relaxed and huddled closer to Tolobe. The reeds shaded him so well, only his eyes were visible in the moonlight. Not too far away, Mubuntu and Chunte searched the reeds. Luckily, it was already too dark to see much.

Finally, Mubuntu said, "It's too late now. For sure the eavesdropper has returned to the village. If you find him speaking against you and your tribe in the morning, you will have to kill Chieftess Jakombe and take her son and her place."

"That's going to be fun." Chunte giggled. "Although Netinu's manhood won't offer me the same pleasure as yours."

"You can always sacrifice him to me later. Also, don't forget to fetch me back my hand. If necessary, kill the witch. At her age, she won't be up to your strength." Mubuntu bit her breast before he disappeared. Chunte wiped the blood from her nipple and a tear from her face, killed the fire, and left.

Tolobe bent to Juma and whispered in her ear. "We need to be very, very careful who we tell about this, or we'll end up with the wrong chieftess."

"Shall we go?" Juma tried to get up, but Tolobe held her back.

"Don't let her trick you into revealing yourself. We'll wait until she's gone."

They lay side by side in the mud waiting for Chunte to leave. Finally, Juma fell asleep. When morning dawned, she woke and looked around. Neither Mubuntu nor Chunte were anywhere in sight. Relieved, she got up and woke her brother. Tolobe stretched and yawned.

"Thank you for rescuing me," Juma said. "How come you were here?"

"I went to spy on the princess's tribe on the other side of the lake. I hoped to find out why they have left their territory." Tolobe got up and patted the dust off his loincloth and skin.

"And did you?"

"The Nameless moved and turned the soil beneath the tribe's feet. Many were badly burnt by molten earth, most of their belongings went up in flames, but the princess led most of them away from the danger. When the earth's shaking wouldn't stop, she sacrificed her mother, their chieftess, to the Nameless, trying to soothe Mubuntu's father. Finally the earth settled and the dust cleared, and they set out to find new land."

Juma tried to imagine the horror the other tribe went through and felt sorry for them. Still, human sacrifice was something her tribe would never tolerate. "We need to tell Jakombe what we found out."

Tolobe nodded slowly, but he was frowning. "We do, but we have to be careful the princess doesn't find out. The hunters and warriors of her tribe still outnumber ours. She could wipe our whole tribe from the earth if she wants."

Hand in hand, they went down to the water's edge, washed, and walked back to the village.

"Try to catch Jakombe when she's all alone," Tolobe said. "She is more likely going to listen to a woman than to me."

Juma nodded. Her aunt had always been slightly snobbish when it came to men. She remembered the last time she had seen her uncle. His small, thin body was worn out from all the tasks she had given him. He'd been working from early morning till late at night with hardly ever a friendly word from his wife. It was no wonder he'd died early. Tolobe was right; it was best if she talked to Jakombe, preferably when her aunt was alone.

Juma got the chance to catch her alone when she visited her father in the healer's hut. His sleep was restless and he turned from side to side until she put her hand on his shoulder and sang him a lullaby her mother used to sing to her. Just as the healer left, Jakombe came in.

"I though the healer said he woke." The chieftess shook her head and frowned.

"He did but he's still so weak, he fell asleep again." Juma got up. "Can I talk to you in private?"

"I'm not going to change my mind about your training," Jakombe said.

"It's about Princess Chunte."

Jakombe crossed her arms in front of her chest. "I noticed the way you try to make Netinu fall for you. Don't think you will be successful. If I deem the princess suitable, he will marry her."

"Would you please stop jumping to conclusions and listen? It's really important." Juma fought hard to keep her anger down. Her aunt's habit of seeing the world the way she wanted annoyed her no end. "I found out that Princess Chunte's whole tribe took shelter on the other side of the lake. Her warriors outnumber ours, and she's determined to conquer our territory one way or the other. She has to. Their homeland was destroyed when the Nameless moved."

Jakombe didn't say a word, but her nostrils flared.

"And last night, I watched Princess Chunte join with Mubuntu." Immediately Juma wished she had kept this to herself because Kandra had slipped into the hut. Kandra's jaw dropped, and her eyes narrowed.

"Are you running around accusing our guests of treason? Chunte might be praying to Mubuntu, but he'd never lay with her."

"Any connection to Mubuntu is suspicious in the drought." Juma shrugged. She didn't want to dwell on last night's details.

"Liar. I saw the princess talking to Mama Lubeda in the evening. Making up stories about an honored guest should get you expelled from the tribe." Kandra lifted her hand as if to slap her.

Jakombe reached out and stopped her daughter.

"Despite her overreaction, Kandra is right. Princess Chunte is an honored guest, and I will not allow you to speak falsely of her. If I hear you going round accusing her of being Mubuntu's bride again without proof, I will punish you most severely." She turned and walked away without another word.

Kandra ran after her mother. "Mother, wait. I meant to ask you something."

Juma's heart sank. What could she do against Mubuntu and the princess if no one would listen to her? A hand touched hers, and when she turned, her father was awake.

"Tell the witch. Jakombe might listen to her," he suggested. His voice was hoarse, and his eyelids fluttered. Juma could see he was still very tired. She smiled at him.

"That's good advice." She squeezed his hand, helped him to drink, and sang another song until he slept again. Since the witch had asked for her to come after the midday meal, she decided to spend some more time at her father's side. Sitting on a stool, she watched his profile. His skin clung to the high cheekbones and his eyes had sunken into their sockets. He looked parched. She remembered how he'd always been there for her, how his eyes had sparkled when she had scaled her first tree, and how proud he'd been when she won her first game of snickets. Everything seemed so far away now.

Lost in thought, she sat at his side for a long time. Finally, he opened his eyes again. His hand found hers and he smiled. "I need you to know something."

She nodded, but first she helped him to drink again.

He sighed, closed his eyes, and stayed silent until Juma thought he had fallen asleep again. But he was awake.

"I've never been one to talk a lot," he said. "It's difficult to find the right words."

"Why don't you start at the beginning?"

He smiled at her. "When I courted your mother, she despised me. I am a warrior and come from a clan where warriors are honored members of the community. Her clan believes men to be inferior to women. I should have stayed away from her, but I couldn't. I loved her too much. It took me a long time to prove my worth to her, but in the end, her love equaled mine." He coughed and drank some more. "We married against her mother's wish. But your mother had already been crowned chieftess, and there was nothing her mother could do against her decision. We lived happily until Tolobe was born. He had a twin brother who died shortly after his birth, and the clan members began to speak of dark magic and offerings to unknown gods. They began to use talismans or signs against evil whenever they met me. In the end, I couldn't stand it any longer. I told your mother I'd leave and released her from the marriage.

"She decided to come with me. As much as I begged her to stay with the tribe she loved, she wouldn't listen. The day we left, she gave her crown to Jakombe and said, 'Care for my people as best you can until I return to claim my crown back.'

"We moved to the little hut at the Endless Well where we lived peacefully for a long time. You were born there, and some time later Lomba, too. One day, you developed a high fever. Your mother fretted over you, but you burned hotter and hotter every day. We watched you waste away. The day before High Moon, your mother told me she'd do the one thing left to her. When the moon was up, she took off a charm she had gotten from her grandmother and called Monnatoba, the Goddess of the Other Side. What I never thought possible happened: the moon-goddess came down to earth and spoke to my wife. I couldn't understand them, but in the end, your mother went with Monnatoba in exchange for your life. Knowing I'd never see her again, I mourned her as if she had died. My duty as a father helped with the pain." Breathing heavily, he put a hand on her arm. "Jakombe shouldn't treat you the way she does. I know you're no liar, and what's more, you are the rightful candidate to become chieftess.

In this tribe, the daughter of a previous chieftess has always been favored as long as was suited to the task."

"I know. I just didn't know that mother never officially gave up her claim." Juma bent down and kissed his cheek. "Thank you for telling me. I'm sure that will help me in getting where I need to be."

"The whole tribe witnessed when your mother handed her crown to Jakombe. Everybody heard that she was planning to come back. Although some might have forgotten, I'm sure the witch hasn't. Selenta will help you. She has always been a good friend for your mother. We should talk to her right away." Her father tried to sit up, but Juma gently pushed him back onto the bed.

"Rest and get better. I will talk to Selenta. Promise me you won't get up before you're better."

Her father smiled, nodded, and closed his eyes. Before Juma turned to leave, his regular breathing filled the hut again. Talking for so long must have been very exhausting for him, Juma thought.

## 9

$\mathcal{S}$HE LEFT HER FATHER AND walked toward the witch's hut, her heart filled with gratitude. She had been awakened to the fact that she loved her father much more than she had thought. Ever since her mother had gone, he had always been there for her. He had done his best to replace the mother she had lost. Tears welled up in her eyes, and she struggled to fight them back. Only when she had composed herself did she push back the hide and enter the witch's hut.

After the politest greeting she was capable of at the moment, she asked, "Why didn't you speak up for me when Jakombe declined my request for chieftess training? Father told me that Mother never gave up her office, so I'm the rightful heir."

"Eligibility is one thing, talent the other." The witch got up and fetched a mug of goat milk.

A mixture of sadness and anger pumped Juma's blood hotly through her veins. She had to force herself not to clench her hands into fists.

"The test showed that I have enough talent to become chieftess."

"True. But we need your magical strength, at least for now. My magic is slowly turning away from the things that concern the living. It's getting weaker. The earth and the herbs don't react to my touch the way they used to." She looked at Juma, who realized there was a deep sadness hidden within the old woman's eyes. "My tribe, the tribe I have sworn to protect, will be no more if we don't manage to contact Vanamate."

Juma couldn't believe it. Surely they would wake the goddess and everything would be all right again. Rain would come then.

"So you're letting Kandra become the next chieftess?" Juma sucked in her lower lip to bite back an impolite remark.

"Kandra is eligible. She might not become the best chieftess we've ever had, but she'll manage. The red cloak totem chose her, albeit a little reluctantly." The witch sat down on her mat again and placed the cup with the milk beside the fire. "Come, sit with me. Your magic is strong. I can feel it. With your help, we'll have at least a chance to wake the goddess."

Juma was still angry but had to admit that waking Vanamate was far more important than quarreling over her training. She breathed deeply and closed her eyes. Soon the witch's reassuring calmness took effect, and she felt less enraged.

"I don't think my magic is special," she said. "I never did anything spectacular."

"I can feel that your talent is great, but it is untrained. We need to find your way to access it." The witch patted the ground beside her. "But first things first. You'll need to learn how to shield. Especially with that princessaround, you have to be able to protect yourself and those you love. I can feel that she is using dangerous magic."

Juma settled beside her, and the old woman went into a lesson much more interesting than the girl had anticipated.

"Magical energy is available everywhere around us, but only witches can gather and channel it," the old woman started. "Every witch has her own way of making magical energy do what she wants it to do. Witches are tied to an element. Mine, like that of most witches, is Earth. The other elements are Water and Air — and Fire, naturally, but I've yet to meet a witch with that affinity."

Immediately Chunte crossed Juma's mind, but she pushed the thought aside and concentrated on the explanations.

The witch bent forward and drew a stick figure into the sand of her floor and lots of wriggly lines around it. "Now, if you use magical energy, it flows into you and does what you want it to do if you've got the right trigger." She drew lines that wriggled out of the ground and into the stick figure. Then, she added straight lines splashing from its hands. "My trigger is herbs. Your trigger will most likely be something completely different, and we need to find it fast. But first, you're going to learn to feel the magic. You won't be able to identify it if you don't know what it feels like." The witch moved her hands in a big circle and then toward her body, as if pulling energy toward her chest.

Juma stared in fascination as the old woman's chest and arms began to glow with a silvery light reminiscent of the full moon. She felt the energy tingle on her skin. It reminded her of the prickly feeling after scrubbing herself clean in a bath. Curious about what tasks magic could be used for, she wondered if there were rules to follow.

With a graceful sweep of her arms, the witch discarded the gathered energy into the earth. "Now you."

Juma waved her arms about. At first, nothing happened, but soon her arms slowed as if moving through water. Prickling sparks danced on her arms, and she was suddenly very aware of the mosquitoes hidden in niches of the hut. The longer Juma waved, the brighter the glowing on her chest became, and the more creatures she could feel. Birds sang in her mind, and she felt a leaf float from a tree near the hut. It felt as if the world had invaded her brain. She spread her arms wide and the energy dissipated. She shook her head to get rid of the buzzing.

The witch frowned. "Why did you let go? You managed to collect a surprisingly big amount of magical energy."

Juma told her about the noises in her mind, the birds' songs, the crickets' chirping, the mosquitoes' humming …

"Wow, it seems that your affinity is not Earth after all. I suspect it's Air." The witch bowed. "I am delighted we've got someone with this talent in our tribe. Now, do it again and find a place in your brain to store the sounds so they will not break your concentration."

Juma did as she was told but it took her quite a while to find a way to lock out the ruckus. Only the crickets' chirping stayed in the back of her mind as a low reminder of what she could sense if she allowed it.

"Are you ready?" the witch asked.

Juma nodded. "My arms are full with magic. What am I supposed to do with it now?"

"If it feels as if you can't hold any more, gently push it outward and form it into a shield."

Juma gathered more magic until her arms were so full there didn't seem to be any room left. Her heart jumped for joy and she began to hum along with the crickets in her mind. She pushed the glowing outward, drawing the form of a shield in front of her. Instead, the power seeped into her body at first. Elation coursed through her veins and burst from her fingertips, filling the form she had indicated. Light flowed into the shape of a shield which stood upright on its own. It wobbled a bit but seemed stable enough. The exhilarating feeling of magic left Juma breathless.

"Are you ready?" the witch asked.

Still humming, Juma nodded, and the old woman hurled a spell against the shield. Both shattered, and the energy dissipated. Juma gasped. Pain shot through her stomach from the sudden drain of magic. She clasped her abdomen.

The witch patted her back and said, "That was very good for a first try. Now, keep up your concentration. When the spell of another witch hits your shield, you are most vulnerable. You need to push more energy into it all the time to keep it up."

They tried again. It surprised Juma that she felt like singing when her arms were full of magic again. This time, her shield held a little longer before the witch broke through. They tried again… and again… and again. When afternoon neared dusk, Juma had learned to raise a sufficiently big shield at an instant and keep it up through the witch's assaults. The whole time, she hummed happily. Using magic is so much fun, she thought. But I could do without the pain. Her stomach hurt as if a zebra had kicked her. With a sigh, she rubbed the sore spot.

"The pain will be gone by morning. Very well done," the old woman said. "It seems you can access your magic just fine. Let's start with the next step." She pulled out one of her herbs. After describing where it could be found, she said, "If you burn it with a white-hot flame, it will pull your spirit from your body and let you travel the sky."

"Did you use it when you chased Mubuntu?" Juma remembered the nightly adventure very well. "He seemed to be quite scared of you."

The witch sat up and stared at Juma. "How did you know Mubuntu was scared? I told no one, not even Jakombe."

"It was written in his face. Didn't everyone notice that?"

"You saw him? In our world? And you tell me you don't have much magic? Even I only saw his fiery tail. No one has ever set eyes on the gods. Even we witches only feel their presence." The old woman's eyes were as wide and round as those of the nightbird.

Juma swallowed. She could do something the wise woman of the village couldn't do? Her mind felt numb, and she didn't know what to think.

"You know…" The witch scratched her nose. "If you really can see the gods, you are truly gifted. Is Mubuntu the only god you saw?"

Juma remembered how she had seen Vanamate in her circle of fire during the first ceremony. She was sure it had been a vision, but what if it had been real? Reluctantly, she told the witch about it.

"You've left your body behind and visited the gods in their realm without any training?" The witch fought her feelings. Juma saw all kinds of emotions flutter across her face; shock, awe, understanding, and finally acceptance.

"So, the water you gave to Netinu was from Vanamate's tears?" The witch's hands trembled as she picked up the cup to drink a little of the goat milk. "It's a pity you gave all to him. A single one would have been enough to heal him. The others would have turned into pearls that we could have used to defy Mubuntu. Vanamate's tears are stronger than his spells. Well, it can't be helped." She sighed.

"We could go back at see if we can get more of those tears." Juma felt elated. "With luck, we might even be able to wake Vanamate and make her leave her ring of fire." Maybe I'm able to save the tribe. That would be a good start for a future chieftess, wouldn't it? She reached for the witch's pouch with the herbs, but the old woman's hand stopped her.

"Your idea is good, but do not forget that Mubuntu might have interfered with her waking. He is a strong and dangerous opponent. We need to be very careful. Let us go when his strength is at its lowest." The witch let go of Juma's hand and looked at her expectantly.

"Tonight?" Juma asked.

"Tonight."

Juma nodded. A little later her lesson was over and she left the hut. She was surprised to see that it was nearly time for the evening meal. She hurried to the Central Hall and took her place beside Sundera. Her heart was overflowing with all the new things she had learned today, and she wanted so much to share them with her friend, but she didn't dare. What if the princess or Kandra overheard?

Soon everyone sat around the fires in the village's open space in front of the Central Hall. Eating and chatting amiably, most people discussed the drought.

"Do you think it will be over soon?" Sundera asked Juma.

Tolobe answered before Juma could think of a suitable reply.

"I do no think the drought will end any time soon. We will have to ration the water even more, since the lake is lower than it's ever been before. Also, we need to strengthen our warriors and train the hunters in warrior skills. The longer the drought lasts, the more tribes will come to this lake for water. There isn't enough to last for everyone."

Juma sucked in her breath. Her brother, the most silent in her family, had dared to interrupt her.

Sundera paled too but for a different reason. "You expect fighting?"

Tolobe nodded.

Before Juma could reprimand Tolobe for his transgression, Chieftess Jakombe's voice rang out over the fires.

"Friends and family. After all the bad happenings of late, we want to share something good with you. Something that will bring us peace and prosperity." She took Netinu's arm and led him into the center of the open area between the fires. "After thinking long and hard about our tribe's future, I have come to the conclusion that it would be best for all of us to form an alliance with the strong tribe from the other side of the holy mountain." She lifted Netinu's hand. "I therefore declare Netinu married to Princess Chunte."

Netinu's jaw dropped. He stared at his mother, unbelieving.

A sharp knife cut through Juma's heart.

No! She slapped both hands over her mouth to suppress a cry.

Princess Chunte shot her a murderous look before she got up and walked to Jakombe and Netinu.

"I am honored, chieftess." She took the hand of Netinu who stood as if rooted to the spot. "Our tribes will become as close as Netinu and I."

All of a sudden, Netinu woke. He ripped his hand from the princess's clutch and turned to his mother. "I will not marry her. I'd rather die."

A collective gasp went through the crowd, and Jakombe looked ashen. Never had a man dared to contradict a woman, especially the chieftess. Everyone felt the chieftess fight her anger.

"You will do as I tell you." Jakombe's voice was very low as she glared at her son. "You might be my son, but you're also the tribe's pledge for peace and prosperity. Your emotions don't matter as long as the tribe doesn't suffer."

"But I thought you loved me."

For the first time, Juma noticed the chieftess's pained expression. "The drought is getting worse every day. The princess's tribe is strong and has many more trained warriors than ours. If we join forces, no one will be able to steal the water from the lake that we so urgently need."

Netinu's shoulders slumped, and he didn't say another word.

Again, the chieftess placed his hand in that of the princess. Her strong voice filled the night and made Juma shiver. "Netinu Botango will follow you wherever you go. He shall catch you whenever you stumble and bear your burden for the time of his life. You, Princess Chunte Matate, will provide for him, warm his nights, and bear his children. I hereby declare that he belongs to your tribe from now on."

With a friendly smile, Chunte raised their joined hands to the cautious applause of the tribe, and Juma saw the triumph in her eyes. Her heart plummeted. Another success for the princess, and this time, it was personal. Juma knew the princess wouldn't keep Netinu as a husband for long. Mubuntu had practically requested him as a sacrifice. She had to warn Netinu. She tried to signal to him, but he didn't look up. Staring at the ground, he allowed Princess Chunte to drag him around to receive the congratulations of the tribe members. Juma felt the crowd's uneasy mood. No one was really happy about the marriage, but everyone had heard and understood. It was inevitable.

With her head hanging low, Juma set aside her bowl and left. Sundera caught up with her near the thornbush hedge. She put her arms around Juma and hugged her. "I'm so, so sorry. I never knew you liked him that much."

"I don't. He's an idiot." Juma pushed her away. "But he's friendly, and I would hate to see him die."

Sundera's eyes widened. "Why would he die as the princess's husband?"

"Because Chunte is in league with Mubuntu, and he has requested Netinu's life. I'm sure she will not wait overly long to sacrifice him."

Sundera put her hand on Juma's arm. "He's her husband. I'm sure, she won't sacrifice him."

Juma snorted. "What's a husband to her? She sacrificed her own mother!"

Sundera's jaw fell open.

Juma kept walking. She needed to get rid of her anger, and moving around seemed the best way. Sundera walked with her in silence. When they had circled the village once, she said, "We can't do much about the princess and her warriors, but if we free Vanamate, she will defeat Mubuntu and Netinu will at least live."

Before Juma could answer, a shadow approached them. It was Netinu. Ignoring Sundera, he took Juma's hands, bent down, and kissed them.

"How I long to kiss your lips instead." His eyes filled with tears. "I am not looking forward to pleasing my wife. She's so… so…" He searched for the right word. "She's heartless and cold. I feel like an animal that's prepared for slaughter."

Juma didn't trust her voice, so she whispered. "Why did you come?"

"I wanted to let you know that my heart will never be in this marriage. I know you don't love me, but I love you. And I always will." He kissed her hands again. "I will not be unfaithful to my wife, but my heart will stay with you. I need your warmth. Will you be my friend even though you don't like my wife?" Netinu seemed to mean what he said.

Juma's heart fluttered. "I will be your friend forever and a day." She reached for his face and traced his cheekbone in the gentle caress of a personal farewell. "Be careful. I am sure your wife plans to sacrifice you to Mubuntu."

His head snapped up. "How do you know?"

"I've got my ways." She smiled, suspecting it looked a lot like the sad smiles she had seen on the witch. "If she tries anything, I will be there to flee with you."

Netinu swallowed hard and nodded. He traced her cheekbone too, and left.

## 10

*J*UMA FELT HIS THUMB ON her skin for ages. When she finally turned away, Sundera stood silently beside her with tears in her eyes.

"You would have made such a beautiful couple," she whispered.

"It was never meant to be." Juma marched on. "I'm fated to become the village witch and therefore have to remain a virgin, or I'll lose my magic."

Sundera tried to voice her pity but Juma stopped her. The moon had risen over the huts, and filled the night with its silvery light. Juma looked up at it. The moon-goddess's face seemed to smile back down. "I need to see the witch tonight," she said to Sundera. "Can you cover for me if the girls ask why I'm not sleeping in our hut? I don't want anyone to know."

"Sure. I'll take our stuff and move out into the open pretending you're with me. It's too hot to sleep inside anyway."

Juma turned to her. "You're my best friend. I'm so glad you made me get to know you."

The girls hugged, and then walked their different ways.

Juma's feelings were in turmoil. She didn't know if she should be glad about Netinu's confession, or scared. A marriage without love or at least respect must be hell, she thought. If I were allowed, I'd want a husband who loves me as much as Father loved Mother. In her mind, she considered all the older boys and the young men she knew, but none came close to what she wanted. Aside from Netinu, not one would be a threat to her magic. But Netinu's solemn face kept appearing in her mind's eye, and it was hard to push it aside. She was glad when she reached the witch's hut. Now she had no time to ponder her future any more. Now was the time to do something against Mubuntu. She entered.

The witch had already prepared everything. Two mats lay in the hut's center. The witch had dowsed the fire. Only a few coals were glowing in a firepot that hung from a pole in a corner. The old woman patted the mat beside hers.

"Sit with me and drink this." She handed Juma a cup with tea. The liquid smelled strongly of herbs. Juma wondered how the witch managed to keep the aroma this strong, until she remembered that it was the old woman's talent. She sipped. The tea was strong with a sweet flavor.

"You put honey in?"

The old woman smiled. "It doesn't taste very well without. Drink it all up and lay down."

Juma obeyed. The minute she touched the mat, her senses seemed to expand. Everything in the hut seemed clearer. The sounds of celebrating people near the village's center were amplified as if she stood beside them. The mat's grassy smell filled her mind and pushed away all thoughts. She tried not to close her eyes.

An old and wrinkled hand slipped into hers.

"Let us go now," the witch said. Juma could see her spirit float over her, and she felt the hand tugging at her, but she couldn't follow. Something was holding her back. In panic, she looked around but there was nothing.

"Free yourself from the earthbound shackles of your body." The witch beckoned to her.

Juma tried hard to free her spirit, but it remained anchored to her body.

"You're trying too hard." The witch's spirit sank lower until she sat beside her. "Close your eyes and listen to the world around you. Then blend out the sounds you hear and concentrate on your heartbeat."

Juma tried. In the village center, someone had begun playing a flute and another person joined with a drum. With all her might, she pushed the sounds from her mind, but the drumming was too similar to the thumping of her heart to ignore it.

"You did it." The witch's spirit voice sounded relieved.

Juma opened her eyes and looked around. She was still holding hands with the witch, who looked a lot younger than in her human body.

"Why was it so hard to get out?" The witch wondered aloud. "I've never had problems pulling someone else from his or her body before."

"Have you ever tried pulling out another person who's got magic?"

"No, I haven't. You are right, that is probably the reason." The witch smiled. "Now, let's go and find Vanamate. Show me the way."

"But I don't know the way." Juma looked down. Thin, semi-transparent tendrils connected them to their unmoving bodies on the ground.

When the witch noticed her glance, she explained. "The bond keeps your spirit tied to your body. It helps to ensure that you'll always find your way back. Only the gods can sever it."

Juma looked at the world. It had changed a lot, and nothing looked familiar any more. The hut was gone, and the mountains looked like black silhouettes against the gray sky. "Why does the world look as if someone drained all the color from it?"

"When you travel the spirit world, you're bound by your own body's restrictions and by those of your travel guide. I'm a plant witch, so all plants you can see will look normal. The ones I can use in my magic will even glow. But everything else is blurry and without color." The witch pointed at something Juma hadn't noticed before. The grass and reeds near the lake showed a healthy green. Some smaller plants glowed between the reeds like burning emeralds.

"Beautiful," she said.

"It is, isn't it? But we're not here to admire the plants. We need to find Vanamate." The witch took both of Juma's hands. "Try to remember what you did when you fetched her tears the day of the ceremony."

"I flew up and up toward the stars." Juma pointed upwards. The uniformly dark gray sky loomed, without any distinguishing features, in all directions. "But there are no stars in your version of the world."

"What did it look like when you accidentally visited?" The witch seemed genuinely interested.

Juma shrugged. "Like always. I didn't notice any difference to the world I should have been in. Maybe the stars were a little closer and brighter."

The witch stared at her with amazement.

After a while, Juma couldn't stand it any longer. "What's wrong?"

"You must have died at some point in your life. Only those returned from death are able to see the spirit world the way the gods see it." The witch breathed deeply. "It's no wonder your talent is so strong. Those who return from death usually have superior magic."

Juma wanted to protest but remembered the story her father had told her. Did her mother give up her life because Juma had died? She didn't really die, did she? It was so hard to remember.

The witch pulled her from her reverie. "We have to try. Give me your hand." She took off, pulling Juma along. "Dear me, are you heavy!"

Juma tried to fly on her own like she had done during the ceremony, but she couldn't. The higher they flew the less familiar the world below looked. Small amounts of green grass and clusters of forests blurred with the gray of the village, the river, the lake, and the soil. The mountains around them seemed to grow higher with every passing minute. Sweat began to form on the witch's forehead.

"I don't think I can keep this up much longer," she said. "If we don't land soon, my arms will come out of their sockets. I don't know why, but you are awfully heavy."

"Maybe next time I should pull you out of your body to take you along." Juma said it as a joke but the witch insisted it was a great idea. Juma coughed. All of a sudden, her throat felt sore. Tiny pearls of sweat appeared on her upper lip and on her bare shoulders. Why was breathing so hard? She looked around but found no reason for the strange sensations. But the witch seemed to feel the same. Her eyes watered, and she coughed several times.

"Let's return to our bodies and try to figure out what you will need to set your spirit free. It obviously isn't herbs." The witch sank toward the blurry gray mass below them. When they came close enough to recognize the village, something red licked at the witch's hut.

"The hut is burning." The witch dove toward her hut so fast, Juma thought they'd crash. She screamed.

Instead of slamming into the ground, she woke with a jolt. Flames and smoke filled the room around her. She screamed again, but smoke and heat burned her lungs, and she doubled over with coughing. I have to get out. Her eyes darted through the room but she couldn't see anything. Staying as low to the ground as she could, she was moving toward the exit when her hands touched the witch's motionless body. She grabbed her by the shoulders and dragged her along. Her eyes watered, and the heat hurt her back more than she could bear. Little bits of burning reeds rained down on her from the roof. At least the tears in her eyes allowed her to see where she was going. The door seemed miles away, and the witch grew heavier with every inch. Juma tried hard not to breathe through her mouth, but panting through the nose was hard. Every so often, she knocked burning debris aside. It seemed as if someone had thrown everything the witch owned onto the ground before starting the fire. Juma was so intent on getting the witch and herself to safety that she didn't understand the implications. The blanket at the door was not in flames yet although some little tendrils already reached for it. Juma pulled the witch through, moved her as far away as her strength would allow, and dumped her.

The old woman's eyelids fluttered. "My herbs. Get my herbs or we're doomed."

Wordlessly Juma hurried back into the burning hut. She found the bag with the herbs beside her mat. Its leather was smoldering but none of the herbs were burning. More coughing doubled her over, but she grabbed the bag and retreated. Then the roof caved in.

"You!" A person made of flames approached her, and the roof stopped moving. She retreated, but Mubuntu blocked the way to the exit. "You can see me."

Juma remembered something he had said to the princess the night they had met. "You can't kill me."

"Not directly, no. But the fire can. And it can burn down the whole village if I'm so inclined. Everything is dry as dust. It would be a marvelous sight."

Juma wondered where the villagers were. Shouldn't they be carrying pails of water from the lake to stop the fire? She inched toward the exit, pressing the bag to her chest while the roof sagged lower with every step she took.

Mubuntu held up his arm, and the flames and smoke froze. Like slices of yellowish-red jewels encased by gray columns of smoke, they stood in the sizzling air, no longer licking on things or whirling upward. He stepped close to her, changing into his red-haired, pale-skinned human form again. "I want my hand back."

"I haven't got it." Juma managed to get past him, but before she could slip though the exit, he grabbed her arm. It hurt as if someone had poured boiling water over her skin.

"Give me my hand, and your tribe will survive."

If Juma had known where the witch had hidden the hand, she would have given it to him right away. But she didn't know. She tried to explain, but he waved her argument aside.

"I don't care who hid the hand, I want it back. You will find it and bring it to me before High Moon, and I will spare you and the village for now."

Juma didn't answer and tried to free herself, but his grip was too strong.

"Promise me by Vanamate's tears, or I swear I'll burn down this village to the ground tonight." He twisted her arm, and Juma yelped with pain.

Bending sideways, she flung the bag of herbs through the door as far as she could. If she had to die, at least the witch would be able to help the healer to save the others.

Mubuntu pulled on her arm until she stood so close to him she could feel his manhood through his loincloth. "If you don't give me back my hand by High Moon, I will come back. I will make you watch as I burn everyone you care for. I'll start with Tolobe and Sundera, follow it with your father, Lomba, and Jakombe, and crown it with Netinu. Their screams will drive you crazy long before I'm done."

Juma shivered. She knew he'd do as he said. But if she agreed to look for the hand, she would at least buy her tribe some time. High Moon was still a few days away, and if she could find Vanamate in time, she would have an ally Mubuntu couldn't overcome.

"I promise by Vanamate's tears I will find your hand before High Moon." Juma put her free hand on her chest. With the gesture, she sealed an unbreakable promise. She would have to stick to her word if she wanted to or not. How to find the hand would be something to worry about when the time came.

Mubuntu grinned and let go of her arm. She stepped back, and he laughed.

"I will fetch it at High Moon." He reached out with his arm, and the flames and smoke streamed into his body as if he was sucking it up. In less than a minute, the fire had gone, and he vanished.

Juma sighed with relief and looked around. The hut's walls were black, the roof sagged and had holes in it, and most of the witch's possessions were charred or at least singed. But the fire was out, and they were still alive. With a heavy heart, she walked outside to the witch. The old woman sat on the ground coughing up soot, hugging her bag of herbs. Not one of her tribesmen was in sight.

The witch stared at what was left of her hut. "Why did no one come to help?" She looked up at Juma, and the sadness in her eyes tore at the young woman's heart.

"Mubuntu is a god. Surely it's easy for him to distract the tribe." Juma crouched beside the witch and told her about Mubuntu's request. "I had to promise him to find his hand or he would have destroyed the whole tribe."

The witch's eyes grew wide with fear and a taste of betrayal.

"But I never promised to give it to him." Juma grinned, happy to see the relief on the witch's face.

"That was quick thinking. I'm proud of you. Now, help me up and let's find out what happened to the others." The old woman smiled and put a hand on Juma's arm. Juma did as she was told, and they walked through a deathly silent village side by side.

"Thank you for saving my body," the witch said when they neared the place in front of the Central Hall.

"Why didn't you wake like I did?"

"Mubuntu put up a shield that kept me from entering my body as long as it was in the hut. When you got me out, I slipped back."

"So he has been after me?" Juma stopped and stared at the witch. "How did he know that it was me who could see him?"

"Gods can taste magic." The witch walked on and Juma followed. "I'm sure he tasted yours when you broke his spell on Netinu during the welcome ceremony. Tonight, he must have recognized it when we left our bodies."

They reached the Central Hall. In the open area, men, women, and children lay around like trees toppled by a storm. Juma's heart missed a beat until she realized they were only sleeping. Then she heard voices coming from Jakombe's hut. She looked at the witch. The old woman nodded, and they walked over to it.

"I don't know anything about a hand," Jakombe said loud enough that Juma and the witch could hear it outside.

"My master wants it back. Force the witch to give it to you if you have to. I can only save your son if you do what I say." The tone in the princess's voice made Juma shiver.

Jakombe's voice sounded resigned. "You've got what you wanted. Please, leave me alone. I can't give you any more."

"Mubuntu will get his hand back, or your son will pay." Princess Chunte seemed to be walking toward the door. Hurriedly, the witch pulled Juma into the shade between two huts. For a second, Juma resisted but then she realized the old woman's wisdom. This wasn't the time to confront Chunte. Not with the amount of magic Mubuntu had given her.

"And tomorrow, I shall announce my plans for this village. I want you to be there on time. Try to look regal. After all, your tribe still thinks you're their leader."

"Please, don't hurt Netinu."

"Thank you for reminding me." The princess giggled. "I think it's time for me to consume… I mean consummate my marriage." She swept through the blanket that covered the door. If Juma had had a club, she would have smashed her skull there and then. She struggled against the witch's surprisingly strong grip, while Chunte marched off toward the guest hut, leaving behind Jakombe's sobs.

When she had calmed a little, Juma wanted to enter the hut to face the chieftess, but the witch advised against it.

"Let this go for now and get some sleep. The day was exhausting, and it's best to discuss this with a clear mind before we can take action. That princess is dangerous."

Juma agreed wholeheartedly with her last assessment. "I have never in my life hated a person more than the princess."

The witch shook her head. "Rid yourself of the hate. It gives Mubuntu an opening. Hatred, desire without love, jealousy, those are the feelings he can use to manipulate a person."

Juma knew she was right, but letting go of the hatred seemed impossible. How could she fight her own feelings?

"I will go and sleep at the healer's hut." The witch patted her arm and walked away without another word.

Lost in thought, Juma walked toward the place where she suspected Sundera had taken her sleeping mat. She was right. Her best friend had found a sheltered spot not too far from the goats. She lay down as quietly as she could, but sleep was long in coming.

The next morning, Juma felt sore all over. Most of all, the patch on her arm where Mubuntu had touched her hurt. A blister in the form of his hand had grown overnight.

"You'd better go and see the healer," Sundera said when Juma told her what had happened. "But don't tell anyone else that you saw the heat dæmon. These days, you don't know whom to trust."

"Can't you take care of it?" Juma glared at the blister, wishing it away, but it didn't vanish. What good was magic if it couldn't rid you of pain?

"I'm not as knowledgeable as the healer, but if you insist…"

Juma did insist, and so Sundera dressed the wound as best she could. When she was done, Juma headed for the witch's hut. Sensing trouble in the air, she tried to discover the cause before the problems found her. She walked past playing children and busy grown-ups. The smell of roasted yams hung in the air, gradually replaced by the charred hut's stench as she got closer. Aside from the hut, everything seemed so normal — too normal for Juma's liking.

When she reached the remains, some men were already taking off the burnt roof, singing a simple working song. The old woman was turning the ashes to see if some of her belongings were still usable. Juma helped her wordlessly.

"We were really lucky to escape," the witch said. "It was careless of me to leave the fire in the firepot untended."

Juma opened her mouth to protest, but the witch shook her head. In a barely noticeable gesture, she nodded toward the working men. Juma understood and searched on quietly. When they were called for breakfast, they had gathered a small pile of intact earthenware and two golden necklaces. The witch had tears in her eyes when Juma discovered the figurines and totems she had used during testing. They were still in good shape.

"Vanamate be praised." She sniffed. "They are the last tie to the man I once loved."

"He made them?" Juma looked up, and the witch nodded.

"It broke his heart when he learned I would never be able to marry him. They were his farewell gift for me. Hunters found his remains a few weeks later. His spirit had gone with Monnatoba."

Juma's heart contracted. Hopefully Netinu would not do the same. After all, he had a wife to care for even if it was a beast like Chunte. Again, she felt the hate rise in her throat. It was hard to fight it back down.

## 11

$\mathscr{A}$FTER BREAKFAST, WHICH JUMA ATTENDED with the witch, Jakombe rose and called everyone to the Central Hall. The tremor in her voice was barely noticeable. She went first, with Kandra at her side. Princess Chunte, with Netinu on her arm, walked right behind her. The rest of the tribe fell in line. Juma and the witch went last, right behind Sundera and Tolobe.

"The princess is up to no good," Tolobe said. "I can feel it in my bones." He turned to Juma. "By the way, do you know that Netinu fled her bed last night? I saw him camp out beside the lake."

Juma's heart somersaulted, but she didn't dare to think about Netinu for long. The tribe filled the hall as they had done for the princess's arrival. The center of the oval hut stayed free. Jakombe went to her throne and sat on it. She looked so dejected and exhausted, Juma felt sorry for her. Aside from her dislike of Juma, Jakombe was a good chieftess and didn't deserve this.

Accompanied by six men with spears, the princess walked up to the throne and turned her back to Jakombe. The tribe gasped collectively at the impolite gesture.

Chunte said, "Since I am the chieftess's son's wife now, I demand access to the lake and its resources because my tribe has come to share my joy."

Jakombe got up, her movements slow but full of hidden strength. "You are not part of this clan. The marriage was meant to form an alliance. Since you came under false pretenses, I hereby annul it, especially since you and your husband didn't consummate it. He told me this morning. Be gone from our lands and take your tribe with you. I am banning you forever."

The crowd gasped. No marriage had ever be annulled as far as Juma knew. She expected the tribe members to cheer but they stayed silent.

The princess's laugh seemed extremely loud in the tense silence. "You can't ban me." She lifted her hand and pointed her index finger at Jakombe. A flame as bright as the morning sun shot out of it and hit Jakombe squarely in the chest. The chieftess's eyes widened, and her body faltered. She held out a hand to her daughter as if she needed help to steady herself, but Kandra made no move to support her. Instead, she glared at Chunte while her mother crumpled to the ground.

The healer pushed through the crowd, but the princess stopped her. "Do not touch her before we're done. Netinu, come here!"

Netinu walked toward the princess as if in a daze. Even from as far as she was standing, Juma could see that his eyes were completely focused on Chunte. The princess must have compelled him in some way. Maybe she used Mubuntu's magic. Juma wanted to throttle her, but she knew she wouldn't stand a chance against her magic and the six spear-bearers surrounding her.

"Undress," the princess ordered, and Netinu took off his loincloth. There was no emotion in his face, and he moved like a puppet. Chunte waved at one of her spear-bearers, who stepped forward and rubbed Netinu's manhood enough that it stood to attention. A low growl rumbled in Juma's chest and she fought hard not to let it out. It wouldn't help anyone if she got killed.

Chunte let her kikoi slip to the ground. Some men goggled at her nakedness. She sat on the throne, opened her legs wide and said, "Fulfill your duty, Netinu."

The chieftess's son stepped forward and did as he had been told. Moving rhythmically, he consummated the marriage, destroying Jakombe's chance of annulling it.

Juma's heart tore. The pain was so severe, she couldn't hold back a small cry. Her legs were suddenly barely able to support her weight, and she stumbled forward. The witch caught her arm and steadied her, but the action didn't go unnoticed.

Netinu's face turned in her direction, breaking eye contact with the princess. He frowned. He stopped moving. His eyes cleared as he looked back at the woman on the throne. He pulled out of her and stepped back.

"I despise you, Chunte. I will never lay with you of my own free will. You can bespell me all you want, but you will never own my heart."

The tribe cheered, but the princess's face turned red.

"You will do as I say." Another bolt of light shot from her fingers. It slammed into Netinu's abdomen. With a cry of pain, the young man clutched at his loin, dropped to the ground and curled up into a ball. Rocking himself, he moaned and cried. Juma wanted to throw herself on the princess, to scratch her eyes out and feed her to the vultures. At the last possible movement, several women beside her grabbed her and held her back. They were scared — scared of a girl barely older than Juma. And she saw the same fear mirrored in the faces of the other tribe members. They probably considered it a wonder that Chunte ignored Juma.

"I am Chunte, the High Priestess of Mubuntu the Wonderful." The princess lifted her arms. "Since Jakombe isn't able to rule any more, and seeing that I am the best-suited member anywhere near this tribe, I am the one you will obey. As of now, I am your chieftess," she announced. "From now on, Mubuntu's laws will guide this tribe, and I shall make you see his glory. His power and strength runs though my veins, and none of you is stronger. Accept my rule and I will be gentle with you — after an initial sacrifice to your new god, of course." She waved to the six warriors. "Fetch all the children and bring them to my hut. If anyone does anything to prevent us, kill them. And make sure Jakombe and her daughter stay in their hut until I decide what to do with them."

Mothers screamed as the warriors tore the children form their arms. Fathers tried to protect their children and the warriors beat them mercilessly. Some of the older children tried to flee, but more warriors arrived outside and caught them, hitting them over the heads with the blunt end of their spears. Juma heard at least one skull crack.

Frozen to the spot, she stared at the chaos around her. This couldn't be true. How could her world go from complicated to impossible in one morning? The witch grabbed her arm and pulled her along.

"Let's get out of here before she decides we're too dangerous to let live." The old woman hobbled to the unconscious boy whose head Juma had heard crack. She knelt and put her hand on the bloody mess, mumbling a few words and pushing some herb into his mouth. Juma saw bluish light flood from her fingers into the head, and the bone moved. In a split second, the skull had taken back its original from, and the boy's eyelids fluttered. The witch slumped and swayed. One of the warriors pushed her aside, grabbed the still dumbstruck boy's arm, and pulled him to his feet.

"Get your ass to the others," he ordered the boy and shoved him hard. The boy stumbled over to a group of children who were crying and sniffling. Juma found it hard to keep from crying herself. When the warrior left to fetch another child, she whispered to them, "Take heart, we'll find a way to get rid of her."

Some of the older children looked skeptical but the others seemed a little comforted. Juma helped the witch to get up and led her away so she didn't have to bear the children's hopeful gazes any longer. The witch staggered and breathed heavily. When Juma asked, she said, "It's the price I pay for using too much magic at once. I should have waited for the healer."

In the witch's roofless hut, Juma sank to the ground and cried. She felt the witch's arms around her shoulders, but her tears wouldn't stop. It took her a long time to realize that they mingled with the old woman's tears.

A sad day followed. Toward evening Tolobe and Sundera joined them in the burned out hut. Juma heard parents lament all over the village, and crying children from the princess's hut.

"We have to get rid of her," Juma said to Tolobe and Sundera. "There has to be a way."

"I could kill her from afar." Tolobe patted his bow. "Although I wouldn't like doing it."

Juma shook her head. "Her warriors would avenge her immediately. Think of all the children."

"If only we could control her like she controlled Netinu. We could make her send the warriors away." Sundera sighed.

The witch shrugged. "I could mix a potion that would turn her into a puppet for a few hours, but how would we get her to drink it? She's extremely suspicious of everyone."

"If it weren't for her warriors, we could kill her like Tolobe suggested. We wouldn't even need the potion." Juma sighed. They discussed their options for a while longer, but found no viable option. Depressed, they went to bed, the witch sharing the healer's hut again.

Juma woke from a commotion at the lake. Animals bleated, and a lion roared loudly. Am I glad it can't cross the fence, she thought. Whoever invented the fence should have been remembered with honor. The prickly thornbush fence had defended the tribe against wild animals more than once. Juma hugged her blanket tight, closed her eyes and tried to go back to sleep. It took her a long time, and she slept badly. Every muscle and joint in her body ached when she woke.

Since no one else was up yet, she walked to the cooking area and found a bucket with water and a cup. Just as she lifted the drink to her lips, she heard a scraping sound. Was someone opening the southern gate? She put the cup away and walked toward the entrance, hiding between the huts as best she could.

Two women resembling the princess entered through the lakeside gate with a small child in their arms. It was badly wounded, and blood dripped from its body to the ground. One of the warriors who had opened the gate cried out, ripped the child from the woman's arms, and pressed it against his chest.

"What happened?" the second warrior asked.

"Lions." The older woman put her hands on her hip. "They killed the healer and a quarter of the herd."

"Chunte promised we would find a better place to live," the younger woman whispered, which made it hard for Juma to understand her dialect. "But things have been getting worse ever since she turned to Mubuntu for help."

"There's a healer in this village," the second warrior said.

"A healer won't be able to save her," the first warrior said. "Without a witch's magic, my daughter will die."

"The witch is dead, burned to the ground with her hut, the careless cow. Princess Chunte was very pleased." The second warrior patted the other man's shoulder. "You'll see. Chunte will make Mubuntu save your child."

"We need to see the princess," the older woman said.

The second guard nodded and led her away while the younger woman and the warrior stood motionlessly, clinging to the mangled body of the child. The wait seemed endless, and the woman's quiet sobbing tore at Juma's heart. Several times, she was tempted to leave her hiding place to comfort the devastated parents.

When the older woman and the second guard returned, their slumped shoulders told Juma all she needed to know.

"I'm so sorry." The older woman put a hand on the younger one's shoulder. The mother pulled away with a small cry that cut through Juma's heart like a knife.

"Maybe you should leave us alone now." The warrior put his arm around his wife and led her between the huts, obviously to gain some privacy, and they came closer to Juma. The warrior's tears glittered in the moon's light, soaking his kikoi. Juma had never seen a warrior cry before. The couple looked so helpless and dejected her heart went out to them. Making sure no one was around, she left her hiding place and walked over.

"Let me have a look," she said, bending over the child in the woman's arms. At first, the mother pressed the child against her chest, but when Juma asked her in Vanamate's name, her arms relaxed. Juma examined the child as best she could. It was a girl, and her breaths were shallow and irregular.

"She's still alive." Juma looked at the woman.

"Not much longer. We have neither a healer nor a witch." The eyes of the woman clung to the little girl, and her lips trembled, but she didn't cry. "I will hold her until she can join Monnatoba."

Juma shook her head. She could still hear the words of her mother when she had nursed one of the river people after a snake had bitten him. A life is always worth fighting for, even if it were that of an enemy.

"Come with me." She led the couple to the healer's hut and entered without knocking.

The woman and the warrior followed her hurriedly. The healer was already up and threw her kikoi over her shoulder. She pointed to a blanket on a bed.

"Put her there. I'll dress the wounds." She reached for a curved needle and placed it into a pan with boiling water that she had obviously meant for an early morning tea. A pot with herbs was standing beside the fire.

Reluctantly, the mother laid down her burden while Juma woke the witch. The old woman rubbed the sleep from her eyes and motioned the strangers to stand beside the door. Then she sat her clay figurine at the child's head, dug some herbs from her bag, and burned them while reciting another of her monotonous singsongs.

Juma felt the strength of the old woman's magic build up. It gathered over the healer and the little girl whose breathing slowed with every passing minute. As gently as possible, the healer began to sew, using the child's hair as thread. Stitch, knot, cut. Stitch, knot, cut, it went.

Juma watched the needle dive in an out of the small body and hoped the two old women would be able to save the child. Watching the healer work, she realized that the witch's magic flowed through the healer's arms into the wounds. The bleeding stopped, and the girl's breathing became more regular the more wounds the healer tended to. When everything was wrapped in clean strips of cloth, the little girl lay motionless, but her breathing hadn't yet stopped and seemed stronger.

"This is all we can do." The witch waved the couple closer. "She's not out of danger yet. Sit with her and soothe her should she wake."

The warrior knelt and lowered his head to the ground in a gesture of ultimate gratefulness.

"I am so glad you're still alive," he said. "I promise not to tell our princess."

The witch nodded her thanks. "I cannot guarantee that your daughter will live. She's in Monnatoba's hands now. Maybe it will help if you pray to her."

"Why don't you pray for our daughter?" the woman asked. "A prayer from a witch will be more valuable to Monnatoba than that of a mere cook."

"Juma and I are needed elsewhere. The healer will go and prepare a strengthening broth for your child. The lion's claws have pierced several organs. Even if she heals, she will require light food like soups, milk, and yam pulp for quite a while."

The girl moaned, and her parents' attention turned away from the witch. Both crouched beside the small head, held hands, and watched their daughter sleep.

The witch pulled Juma out of the hut.

Outside, Juma whispered a question that had been burning on her tongue. "Why didn't you heal her like the little boy this morning?"

"It would have drained me too much, and I need my strength."

"Did I do wrong?" Juma asked.

The witch shook her head. "A child's life with all its potential is as important to a tribe as that of an elderly member with all its memories and experiences. You did well, even if it will complicate our lives a little. Let's pack our belongings."

"What for?" Juma frowned. "You think they will tell Chunte about us?"

"If they don't, Mubuntu will. I just realized that. Maybe he already did. It's best to leave the village for a while."

Juma had to admit that the old woman was right. Before the village had fully risen, they had their bags packed, ready to leave. Secretly, they said their farewells to the healer, Tolobe, Lomba, Sundera, and Juma's father. When the water-bearers left, they walked through the opened gate, hiding in their midst. None of the enemy's warriors ever saw them.

From among the reeds, Juma looked back at the thornbush fence. She thought of the safety they were leaving behind.

"I wish we could stay." She sighed.

The witch wiped away a tear and pulled her along. "I've got a small hut on the eastern shore of the lake. My teacher used to live there, many, many seasons ago. It might not be very clean but it will provide shelter. And it has a thornbush fence too."

Juma followed her with a heavy heart. When she thought of leaving her tribe in the clutches of Princess Chunte, she felt as if she was betraying them. They walked for half an hour along the lake's edge. Since they tried to keep out of sight of the water-bearers, they had to find a path through the reeds, which slowed them down considerably. The sun was already high over their heads when they heard running feet behind. Juma turned.

"Wait!" Tolobe came running after them. "Juma, Old Mother, please wait."

They stopped. Juma wondered how her brother had found them, until she noticed their footprints in the powdery red dust that covered the cracked soil.

When Tolobe had caught his breath, he said, "You don't need to leave."

"Explain." The witch sat down. Juma and Tolobe followed her example.

"When the injured girl woke and recognized her parents, Morva and her husband begged princess Chunte to keep you alive," he said. "They reminded her that more of their tribe members might needed the skills of you and our healer. After some consideration, the princess complied with their wish. The only condition is that you won't oppose her."

"But we are opposing her." Juma frowned.

"Yes, but we'd be stupid to do it openly." Tolobe grinned at her.

"So we can come back?" Juma's mood brightened considerably.

Tolobe bent forward. His eyes sparkled. "More than that. Morva and her husband are part of a small but growing faction of their tribe who want to return to worshiping Vanamate. They are prepared to help us if we promise that the princess will never return to their tribe."

"We can't kill her," the witch said. "And with Mubuntu's magic in her, we can't control her."

"We could keep her drugged," Tolobe said.

The witch shook her head. "Drugs kill a person bit by bit. The more often they are used, the faster the person dies. I will not be guilty of taking Princess Chunte's life."

"What if we build a fireproof stone hut for her and lock her up in it?" Juma suggested. "Also, we can keep her as wet as possible. It might douse her borrowed magic. It's not as if she has much power of her own."

"That's way too complicated, especially with the drought," the witch said.

Juma knew she was right, but she had another idea. "We can tie her to a rock in the lake in a way that only her head is above the water. Probably Mubuntu won't go near her there. I'm sure that he'll grow tired of her soon enough, so she won't be able to refill her magic."

The witch considered her idea for a while and nodded. "It is a possibility. You are right about Mubuntu. He isn't known for his loyalty. He'll surely abandon Chunte. Let's go back." She got up. "You, Tolobe, will let the others know that I am returning."

They reached the village before nightfall and managed to slip back in with the last group of water-bearers. The witch walked straight to the princess's hut. It aggravated Juma that she had to kneel in front of Chunte beside the witch.

"It's so nice of you to come and pay your respects — even if you're late." The princess snickered, but the witch ignored her.

"I've grown old protecting this tribe, and I'm not going to stop now." She looked Chunte straight in the eye. "Still, I hereby swear that I will not oppose you unless you hurt any of my people."

Chunte laughed. "As if you're a threat to me. Your magic is mostly with Monnatoba anyway." Her gaze traveled to Juma. "What about you, witchling?"

"I only began the training a few days ago and have not found access to my magic yet, although the tests claim I've got the talent." Juma forced herself to tell the truth. As much as she disliked giving Chunte the time of day, this information might make the princess underestimate her opposition — at least until Juma managed to connect with her magic.

"Well, as long as you lie low, you may stay." Chunte waved them away. Juma helped the witch to return to the healer's hut, fighting down her loathing.

## <u>12</u>

$\mathcal{W}$HEN THE MOON HAD RISEN, the conspirators met in the remains of the burnt hut. The wounded girl's parents expressed their gratitude to the witch over and over, until Juma cut in.

"We need to find a way to deal with Princess Chunte."

Morva nodded and sat. The others followed her example.

"Palok and I will help any way we can if it means we won't have to see her again," the cook said.

"Why are you willing to help us?" Sundera asked. "She's from your tribe."

Morva didn't answer for a while, staring at the ground. Then she said, "In stark contrast to Chunte, your witch did her best to save our daughter. We don't know yet if she will live, but the healer gave us hope. She said it was a good sign that our precious recognized us upon waking." She looked up into Sundera's eyes. "Also, Princess Chunte is not a good chieftess. Ever since she became our tribe's leader after the Nameless moved and our lands erupted into flame, things went from bad to worse. We lost too many people already and she's putting the rest in more danger than necessary."

Palok added, "On the long track to this lake, Chunte dispatched our witch because she refused to worship Mubuntu. Selto, the husband of our former chieftess, and four of his best friends tried to protect the witch but failed. They were never seen again. When we arrived here, our elders weren't happy with the way Chunte ran things and declared that we needed to elect a new leader, so Chunte killed them too. She gave power to some of the younger men. Now, they will do anything for her."

"How do we know we can trust you?" Tolobe looked stern with the frown on his face.

"Our daughter is still in your hands, and probably will be for a long time to come." Morva smiled. "You can trust us with your plans."

Juma knew they didn't have a choice. These two were valuable allies.

"We've been thinking about drugging her," she said. "If we tie her to a rock in the lake with only her head above the waterline, she might not be able to get in contact with Mubuntu. But we don't have anyone she trusts enough so she would take the drug. It will be a very dangerous task."

"Do you think the lake's water will stop Mubuntu? As long as Vanamate is not with us, he'll be able to find Chunte if he wants. We won't be able to stop him."

"True enough. The whole plan is dangerous and we cannot guarantee positive results," Tolobe said. "But it's the only option we have. The witch refuses to poison Chunte, and a fight with her and her tribe... I mean, your tribe, will cost us all dearly. We need to get control of her so she'll at least send her warriors away."

Morva looked at her husband, and he nodded. Staring at his fingers, he said, "Chunte orders the best-looking warriors to her bed every other night regardless whether they're married or not. At first, she chose our former chieftess's husband, Selto. After he opposed her, she selected several men. She forced me to come several times already. Before I share her mattress, both of us drink a potion that enhances our stamina. The next morning, I feel used, sore, and I hate myself. If it weren't for Morva's care and understanding, I would have gone with Monnatoba of my own free will already."

"When will she call for you again?" Juma hardly dared to breathe. If it was soon, it could be the very chance they had hoped for. High Moon was only a few days off, and Mubuntu surely hadn't forgotten about his hand. They needed to get rid of Chunte before then, hopefully without him noticing. Her thoughts were churning so much she nearly missed the warrior's answer.

"I am to lay with her tonight."

Juma realized that if Netinu could perform, Palok wouldn't have been called. Thinking of Netinu cut into her heart. How much longer would it take him to recover from the attack on his manhood? She dragged her thoughts away from Netinu's injury when Palok continued to speak with his low voice, filled with the sadness of painful memories.

"I am supposed to burn Chunte's husband tomorrow morning. It's probably what she did with Selto and his friends too."

Juma gasped as a jolt shot through her heart. Netinu! No!

"We've got to act tonight." She barely controlled the shaking of her voice.

The witch nodded. "You will need this to manipulate Chunte. It will make her follow anyone's orders for a while. I cannot say how long it will hold, though." The witch pulled a tiny earthen bottle from a pouch on her belt. Carefully, she dripped three drops of a greenish liquid into a small bowl on the ground. "You don't need more than that. This potion is dangerous, and I refuse to give her more than the one dose. I can follow it up with a tea that will make her sleep for two or three days at the most. If we haven't found a way to keep her from Mubuntu's magic, I fear that drugging her will only add to our problems."

"We might need to kill her," Tolobe said. "If she sends away her warriors, I am willing to face her. Will you protect me, Old Mother?"

The witch sat up straighter. "I refuse to take her life. It would not please Vanamate."

"I understand that. However, as a warrior, I have sworn to protect this tribe with violence, if necessary, and I'm prepared to die trying." Tolobe's eyes sparkled with an intensity Juma had never seen in her brother before.

"Do you think it's possible to fight Mubuntu's high priestess with Mubuntu's gifts?" Palok frowned.

"A good warrior can contain the bloodlust," Tolobe said.

"Possibly," Morva said. "But are you a good warrior? Our former chieftess's husband, Selto, was a formidable warrior, and he did not have a chance against her."

"If our plans fail it is our last chance. If bad comes to worst, I will fight Chunte to the death. Maybe some of the other warriors will understand and help me." He turned to the witch. "However, we will never be able to send her to Monnatoba without your help, Old Mother. Will you support me if she attacks?"

"She's too dangerous," Juma said. "If we need to kill her, we'll have to do it when she's asleep."

"I am an honorable warrior. I can only fight her if she attacks me or one I love. But with Vanamate's help and the witch's drugs, I might win."

The witch frowned. "Juma and I will keep you shielded against her magic as best we can, but we will not participate in the killing. If you have to fight Chunte after she wakes, you are on your own. And if you lose…" She left the consequences hanging in the night's air. Juma shivered.

"If necessary, I shall prevail." Tolobe sat up as straight as he could, but his words didn't ease the feeling of dread in Juma's heart.

"Are you sure you want to risk this?" Morva put a hand on her husband's arm. Her smile was terse. "If you fail…"

He pulled her hand to his mouth and kissed it gently. "This is the first time since she called me that I feel hope," he whispered. "Even if I fail, I have at least tried."

They stared at each other wordlessly for a while, and then Palok turned to the witch. She helped him to apply the drug to the nail of the smallest finger on his left hand, where it dried, leaving barely more than a greenish sheen.

"Dip it into your drink for a few seconds so it can dissolve," she instructed him. "But make sure you don't accidentally ingest it yourself."

He nodded. Since everything that could be prepared had been tended to, and because morning was drawing nearer, the conspirators dispersed.

Juma stayed by her father's side with Sundera and Tolobe in the guest hut. For a while, she didn't even realize how much this went against her normal way of life. After all, it was long past bedtime. Everybody must be too preoccupied by Chunte, or one of the grown-ups would already have fetched her and Sundera long ago. She was grateful for her chance to stay. Although her father was still weak, she felt protected and safe.

Listening to the sounds of the night, she tried to sleep, but sleep wouldn't come. Her heart beat too heavily. What if things went wrong? It would be a nightmare if Chunte used the drug on Palok instead. Then Juma would wake to see Netinu burn. Why did every thought of Netinu hurt so much? She surely hadn't fallen for his charm. As long as she was a witch's apprentice she couldn't even dream of marriage. So why did her heart ache so much? With her mind in turmoil, Juma pondered and worried until the first rays of the sun rose over the horizon.

Unable to wait any longer, she left the hut and strolled closer to the second guest hut where Princess Chunte stayed. The two warriors usually standing in front of her door were nowhere in sight. Still, Juma didn't dare to call. Before she could turn and leave again, the blanket moved aside and Palok came out.

When he saw her, he smiled. "It worked very well. I already told her to send away the guards at the door, and she did. What shall we tell her next?"

"Make her set the children free, so they can return to their parents." Juma hadn't been able to shake the children's tears and their parents' stony faces. "After that, we need to get the warriors of your tribe out of our village."

"Consider it done. Will you fetch the others here, please?" Ready to go back inside, he waited at the door until she nodded before he turned.

Some time later, they all gathered in the second guest hut. Princess Chunte sat on her bed staring into space motionlessly. A cold shiver ran down Juma's spine, and she understood why the witch didn't like using this drug. It felt wrong, no matter how necessary it had been.

"The warriors are ready to leave," Palok said. "Only a handful will stay. I made sure they are the ones that will support our rebellion."

"Where will your people go when you leave Chunte's followers?" Sundera adjusted her kikoi.

Morva shrugged. "If you allow us to take enough water to reach the next river, we will keep traveling until we'll find a place to stay. There is nothing else we can do."

"Will you have enough provisions?" Sundera asked.

"We've got the herds and all the grain we were able to rescue. It's not much but we'll get by as long as we have enough water."

Juma thought about the harvest they had stored. If they rationed it, it should be enough for all. "Why can't Morva go and fetch those of her tribe that want to break with the princess? We could use the support if Chunte's followers decide to attack."

"That's for Jakombe to decide," the witch said.

Tolobe nodded. "Hopefully she'll wake soon. We'll get into trouble if she doesn't."

"The healer and I mixed a strong magic for her when she fell unconscious. It should show effect today or tomorrow at the latest. The tea I'm currently preparing for Chunte should keep her sleeping until then."

"So can't Morva's tribe stay until Jakombe is fit enough to decide?" Juma asked.

Everybody agreed that it would only be fair to take in Morva's people for a while. After all, Palok had taken a deadly risk to help them.

Expressing their gratitude, Morva and her husband left to fetch their fellow tribe members. Juma, Sundera, and the witch went to see how Jakombe fared, while Tolobe stayed behind to guard the mindless princess.

The women found Kandra slumped over her mother, holding her hand and snoring. When the three women entered, sunlight fell on Jakombe's face, and she opened her eyes.

She smiled weakly. "I never thought the princess would hurt me," she croaked.

The witch didn't get to answer. A loud thumping noise vibrated through the village. The Big Drum! Juma had heard it in use during ceremonies but never unannounced like this. It could mean only one thing: a fight! Had they made a mistake to trust Morva and her husband? Everybody's eyes clung to the door.

"We're under attack!" Mama Lubeda's voice carried over the drum's heartbeat rhythm and the stunned silence. "Women and children into the compound! Warriors and hunters gather at the northern gate."

Instantly, running feet passed the hut, and a cacophony of voices filled the air, mixed with bleating and lowing. The witch grabbed Jakombe's staff that stood beside the door and hurried out. Sundera followed her immediately, but Juma stood rooted to the spot. Open-mouthed, she stared after them, then turned her gaze to Jakombe. The chieftess shook Kandra's shoulder until the girl woke with a start.

"You need to help fight off the invaders." Urgency filled Jakombe's voice. "Selenta has the lead. I'm too weak."

"Selenta?" Kandra seemed confused. "Who is attacking us?"

"I don't know. Assist the witch any way you can. The tribe has to survive." Her mother pointed to the door.

Kandra jumped to her feet and glared at Juma. "What are you waiting for? We have to win this battle."

The girls ran out and looked around. Women and children were hurrying toward the Central Hall. Many children, even older ones, cried or screamed. Herders tried to gather the bleating, panicked animals in one place, but frightened people accidentally scattered them again and again. Juma tried not to hear the chaos of noise around her. She spotted the top of Jakombe's staff close to the northern gate amid a group of hunters and warriors. As fast as she could, she ran after Kandra who tried to catch up with the witch. Juma marveled at how fast the old woman still was.

"Who's attacking us?" Kandra jammed an elbow into one of the hunter's ribs.

He gasped, but his neighbor answered.

"The river people."

"They don't have many warriors, so who is fighting?" Kandra ripped the staff from the witch's hand. Due to its weight, the heavy staff twisted unexpectedly and knocked the old woman on the head. Kandra didn't spare the witch a glance as the old woman crumbled to the ground soundlessly. The hunter paled. Juma's heart plummeted. Why had Kandra done that? Without the witch they'd be lost. What should she do? Confused and scared, she knelt beside the old woman, barely hearing the hunter's shaky voice.

"It seems like all available men are in the attack, and I've even seen some women."

"Did you get all of our people into the compound?" Kandra asked.

The hunter nodded. "The warriors are still out there, but they're outnumbered. Once they're overrun, the river tribe will most likely put fire to the thornbush fence. It's so dry it will—"

"Stop it," Kandra interrupted him and turned to the other men. "We need to defend our village before they get too close. Storm out of the northern gate and help our warriors kill everyone we see. Hurry!"

Kill? Juma's stomach clenched. How could a day that started so well go downhill so fast? She didn't think anyone aside from the warriors had it in them to kill humans, but the men seemed to accept Kandra's orders. They ran toward the gate.

Kandra turned to Juma, who still squatted beside the unconscious witch. "We'll need a witch to drive them back, and the old bag of bones is not up to it. Come!"

Juma had already opened her mouth to refuse when the witch's eyes fluttered and opened. The old woman moaned, and her lips moved as if she wanted to say something. Juma bent over her.

"Go with her. Make peace. The river people are just desperate." She breathed as if she had run a marathon. Reluctantly Juma got up to follow Kandra. She looked back every so often, realizing that Sundera had taken care of the situation in the village. The young herder apprentice made some women pick up the witch and carry her toward Jakombe's hut. Others she sent to collect water pails and grass rings. When she noticed Juma, she waved and called, "The children are fetching water. They're using the lakeside gate. We will alert you should the attackers round the village."

Relieved, Juma nodded and followed Kandra and the hunters through the gate. The men yelled at the top of their lungs and shook their clubs, spears, and flint knives. Juma stopped to pull the gate closed behind them, just in case. She knew she was dawdling but couldn't bring herself to move faster. How could she bring peace with everybody set on killing?

Dragging her feet, she watched the men of her tribe race to where their warriors fought with the river people. They met the fighting group halfway up the hill.

Piercing screams and clouds of red dust filled the air. Juma forced herself not to put her hands over her ears or close her eyes. Men fell on men, pounding, hitting, stabbing and slicing left and right. The attackers slowed to a standstill. Blood soaked into the red earth, and Juma felt sick to the bone. Her heart contracted. How many mothers and wives would cry tonight?

Suddenly she felt very much alone. And cold. As if there was no place in the world where she could hide from the chaos of screams, blood, sweat and shouts.

Kandra kicked her viciously against her shin. "Do your magic! Make them freeze or melt them. Anything to kill them!"

Since several warriors fought in a half-circle close to them to keep her and Kandra safe, Juma closed her eyes, turned her back to the battle, and tried to think of something. It was so hard to concentrate and she felt so lost. She couldn't kill the attackers but she also didn't know how to bring peace to the people around her. Only gods could do that, right?

To block the screams and shouts from her mind, she began to hum a prayer to Vanamate, begging for peace and rain. Her skin tingled as magic gathered around her. Although she wondered how she had managed that, she grasped as much of it as she could hold and opened her eyes. Since her back was turned to the fight, she saw the men from Chunte's tribe run up the slope toward them. With the princess still subdued, they obviously meant to help. The river people would be slaughtered. Her heart felt as if it turned in her chest. The river people are fighting for their tribe's survival, she thought. All they want is water. I need to calm the fighters now. She turned back to the chaos.

"Calm — all of you!" she called and pushed the magic she had gathered outward. A tingling sensation on her skin told her how fast the power sped forward. In the blink of an eye, it reached Kandra and their protective circle. They toppled and fell.

Thinning, it reached more fighters. They swayed. Their movements grew sluggish for a little moment as her power surged over the battlefield. However, it dissolved too quickly and the fighters resumed their bashing. The only people clearly affected were Kandra and five of her guards, lying on the ground like crumpled kikois. Juma sobbed.

A hand fell on her shoulder, and Tolobe said, "The men need a leader." He picked up the staff and pressed it into her hand.

Juma tried to focus on the fighters but she didn't know where to start. Her jaw worked up and down until an idea flashed through her mind. "You're a warrior. You know how to fight. Can't you lead them for now?"

Tolobe nodded.

"Then play along with me." She took his wrist and raised it together with the arm that held Jakombe's staff, and yelled. "Kandra has fallen; I am your leader now. Hark Tolobe's commands." She nudged his arm even higher and let the staff slip into his hand. The fighters hesitated for a moment — a man carrying the chieftess's staff was unheard of. This tiny break gave the river people the advantage. They surged forward.

Instantly, Tolobe began ordering the fighters. Since Juma made no attempt to take back either command or staff, the fighters obeyed.

"Get Kandra out of here. I'll make sure we're not overrun." Tolobe swung his club against the hip of an attacker.

Juma grabbed Kandra's shoulders and was dragging her toward the gate when the men from Chunte's tribe passed her with a war cry. She shivered, stopped, and looked back at Tolobe. He stood proud and fierce and directed the fighters with few gestures and even fewer words, and they obeyed without questioning. When the river people realized that reinforcements were coming, they turned and fled, dragging along their wounded.

Juma bent down and grabbed Kandra's shoulders once more. Her heart was heavier than ever, despite the retreating enemy. When everything had depended on her, she had failed. She swallowed several times but the lump in her throat stayed.

At the gate, Sundera met her to help.

"It was a splendid idea to hand the command to Tolobe," she said as they carried Kandra toward her mother's hut. "He knows all about fighting and is level-headed enough that he won't allow unnecessary killing. You'll be a great chieftess one day."

Juma knew that to be wrong, but a tiny flicker of hope moved in her heart like a butterfly wing. The attack had come unexpectedly. Surely the training would teach her how to be a good chieftess, one who'd be able to cope with a situation like this.

## 13

*T*HEY ENTERED THE HUT AND laid Kandra on a mat beside the witch.

"Now it's getting crowded." Jakombe's voice shook, which voided her attempt to hide her worry behind casual words. "Where is Netinu?"

Juma wondered the same for a moment until she realized she had not seen him with the fighters. All of a sudden, her tongue went dry and stuck to her palate. She shook herself. *He's probably still recovering from Chunte's attack. Forget him. There are more important things to think of right now.*

"I'll go and help Morva bring her people through the lakeside gate," she said to Sundera.

Her friend smiled. "I already took care of it. Let's go back and see how Tolobe and his men are doing."

They left Kandra and the witch to the healer and ran back to the northern gate together. The fighters carried Tolobe on their shoulders, singing as they approached the gate. Many men were wounded, but no one seemed to have died, and the river people were nowhere in sight. Juma sighed deeply.

When they had marched through the gate, Tolobe ordered the men to set him down. He held out the chieftess's staff to Juma. "Thank you for trusting me with the staff and the lead. If I've made mistakes, please punish me accordingly." He lowered himself to one knee.

Juma blushed and took the staff. "I think you did well. Any question of punishment is for Jakombe to decide." She turned away and went to close the gate behind the fighters.

Sundera rounded up some of the older women and set them to dress the men's wounds under the healer's watchful eyes. Others set up comfortable beds in the Central Hall. Juma marveled. She knew she would have thought about the same measures but with more delay, and she wouldn't have been able to run everything so efficiently. It dawned on her that Sundera would make a splendid chieftess — surely a much better one than she would ever be. No wonder the totems chose her. But then she remembered that Sundera would have to marry Netinu if she became chieftess, and she was rather glad her friend had chosen a different path.

From the northern gate, the sound of unfamiliar drums filled the air. A warrior approached Juma.

"It's a delegation from the river people," he told her. "They demand to see our chieftess. Will Jakombe be able to receive them?"

Juma nodded. "We will get her ready. Make sure they don't enter the compound."

The man bowed and hurried away. As soon as she told Sundera, her friend turned to one of the women.

"Prepare some food and drink for the envoy." Sundera smiled at Juma. "Oops. Here I am, behaving like Princess Chunte already, taking away your place. I'm sorry."

"You're doing a great job." Juma waved her apology aside. "Let's fetch Jakombe. She'll be glad to be back in charge."

In the hut, Juma handed Jakombe the staff and told her what had happened during the fight. The chieftess sighed and scratched her chin. Finally, she said, "You gave command to Tolobe, so I'll have to judge your actions, not his. I must think about that. Let's negotiate with the river people first."

The sun had barely moved a finger's width over the sky when four strong men carried Jakombe in a chair decorated with greenery out of the northern gate. Juma, Sundera, and a handful of warriors followed them.

Close to the battlefield, they met with the delegation of the river people. Juma's gaze flickered to the brown patches in the parched earth several times before it settled on the river tribe's chieftess. She was dressed in a blue and yellow kikoi and hung with more gold than Juma's whole tribe owned. A hawk-like nose jutted over full lips. She clenched her spear as she bowed.

"Honored to meet you, Mother." The traditional greeting sounded forced, but so did Jakombe's reply.

"Be my guest, Daughter."

The carriers set down the chair, and Juma hurried to provide the river people's chieftess with another one they had brought. The young woman sat. For a long time, the two women stared at each other. Finally the young chieftess broke the silence.

"The water of the Endless Well is dwindling. Our children cry of thirst and our cattle are dying. We need access to the lake."

"We cannot allow you to go there." Jakombe spoke so low, Juma had to strain her ears to understand her. "The lake is nearly empty. There isn't enough left for another month."

The young woman half rose, clenching her fist over her spear, but she caught herself in time and sat down again. "My tribe will not survive without water."

"Neither will mine. And we've been burdened with friends from the other side of the holy mountain where the Nameless moved and devastated the earth."

The young woman's chin jutted out. "The water in the well will last for one week at the most. If you do not give us access to the lake, we will attack until we get there. We will rather die fighting than watching our children die of thirst."

Jakombe ground her teeth. "In that case, we'll be at war with you."

Sundera stepped forward and put her hand on Jakombe's shoulder. "May I ask a few questions, Good Mother?"

Frowning up to her, Jakombe nodded. Sundera thanked her with a smile and turned to the river people's emissary.

"Why have you left the river? Surely Mubuntu's heat isn't strong enough to dry it out."

The river tribe's chieftess snorted. "There is nothing but dry, cracked earth in the river's bed. We stayed for as long as we could, but there is no surviving in our old village."

"But that should be impossible," Juma said. "The river comes from the holy mountain. Even Mubuntu shouldn't have been able to stop it."

"Well, I don't know who or what stopped the water, but fact is that the river ran dry. We sent several men to find out, but none of them returned. When the old chieftess died, I decided it was time to spare the lives of our men. So, we left our homeland."

"Did the earth shake near your village?" Sundera asked.

"Not that I noticed." The river tribe's chieftess leaned back and frowned. "Why are you asking all these questions? Are you suggesting we didn't do everything we could think of?"

Sundera lifted her hands, palms facing the woman. "I did not mean to offend you. I'm just curious and wondering if there might be a different reason for the strange disappearance of the river." Her gaze wandered into the distance. "My mother's mother was from your tribe, and she once took me to visit her sister. I remember your village well, although I was quite small at that time. It's no easy feat to dry out a river as wide as four grown men are long."

"If it hadn't truly happened, we wouldn't be here." The young chieftess scowled.

Sundera bowed politely. "You said the water in the Endless well would last one more week. Shouldn't we use the time to try once more to find the reason the river vanished?"

"What good will it do? We've lost ten of our best hunters that way." She crossed her arms over her chest.

"I hate the thought of starting a war if there is hope still," Sundera said. "Let us send out a group of capable men to see if they can find out what is wrong with the river. I am sure my soon-to-be husband and some of his friends would gladly go if some of your men would accompany them."

"They won't be able to do much in one week."

"It would be worth a try," Jakombe said.

"We will send three men, and wait for three nights. If they don't return before then, we will attack." The young chieftess got up. "This consultation is over now." She turned and walked away, ordering three of her men to stay.

Juma suppressed a grin. Sundera was so subtle, the river tribe's chieftess hadn't even noticed she had been manipulated.

"Three days isn't much," Jakombe said, signaling the men beside her to carry her back.

"In three days, a good walker can reach the top of the holy mountain and return without breaking a sweat," Sundera said. "As you said, it's worth a try. Anything will be better than war."

There was nothing Jakombe could say to that.

A few hours later, Tolobe, two of his friends, and the three men from the river tribe set out toward the mountain. Jakombe had made sure they were well fed and provided with everything they might need. Juma and Sundera watched them leave until their silhouettes merged with the scenery. When they turned to go back, Juma stifled a scream. Mubuntu stood right behind her, grinning broadly.

"They won't come back. There is no one on earth who can undo what has been done." He giggled. "Give my hand back to me, and I will make sure that at least your brother returns."

"Leave me alone." Juma frowned.

Sundera's eyebrows shot up. "What did I do wrong?"

"Not you. Him." Juma pointed at the heat dæmon and walked past him. Laughing madly, Mubuntu vanished.

"There's no one there," Sundera said.

Juma shrugged and forced a smile. "It seems I'm more exhausted than I want to admit."

Of course she worried about her brother and the other men, but for now the weariness deep in her bones numbed her mind. The exciting events of late and the little sleep she had gotten had made her too tired to feel much. She wondered why Mubuntu's threats didn't scare her as much as before, but her mind refused to ponder the question and shut down. She didn't feel Sundera lead her to her bed, more asleep than not.

The next morning, Juma woke fresh and well rested. First thing after checking on the sleeping princess, she went to see her father to tell him about Tolobe's dangerous task. Then she went to the healer's hut to visit the witch. The old woman had recovered enough to sit and drink tea from a bowl.

Juma smiled. "It's so good to see that Kandra didn't hurt you too badly."

"This old head of mine," the witch tapped against her skull with a finger, "survived far worse. I heard you managed surprisingly well." It sounded more like a question than a statement, so Juma told her what had happened. She found approval in the old woman's eyes.

"Well done. If someone will bring back the reason the river vanished, it is Tolobe. I've never seen a man as resourceful as him. It's a pity he's no woman." The witch closed her eyes. "And how is our unwanted guest?"

"Your potion is still working, but her sleep is restless." Juma slapped her forehead. "By Vanamate's tears, we forgot that Tolobe meant to fight and kill her when she wakes. What will we do now that he's gone?"

"With luck, he will return in time," the witch said. "It was a very strong potion."

Juma wasn't comforted. "She is filled with Mubuntu's magic. What if it counters the effect of the potion?"

"We'll have to create a very strong shield." The witch stared grimly into her tea. At that moment, Kandra burst through the door and threw herself on Juma.

"You did that on purpose!" She slammed a fist into her cousin's belly. Pain exploded in Juma's body, and she doubled over, gasping for air. Kandra pummeled her bowed head with her fists. "I'll never forgive you!"

Juma threw her hands protectively over her head and twisted away from her cousin's fists. Kandra kicked and screamed, trying to get hold of her again.

"I didn't do anything." Juma danced around the witch to stay out of reach.

The old woman rose, her face contorted with the effort, and put a soothing hand on Kandra's shoulder. The young woman tried to get away but the frail witch didn't let go. Although she gripped the young woman's shoulder only lightly, Kandra couldn't break free.

"What did she do on purpose?" the witch asked, but Kandra just swore and struggled on.

Pushing ever so gently, the witch forced her to sit on the ground. The young woman glared at Juma, but the witch didn't let go.

Still fighting for air, Juma wondered about the old woman's strength until she realized that the buzz of magic tingled on her skin. Selenta probably knew many more tricks like that. Juma's breathing normalized and she was able to focus on the world around her again. The witch murmured soothingly. Her magic tugged at Juma's nerves, but it also calmed the raging girl. Soon Kandra relaxed, and Selenta let go of her shoulder. Kandra put her face in her hands and cried.

"What's wrong, dear?"

"If she hadn't knocked me out by magic, I could have proven to my mother that I can be a good chieftess," Kandra sniffed but didn't look up.

The witch pulled up an eyebrow and looked at Juma.

"She told me to do something with magic, and I tried. But the discharge I used went astray and hit her. I'm really sorry."

"See, it was an accident." The witch patted Kandra's back. The young woman didn't answer and kept sobbing.

"It is very dangerous to use magic without training. You should have known that, Kandra. Your mother taught you the rules." The witch looked up at Juma. "We will train again after the midday meal."

Juma nodded, said her farewell, and left the hut. Since there were still a few hours to go, she checked on the princess again. Palok was currently guarding her. She lay on a mat with her hands tied, tossing around in her sleep.

"We'll need to prepare a way to imprison her in the lake," Juma said. "Let's hope she'll sleep until we're done or until Tolobe returns."

Palok agreed. "I don't think I'd be able to kill her. After all, she's still the leader of our tribe. Even if she's truly evil, I'd feel like a traitor."

"I just hope the witch and I can create a shield strong enough to keep her from harming anyone," Juma said.

The warrior smiled. "I'm sure you will." He put a hand on her shoulder. "You remind me of the princess's mother. She was as straightforward as you are, and she always found a way out of any predicament."

Warmth spread through Juma's body at the compliment. She left the hut smiling, although she did wonder why a man's praise meant so much to her. She walked through the village, asking here and there if she could help, but everybody politely declined. For the moment, life had more or less returned to normal. Children ran around the huts, now and then hugging their mothers, and everybody seemed busy with the usual everyday chores. Still, tension filled the village and made the hairs on Juma's arms rise. She frowned at the sun. Hopefully Mubuntu hadn't yet noticed his priestess was missing. They'd need to move Chunte to the lake soon.

The sun had to move a lot more until the midday meal, so Juma went to look for Sundera. Her friend was feeding the goats. The scrawny animals pressed against her legs as if she was their savior.

"We need to put a pole in the lake so we can tie Chunte to it before she wakes." Juma bent down and patted a black and white goat. "She needs to be up to her chin in water soon."

"Morva already took a couple of her husband's friends to find a suitable tree trunk." Sundera dumped another armful of hay onto the cracked ground. "It's going to be really hard to put it in the middle of the lake."

"It doesn't have to be in the middle. Just deep enough that Chunte's body will be under water." Juma stretched. "Or we can tie her legs to a heavy rock."

"Good idea. It would make it easier to move Chunte when the lake's water level drops. But for the moment, there's nothing we can do." Sundera stretched too. "So, what will you do next?"

"Nothing's scheduled before the afternoon. I've been dismissed." Juma shrugged. "Kandra had a breakdown and tried to punch me to pulp."

"She's a very unhappy woman. I feel sorry for her."

"Me too." Juma was surprised to realize that she truly did. "It must be hard to have a mother who prefers the brother."

"By the way, have you seen Netinu?" Sundera asked. "It seems he went into hiding as if he were too embarrassed after the forced incident with Chunte."

"I don't care where he went." Her own words sounded hollow in Juma's ears.

"Stop pretending you don't like him." Sundera grinned.

"I…" Juma glared at Sundera but her ears grew hot. Her friend just smiled, fetched the next armful of hay, and carried it to the goats. Juma turned her back on her and watched three girls bring more hay. It's none of Sundera's business if I do or don't fancy Netinu. Memories of Netinu sent a pleasant tingle down her spine, but she refused to go looking for him. She ground her teeth. As hard as it was, she had to admit that Sundera was right. She did care for him. At least a little bit.

When the girls had left, she turned back to her friend. "If he doesn't search me out, I'm definitely not going to run after him like a love-stricken antelope."

Sundera's smile didn't reach her eyes, where an unshed tear sparkled. "At least you can see him if you want. I just wish Tolobe hadn't left. What if the river clan's chieftess was right and he doesn't return?"

Juma had an idea. "You know what? I'll go and search for him to see how he's doing."

"You can't leave. The witch would get a fit, and so would Jakombe."

"I'm not planning on taking my body along." When Sundera's jaw dropped, Juma grinned.

With so much time on her hands, she would be able to experiment with her out-of-body experiences. Checking on Tolobe seemed to be a good start.

She found herself a quiet corner in the compound, lay down, and closed her eyes. She gathered magic around her, struggling to build it up. It felt like moving though mud but she managed to collect some to her chest. When the magic glowed like a small star, she tried to use it to pull her mind out of her body. The magic dissipated without taking effect. She tried again and again, but nothing happened.

She frowned in concentration. It had to work. When Selenta did it, it had been so easy. And when she had visited Vanamate during the ceremony, she hadn't even noticed she had left her body behind. She tried again and failed.

With hands balled to fists, she sat up, put her elbows on her knees and supported her forehead with her knuckles. What was she missing? What had been different when she had left her body during the ceremony?

It had been night. There had been a big bonfire. And lots of people. Netinu had been in danger.

She would have to test the individual elements to see which one she needed to fully use her magic. She couldn't start with fire. The flames might call Mubuntu. Although boring, it was safer to wait for nightfall. If it wasn't enough, she would have to try fire next, but she'd need the witch's help just in case. *What if I need someone to be in danger for my magic to work properly?*

The answer hit her like lightning. *It can't be, or the spell I used on the river people would have worked the way I wanted it to. Instead, it knocked down Kandra. Well, it's a relief to know. It just wouldn't have done to endanger someone on purpose just to find out.*

She lay back again and looked at the bright blue sky. If only there were clouds — fluffy white ones providing a little shade from the celestial glare would be a good start, but she preferred the dark gray ones promising rain. She sighed and got up. Lying around lazily in the sun wouldn't do as long as the others were still working hard. She would find something she could do. Maybe she could help the men who were putting new reeds on the witch's hut. *I'm thinking of helping men without having been forced to? Oh Vanamate, how did it come to that?*

## 14

$\mathcal{S}$HE HAD HARDLY REACHED THE place in front of the Central Hall when people ran past her, screaming for their children and moving them out of sight into their huts. Before Juma realized what was going on, Princess Chunte walked toward her. She swayed and seemed to have problems focusing on the world around her. Her hands glowed ghostly blue, and sparks sprang from her fingertips. It was only luck that kept the huts from catching fire.

Juma frowned and gathered magic around her as best she could. Chunte shot a bolt of fire toward her. Juma jumped aside and it hit the ground instead.

"Get out of my way, little witchling." Chunte's voice was hoarse, and her eyes glared with a hatred Juma had never seen before. "If you stay where you are, I will wipe you off the face of the earth."

Pretending not to care, Juma stood straighter. "We threw your people out. You don't have any followers left in this village. And although you might kill many of us, the magic Mubuntu gave you is limited. Sooner or later, the witch or I will get you."

Chunte screamed and threw her arms forward, hurling another ball of fire toward Juma. This time it slammed into Juma and sent her flying. Fire raced through every fiber of her being, drowning her in pain. She screamed. Only vaguely, she noticed that Netinu stepped from the shade of the huts, stood over her, and shielded her with his body.

Chunte laughed. "Do you really think you can oppose me?"

The words cut through Juma's pain. She knew Netinu would die if she let him fight Chunte unprotected. Struggling against the fire raging in her body, she tried to find her magic. Only a small drop. Just enough to protect Netinu from the crazy princess.

He lifted his hunting spear. "Leave her alone, or I will kill you."

Chunte laughed again and charged. Despite her disorientation, she moved as fast as lightning. Juma's heart was bleeding when, abruptly, the feeling of being burned alive stopped and the princess slammed into an invisible wall. Surprised, Juma looked around while picking herself up. The witch was standing between two huts, holding her hands over her head and spreading magical energy. Soothing greenish light spilled from her fingers and formed a dome over Netinu, Juma and her.

Chunte screamed again and shot bolt after bolt at the witch's shield. Every single one bounced off and died in the ground, but beads of sweat ran over the witch's face. With every attack, she breathed harder and slumped a little more.

Netinu jumped forward and thrust his spear at Chunte. It slipped through the witch's shield without a problem, but he missed the princess, who moved too fast. Thrusting, evading and hurling fire balls at the shield became a mesmerizing dance that seemed to tire the witch considerably.

Wondering how much longer the old woman would be able to hold out, Juma hurried to her side, collecting magic along the way as best she could. She touched the old woman's arm, letting the magic flow into Selenta. It was the only thing she could think of, and it seemed to help. The witch's breathing became more regular again, and she straightened.

"Leave us alone." Netinu feigned an attack and thrust his spear in a different direction at the last possible moment.

It glanced off Chunte's ribs, and she yelped with pain. Blood flowed over her bronze skin. She lowered her hands and glared at Netinu.

"You will pay for this." A swiping over the shallow wound closed the cut. Instantly, the blood began to dry. Chunte turned to the witch with a frown. "For now, you win. But I will return with my warriors and with Mubuntu. Then you will give me Mubuntu's hand and crown me queen of two tribes, or I will burn your huts to the ground."

With her head held high, she stomped toward a path that led to the lakeside gate, faltering every few steps. Juma was glad she seemed as exhausted as the witch. Maybe they could overpower her still. Together with Selenta, she followed the princess. They shielded people and huts along the way as best they could. But Chunte stayed alert enough to avoid any attempt to subdue her, so they had to let her leave the village. When the angry princess was out of sight, the witch let her shield down. She faltered and Juma took her arm and steadied her.

"Thank you for strengthening me. I never knew magic could be passed on." The witch panted like a dog that had been running in the sun. "Let's get something to eat."

Only now did Juma realize she was starving too. Obviously it was quite strenuous to use magic this way. They turned and walked back to the place in front of the Central Hall where the cooks would soon serve the midday meal.

Netinu waited for them. When Juma had seated herself beside the witch, he approached and knelt on the ground before them.

"I would like to apologize for my behavior. I should have fought Chunte's spell before she forced me into fulfilling a husband's…" He seemed lost for words.

The witch put her hand on his shoulder. "There is no need to apologize. It was a miracle that you managed to break free at all." She glanced at Juma. "Methinks love really is stronger than anything on earth."

Netinu blushed, and Juma grew hot as well.

"We're not in love," she protested.

"Well, I am," Netinu said, not looking at her.

At that moment Morva joined them, supporting her husband, who looked like he had been trampled by elephants.

"I'm sorry, but I couldn't hold her back," he said and lowered himself beside Netinu.

"You look as if you tried." The witch smiled at him. "You should see the healer."

"She pinned me to the hut's wall after slamming me into it a couple of times." His face twisted with pain. "I will survive."

The cooks arrived with the food. Juma noticed that they kept glancing around as if Chunte would jump them any minute. The tension eased somewhat when Morva confirmed that the princess had taken her loyal followers and left the rest of the tribe. Everybody knew it was a respite on borrowed time, so they ate in silence.

Sweat ran over everyone's bodies. Juma wiped her face and gazed around. The air flickered, even blurring people sitting close by. The heat had increased again. Juma listened as Jakombe told the herders to take the animals to the lake a second time. She wondered if she would have to tell the chieftess about Chunte's threat. Relief flooded her when the witch got up and walked over to Jakombe. After a low exchange of words, Jakombe sent two men out to keep an eye on the princess. For now, there was nothing much they could do.

To avoid the worst of the heat, everybody retreated into their huts after the meal. Juma followed the witch. The repairs of her hut wouldn't take much longer, maybe two more days, but it would take ages to get rid of the stink of burnt furniture. The witch pulled a face and went in search for a different place where they could practice without being disturbed. When they left the compound, two fighters with spears followed them. Even though Juma didn't like it, she understood that the witch was too important to lose.

The women settled on a small patch in the reed field near the lake. The warriors found two places nearby and turned their backs to the women. Juma was grateful that they tried to give them privacy as best was possible. Through the reed's stems, the witch and Juma looked at the lake. A lot of its bed was dry and cracked. Shriveled plants covered the previously shallow areas, and a couple of dead fish lay around.

"Chunte and Mubuntu are getting out of hand. We need to wake Vanamate urgently," the witch whispered. "Therefore, we need to train you. I will not be strong enough to confront Mubuntu on my own."

Juma pointed to the distant shore. "See how many animals have come."

Antelope, wildebeests, zebras, hyenas, and monkeys swarmed the lakeside, trying their best to stay out of each other's way. In the shade of a tree, a pride of lions dozed. Juma's heart accelerated. What if they attacked the herds on their trip to the water? It was a worrying thought, but there wasn't much the tribe could do. It would be too much work to carry the water to the animals. Juma watched the herders move their animals toward the water's edge, first the cows then the goats. Two men played drums, and the wild animals fled from the sound. The lions barely looked up. Juma understood perfectly well why. The air was so hot, every breath burned in her lungs.

"Let's get started," the witch said. "You need to know how to leave your body deliberately, since you will have to lead the way to Vanamate this time. If you can't control it, we can't wake the goddess, which means the tribe will be doomed."

"Not as long as you're there," Juma said.

The witch smiled. "We do not know how much time Monnatoba still has allotted to me. Now, lie back. We need to hurry."

Juma obeyed. She didn't think it would do much good to try again. Surely she'd need the darkness, and night hadn't fallen yet, but she didn't want to disappoint the witch. The men's drumming filled the air like a low heartbeat. Juma closed her eyes and collected the magic around her as she had learned. The thumping of the drums made it harder because the sound hummed through her body and made it sing. The more she concentrated on gathering magic, the more her mind drifted away. Finally, she opened her eyes to tell the witch that the drums were distracting her too much.

Her jaw dropped. She hovered above the lake's water with a good view of the scenery around her. Big herds were wandering toward the lake. The grass glowed a brilliant green, and the water sparkled. At the rim of the small wood in the south, Princess Chunte and her remaining followers had set up camp, a patch of flickering red among the trees' greenness. The men were sharpening the wood of their spears. Juma shuddered and looked back to where her body lay. The pale tendril she had experienced before connected her to it. *I didn't know it was so easy to send my spirit out.* She soared over the plains to look for Tolobe and discovered him halfway up the holy mountain. He and his men were just setting up camp for the night when Juma arrived. Her tribe members seemed to be on friendly terms with the men from the river people. *If I can find the reason why the river is blocked, I can spare them the journey.* Juma sped along the mountain slope.

She came to with a start. The thumping of the drums had stopped, and the witch was holding her hand, whispering, "It's time to come back, dear. Please return." There were worry lines on her face.

"Drat." Juma sat up.

"Thank Vanamate you are safe." The witch relaxed and smiled, her relief plainly visible. "You had me really worried when I realized you left your body."

"I was so close to the river's well. Just a moment longer and I would have found the water." Juma lay back. "I'll try again. I'll be fast about it. Promise."

"I understand your impatience but traveling outside your body is exhausting work. You will not go out again today. You might damage your health." The witch smiled to take the edge off her words. "The next time we try, I will come along. But now, the day has come to an end."

Juma looked around with surprise. Night was approaching fast. Had she really been out of her body for that long? She shook her head to clear it. Obviously it was easy to forget about time without a body. She'd have to be more careful when she tried it next. If I manage to get out of my body again, she thought.

At the witch's side, she walked back to the village pondering what had made it so easy to leave her body this time. Since it hadn't been dark when she had succeeded, it couldn't have been the approaching night. The only thing that came to mind were the drumbeats. The night of the ceremony, there had been drums too. She glanced at the witch. She needed to talk to her, there was no doubt about it. However, it was probably better to confirm her suspicion before raising the old woman's hopes in vain. What if she was wrong and the drums weren't her trigger? It wouldn't do to disappoint the witch—the whole village—with a claim she couldn't prove. She needed to make sure. Juma decided to keep her secret for one night. Tomorrow, when she had confirmed her find, it would be early enough.

When everybody was asleep, Juma and Sundera rose. As quietly as they could, they opened the northern gate a tiny bit and slipped out, pulling it close behind them. Juma knew it would be dangerous outside with the lions so close, but drumming inside the village would wake too many. Sundera had come of her own free will when Juma had asked her, although she disagreed with Juma's reasoning on why they shouldn't take the witch along. They walked to the plain where the witch had hunted Mubuntu and where the risk of meeting a lion was low. Juma spread out her mat and lay down. Sundera sat beside her, pulling out her little drum. She seemed a little nervous.

"So, I shall start drumming when the moon has moved one finger's width over the sky, and stop after another finger's width, right?"

"It's important not to start right away. I need to see if I can do it without the drum, first." Juma closed her eyes and gathered as much magic as her chest would hold before she tried to get it to pull her out of her body, but it didn't work. When the drum started, it surprised her. She hadn't realized trying had taken her so long. She meant to tell Sundera, but when she opened her eyes, she was already hovering above her body. This time, she didn't fly far. She flew a little round over the village. Elephants were moving through their fields, trampling more than they ate. Jakombe will be furious. We need to put up guards again, she thought, or there will be nothing left. With the drought, the harvest will be barely enough anyway. She listened if she could still hear the drum and felt the beat reverberate in the bones she had left behind. The time was over soon, and her friend stopped drumming. This time, Juma concentrated on staying out of her body, fighting the pull, but it was no use. Faster than a cheetah, she zipped back into her body. Opening her eyes, she smiled at Sundera.

"I was right. It is the drum."

Her friend hugged her. "Do you think knowing will help you to find Vanamate?"

Juma shrugged and rolled up her mat. She knew exactly where Vanamate was, but would her newfound ability help to wake her? She would have to try. But this time, she would take the witch along. Together they stood a better chance.

The next morning, the girls were very tired. Juma tried to stay out of Kandra's way as best she could. She was glad her father had found the strength to leave his bed and join them for breakfast. He sat with

Lomba. When they had eaten, Jakombe got up and announced the extent of the damage the elephants had caused during the night.

"If this happens again, we will starve," she said.

"If the drought doesn't end soon, we'll starve anyway," a woman beside Juma mumbled, but Jakombe didn't hear. She went on, unperturbed.

"Luckily my sisterman has agreed on training every available man in combat skills. That will also come in handy if the river people or Princess Chunte's warriors attack again. All men will follow him through the northern gate for training. Just make sure that you catch up on your regular duties after the midday meal."

It's high time to take the witch to Vanamate, Juma thought. I'm sure everything will return to normal when Vanamate is free to send rain. She walked to the witch's hut right after the meal was over. Due to the rationed portions, her stomach still grumbled. Magic really did cost a lot of energy. She sighed and sat down in front of the hut, waiting for the witch. The old woman arrived with a young girl at her side.

"Today, you will take me to Vanamate. The child will call for help, should we stay out too long or if Mubuntu attacks the hut again," she explained.

Juma applauded her on the idea, then told her about the drumming. Since she had brought a small drum, she handed it to the girl.

The witch sat beside her.

"I'll wait for you to fetch me as soon as you find Vanamate," she said.

Juma shook her head. "I know where to find her. She has been captured by Mubuntu. I need you to come along right away because I can't free her on my own."

"I'm old, and my magic has never been strong." The witch stared at her hands. "You will have to drag me from my body so I can see what you can see."

Relieved, Juma lay down on the ground and told the girl to drum. A little later, she stood beside her body and took the witch's spirit by her hand. It slipped from the body as easily as hers had slipped out. Together, they flew up.

The witch looked around at the world in amazement. "This is how you see the spirit world? Oh, I so envy you. It's wonderful."

The world they had entered was flooded with light. The huts seemed to glow with the soothing yellow of ochre, the wilted grass held a greenish tinge, the lake sparkled in the distance, the sky held myriads of stars, and every living being on the ground consisted of a small flame of life. Juma had to admit that the witch was right. The spirit world as she saw it was very beautiful, but they hadn't come for sightseeing.

"We need to go up." Juma pointed to the stars. She didn't remember exactly where Vanamate had been, but she remembered going up to the sky, so she dragged the witch higher and higher. When they got closer to the stars, they seemed to sing to her.

"Go to the mountain," they chanted. "Don't touch the fire. Go to the mountain."

Juma stopped and looked around. In the distance, she saw a mountain. A big fire blazed into the night.

The witch pointed to it. "Do you see the flames atop the holy mountain? I am sure it's Mubuntu's doing."

Juma approached slowly. She wanted to make sure that Mubuntu wasn't anywhere near. It would be too dangerous to face him without freeing Vanamate first. He was a god, albeit a lesser one, but they were only human. The witch agreed when Juma explained her need for secrecy. They landed some distance below the fire. Using bushes and rocks for cover, they walked uphill. At the top of the mountain, a gigantic ring of fire rose to the sky, higher than anything Juma had ever seen.

"When I was here during the ceremony, the flames weren't this high," she said.

"Mubuntu is getting stronger." The witch walked slowly closer to the circle, and Juma followed her. Through the flickering, they saw a woman, bigger and more beautiful than any woman they had ever met before. With gracefully slender limbs and a bust like carved ebony, she sat on a stone sleeping while tears welled from her eyes. They vaporized when they hit the flames and dissipated into the sky.

"I bet the stars get more rain than they like." The witch grinned, but not in a friendly way. "Now, how do we open this circle?"

"I don't know. Can we return to the lake and bring water up here?"

"I'm not sure if our spirits can take along something tangible. Also, if Vanamate's tears don't quench the flames, will normal water be able to?" The witch stepped closer and reached for the fire hesitantly. A small flame lashed out, so she jerked back.

"Don't touch the fire," Juma said. "The stars warned us, remember?"

The witch nodded. "I've got another idea that might work. Let's try it." She knelt and filled both hands with earth. Then she began one of her unmelodious singsongs and flung the soil toward the ring. More and more earth rose from the ground and followed her two handfuls. At first, nothing much happened, but the more soil hit the flames, the smaller they got. It took a lot of chanting and throwing, but in the end, a good part of the fire was dead. There was a breach in the ring. Sizable drops floated out, dropped to the ground, and sank into the parched soil. Juma caught some, enjoying the wetness on her hands. She wiped the water onto her hair, feeling much refreshed.

"I'll go to wake Vanamate. We need to get her out of the ring before Mubuntu returns and notices what we're up to." She darted toward the breach, but the witch held her back.

"I am the one with the earth magic. I will go." She crossed the pile of earth that had smothered the flames, walked over to Vanamate, and shook her. The goddess didn't move. With her head on her hands, she slept on.

## 15

"CAUGHT YOU!" MUBUNTU'S LAUGH FILLED the air, as he appeared in the breach. "And I'll make sure you won't be able to return that easily.

Juma ducked behind a rock instinctively. Her heart raced. How could they have missed the heat dæmon's arrival? His skin and hair was aflame, and fire was already eating through the pile of earth again. The witch needed to get out right now, or she would be as caught as the goddess. Juma's thoughts whirled but she couldn't think of anything that might distract Mubuntu long enough to let the witch escape. Squatting behind her rock, she saw the old woman scoop up Vanamate's tears in a small clay bowl and fling some of them at the heat dæmon. He howled in pain and retreated. The witch jumped through what was left of the breach. He grabbed for her but used the arm where his hand was missing. Agile, the old woman ducked his stump and raced past him with the small clay bowl filled with Vanamate's tears in her hands. As she dove into the rock's shade, she pressed the bowl into Juma's hands.

"Get this to safety. I'll distract Mubuntu." She sped on, pretending she still held the bowl. Mubuntu shrieked and raced after her. Juma saw the two zigzag through the sky. Tears ran down her cheeks. She knew the witch was a good fighter, but this time, she hadn't prepared for battle. Mubuntu was bound to win. Still, the witch had given her a task. As soon as the last fiery blur of Mubuntu had vanished, she hurried down the mountain. Only when she saw her village did she dare to fly again. She sped through the sky as fast as her mind would carry her.

She had just reached the lake when the witch zoomed past her, followed by Mubuntu. Selenta dove into the water with her follower close on her heels. Water evaporated as it hit the god's burning skin. The witch and Mubuntu raced past Juma again when they left the lake, coming so close, Juma dropped to the ground like a stone. Half of the water in her bowl spilled. The sound it made when it hit the lake's surface reminded Juma of gently falling rain. Glad that Mubuntu hadn't taken any notice of her, she hurried onward to the witch's hut. She jumped into her body so fast, she woke with a start. Surprisingly, she still held the bowl in her hands, but instead of water, it was filled with pearls. She set it aside and turned to the witch. Her body was breathing but her spirit hadn't returned yet.

The girl had stopped drumming and looked at Juma, wide-eyed.

"Keep drumming," Juma said. "I need to help the witch."

The second the girl resumed her rhythmic thumping, she was out of her body again, speeding through the sky, looking for the witch. When she couldn't find her, she returned to the circle of fire in the hope that the witch had hidden somewhere between the rocks. She set down near the summit and walked uphill using the rocks for cover. At the top, she found Mubuntu, gloating at the witch.

"Don't think I'll let you touch the earth ever again." He floated the cage of glowing reeds that held her several inches higher. The prison was big enough for her to move, but not big enough to lie down and reach for the earth.

The witch smiled.

"You will not able to hold me forever," she said. Then she fell silent and refused to talk to Mubuntu no matter how much he taunted her.

Juma admired the old woman's self control while she waited for the heat dæmon to lose interest. Soon enough, he dashed away. When he was gone, she walked toward the cage.

"I'll get you out." She put her hand up and tested the glowing reeds. They were hot but didn't burn her, yet when she tried to pull them apart, they fired up, sizzling angrily. Juma withdrew her hands.

"It won't work that way," the witch said. "We need water or earth to kill the fire."

Juma crouched and tried to scoop up soil like the witch had done. Not a single grain of sand moved.

"Why can't I do that? It looked so simple when you did."

The witch shrugged. "My magic comes from the earth, so I can use it even when I'm in spirit form. Your magic seems to be more related to the air and the sky, maybe even to water."

"But I was able to hold the clay bowl."

"Because I gave it to you. If I could reach the ground and hand you some soil, you'd be able to hold it just because I want you to. That's the way my magic works."

Juma scratched her nose. "But how do I get you out of this?"

"Don't worry about me. I'm old and would have gone with Monnatoba soon anyway. You need to free Vanamate, or our whole tribe—no, the whole land—will parch and die."

Juma's heart twisted at the thought of leaving the witch behind. Tears filled her eyes, and she swallowed to keep them down.

"You need to walk to the top of the holy mountain in your body. There is a gate which will take you to the god's mountain in a more solid way, not as a spirit. You might be able to bring water or earth to kill the ring of fire around Vanamate. It's essential to free her." The witch pushed her hand through a gap between the bars and patted Juma's arm. "Now hurry, before he comes back."

With tears streaming over her face, Juma hurried back to her body. The sun had long risen, and the spirit world around her shone with colors. She barely noticed. Leaving the witch behind hurt so much, she couldn't think clearly. Her vision blurred, but she reached the hut in the village without trouble. Back in her body, she curled up and cried. Who would have thought I'd grow so fond of the old lady. She hugged her knees and rocked until running feet approached her.

"What have you done to the witch?" Jakombe's voice cut through her sorrow like a knife.

"Mubuntu caught her." Juma tried to explain what had happened, but Jakombe didn't understand why a caged spirit posed such a problem.

"Why don't you go and fetch her then? Really, some people are as helpless as a man when it comes to solving problems." Jakombe snorted and turned to go. "I'll tell the healer to look after Selenta's body until you bring her mind back."

Juma bit her lip not to shout, but she didn't hold Jakombe's ignorance against her. The chieftess had never fought Mubuntu the way the witch had. An idea shot through her mind.

"I need his hand," she said, swallowing her tears.

"I haven't got the slightest idea where Selenta put it." The chieftess left without looking back.

In her place, the healer entered. She examined the witch's body thoroughly and nodded sadly. "Her bodily functions are all fine, but I don't think she'll live for much longer."

Her words were another stab at Juma's heart. "Can't you help her?"

"I will try to feed her as best I can, but a body will not survive more than a few days when the mind is gone." The healer stroked Juma's cheek. "Don't be too sorry. She is old. She would have liked to leave this way, without pain."

"But I don't want her to die."

"There isn't much you can do. If her spirit doesn't return before High Moon, her body will dwindle until nothing is left to return to. I've seen it before." The healer got up. "I'll find Sundera. She'll be the best one to look after my old friend."

As the healer left, Netinu slipped in and sat beside Juma. He bowed his head.

"May I talk?"

"Since when did a 'no' ever stop you?" She glared at him, trying to indicate she wanted to be alone without actually sending him away.

"I'm hopefully learning to be more considerate."

"Go ahead." Juma sighed.

"I listened at the door, and my heart knows you well. You will try to save the witch, won't you?"

"So what? She's my friend." Juma realized that her words were true. From the first second, the witch had been there for her and helped her whenever she could. "I want her back safely. Also, I'll have to free Vanamate. Mubuntu holds both of them prisoner. I wish your mother would listen to the whole tale."

"She's not used to handling a crisis like this drought. Also, Kandra tries hard to make you seem incompetent."

"I'm doing a good enough job with that myself." Juma picked up the bowl with the pearls and dumped them in a piece of cloth. She knotted it so none could fall out. "I need to do something right for once."

"Don't leave us— me." Netinu looked at her pleadingly. "I couldn't live without you, knowing the whole tribe will die from thirst soon."

"If I can free Vanamate, no one will die."

"Some of the elders and two children already suffered heat stroke. It's been getting hotter ever since Princess Chunte fled. The lake is down to a dwindling puddle that won't last more than a few days." Netinu stood up and held out his hand. "Come, I'll show you."

Since Juma had everything she needed from the witch's hut, she got up and followed Netinu outside. Sundera hurried past them with a hasty greeting. Juma only nodded at her. She knew that between the healer and Sundera, the witch's body would be in good hands. Now she only needed to pack her things and start walking. It would take her a day and a half to reach the summit of the holy mountain. She remembered that her father had once gone when she had still been a small child.

Netinu pointed to the Central Hall. Women ran to and fro, feeding drops of water to feverish children. The healer walked from patient to patient, handing out support or medicine as needed. Juma stared at the number of people lying on mats in the hall's shade. Had all this happened overnight?

Jakombe noticed her, and a smile smoothed her worry lines. With hurried steps, she approached Juma. "You must help the healer. The tribe needs to witness a witch in action during this crisis."

Juma bowed her head. "I'll do my best, but Selenta never taught me anything about healing, so I might not make much of a difference."

"I'm not asking for miracles, but we need to keep the tribe from panicking." Jakombe turned and spoke to the crowd. Her voice quieted the subdued babbling instantly. "Tonight, we'll celebrate the ascent of our new witch, Jumatoa Botango."

Juma gasped for air. What was Jakombe thinking, instating her as the new witch now? What about the old one? This was so unfair.

Surely it was Kandra's idea to use this opportunity to get rid of the unwanted competition. But she wouldn't let the others push her around.

"Selenta is not dead yet," she shouted over the cheering. People around her fell silent as she glowered at the chieftess. "I refuse to take up the office until either Selenta officially hands it over to me, or until the healer confirms her death." She folded her arms in front of her chest. "Until then, I keep up my claim on the leadership for this tribe. I am of royal blood, after all."

"Selenta won't survive another week, and the tribe cannot be without a witch." Jakombe put her fists on her hip.

"A lot of things can happen in a week."

Jakombe ground her teeth. Netinu put his hand on his mother's arm and whispered into her ear. She frowned at him. "How dare you?"

Juma wondered what he had told his mother. What if he insisted that he wouldn't love anyone but Juma? A storm of confusing emotions churned through her, rooting her to the spot.

He stared at Jakombe and not a single muscle in his face twitched. "I swear," he said.

"Very well. We'll have to make do with what we've got." The chieftess glared at him and turned to Juma. "You will temporarily replace Selenta until she passes on to Monnatoba. But then you will assume her office without delay." She turned and stomped away.

Silence filled the Central Hut. Juma felt all eyes on her. The faces around her showed all manner of emotion, disapproval, disappointment, and confusion, but no one uttered a word.

Juma's ears smarted. Why did she have to confront Jakombe like that? Wasn't it enough that her aunt already disliked her? She couldn't afford to have Jakombe hate her. Worse, the chieftess had been right. The tribe needed a witch.

Lowering her gaze, Juma approached the healer. "What can I do to assist you?"

As the healer explained in a low voice how Selenta had strengthened her medicines, men and women took up their tasks again. Still, Juma felt their stares tingling on her back until a boy came running.

"A miracle! Come and see. A miracle has happened." He turned and ran right back. Everybody who was able to followed him. Juma allowed Netinu to pull her along. They ran through the lakeside gate and down toward the shore. There, the boy stood and pointed to the water's edge. In gentle waves, it lapped at its old shoreline as if it had never lost water. Someone started to cheer, and soon the air was filled with shouts of joy, drumming, and happy voices. The animals on the other side of the lake fled in panic from the noise, and the rest of the tribe, including Jakombe, came to investigate.

Juma wondered where the water had come from. The answer came to her, when she dipped her hand into the cooling wetness. Vanamate's tears! She had spilled half of the bowl's contents, and the tears had dropped into the lake. They must have replenished it. All around her, happy thank you songs rose to Vanamate. It hurt her to know that the goddess didn't hear them. Gratefully, she drank a handful of the sweet, cold water. >From the corners of her eyes, she saw Kandra whisper with her mother. When Netinu crouched beside her to drink too, a flash of fire streaked across the sky. Juma jerked back.

Mubuntu hovered over the lake, glowing like a small sun. "This puddle won't take more than a day or two to dry out. You should have kept them from singing to my sister."

Juma could only imagine the grin on his face; he shone too brightly to look at. Instead, she stared at the lake. Was the water level dropping already?

Suddenly, Mubuntu looked toward the holy mountain. "Oh no, you're not!" He rushed away, calling "I'll be back" over his shoulder, just as Jakombe's voice silenced the crowd.

"This miracle bought us a little time. We do not know where the water came from, nor do we know how long it will last. Let us make the best of it." She turned to the herders. "You will take the animals down so they can drink. All mothers take their children to bathe and drink, and every able-bodied person helps to carry water to the sick." Next, she turned to the cooks. "You will fetch as many calabashes and bowls as possible and get the children and youngsters to fill them with water. We'll place them in the Central Hall and cover them so the water can't get out. That way, we'll have at least a little reserve."

Juma marveled at Jakombe's brilliant thought. When she noticed Kandra's smug smile she realized it hadn't been the chieftess's idea after all. If Kandra would stop being so nasty, she might make a decent chieftess after all. She wondered why she didn't feel jealous at this thought. Was it possible that the work of a chieftess had lost some of its appeal? No. She still felt the fire burning in her chest. It was just that at the moment she had more pressing matters than fighting with Kandra. She had to save the witch and fetch rain before Mubuntu returned to deplete the lake. Biting her lower lip, she walked to her hut and began to pack her things. It was time to find the gate to Vanamate the witch had told her about. She would leave when night fell. With the celebration of her ascent postponed, everybody would be preparing for sleep. No one would notice her leaving, not even Sundera, since she'd be sitting with the witch.

Juma finished packing long before it grew dark, but she stayed in the stifling mugginess of the hut. She didn't want to be held back by anyone, especially not by her aunt. If only the witch would wake. She would have been able to mend the situation. Juma curled up on her bed and cried a bit. After a while, she fell asleep, but her dream offered no solace.

The drums' steady rhythm shook Juma's bones and made her stumble in her haste. It was early morning, and High Moon hung low and orange over the horizon. The clouds around it looked as if they were burning from inside. She needed to stop the ritual before it was too late. Vanamate did not approve of a human sacrifice. Juma ran as fast as she could along the path they had taken the night the witch had chased Mubuntu. Cursing, she shot past the giant stone that marked the road's summit and raced down toward the plain of red sand, leaving dust clouds in her wake. The drums were getting louder, and she could see the dead tree and the people who had gathered around it. Four small fires burned with flickering flames, and the people chanted.

The second she reached them, gasping for air, she scanned the sky for a sign of the heat dæmon. He wasn't there yet. Two villagers stepped forward, dragging Netinu along, who hung limply in their arms. Darn, they had drugged him.

A streak of red shot across the sky. Time. She needed more time! Too winded to speak, Juma stumbled forward holding up her hand to keep Jakombe from continuing, but her aunt ignored her. Tears ran over the chieftess's face as she and Kandra tied Netinu to four wooden pegs that had been hammered into the dusty ground.

She walked closer, but no one took notice. Everybody stared at the bound person. Juma's knees shook from exhaustion and fear.

Jakombe stood, silently crying, but Kandra resembled a cat who had stolen the cream. Proud and erect, she stood and said, "Now it begins. Rejoice."

How Juma longed to wipe the smug smile from Kandra's face!

The sun rose over the mountain and filled the plain with light.

"Stop this at once." With every breath, Juma's strength returned. "I forbid you to praise Mubuntu."

"Too late." Kandra pointed to the red-haired man who floated out of the sun toward them. The color of his skin resembled the pale ashes of a fire burnt down.

Reluctantly, the villagers began to sing a song that praised Mubuntu. The heat dæmon took his time coming closer. The air grew hotter the higher the sun climbed the sky. Its fiery fingers drummed the earth relentlessly. Netinu begged for water. Juma ran to him. She tried to undo his bonds, but her fingers slipped off the knot. Sobbing, she whispered nonsensical words, but Netinu didn't seem to hear. Gasping for air, he called to his mother.

Jakombe fled with her hands over her face. The villagers followed her lead. Only Kandra stayed behind. When Mubuntu set down, she laughed.

"This time, she cannot help you, brother. This sacrifice is too important. What is the life of a single man compared to the lives of the whole village?"

"Why?" Juma's voice was hoarse.

"Because a person is the most valuable sacrifice our tribe has to offer, and men are more expendable than women."

"But why him?"

"Of all the men, he is the most valuable. And I hate him." Kandra spat at Netinu. "He took away Mother's love, and he wasn't even female. Mother should have cared for me more. Actually, I am very glad the choice fell on him. Now everything will be as it should have been from the start."

She laughed again. Netinu closed his eyes. His breathing became more labored. Beads of sweat ran over his face and body. Juma bent to kiss the cracked lips but couldn't touch him. Her hands went through his arms as if she wasn't there any longer.

What's wrong? Am I dead? She tried to remember what she had done before she raced to stop the sacrifice. Didn't I go to sleep? Did I go on a spirit journey without noticing? She closed her eyes and felt for the bond connecting her to her body. It wasn't there, so she couldn't be out of her body. But why wasn't she able to touch Netinu? And if she was spiritwalking despite the fact that she couldn't feel the bond to her body, how was Kandra able to hear her and talk to her?

Screaming with frustration at her inability to help, she sat up and found herself in her hut. Her heart raced, and sweat pearled on her forehead. Her hands shook. She hugged her knees and cried. It was a dream. Nothing but a dream. She sobbed so much, breathing became hard. It took her quite a while to calm down. I've never had a dream this vivid. Maybe it's more? It could have been a vision of future events. Gazing out of the door, she wondered how long she had slept. She was running out of time. Maybe she shouldn't wait for nightfall. She decided to fetch some provisions and leave right away. To avoid drawing attention, she left her bundle behind. Hiding in corners and in the lengthening shadows of the late afternoon, she slipped through the village, not wanting to be seen.

## <u>16</u>

$\mathcal{T}$HE CATTLE PEN WAS EMPTY because the herders had taken the animals to the lake. Still, Juma heard someone whisper in the herder's hut. She walked faster to reach the safety of the hut's shade. Here, the voices were clearer.

"If I don't get my hand back soon, I'll burn down the village," Mubuntu said.

"The old hag hid it too well, and now she's out of her mind."

Juma froze. Those words had been spoken by a female. Had the princess returned?

"I don't care; I want it back." Mubuntu's voice was filled with anger.

"Take me on a spirit journey tonight. I will talk to her. If I pretend I came to free her, she'll tell me where the hand is. You'll see."

"You know it's dangerous if I take you out of your body."

"I trust you to bring me back, but I assure you that this is the easiest way to find out where your hand is."

Juma grew cold at the thought that the princess was able to leave her body with Mubuntu's help. She listened closely, hoping to identify the speaker, but the voice was too low to determine whether it was Princess Chunte or not. Juma tiptoed closer to the voices.

"I still feel like burning down something."

"Not the village. I have plans with it." The female voice was firm although it didn't get any louder. "By the way, I settled on a date for the sacrifice."

"What if the chieftess doesn't agree? After all, it's her son you plan to burn." The cackle in Mubuntu's voice sounded like the cracking of burning timber.

"I know exactly how to convince her. Just make sure it gets hotter every day. Don't forget to evaporate the new water in the lake. In the end, Jakombe is not woman enough to stand up for her tribe in a crisis." The female's voice held so much contempt it sent shivers down Juma's spine. She knew no one in the village who hated Jakombe this much. It had to be Chunte.

As silently as she could, she sneaked away to fetch the guards, wondering how the princess had managed to slip back into the village. It probably wasn't all that difficult. The witch and Juma had done so too, a while back.

She had hurried all the way to the northern gate when she realized Chunte and Mubuntu had talked about the sacrifice she had seen in her dream. Her jaw dropped. What if it hadn't been a dream but another vision? None of the witches of at least three generations have had visions, and she had her second one already. Why did the gods consider her special? She stopped mid-stride and put her hand on the wall of a hut to steady her shaking knees. What did they expect from her? She remembered the tales about the last witch with visions. She had sacrificed herself to Monnatoba so that the goddess would calm the Nameless. Did the gods expect her to sacrifice herself instead of Netinu? Would her sacrifice free Vanamate and save the tribe? Juma sank to her knees and begged the gods silently for mercy. She didn't want to die. Was it possible to change the events? It had to be. What good was a vision otherwise? Closing her eyes, she tried to remember details.

The moon! The morning she had seen was High Moon. How many days did she have left? She counted it on her fingers. High Moon would be after the third night. Would that be enough time to find and free Vanamate? Juma was sure she could prevent her vision if she could win the goddess's help. She wiped away her tears. One step at a time. First, she had to make sure Chunte would be caught and sent on her way. This time, Juma would have to shield her tribe from Mubuntu's magic. And she would have to do it alone. Would she be strong enough?

She got up and walked toward the northern gate. As she neared it, the guards opened it wide, and a sad procession walked in. Two men of her tribe and two of the river people carried a stretcher with Tolobe on it. He was badly burnt. A strangled cry escaped Juma, and she hurried to his side, Chunte temporarily forgotten. Her soul cried fiery tears. Gently she took his crippled hands into hers.

"Get the healer." She hummed a low melody, gathered magic, and tried to push it into her brother. She felt the familiar tingle build up, but it evaporated, doing nothing to help Tolobe. She bit her lip not to cry. The men carried the stretcher to the Central Hall, and Juma went with them, holding her brother's hand. They set the stretcher down and stepped back just as the healer arrived. She held a bowl with a greenish liquid and knelt beside Tolobe. Lightly, she lifted his head to help him drink. He moaned, and Juma's heart contracted painfully. Where his skin wasn't covered in blisters, it was more red than brown. His breathing came in shallow bursts.

"Add your magic to the medicine," the healer said. "It's the only way to get it inside of him."

Again Juma hummed her song and gathered magic until her fingers tingled. Gently, she eased it into the medicine, surprised by the rush of energy. It was as if the medicine sucked the tingling sensation from her hands. As the healer fed the injured more medicine, Tolobe's features relaxed. He fell into a restless slumber as soon as the last drop vanished down his throat.

Juma closed her eyes for a second and thanked the gods. Her father came running, followed by Sundera. The young woman sank to the ground beside her fiancé with tears running over her face, but she didn't wail.

"Will he live?" Her voice was hoarse and trembled a bit.

The healer shook her head. "It doesn't look good."

Juma bit her lip. Sundera's sorrow and her brother's pain were hard to bear.

A hand warmed her shoulder, and her father's soft voice whispered in her ear. "Don't torment yourself. He knew the voyage would be dangerous."

Jakombe arrived slightly out of breath with Kandra in tow. She turned to the men who had carried Tolobe.

"What happened to him?"

The two men from the river people crossed their arms over their chests refusing to speak, but one of the other two men stepped forward. He didn't lower his gaze when he spoke.

"We found out why the river disappeared. A huge bolder blocks the water's bed, so it looked for a different path. It vanishes into a cave, never to be seen again."

"What does that have to do with my question?" Jakombe put her fists on her hip. "I need to know what happened to my sisterson."

Juma got up and put a hand on the man's shoulder, half turning him away from Jakombe. She had misbehaved already, so it didn't matter if it was her turn to speak or not. "How is the blocked river connected to my burned brother?"

The warrior ignored the chieftess's furious glances.

"We found the river people's missing men in the cave the river runs through. They were afraid to leave. We convinced them to help us free the river, but when we tried to move the boulder, we found ourselves facing five magical animals. They were made of fire, and flames licked at us as we clambered to the cave for safety." He wiped his eyes at the memory. "We soon found out that our weapons were of no use. They burned before they touched the animals' skins. The lion prowled so close to the entrance, we didn't dare leave. Luckily he didn't enter. Tolobe thought he might have been scared of the water. The elephant blocked the path back to our village, and the hyena sat on the boulder laughing as madly as only hyena do. Since the rhino and the cheetah weren't anywhere in sight, Tolobe estimated our chances to flee were high. He managed to convince everybody with his plan.

"We soaked our blankets and kikois with water and hit the lion with it. It roared and fought like a maniac, but we didn't let it escape. We sprayed it with water until it stopped moving. Then we climbed past the boulder and ran along the dry river bed. The other animals never saw us leave. When we thought we had made it, a flash of fire raced after us. The cheetah had found our tracks. Tolobe told us to hurry on, and we did since we had elected him leader. But he stayed behind to fight the cheetah. We ran and ran. When we were sure the cheetah didn't follow us any more, two of us volunteered to go back. They found Tolobe as you see him now. The fire cheetah was gone. We do not know if Tolobe killed it or if it was satisfied when it had mangled one of us. We didn't stay to find out if it was still alive. The men carried Tolobe to where the rest of us were hiding. We built the stretcher to bring him home. He returned the river tribe's men to their tribe unharmed. If the gods wish, he will wake once more before he goes with Monnatoba. He is a hero."

No one had interrupted his tale, and even when he finished, no one dared to speak. Juma turned back to Tolobe and knelt beside Sundera. In her mind's eye, she saw Netinu parching in the merciless sun. She knew exactly how her friend must feel. She took her hand.

"I will find a way to save him." She didn't have any idea how to go about it, but she intended to keep this promise.

Jakombe congratulated the men on their return. "Methinks we did what we so rashly promised." She shot an angry look at Sundera, who was oblivious to her surroundings. "The reason for the vanished river has been found. Remind your leader that there is no reason to attack us again."

"The river is still blocked," one of the river people said.

"I don't care. We did what we promised to do. More, if Tolobe truly brought back the missing men. You can't ask anything else from us now. The price has been too high already."

The men shrugged and left without saying their farewell. Jakombe's face burned red with anger, but Kandra held her back.

"We can reprimand them for their impoliteness some other time," she said. "It's more important to appease Mubuntu. We will not survive another week without rain."

"You are right." Jakombe turned to Juma. "Witch, you will come with us to discuss our next step of action."

Juma would have preferred to stay with her brother, but she followed. Maybe it was time to tell Jakombe about Vanamate's prison. They sat down in front of the chieftess's hut. Kandra fetched tea and sat with them. Juma frowned.

"Since when have you been named chieftess in training?" she asked.

Kandra clenched her fists but kept her temper. "We will discuss my idea, so mother asked me to come."

"Desperate times need desperate measures." Although she didn't feel like smiling, Juma grinned.

"Enough." Jakombe set down her mug. "Set aside your petty rivalry. Our tribe is dying. We need to find a way to stop the drought, and Kandra suggested something than might actually work — if we work together."

Juma pulled up an eyebrow and sipped at her tea deliberately, slowly. Jakombe nodded at Kandra, and the girl started to explain.

"We know that Princess Chunte believes she's favored by Mubuntu. We also know that she hasn't yet left the camp on the other side of the lake, and that only ten of her warriors remain with her. With your help, we could drive them into the lake where Chunte can no longer access her magic."

"How can you be sure about that?" Juma interrupted Kandra without a second thought, pushing aside the thought that they had assumed the same when they had planned to tie Chunte to a pole in the lake. "Are you now best friends with the gods?"

"She's Mubuntu's High Priestess, and Mubuntu is a fire god. Of course the magic she got from him will not work in the lake."

"Why not simply kill her then? It'd be one threat less."

"We need to talk to Mubuntu, and since we're not his followers, there's no use in simply calling him. But I am sure he will show up to save Chunte."

"And what are you going to do if he shows up showering the village with fire instead? Also, Selenta is in his power. He won't play by our rules." Juma set down her tea and bent forward. "One more thing to remember is that Chunte is a very dangerous woman. I don't know if I'll be able to create a shield as strong as Selenta's. I haven't had much training as a witch."

Kandra glared at her. "You're only jealous because I had a good idea and you didn't."

Before Juma could say a word, Jakombe spoke.

"You are right in many respects, Juma. I know this is risky, but we're running out of time. We must stop Chunte and Mubuntu, and the princess is the only one we can reach. You'd better start training the creation of a shield strong enough to contain Chunte's magic, because we are going to do this."

"What if Chunte defeats us and decides to sacrifice Netinu instead?" Juma remembered her vision but didn't dare to talk about it. Admitting to having visions would seal her into the job as village witch instantly.

"Truth be told, we don't have many options." Jakombe was surprisingly calm. "The lake is going to dry out sooner or later. The water level is already sinking again at an alarming rate. The river tribe will attack us at some point to get access to whatever is left of its water. If they bend to Chunte's will, our whole tribe will perish. And it won't be a consolidation that the other tribes will die from thirst soon after."

Juma remembered what the fire god was after. "I'm sure we could get Mubuntu to talk to us if we're willing to give him back his hand."

"I would if I could, but someone stole it." Jakombe got up. "You have one more day to prepare your shield, and that's the end of the discussion." She walked into the hut.

Juma stared after her with her mouth hanging open. Someone stole the hand? Who was so stupid to have risked Jakombe's and Selenta's wrath? Kandra smiled smugly and sipped her tea. Had she...? Juma's eyes narrowed. No... if she had stolen the hand, she wouldn't have come up with this nightmarish plan.

Knowing that she wouldn't be around to see it carried out, Juma suppressed her frustration, got up, and left wordlessly. Slowly, she walked back to the Central Hall. The rays of the sun painted the sky with red and orange. The huts and trees were only black silhouettes against the fiery firmament. Despite the horrible drought, it was a marvelous sight. Juma looked up to where the first stars appeared. She would leave as soon as everybody was going to bed. Surprisingly, it didn't please her as much as she would have thought that she was ruining Kandra's perilous plan.

People hurried past her on their way to their huts, but she didn't take notice. She watched the sky grow darker with more and more stars lighting up every moment. Soon, the moon rose over the horizon, big and nearly full.

A hand alighted on her shoulder, and jerked her from her reverie. To calm her racing heart, she turned slowly. Netinu put his other hand on her second shoulder.

"You have to leave." He didn't bother with niceties. "I overheard Kandra talk to a man from Chunte's tribe. He's supposed to kill you as soon as Chunte is caught."

"It's very good of you to feel concerned for me, but I don't need your help." Juma pushed his hands off her shoulders.

"I know you can handle this, but I wanted to let you know how deeply Kandra's hate runs," Netinu said. "And I cannot bear the thought of you getting hurt."

Juma looked at the ground. Should she tell him about her vision? She decided against it. What good would it do? She was determined to prevent it anyway. She looked up at his face. The rising moon cast a silvery glow over his ebony features. He looked so good, her heart stumbled. And the concern in his eyes melted the wall she had built around her heart. She swallowed.

"I didn't plan to stick around anyway." Her voice sounded strange to her ears, but Netinu smiled.

"Thank Vanamate." He bent forward and kissed her cheek. In the deserted village, no one noticed. "You'd better pack your belongings and leave now. I'll distract the guards at the gate."

"I already bundled up what I will need, but I have to see my brother before I leave. I might not... he might be... Monnatoba will..." Her voice broke. Wordlessly Netinu put his arm around her shoulder and stroked her back. When she had regained her composure, he took away his arm and accompanied her to the Central Hut. A low fire burned inside. Sundera was still sitting beside Tolobe, who lay motionless, breathing very shallowly. She looked up with tears in her eyes.

"If only Vanamate would hear our prayers," she whispered.

"I know she does." Netinu put a hand on Sundera's shoulder.

Juma stepped closer and said, "I'm not so sure about that. She's sitting in a ring of fire, and I suspect Mubuntu keeps our voices from reaching her." She knelt beside her friend and took Tolobe's hand.

Sundera's eyes widened. "How do you know?"

Juma told her about her spirit journey.

"You really saw Vanamate?" Netinu's eyes were as round as a full moon. "And Mubuntu?"

"He caught the witch." Juma wiped away a tear. "But I will defeat him somehow. Selenta told me how to help her, and together we'll find a way to free Vanamate. I swear."

"Mubuntu can't be defeated," Sundera looked at Tolobe again, and tears ran over her cheeks. "No weapon can hurt him, no fire can burn him."

"But maybe water will douse him," Netinu said.

Juma shook her head. "I've seen him fly through the lake's water, and it just vaporized around him. Only Vanamate can defeat him." A memory lit up in her brain. "I'm so stupid." She slapped her forehead, got up and ran, ignoring her friends' surprised stares. In the blink of an eye, she reached her hut, grabbed her bundle, and ran back to the Central Hut. How could she have forgotten her most valuable possession? She knelt beside her brother and dug into her bundle.

"Yes!" With a shout of triumph she pulled out the cloth where she had wrapped the pearls. If half the bowl of water refilled the lake against Mubuntu's intent, maybe one of the pearls would save her brother's life. A song of hope filled her heart and mind. If anyone could heal Tolobe it was Vanamate — and the pearls were the closest they would be able to get him to the goddess. Considering carefully, she picked a small pearl and pushed it between his lips.

## 17

*H*E GASPED, BUT SWALLOWED. FOR a moment, nothing happened. Then he curled up hugging his belly, gasping, and breathing really fast. He moaned and whimpered like a newborn as shivers ran through him. Juma's heart broke even before Sundera clutched her arm.

"What have you done?"

Incapable of moving a single muscle, Juma stared at her brother. Had she killed him? She hadn't meant to increase his pain. Blood roared in her ears like Mubuntu's fire, and she had no tears to douse it. Why didn't the pearl help? Juma cried without noticing. Black crusts crumbled and blisters deflated while Tolobe's body shivered. Skin as light as that of a newborn replaced the burns. Still Tolobe's body jerked like a reed in a storm. Finally, his back bent as far back as it would go, making Juma think he'd break in two any second, and a long moan escaped his lips. When his body stilled, Juma stared at the irregular pattern of the two tones of his skin. Tears filled her eyes as she reached for him with trembling fingers. Please, Vanamate, don't let him be dead. It required all her strength to inch her hand forward. Before she could touch him, he sat up and breathed in deeply.

"My, oh my, that was quite the experience." Then he looked around, smiled at the three people close to him, and embraced Sundera. "All the time as I lay there, I wanted to do this. Who cares about etiquette anyway?"

Juma felt light as a feather. She hadn't been wrong after all. The song in her soul returned when she realized that even his crippled fingers were as straight and gentle as they used to be, and the lighter patches on his skin were already darkening. With a little luck, or goodwill from Vanamate, it would soon be hard to make out the scars. She wiped away her tears and put the remaining pearls away, enjoying Tolobe's and Sundera's obvious happiness.

After a while, Tolobe let go of his fiancée and hugged Juma too. "Thank you for saving me, little sister."

"It wasn't me. Vanamate gifted me some of her tears." Juma clung to him, sucking in his familiar odor and feeling protected like a child. Holding her with one arm and Sundera with the other, he asked, "May I suggest something?"

Why was he asking? Didn't he just do away with tradition? Juma grinned and nodded. Some old habits seemed to die hard.

"Despite my state, I heard your tale, Juma, and I agree that you'll have to free Vanamate." He kissed her forehead. "But I insist that Netinu accompanies you."

Juma opened her mouth to protest, but Tolobe didn't give her a chance.

"He is madly in love with you, Juma, which means he will give his life to see you safe. Just as I would give my life for you if I were to come along. But I cannot leave. I have to protect Father and Sundera."

Juma looked up at Netinu. He fiddled with his hands and stared at the ground. Suddenly, his head jerked up. "Would it help to have the hand Princess Chunte seemed so eager to get?"

"Do you know where it is?" Juma jumped to her feet and grabbed his arm. A tingling sensation spread from her fingers through her body, and she had to fight to concentrate on the matter at hand. "I thought someone stole it."

"I did. Everybody was so eager to get hold of it, I thought it best to hide it so no one could find it."

"Show me." Juma flung her bundle over her shoulder and waited for Netinu to lead the way. Silently they walked to the chieftess's hut. With her heart beating wildly, she followed him inside. A low, smokeless fire burned in the middle of the hut, illuminating it just enough that they could see. Aside from two beautifully woven blankets covering the walls, it looked like every other hut Juma had seen. Jakombe lay snoring on her raised sleeping platform, but Kandra's bed was empty. Where was she? Did she have a secret lover? When would she be back? Juma stood with her back against the doorframe and half gazed out of the hut and half in.

Netinu tiptoed to a mat beside the fireplace. He crouched, pushed it aside, and began to dig. Juma's gaze clung to his silently moving hands. Tiny mounds of earth piled up beside the hole. She held her breath when the corner of a piece of whitish cloth peeked through the dirt. Soon, Netinu unearthed something wrapped in a cloth. Grabbing a blanket and his kikoi, he got up and handed the parcel to Juma. The door-curtain beside her swung open, admitting the cool air of the night.

"Give the parcel to me." Kandra's voice cut through Juma like a knife. There was a lot of magic behind it. Instinctively she pulled up a shield. Netinu grabbed her free hand and dragged her past his sister out of the hut. A blast of magical energy that would have killed them without the shield pushed them on.

Once Juma's initial surprise wore off, she ran while stuffing the parcel with Mubuntu's hand into her bundle. Kandra followed them, screaming. It didn't take long to reach the northern gate. The guards had lowered their spears to stop them, but when they recognized Juma and Netinu, they moved their weapons aside.

"Running away like your parents, are you?" One of the guards grinned at Juma. "I wish I could."

She ignored him and opened the gate wide enough for them to slip through.

"Please keep my sister from catching us," Netinu said.

"Will do," the second guard said with a nod.

Juma and Netinu escaped through the gap just before Kandra reached the guards.

"Halt! Who's there?" The first guard's voice rang though the night, holding an undercurrent of amusement.

Juma ignored Kandra's bickering. Hand in hand, she and Netinu ran toward the holy mountain. Netinu had to hold his side because he was laughing so hard.

"Did you see her face? She was so pissed." He stumbled and Juma had to steady him so they could keep running. She glanced over her shoulder. Kandra was following them, and she was gaining. Burdened with their bundles, Juma and Netinu couldn't run as fast as she could. Juma tried to accelerate, but her lungs burned already, and she knew she couldn't keep up the speed for much longer. *The two of us should easily be able to cope with Kandra if she didn't have this new magic,* she was thinking, when a shadow grew out of a bush.

"Halt it right there!" he cried.

"The river people!" Juma grabbed Netinu's arm as he was about to swerve past the warrior. Surely there were more guards somewhere close. Well, this was a good a way of losing Kandra. She only had to make sure the river people would let them go again. She lifted her hands at shoulder height with the palms facing the guard.

"We came in peace," Juma panted, but the guard must have understood her.

He lifted his spear and told them to walk. A second guard appeared from the dark and took the first man's place while the first guard accompanied them. Glancing back over her shoulder, Juma saw Kandra standing in the moonlight, watching. Despite the distance, she could make out the hatred in her cousin's expression. She turned away and focused on the way ahead.

When they reached the camp, the river people's chieftess was still awake. It was the same woman who had talked to them as emissary. She sat beside a fire in front of a tent surrounded by warriors. Everyone else seemed to be sleeping. Juma swallowed her surprise, knelt, and paid her respect in the traditional way. The chieftess nodded her approval.

"Why have you come?" she asked.

"We needed to escape our enemies and knew they wouldn't risk coming here." Juma thought it best to stick to the truth as far as possible. "We are on a journey to save Vanamate." She told the chieftess about the goddess's fiery prison.

"Maybe it would be best to return you to your tribe. Somehow, I'm sure they won't give up on you so easily, which might lead to more fighting. We are prepared for that, but I had planned on more negotiations first." The chieftess put another branch on the fire. "I need good proof of your claims if I'm to risk my tribe members' lives for you."

"I don't know how to do that," Juma said.

Netinu winked at Juma and bent forward. "Don't you have someone who suffered from Mubuntu's fire?"

The chieftess's eyes narrowed in suspicion. "What would you do with such a person?"

"Juma can help, and it would prove her claim is right." Netinu pointed to Juma. "But you'd have to trust her."

The chieftess closed her eyes and thought for a long time. Juma's heart beat furiously. She knew what Netinu meant her to do. What if the chieftess said no? Waiting for a decision, Juma's mouth grew dry, and she swallowed. It was a pity she would have to use another of her pearls, but if the chieftess didn't trust them, their journey would be over before it began. The only advantage would be that she could keep Vanamate's tears. There were so few of them, and they might need them later. And later would never come if the river people sent them back. Juma chewed the inside of her lip. She held her breath when the chieftess spoke to one of the warriors at her side.

"Bring my daughter."

They waited in silence until the man returned with a toddler in his arms. He knelt and laid her down on the chieftess's crossed legs, never taking his red-rimmed eyes off her. The chieftess stroked the little girl's cheek, unsuccessfully fighting back tears. Her lips trembled but she managed to keep her legs steady.

The little girl was in bad shape. Her arms were blacked in places, and she had lost all color. Red sores bloomed on the pale skin. Juma thought they were too late, until she noticed the barely visible rise and fall of the chest. It was obvious the little girl wouldn't live much longer.

"It's a miracle she survived as long s she did. If only I could…" The chieftess's voice broke.

Juma felt a lump in her throat.

"What happened to her?" Netinu asked.

"Yesterday she was playing with her friends near the animals' pen when a stranger with red hair showed up. The children say he seemed angry. He grabbed her arms, swung her around, and let her

172

fly. When she hit the ground, she fell unconscious and her arms had all but burned away."

"That sounds very much like Mubuntu," Juma whispered. She dug through her bundle and pulled out a single pearl. "Please, don't be alarmed if she seems to get worse first. This will help. I promise."

Hoping the pearl would work just as well against Mubuntu's burns as it had against the fire animals' wounds, she pushed Vanamate's tear between the child's lips. Please Vanamate, let the little one be strong enough, she prayed silently. When the child didn't swallow, she pushed the pearl deeper into her throat. Finally the girl gulped it down. Like Tolobe, she convulsed and shook. Alarm spread over her mother's face. The guards lifted their spears and pointed them at Juma, ready to kill her at a word from their chieftess. But the woman was too mesmerized. Her alarm turned to awe as she watched the skin on her daughter's arms and hands grow back. A few heartbeats later, the girl calmed. She yawned and opened her eyes.

"Mama." She reached for her mother with unblemished limbs. Wordlessly, the chieftess hugged the child. Tears ran over her face, and Juma discovered some of the men wiping their eyes too. She sighed with relief. Thank you, Vanamate. Using the pearl had definitely been worth it.

The chieftess's gratefulness couldn't have been any greater. Equipped with enough provisions to last them a week, Juma and Netinu set out for the holy mountain a short while later. With the child in her arms, the chieftess stood at the border of her tribe's camp and waved until they were out of sight.

"Thank you for thinking about the pearls," Juma said to her companion.

"What's this?" He lifted an eyebrow in mock surprise. "Were you shocked I got a brain to use too?"

Juma laughed and reached for his hand. "I think I'm getting used to it."

When the sun rose, they had left the plains behind and were walking up the mountain's flank. Juma wondered how long it would take them to reach the summit. It seemed so close and yet so far away. Boulders the size of houses grew from the ground, and small stones dug into the soles of their feet. Juma tried to walk on the dried grass as best she could. Netinu went first, with his spear at the ready. He had warned her about snakes and scorpions, but so far they hadn't seen any.

Juma glanced at the sun. It was high in the sky already.

"We should find a place for our midday meal." She knew they didn't have the luxury to wait out the worst of the midday heat.

Netinu pointed ahead. "There are a couple of trees ahead. I bet we'll find something there."

He climbed the last stretch a bit faster. Juma smiled. He's so eager to please me. She kept her pace to give him a chance to prepare the meal before she reached him. When she turned around the last boulder, Netinu ordered her to stop. She obeyed without thinking.

Not far from her, Netinu hung in the branches of a tree with an angry rhinoceros stomping the ground beneath him. She pressed close to the boulder hoping the nearsighted animal wouldn't notice her. There was nothing she could do to help Netinu. They would have to wait out the animal's anger and hope it would leave when it calmed. Juma climbed onto the boulder and settled down to eat when she saw that Netinu had made himself comfortable in the tree.

The day dragged on, and the sun burned relentlessly on her scalp. She wished the rhino would stop running around. To pass the time, she pulled out her drum and began to play herself a little song. Bits of an odd melody floated through her mind, and she tried to capture them as best she could. The blood in her veins hummed the counterpoint, and soon music filled her soul.

"Nice song." Juma had never heard this voice before. She stopped to look around, but except for Netinu and the rhino, no one was near. With a shrug, she resumed her song.

"Monnatoba's teaching?" The voice filled her mind, weaving into her melody like an obbligato.

Juma looked around again, stopping her music. Still, there was no one in sight, but the rhino had strolled away from the tree closer to her boulder. Its tiny eyes seemed to watch her.

"Who's talking?" she asked. When she got no answer, she simply played some more. Maybe the music would draw out whoever was talking.

"Animal music," the voice said. "Play is talk."

The rhino is speaking to me? Juma's jaw dropped, but she played on.

"Why come here?" the rhino asked. His voice complemented the song in her mind wonderfully.

"We are going to free Vanamate."

"Good reason. Down come? I friendly."

Juma looked at the gray colossus below her and swallowed. Did she dare to trust the voice? What if it wasn't the rhino after all? What if Mubuntu had found a way to trick her into believing she heard the rhino's voice?

"Me friendly," he repeated and turned to graze.

Slowly, Juma slid down from the boulder and walked over to the rhino despite Netinu's alarmed shouts. She settled on the ground and resumed her music.

"May my friend join us?"

"Sure." The rhino chewed and looked at her. "Weaklings strong? Fight Mubuntu?"

"We'll try," Juma said. "If we manage to free Vanamate, we can banish him."

She called Netinu from his tree. He only climbed off his tree when she had explained what had happened. "Music seems to trigger all sorts of magic for me." Her heart danced to her song.

When the rhino remained peaceful, Netinu picked up his spear and sat beside her. He opened his bundle and took out something to eat.

"What do next?" the rhino asked.

"We will try to climb the mountain as fast as we can. We lost a lot of time already," Juma said.

"Me help." The rhino ripped another mouthful of grass from the ground, then walked toward them. "Climb me."

Juma's jaw dropped. "You want us to ride on you?"

"Me strong. Me fast."

Tentatively Juma touched the gray skin. It was warm and a lot coarser than she had expected. It felt like very thick, sand-covered leather. If she rode it without protection, it would rip the skin off her legs. She spread her blanket over the rhino's back and climbed up using a stone for help.

Netinu watched her frowning. "Are you sure it's safe?"

When she nodded, he climbed up and settled behind her. The rhino trotted off while Juma kept drumming. For a few hours the rhino carried them up the mountain, and they made good time. Halfway up, the animal became restless.

"What's wrong?" Juma asked still drumming.

"Smell fire." The rhino slowed. "Can't fight fire."

"What did he say?" Netinu wanted to know. Juma translated, and he nodded. "The way the men described it, we're close to where the river is blocked. Maybe he smells the burning animals."

Juma agreed. Since she didn't want to endanger the rhino, she told him to stop to let them down. "You'd better head back to your territory," she said.

The rhino stopped, outwardly unmoved. Rhinos weren't made for showing their emotions, but Juma felt his relief. When Netinu had slipped back down to the ground, she climbed off too and took her blanket. She thanked the rhino, scratching him behind the ears — something he very much liked, as she had discovered during the ride.

He snorted. When she resumed her drumming, he said, "Stop Mubuntu. Best thank you."

A slight trembling went through the earth like a shiver. Wide-eyed, Juma stared at Netinu, and the rhino swung its great head from side to side. The tremor repeated, slightly stronger this time. Smaller stones rained from the rocks around them. The rhino bolted. Netinu put his arms around Juma and pulled her to a place with only a few smaller rocks around them. For a third time, the earth shook. Juma's knees followed suit.

"The Nameless is waking," she whispered.

"I'm sure it's Mubuntu's doing." Netinu's hug grew stronger. "But I'm also sure he will not risk waking his father."

"What if he does?" Juma's voice trembled nearly as much as the ground under their feet.

"We can only hope that, once we wake her, Vanamate will know how to calm her father."

Despite her trembling, Juma freed herself from Netinu's arms. "We need to hurry. The faster we reach Vanamate, the better." She shouldered her bundle and walked uphill swiftly. Netinu fell in step behind her, keeping up easily.

The path narrowed with a steep decline on one side and a rocky cliff at the other. Juma prayed to Vanamate that the Nameless wouldn't choose to turn just now. They'd loose their footing if the earth shook again. Fighting against the weakness in her legs, she walked on.

When they rounded a corner, the path widened enough for them to walk side by side. Juma sighed with relief. A little later, a big pool spread in front of them with a wide river flowing out on the other side. It ran downhill for a bit and vanished in a gigantic cave.

"If Tolobe is right, the fire animals are guarding the pool. We need to make sure they won't see us." Netinu showed her how to stay in the rocks' shadows. They passed the pool without seeing any of the animals. Only a faint reddish glow flickered near where the river vanished.

When night fell, they were long past the danger and a good bit up the mountain. The earth had trembled a few more times, but not strong enough to dislodge bigger stones. A narrow rivulet had joined the path and was flowing downhill toward the pool. Normally its bed would have been wider but with the drought there was barely any water left. They found a sheltered spot and decided to camp a few hours. Netinu built a small fire.

"I will keep first watch," he said.

Thankful, Juma curled up in their blankets to sleep. She woke to the sound of voices. When she opened her eyes, Netinu was talking to an old woman who warmed her fingers at their fire. Her bent form suggested an age close to the village witch's, and her kikoi and skirt had been mended often.

Juma sat up and looked around, wondering how much of the night she had slept through. She wasn't fully rested but felt much better than before. The old woman smiled at her, and something in that smile triggered a memory. All of a sudden, Juma felt loved. Warmth spread through her body, and she didn't ask the questions she had meant to ask.

"Your friend has been so generous to let me stay near your fire," the woman said.

Juma smiled. "Did he remember to offer you something to eat?"

"Of course I did." Netinu's indignation made Juma laugh. He huffed and curled up beside the fire. "I think it's time for me to go to sleep."

For a while, the two women sat silently. Juma kept wondering why the old woman seemed so familiar. She didn't know many people this old aside from Selenta. In the end, she couldn't stand it any more.

"Have I met you before?" she asked.

"Monnatoba sends me. I am sure you noticed the slight tremors of the earth today."

Juma nodded, slightly annoyed that the old woman hadn't answered her question.

"Mubuntu is teasing the Nameless. He doesn't intend to wake him, since that would be the end of the world as we know it, but he's playing a dangerous game."

"We are on our way to free Vanamate. She will take care of Mubuntu, and that should put the Nameless at rest too." Juma tried to sound more confident than she felt.

The old woman smiled. "Monnatoba knows this. But stopping Mubuntu won't be enough. You will have to help Vanamate to calm her father. And you will have to hurry. He's as close to waking as never before."

Juma looked at Netinu. "Shall we leave at once?"

The old woman shook her head. "Let him rest a little longer. You will need his strength." She looked at the sky where the nearly full moon shed its silvery light on the world. "I will tell you when it's time to go."

Juma sighed with relief. Her legs still felt tired from all the climbing, and she was glad for every minute she could sit. Fighting her exhaustion, she waited.

The crone cleared her throat. "Monnatoba insists that you will need to remember a story your mother told you before she died."

"I don't remember much at all. I was too small."

"That's why I'm here." The old woman reached out and rested her hand on Juma's cheek for a fleeting moment.

And Juma remembered.

## 18

$\mathcal{O}$NE NIGHT, WHEN SHE WAS little, she hadn't felt well. Instead of sleeping inside the hut with her brothers, she had been allowed to cuddle into the depression between her mother's crossed legs. Night had already fallen, and the stars sparkled so merrily she wanted to dance along with them. Her mother had stroked her hair, and the air smelled of her sweet perfume.

"Mama, why do the stars dance?" she asked.

"They are happy." Her mother smiled. "People who love unconditionally cannot be sad for long."

"How do you know they are people and not mice or lions or elephants?" Juma cuddled deeper into her mother's embrace.

"Generations of witches have assured us that the stars are our ancestors. When they leave their bodies behind for us to mourn, Monnatoba guides their souls to the Merry Fires. From there, they will watch over us and guard us as best they can."

"Will I go there too?" Juma yawned.

"When the time comes, everyone will see Monnatoba, but only those who know how to love unconditionally will sit around the Merry Fires." Juma's mother placed a kiss on her daughter's scalp. "I am sure we will see each other there."

179

"Hopefully it will be a long time in the coming," her father had said. After that, Juma had fallen asleep. It had been a long, feverish sleep, and when she woke, her mother had gone with Monnatoba.

The memory brought tears to Juma's eyes. She hadn't known it was still there. Shouldn't she have been able to forget the sorrow she'd felt back then? Why did Monnatoba insist she know this tale? Was it because Netinu was able to love unconditionally while she didn't even manage to stop wanting her mother close? She should be happy to know that her mother was favored by Monnatoba and danced with the stars.

A moonbeam bathed the old woman, and for a split second she looked much younger. Juma gasped. Young, the woman reminded her of someone she couldn't fully remember. Had they met when she was still a child? Was it…? No, it couldn't be… Her heart contracted. She opened her mouth to speak, but the woman was faster.

"Wake Netinu. You'll have to leave right away. Mubuntu is on your heels, and he's leading Princess Chunte and her men so they can do his dirty work."

Juma did as she was told, and a heartbeat later, they were ready to leave. The old woman put her hand on Juma's arm.

"Put Mubuntu's hand and Vanamate's tears in a bag at your belt. They're safer there. And always remember that Mubuntu cannot hurt you directly."

Juma dug through her bundle and pulled out the wrapped hand and the pearls. As an afterthought, she added her drum. She knotted everything into a small bundle and tied it to her belt.

The woman shooed them away. "Now, hurry. I'll try to hold Mubuntu for as long as I can."

"He'll hurt you," Juma said.

"He can't. I'm Monnatoba's emissary which means I'm no longer part of this world." Gently, she shoved Juma and Netinu to the path leading up the mountain. "Hurry."

They ran through the night. The bundle with the pearls, the hand, and the drum thumped on Juma's thigh, urging her to go faster, but despite the moonlight, she stumbled over rocks and lumps of dried grass often. Her heart raced with her, and the blood roared in her ears. She knew they had to get away before Mubuntu discovered them. The princess would show no mercy. Faster.

Netinu took her arm and helped her over a particularly steep climb. Juma envied him. He was barely breathing harder than usual, and she was panting like a baboon in the sun. Hand in hand, they hurried through the dark. Juma hoped that Mubuntu wouldn't find them. When they reached a fork in the path, they stopped to catch their breath.

"Which way?" Netinu asked.

Juma put her hands on her knees, breathing hard, and looked at the two paths. One led upward along a small rivulet of water. The other led sideways, and it wasn't evident where it went. She pointed to the one leading up.

"We need to get to the summit as fast as possible."

They set out again. As little water as was left in the rivulet's bed, it moistened the air which made running bearable. Still, Juma's chest burned, her sides hurt, and her feet seemed to have given up signaling their pain. Her breath came in short bursts. How she longed to drink some of the rivulet's water and rest.

A streak of fire shot through the sky and landed ahead of them. A bush went up in flames, illuminating the path where the fugitives stumbled upwards. Netinu lowered his spear at the burning bush, and Juma stopped. Mubuntu stood right besides the bush, laughing.

"Do you really think you can escape me?" He took a step toward them. "Now, give me my hand." He reached for Juma, and she stumbled backwards.

"Never," she said.

Mubuntu took another step forward. He glared at her. "I killed that flimsy mother of yours and sent her back to Monnatoba. You'll join her in no time."

"My mother?" A pang of loneliness shot through Juma's heart.

"The hag on the way up," Mubuntu sneered.

Her suspicion confirmed, Juma sucked in her breath. Why hadn't her mother revealed herself? Then she remembered how very little time they had, and she understood.

"You're a liar, Mubuntu." She stepped as close to Netinu as she could without hindering his movement. He pointed his spear from side to side as if searching for the enemy. With her hand on his shoulder, Juma stood as tall as she could. "She has been with Monnatoba for a long time. You cannot kill someone who is already dead."

Mubuntu snarled. "But you are not dead yet, are you?"

His spear still lowered, Netinu looked around with confusion written all over his face. "Who are you talking to?"

"Mubuntu."

"He's here? You can see him?"

Juma nodded. She grabbed his arm and pulled him backward into the ankle-deep water.

Mubuntu laughed. "That won't help you, you know? I'll make the water boil, and Chunte with her warriors will be here any minute." He waved his hand, and the bundle on Juma's back flared up.

With a small scream, she dropped it into the water. The fire didn't die easily, enveloping the couple in clouds of steam. Juma grabbed Netinu's arm and pulled him uphill. The vapor covered their flight. Sure, Mubuntu would find them in no time, but as long as they kept moving, at least Chunte wouldn't catch up.

After a while, the rivulet ended, and Juma stumbled over a rock hidden in the sand. Pain shot through her foot, but she hobbled on. How far was it to the summit anyway? Shouldn't they be close already? She stumbled uphill and tried to ignore the pain. Once in a while, she looked back.

Not far below, the flickering sparks of torches moved slowly up the path they had come. It must be Chunte with her warriors. Juma scanned the land around her, but there was no sign of an advance guard. If they found a way to shake Mubuntu for a short while, they might find a place to hide from the princess and her warriors.

The path widened to a gently rising rocky plain. In the moonlight, the top of the mountain rose clearly visible ahead of them. Two vertical stones marked the summit less than the village lake's width ahead of them.

Juma ran over the flat area with Netinu at her side. All of a sudden, his bundle burst into flame. He threw it to the side and it landed at Mubuntu's feet.

"You can't escape your fate." The heat dæmon raised his arms and began to dance. Blue magic swirled around him, condensing with every jump. His private parts bobbed and slapped in rhythm. If it hadn't been so scary, Juma would have laughed. As it was, she didn't even have enough air left to breathe normally.

Netinu dragged her on.

"Whatever you see, ignore it," he said. "We need to get to the top."

"Give me my hand!" Mubuntu lifted his right foot.

Juma shook her head, and he slammed his heel into the ground.

The earth moaned and shook. It lurched violently. Juma bumped into Netinu who barely managed to keep them standing while stones and debris flew through the air. Most missed but a couple slammed into the fugitives. Juma's skin broke and pearls of blood ran over her arms, shoulders, back, and legs. She bit her tongue not to cry out. She wouldn't give Mubuntu the satisfaction. As soon as the earth had calmed, she set out toward the mountaintop again.

A warrior stepped out of the shadow, and Juma's heart missed a beat. So Chunte had sent an advance guard after all. She turned. A few more warriors trotted up the path, carrying torches. The flickering light was enough to see Chunte running ahead of them. Leading her men, she blocked the only route of escape. Netinu pushed Juma behind his back and lowered his spear.

"It's so nice to see you again, dear husband." Despite being winded, Chunte grinned and raised her hand.

A beam of blue fire sped toward the two. Instinctively, Juma pulled up a shield big enough to protect her and Netinu, silently thanking Selenta for her training.

Chunte didn't shoot a second bolt, which surprised Juma, so she lowered her shield. The princess walked closer swinging her hips. "Since you can see my beloved master, I take it you were the one eavesdropping on us. I bet you would want to share his love, but he's mine. I'm the only one who partakes of his power. The world will be mine to rule, and everybody will bend to my will."

Juma couldn't believe her ears. Chunte couldn't be so blind, could she? "If you don't stop, Mubuntu's folly will wake the Nameless."

"So what? We can always go and look for a different place to live. Too bad about your tribe. But since it didn't embrace me the way I deserve, I won't shed a tear on their passing." Chunte stepped close to Juma, who stepped back. However, the soldier who had overtaken them blocked her. He grabbed her with an iron grip.

Chunte stepped so close, her breath hit Juma's face. "I think my lover will enjoy your death. I will make sure it is a very slow one." She shot round. "We'll stop here." She waved to the guards who had stayed behind, and they busied themselves with setting up a camp.

Soon a big fire burned in front of a tent. Juma and Netinu sat side by side with their hands and feet bound. Chunte picked up Netinu's singed bundle.

"Where is that damned hand?" She searched frantically.

Juma wondered why the princess hadn't taken the bag from her belt. Glancing down, her heart dropped. The bag wasn't where it should be. The belt was empty. She must have lost it. On the one hand, that was good news since it meant Chunte wouldn't be able to get it. On the other hand, it was bad news, since Juma couldn't remember where she had seen it last. She pressed her lips together, trying to keep her panic down.

Netinu's knee nudged hers. When she looked up, he winked. She bent sideways until her head lay on his shoulder.

"Don't worry about the hand. I hid it when he attacked the first time. I seem to have a knack for stealing things." He spoke so low, nobody heard his words but her.

Chunte got up and walked over to them. "Dear me, what a romantic picture. I'll have to make sure my husband will satisfy your appetite before I turn him into an animal."

Juma sat straight and snorted. "You couldn't turn a beetle into an ant if your life depended on it." Annoying Chunte felt good, although it was a dangerous game.

The princess frowned. "You need proof? Don't worry, you will get it. Tomorrow we'll take you down to the pool where the river wells up. My creations will crisp you to cinders."

"You created the fire animals?" Juma's eyes widened.

"They are the most powerful, the most beautiful creatures that ever walked the earth, and I made them." Her eyes sparkled. "As soon as Vanamate has faded away, killed by the vapor of her own tears, I shall join Mubuntu in his realm. Together, we will be the new gods."

Juma lowered her head. This girl was stone crazy. It was no use talking to her. The bad thing was that her plan might work. Even if Mubuntu wasn't faithful to Chunte, which was very likely, he had imprisoned Vanamate. What if he really killed his sister? Juma's already heavy heart felt like a stone in her chest. What if he woke his father? Who would survive if the Nameless walked the earth again? She had to stop Chunte.

Despite the turmoil in her mind, a memory surfaced, and a thought formed. Whenever she had looked back when they climbed the mountain, there had not been a trace of Chunte and her men. Juma hadn't even known they were following. They must have hidden. Why would they do that if they didn't expect to meet something scarier than an insignificant witch and a lone warrior? A smile grew on Juma's lips. They had been hiding from the fire animals. The warriors had to know something no one else did. A plan formed in her mind, and she decided to risk Chunte's wrath for it.

Looking up, she smiled. In a singsong voice, she said, "If you're such a great witch, how comes that you cannot control your own creations? You hid like a coward when you neared the pool, and your warriors are scared by the very idea of meeting the fire animals."

"That's not true." Chunte kicked her viciously. "My fiery pets worship the ground I tread on."

"Why didn't you bring them with you then? By all Tolobe told me, they're much faster and much more dangerous than a bunch of useless warriors." Juma tapped the ground with her foot in a counterpoint to the song her words formed. In the bushes, an early bird joined her. "These warriors aren't worthy of the spell of any witch even an untrained one like me."

One of the men yawned. Two others sat beside the tent and leaned against each other. Juma was delighted when she saw their eyelids droop. Chunte didn't notice, but Netinu did. He clicked his tongue in a rhythm complementing her own and picked up a sharp sliver of stone. Juma marveled at his perception. He helped although he didn't know what she was up to. No time for analyzing now. She concentrated on the song in her mind.

"I bet the animals would burn you to cinders too."

"They are mine. I created them, and they obey every word I say. You'll see." Chunte stomped her foot. "Now, tell me where you put Mubuntu's hand and I might let you live."

"Why is this darned hand so important?" Juma asked. "He obviously isn't in pain. Can't he fill your magic again without it? I thought prostituting yourself would be all that's required."

Chunte pressed her lips together and kicked Juma again, real hard. The pain nearly killed the song and sent tears into her eyes. In a fluent motion, Netinu rose. The bonds on his wrists fell away, and he jumped Chunte. The princess hit the ground and cracked her head on a stone. None of the warriors moved. Juma blinked away the tears, breathed deeply, and increased the seduction of her song while Netinu untied his feet. One of the warriors snored loudly. Netinu didn't need particular skill to steal his knife. He knelt beside Juma and sliced through the rope with the sharp edge of the stone blade.

When she was free, he turned to Chunte and sliced across her throat. A bluish glow lit up Chunte's throat briefly and the blade splintered without leaving a trace on the princess's skin. Netinu swore.

"Let's go." Juma took his hand and pulled him up. "I need the bundle."

Wordlessly they ran down the hill. Already the horizon brightened ever so slightly. Dawn was approaching fast. When they reached the crossing where the second path veered off from the main path, Netinu pushed his hand into the water and lifted a stone. Her bundle lay beneath. Fearing for her pearls, Juma tried to remember if the rivulet had held less water on the way up, but she couldn't say. Netinu handed her the dripping bundle, and she began to dig around.

"My hand! Give me back my hand." Mubuntu appeared beside the rivulet. Netinu flinched and paled. Obviously the god had decided to become visible to him as well as to Juma.

"Chunte!" Mubuntu's scream echoed through the early morning, drowning out the voices of birds and other animals.

Worried, Juma gazed at the sun's reflection in the sky. Not much longer and it would rise over the horizon, feeding Mubuntu with more power. She had to hurry. Her fingers found what she had been looking for. She pulled out one of Vanamate's tears and flung it at

Mubuntu. It hit him squarely in the face. His jaw dropped, and he stared at her, unbelieving. Then he crumpled to the ground.

"You did it!" Netinu hugged her.

Juma shook her head. "He'll come round when the sun rises. We need to get away fast."

Netinu set out uphill, but Juma called him back.

"If we go there, they'll find us immediately. We need to find a different way up, even if it means climbing over the rocks on the other side of the mountain." Hand in hand, they hurried up the second path, the ever-brightening sky at their backs.

Soon the path narrowed and they had to walk one after the other. For a while, it led downhill. Juma worried it might lead them all the way back to the foot of the mountain. Looking around, she saw a craggy cliff that rose over the other rocks on their right side. The two stone pillars of the summit stood right at its top.

"We need to climb up there." She pointed, and Netinu left the path. She followed him over the bed of loose rubble. It was hard going. The rocks were sharp and cut the soles of her feet through her sandals whenever she wasn't careful enough. Biting her lip, she walked on. Whenever climbing became too difficult, Netinu helped her.

"Do you think they will be waiting for us at the top?" he asked.

Juma had wondered the same. She would if she were in Chunte's place. Also, the sun lit up the sky already. Mubuntu would be on their heels any minute now. She tried to reassure Netinu and herself. "If they do, we'll think of something. I promise."

"It's not as if we've got another choice." Netinu smiled and held out his hand again.

A low growl shook Juma to her bones. A cheetah walked around a big boulder. Instead of the usual dotted fur, flames flickered around the body. It pulled up its flews and hissed. Holding her breath, Juma clung to Netinu's arm. Together, they stepped backwards. The cheetah followed.

## 19

"*D*ON'T RUN, AND DON'T TURN away," Netinu whispered.

"Do you really think a magical animal will behave like the real thing?" Juma's fingers slipped on his arm because she sweated so much. Her heart raced, and her feet longed to follow its example, but she forced herself to stay calm.

Step by step, the couple retreated, followed by the cheetah. It hissed and growled at them but didn't attack. It drove them back to the path and further down the hill. The higher the sun rose, the higher the flames on the cheetah burned. Only now did Juma see what the night had hidden.

All the trees and rocks around them bore scorch marks. Even the grass was black and dead. She swallowed.

There was an intelligence in the animal's eyes that scared her stiff. Still, she moved backwards slowly, clinging to Netinu's arm. They walked in silence for a long time, always facing the cheetah. When they tried to walk sideways or even uphill, the animal blocked their way and growled. After a time that felt like an eternity but couldn't have been more than an hour, they reached the pool where the river began. The cheetah howled, and a fiery rhino joined it. A little further down the path, an elephant, a hyena, and a lion appeared. The lion roared, and the cheetah hissed, but none of the animals made a move to hurt their captives.

"They are communicating with each other," Juma said in awe. She sat down and tugged at Netinu's arm.

His gaze flickered from her to the animals and back. "Are you sure that's a good idea?"

"I think they want something from us," she said. "The cheetah alone could have killed us in the blink of an eye. Instead it herded us to its companions. It is trying to tell us something, and I know how to talk to them."

"I can't protect you when we're sitting."

"You can't protect me against fiery animals whether we're standing, running, or sitting. It doesn't matter. If they wanted to kill us, they would have done so already."

Reluctantly Netinu sat down with his back leaning against hers. She pulled out her drum and began to play, focusing on the animals.

"Can't you send them to sleep?" Netinu whispered.

"I'll try as soon as I know what they want." She drummed on and on. After a while, the cheetah's hiss began to make sense.

"You witch?"

She nodded. "Yes, I am a witch."

"Turn back," the elephant said.

"Yes, turn back," the others said too.

"We can't turn back. We need to go up the mountain to free Vanamate and stop Mubuntu."

The lion roared, a frown on its face. "Us. Turn us."

Like pieces of a puzzle, everything fell into place. Chunte had turned her own men into animals made of fire, and the animals seemed to remember. All they wanted was for Juma to return them to their human form. But could she do it? The spell Chunte had used must have been a very strong one, and her magic was borrowed from Mubuntu, not natural like Juma's. Would Juma be able to counteract it?

"I will try, but you need to lie down where I can see you all," she said.

"Come." The cheetah walked past them to the pool, and the other animals followed. At the shore, it looked back. Juma helped Netinu to his feet.

"I have to go with them and see if I can help. But you don't have to come."

He pulled her hands to his chest and looked deeply into her eyes. "I will go wherever you go regardless the danger."

Juma's skin grew hot. She tried to pull away, but found she couldn't. Her heart raced, and she held her breath. What was happening? Ever so gently, Netinu's lips touched hers. Fire raced through her veins, and her body wanted to melt into Netinu's. She gasped. This much desire would surely call Mubuntu. Also, if she was no longer a virgin and could not use her magic any more, how would she free Vanamate? She jerked free.

"We have things to do." She turned away, trying to ignore the hurt expression on Netinu's face. The pain in her heart drove tears to her eyes, but she blinked them away and followed the animals. Juma knew she'd only need to stay a virgin until Vanamate was free, but Selenta had been a witch for all her life. How had she been able to stand it? She would have to explain to Netinu at one point, but right now, she didn't feel up to it. The sensation of his lips touching hers still lingered, and she needed to savor it. Blind to her surroundings, she walked behind the animals. When she looked up, she stood in front of a cave right beside the pond. An overflow from the pond the size of the river flowed right into it. A wide stretch of sand provided enough room for the animals to lie down side by side. Juma sat down and picked up the drumming again with Netinu standing behind her.

"Turn us," the cheetah hissed.

"I will try, but I can't promise you anything. I haven't been a witch for long, and Chunte's spell is very strong," Juma explained.

"Turn us or die," the lion roared.

"Silent," the cheetah growled at it. "She help. Animal or human. She live." The lion lowered its head and fell silent. The cheetah turned back to Juma. "Do best."

Juma's smile was a little crooked but genuine. She concentrated on her drum and changed the song. A melody floated just out of reach. She tried to capture it, but to no avail. She played until her fingers hurt, but all she managed to do was to send the animals to sleep. The flames on their bodies flickered less although the sun was high over their heads already. With a sigh, she gave up.

"I can't do it."

"Let's hope they will understand." Netinu put his hand on her shoulder, sending a jolt of longing through her body.

"If only Chunte hadn't used Mubuntu's magic. I'm sure I could have countered anything else." She got to her feet and walked closer to the animals. They were sleeping peacefully. Maybe she should flee with Netinu before they woke. The lion at least wouldn't be very happy, and Juma wasn't sure if she could trust the cheetah to keep its promise.

"If we free Vanamate, maybe she will be able to…" Her jaw dropped. Of course! She dug through her bundle and took out the pearls. There were only six left. Should she really squander them on the animals? For a moment, she tried to imagine what it must be like to be separated from your tribe and forced to live as a creature of nightmares. She couldn't ignore the fire animals' plight. Picking one pearl from the cloth, she approached the cheetah. Hopefully it won't wake just now, she thought. With trembling hands, she reached for its muzzle. Despite the heat, she pushed the pearl between its flews. When it didn't swallow, she pried apart the jaws with trembling fingers and pushed the pearl deeper. It gulped and sighed. Hurriedly, Juma stepped back and watched.

The cheetah's legs twitched, and it shivered. It curled up. Steam rose from its body, wrapping it in a cloud, hiding it from view. A gentle wind blew the vapor away and revealed a naked man. He blinked and opened his eyes, looking around in confusion.

"I've had the most terrible dream." His voice was hoarse. Then his gaze fell on the other burning animals, and he jerked back. "It was real, wasn't it?" His gaze searched Juma, and she nodded. He looked at his comrades again. "Why haven't they changed back?"

Juma explained about Vanamate's tears. "I tried it on you first to see if it would work." She walked to the rhino, pushing another pearl between its lips. It was much harder to open the jaws wide enough to slip it in, and she burned her fingers a little. Then she gave one each to the elephant, the hyena, and the lion. Soon, clouds of steam billowed over the small patch of sand between the pool and the cave. When it cleared, four more men sat up trying to get their bearings in the world again. Juma averted her eyes as best she could since none of them wore anything, not even a loincloth. Netinu ripped part of his kikoi apart for their need while Juma carefully stored the last pearl in her bag again.

When everyone was decent, ex-cheetah bowed to Juma and expressed his thanks in the most appropriate manner.

"We are aware that giving up Vanamate's tears for us might cost you dearly later on, and we are prepared to protect you with our lives in return." He knelt and rested his right hand on his raised knee, lowering his head until his chin touched his chest. The other warriors followed his example.

Juma was delighted until she remembered that they'd have to climb back to the summit with only a single pearl left. How could they oppose Mubuntu if they didn't have anything with which to fight him? She sighed. "If only we could weaken Mubuntu before we begin to climb."

"That should be possible," ex-rhino said and pointed to the pool. "He thrives on heat, sun and drought, right? If we free the river, it should weaken him somewhat."

Juma knew immediately that he was right. "Can you help me get the boulder out of the river's bed?"

Without an answer, the men ran to fetch strong, flexible branches that could be used to move the boulder. They returned with the spears Tolobe and his men had left behind when they fled the fiery animals. Three men climbed over the boulder to the other side, while the other two stayed with Juma and Netinu. When she took the first step toward the boulder, Netinu put a hand on her arm and held her back.

"You will have to watch out for Mubuntu. I'm sure he'll try to keep us from freeing the river. He seems to feel it when we do something that opposes him."

Reluctantly, Juma nodded. Just in case, she dug out the last pearl again and stood at the side of the pool, close to the burnt remains of a big bush. The men dug the tips of their spears into the soft bank and put their whole weight on the shafts to move the boulder. It wobbled a bit. With delight, Juma saw a thin line of water trickle into the old riverbed from under the stone. The men heaved again, and the boulder rocked, spilling more water into its former bed.

"Stop that right now!" Mubuntu's voice was low and controlled. It sent icy shivers along Juma's spine. She stepped closer to the dead bush, sure that the heat dæmon hadn't seen her yet. He was too focused on the men. A spear went up in flames, and ex-hyena jumped back. The others heaved again, and the boulder rolled a few fingers' width forward. Mubuntu roared, but before he could do anything, Juma hurled the last pearl. It hit him at the temple. A tiny cloud of steam rose from his head before the pearl bounced and dropped into the pool. Despite the seemingly gentle touch, Mubuntu crumpled to the ground.

The earth began to shake. Juma clung to the dead bush to stay on her feet, but the men toppled and fell. They dug their fingers into whatever plant they could find. The earth's tremor grew stronger, and the boulder slipped some more. The amount of water in the pool seemed to increase, although it was hard to tell since it sloshed from one side to the other. The waves grew bigger the longer the ground shook. When the quaking subsided, a wave higher than an elephant rolled toward Juma and the men. Roaring like fire, it slammed over them. With all her might, Juma clung to the bush's branches, glad they were still strong enough. She pressed her eyes closed, and the water soaked her and filled her mouth and nose. She held her breath until her lungs burned and stars danced on the inside of her eyelids. Then the urge for air became too big, and she gasped. Instead of the water she expected to run down her throat, fresh air revived her.

She opened her eyes and looked around, enjoying every breath as if it was her first. A thought crossed her mind. Too much water was just as dangerous as too much fire. She knew she should be thinking about this some, but there were more pressing matters at hand.

Mubuntu was gone, and so was the boulder. Netinu! Where was he? She inspected the area more closely. The river had returned to its former bed, glittering merrily in the sun. Netinu clung to a rocky outcrop at its bank. Relieved, Juma sighed. Two other men clutched his legs. As soon as they noticed that the water had gone, they rose. Juma got up and searched the other bank for the rest of the men. She found two of them beside a big rock the wave had smashed them against. The ex-lion waved and the ex-hyena vomited. Scanning the ground for the third one, Juma stepped closer to the river.

The body of ex-cheetah hung limply in a dead tree on her side. She ran to him. It wasn't easy to pry him out of the branches, but she managed. She felt for a pulse, but her fingers were too numb, so she bent over his mouth and listened. He wasn't breathing. She put her lips against his throat. Like the tips of a butterfly's wings, his pulse throbbed faintly against her skin. He needs air, she thought. Maybe if I help him, he'll start breathing again. She bent over him, supporting her weight on his chest with an arm, pressed her lips to his mouth and breathed into him.

A gush of water shot out of his mouth, and he gasped, coughed and spat. Juma sat up and watched him breathe on his own until he vomited more water on her feet. Withdrawing a little, she felt as relieved as if the big boulder had been removed from her heart, not from the river. Ex-cheetah had been the nicest man of the lot and it would have pained her had he gone with Monnatoba. When Netinu and the others reached her, the man was already recovering, thanking Juma over and over.

"I'm Selto and will be forever in your debt," he said, trying unsuccessfully to kiss her hands.

To change the subject, Juma said, "I need to reach the summit before Mubuntu wakes again. I used my last pearl on him."

"Do you think Vanamate's tear caused the trembling and the wave?" Netinu wondered.

"I think so, but only the gods can say for sure." Juma shrugged. "Let's leave now. We've lost enough time already."

"These men need to rest." Netinu pointed at the former animals. Ex-hyena's skin held a grayish tinge, and sweat stood on his forehead.

"They will go back to our tribe," Selto, the ex-cheetah, said. "Only Molo and I will accompany you."

Netinu explained that most members of Chunte's tribe were now living with their clan. He gave detailed directions to their village. Ex-lion and ex-elephant shouldered the former hyena and walked downhill along the river.

The other two followed Juma and Netinu back up the hill. When they reached a bush that hadn't burned, they broke off several long staffs since the water had carried away the spears. They climbed slowly and steadily. With worry, Juma noticed how far the day had already come. He stomach grumbled but there was no time to eat. With bowed heads, they walked higher and higher. Soon, they reached the place where the cheetah had forced them to turn back. Netinu took her hand and smiled at her, sending a tingle through her body.

"If anyone can do it, it's you," he whispered. She leaned her head against his shoulder. If only she weren't so tired. Holding his hand, she began to climb. She tried to be careful about where she put her feet, but her weariness made the stones blur. Ever so often, one of the sharp points cut through her already worn sandals into the soles of her feet. Soon the sandals were so shredded that she took them off and threw them away. Netinu and Selto joined hands to form a seat and ordered her to sit on it. With her arms around their shoulders, they carried her over the sharp stones. Molo carried their staffs as well as his own. Juma rested her weary head against Netinu's shoulder and dozed. When they reached the base of the steep decline, she felt much better, but a look into Netinu's eyes told her the price. He sank to the ground and breathed deeply.

"I need a short break," he said.

Selto sat beside him wordlessly; Molo stood to the side watching the slope they had just climbed. Further down, a group of men stepped from the bushes that lined the path. Chunte's warriors had found them, and Juma groaned. Why couldn't they have a few minutes to rest? Surely Chunte and Mubuntu would show up now. One man pointed at them, and began to climb. The others fell in line.

Selto narrowed his eyes and gazed at them. "I can handle them. They're from our tribe."

Netinu shook his head. "Don't try. They are loyal to Princess Chunte."

"Princess." Selto snorted. "She's as much a princess as I am female. The beast took over my wife's office by murder."

"Your wife was weak!"

Juma's head shot round at Chunte's voice. The woman stood beside them in the shade, glaring at Selto. Her face was filled with hatred. "I am your chieftess and your princess now. You will do my bidding or lose your honor forever."

Neither Selto nor Molo reacted to her words. Not even Netinu took any notice. Juma frowned. Then Chunte took a step forward, and Juma could see the rock behind her through her body. The young woman must have sent out her spirit. How had she done that? Did

Mubuntu pull her out? She remembered that she'd heard him mention how dangerous that was. Well, she wouldn't cry if Chunte didn't find her way back into her real body.

"Mubuntu. Come and help!" Chunte screamed, but the heat dæmon didn't show up. Juma hoped that he was still suffering from the pearl's impact.

"We need to leave now," Juma said. "Chunte's spirit is here. She will lead Mubuntu to us as soon as he shows up."

Selto nodded. He sent his companion down toward the other men of his tribe. "Tell them to go back. Tell them that the one they're chasing saved my life and our souls, and that she returned our bodies to human form. Tell them she will foil Mubuntu's plans. They are to leave Chunte regardless what she's threatening. Here is a woman who's a good match for Chunte's evil magic."

The certainty in Selto's words felt good but Juma wasn't sure she deserved it.

"And if they don't listen to me?" Molo asked.

"In that case you'll follow our brothers." Selto touched Molo's shoulder quickly and turned away to face the mountain. Molo left while Chunte howled insults at Selto, which he clearly didn't hear. Juma blushed. Ignoring Chunte, she followed her two remaining men who walked first to find the easiest route. Walking around the base of the cliff, they looked for a place where climbing wouldn't be too dangerous.

Chunte's spirit stepped in front of Juma until their noses nearly touched. "Go back right now. I order you to."

"Leave us alone, Chunte," Juma said. "None of your men can hear you, and I will not make them turn back. You should be more worried about your body. Are you sure you can return to it?"

Howling like a rabid dog, Chunte's spirit raced off. Relieved, Juma walked on until she bumped into Netinu. He pointed upward.

"There is a cave, and it looks as if there is a path from it to the summit."

Juma's gaze followed his outstretched finger. True enough. There was an entrance to a cave in the cliff, and a narrow path led from it to the top of the mountain. The question was how to get to the cave.

Selto put down his staff. "If you give me your kikois, I will help you to climb there." Juma handed him her kikoi, and Netinu did the same with what was left of his. With nimble fingers, Selto ripped them into long strips and braided them into a sturdy rope. Juma and Netinu used the time to rest.

Juma slept fitfully, always expecting another attack from Mubuntu. Selto's hand on her shoulder woke her. "I am ready. You will need to watch me closely. When you climb, you need to put your hands and feet exactly where I put mine."

Juma nodded, then looked around for the telltale fiery streaks of Mubuntu's approach. Nothing.

"Good luck," she said.

Selto began his ascent. Pushing his fingers and toes into tiny cracks, he moved higher and higher, the rope wrapped around his belly. Juma chewed her fingernails in concentration as she tried to remember every crevice he used as a foothold. It seemed to take him ages to reach the cave. When he did, he tied the rope to a rock beside the entrance and let it down.

"The staffs first," he called down.

Netinu tied the staffs into several coils of the rope, and Selto pulled them up. After putting them aside, he lowered the rope again.

"One after the other," he instructed them.

"You go first," Netinu said and tied the rope around Juma's waist. "If you fall, I might be able to catch you."

## 20

*J*UMA'S MOUTH WENT DRY AS she approached the cliff. She had never climbed anything higher than a tree before. The gentle slopes of the mountain didn't count. With cold fingers, she pushed the rope out of the way and felt between the stones for the first handhold. Slowly, she pulled herself up before she placed her foot into a different crevice and pushed herself higher. Her heart beat faster as she pulled herself higher again. Her arms were tiring fast. Maybe she wouldn't make it to where Selto waited. She tried not to think about what would happen if she fell. Instead, she moved her feet from one foothold to the next and pulled with all her strength. Foothold, push, handhold, pull. The rhythm of the climb numbed her fear but her body began to complain. Her breathing became harder. Her hands felt as if a cheetah had chewed on them, and her arm muscles trembled.

When she reached the cave, she was glad the climb was over. Gratefully, she sat down cross-legged beside Selto and allowed him to remove the rope from her waist. She rested her hands on her knees and tried to relax. Her muscles twitched for quite a while. Closing her eyes, she hoped Netinu would make it. Even with the rope, it was an exhausting climb. She thanked Monnatoba that she'd made it without a hitch.

When she opened her eyes again, Netinu crawled over the rim to the cave's entrance. His body shook just as much as Juma's had, and he panted, but he smiled at her in a way that said, "Did you worry about me?"

Blushing, she looked away, and her gaze fell on the steep path that rose to the summit. It would be a lot easier to walk up there.

A red flicker appeared at the top of the path, and Mubuntu's voice drifted down to them. "I won't fight them down there. It's way too close to him."

"Don't you want your hand back?" Chunte's voice sounded angry.

"Would you like to be hit by one of Vanamate's tears? They hurt. A lot."

"It's your own fault for getting too close. You should have dropped something burning on top of them."

"Why don't we just wait? They're bound to show up here, sooner or later."

Chunte didn't answer, but she stepped onto the path leading down with two warriors in her wake. So she obviously had found her way back into her body. Juma got up and waved for the others to go into the cave. They crouched under the drooping ceiling, whispering to each other.

"We can't fight them," Selto said. "Our staffs are no use against real weapons."

"Won't the men listen to you?" Netinu asked.

"I don't think so. Some men in our tribe helped Chunte turn me into a cheetah, and I'm sure they're with her now."

"We could go deeper into the cave," Juma suggested. "It's very tight in here, and dark. That way they won't be able to use their spears, and we would see their outlines against the sky outside. We might be able to protect ourselves here."

The men agreed, and they slid further into the darkness. The ceiling bulged so low, they had to lie on their bellies to move, but after two body lengths, the ceiling rose again, and they were able to stand. Juma knelt and looked through the gap they had just passed.

"They're here," she whispered. "Maybe they will leave if they can't find us."

"What do you mean they're not there?" Chunte's voice screeched. "They didn't climb down again. Find them. Burn them out if necessary."

Netinu and Selto knelt beside Juma. Together they watched the shadows move in and out of the cave. Then Mubuntu entered and set a pile of wood aflame that the men had carried into the cave. The flickering of the flames shed a little light on part of their hiding hole too. Smoke gathered at the cave's ceiling.

"If they keep the fire up for any length of time, we'll have to come out," Selto said.

Juma looked around for stones they could use as weapons. At least the entrance to their hiding place was so narrow they stood a good chance at defending it.

"Look at this." Netinu carried two unlit torches toward them. "It seems people have been to this hole before. There are even two fire stones and dry grass to light the torches."

"Why would anyone deposit torches when this hole leads nowhere?" Selto looked confused.

A draft caressed Juma's cheek, and it didn't come from the narrow entrance. She closed her eyes and felt for it. Cold, musty air flowed past her from her right. With eyes still closed, she followed the flow of air to a dark corner and explored it with her hands.

"There is a passage here," she said.

Netinu thrust the torches at Selto, grabbed the stones and the grass, and walked over to Juma. Right around the bend, he crouched and struck flint against fool's gold. Tiny sparks rained onto the grass. Soon, it smoldered. He blew gently on it until it burned. Selto held the tips of the torches into the tiny flames until they caught, then held them out into the darkness ahead.

"Let's see where this tunnel will lead us." He handed one torch to Netinu and took the lead. Juma followed him, with Netinu bringing up the rear.

"There is a gap at the back," a male voice behind them shouted. "They're probably hiding in there."

"What are you waiting for? Check it out," Chunte ordered.

"The fire is right in front of it," a male voice called.

"Mubuntu, put out the fire."

"I'm don't put out fires, I start them."

Another male voice said, "Honorable princess, I advise you to keep smoking them out. Anything else is too dangerous. They've got spears or at least wooden poles and stones."

Juma walked faster. It wouldn't take their followers all that long to realize that no one was defending the hiding hole.

"Hopefully, the tunnel won't take us back down," she said. "What if it ends in the cave where the river went when it was blocked?"

"Don't worry." Netinu touched her back from behind her. "So far, it's sloping upward. Maybe it will even take us to the mountaintop."

"I hope so. We've lost so much time already." She hurried after Selto. The light caused moving shadows which made the tunnel come alive. The walls seemed to contract and expand. Juma felt the weight of the mountain press in on her. All that kept her from screaming was the comforting flickering of the torches ahead and behind. Sweat ran down her body as if she was standing right beside Mubuntu. She tried to calm herself. *This tunnel has existed for countless years; it won't collapse right now.* The passage split, and Selto chose the branch leading up. Soon it leveled out, and a little later, they stood in front of a cliff slightly less than the height of a man. Juma wiped her hands on her loincloth and stared up. The darkness seemed to mock her.

Without a word, Selto climbed the hurdle, leaving the torch behind. At the top, he lay on his belly and reached down. Netinu handed him first one, then the second torch. Juma bit her lip when the light dimmed around her. She kept her gaze fixed on its flickering on the ceiling when she climbed. Netinu gave her a lift, and Selto helped from above. She reached the top of the cliff in one fluent motion. Her gaze fell on another cliff of the same height which loomed ahead.

"Stay with the torches while I help Netinu," Selto said. Gratefully, she sat as close to the light as she could manage, listening for muffled voices. Surely Chunte and her followers had discovered their escape route by now. Juma swallowed, wondering what she feared more: Mubuntu and his princess, or the pressing weight of the mountaintop. Wiping the sweat from her forehead, she picked up the torches.

"We could stay here and defend ourselves against Chunte and her men. This'd be a good place," Selto whispered. Did he feel uncomfortable too?

"It's more important that we reach the mountain's summit," Juma whispered back, thankful for the admittedly short distraction.

Selto gave a curt nod and climbed the next cliff. Juma fought down her urge to scream, handed him the torches, and followed him with Netinu's help.

Mubuntu's voice sounded from a distance. "I will not follow them, and that's my last word. There's no harm in teasing the Old Man so he twists and turns in his sleep, but I'm not suicidal. If I wake him, it will be my end too."

Chunte said something, but it wasn't loud enough for Juma to understand. Setting her jaw, Juma walked toward the next cliff. If Mubuntu refused to follow, they had a chance to escape.

Thankfully the ground leveled again after they scaled the next cliff.

"Look, there is a peg in the wall." Netinu pointed to a wooden stake the size of her arm. It looked strong enough to fasten a rope to. "It seems as if this passage has been used by people in times gone by."

Fighting her discomfort, Juma decided to ask Selenta about it if she ever got a chance to talk to the old witch again. She took a step forward and stopped. The stone under the soles of her feet was warm to the touch. Lifting the torch as high as she could, she looked around. A rather big cavity opened ahead of them, and their light didn't reach the other side. The cave's ground stood in dark contrast to the ochre walls. Juma knelt and touched the granite surface. It felt as if the people who used the passage before them had smoothed the ground meticulously. Why would someone do such a thing? And how did they manage to even out so much of the ground? It must have taken ages. She got up again and set out over the strangely smooth surface. After a few steps, the ground rippled under her feet. Like a lightning strike, Mubuntu's words registered.

"The Old Man he referred to must be the Nameless," she whispered and looked at her companions. Their faces paled. Juma looked around again to find out if they were really walking over some body part of a god who could destroy the whole world. To her right, the ground sloped downward to a deep depression. Even when she stepped closer, she couldn't see the bottom. Beside it, a ridge rose toward the ceiling. Could it be the bridge of a nose? In that case, the depression would be an eye, and there had to be a second one on the other side of the ridge. Blood roared in her ears, making it impossible to determine if someone was breathing close by.

Well, god or no god, they'd have to cross unless they wanted to go back and face Mubuntu and Chunte. Closely followed by the two men, Juma tiptoed onward. Sweat wet her armpits, and she panted slightly. Her mouth dried out and her tongue stuck to her palate. The smooth ground beneath her naked feet rippled again, and her heart nearly missed a beat. She stopped and held her breath until the movement ceased.

"I'm scared." Netinu's words were barely more than a breath. Still, they hung in the air like the echo of a bell. When he took her hand, his fingers trembled. Wordlessly, Selto took her other hand. Huddling close, they moved with utmost care. They walked for a long time. When they had passed the point where the ridge began, another depression became visible in the unsteady light. So it was a face after all.

"We are walking over his forehead." Selto's voice was so low, Juma barely heard. She nodded and tried to tread even more softly than she already did. A loud sigh echoed through the cave, and the ground shifted again. They toppled and fell, and Juma needed all her strength to suppress a scream. One torch died as it hit the living ground. It rolled down the gentle slope of the forehead and hit something somewhere in the darkness with a thud. Luckily, Netinu had been able to hold the second one aloft. Selto crawled closer to the depression as if to search for the second torch, but Juma held him back.

"Let's get out of here as fast as we can," she whispered. She didn't want to spend more time than absolutely necessary on the Nameless's forehead. With her heart racing, she dragged the two men across the uncomfortably warm stone, trying to forget it was the skin of the gigantic god. Please, Vanamate, let there be a second tunnel on the other side. Despite the scariness of the situation, she realized how funny it was that she considered a tunnel like the one that had scared her so much a safe haven. It was all a question of perspective.

The way over the god's forehead seemed endless. Juma hoped and prayed they weren't walking in circles. It was hard to tell in the dark, and the one torch they still had didn't help much. Finally, a wall grew out of the darkness. Starting as a reddish hint in the fluctuating shadows, it grew brighter the closer they came. Juma discovered a dark opening a bit to the side and headed toward it. With relief, she set her feet on packed earth and rocks again. Her knees trembled so much that she sank to the ground a few steps into the tunnel. If the men hadn't been there, she would have kissed the soil. Netinu and Selto sank down beside her. The relief on their faces was plainly visible despite the bad lightning. Juma listened, but there were no sounds, not even the giant's breathing. The Nameless slept on. Hopefully that won't change. She wondered if Chunte was mad enough to wake the sleeping god to catch her, but didn't think she would. Thinking of Chunte reminded her of the task she was still facing. Despite her fatigue, she got up and took the torch. She walked on, knowing the men would follow her. Although the tunnel was even darker than the other one they had walked, it had lost its fear-inducing oppression.

Soon the flame of the torch flickered stronger, and Juma felt a cool breeze tug at her loincloth. It dried the sweat on her skin and made her shiver. A little later, around another bend in the tunnel, a pinpoint of daylight appeared and grew with every step. Involuntarily Juma walked faster. When she left the tunnel, she sighed with relief. She dropped the torch on the ground and shoved sand over it with her feet until the flame died. Then she looked around.

The sun was just setting, and they stood on an outcrop of rock near the summit. Hugging the steep slope, a narrow path led to another path that meandered up from the other side of the mountain. Juma walked forward, but Selto and Netinu held her back.

"We go first," Netinu said. "You're too important. What if Chunte shows up at the same time as we do?"

Selto agreed. "We might not be able to protect you from Mubuntu's spells, but we know how to handle her warriors."

Slightly annoyed but knowing they were right, Juma walked behind them. When they passed a bush, the men broke off flexible staffs before they walked on. The closer they got to the plateau on the mountain's top, the darker the world around them grew. When they reached the summit, the moon was just rising between the two stone pillars standing at the upper edge of the cliff. They stepped closer to the edge, and Juma bent forward to gaze down the cliff. The portal led to a deep fall. Despite the dark, she could see Chunte and her warriors halfway up the path that came from the lower cave entrance. They would have to hurry. She breathed deeply and took a few steps toward the gate.

A figure appeared between the two stone pillars. Against the moon, it was barely more than the shadow of a woman, but Juma recognized her immediately.

"Mother!" She hurried forward into her mother's embrace. She had her mother back; now everything would be all right. She closed her eyes to blink away the tears. Father will be so happy. And the boys... Tolobe can get her blessing for his wedding after all. She sniffed and hugged harder.

Her mother returned the hug with fervor, then freed herself and held Juma at arm's length. "I'm sorry to cut this short, but we don't have much time left. It's the evening before High Moon. Monnatoba is very worried that you might have cut it too close."

"Will you help us again?" Juma drank in the beloved face. Her mother smiled.

"So you recognized me after all? I told Monnatoba that you would, but she didn't believe me." She sat down slightly to the right of the gate. "Come, sit with me. I am here to explain what you are facing."

Juma eyed the stone pillars. "Selenta said we'd have to go through the gate to reach the real summit, the one where Mubuntu holds Vanamate prisoner."

"That is true. What she doesn't know is that to use Monnatoba's gate, you will have to die."

Juma's jaw dropped, and she stared at her mother in disbelief. So she really was supposed to give her life for her tribe's survival. She closed her mouth and swallowed. I don't want to die. Just when I realized... She looked at Netinu, who seemed just as shocked as she was. She turned back to her mother.

"Why can't we go the way we are?" Selto asked.

"The god's mountain only exists in the spirit's world. No one can take his or her body along. Only the spirit can survive."

"But when I go on a spirit journey, I don't die," Juma said.

"With that kind of travel, you only send out your spirit, your conscious mind. Your soul, the center of your being, your character, stays behind in your body. The link between your spirit and your soul will always guide you back." Juma's mother wiped her eyes. "To free Vanamate, you will need your spirit and your soul. When you step through this portal, your body will be separated from the two, and you can enter the world of the gods as a spirit-soul."

Juma understood. "Without a connection to the body, we won't find the way back to it. Is that so?"

Her mother nodded.

"Can't you guide us back?" Netinu asked. "You seemed to have come from the other side."

"That I may not do. I am Monnatoba's now, and have to follow her wishes."

"Can't we make a bargain with her the way you did?" Juma took her mother's hands. "We'd be willing to trade anything if she would let us return to our bodies."

"Monnatoba is a hard one to bargain with, but she told me to put an offer to you. If you manage to free Vanamate, she will allow one spirit-soul to return to its body."

"In that case, I will go alone," Juma said.

"No way." Netinu glared at her. "Even if it means I can never return, I will not leave your side."

The stubborn fool. Before Juma could express her anger, her mother lifted a hand. "Do not quarrel, and do not decide rashly. A loving heart is worth more than anything in the world. Why did you think I left my crown behind when your father decided to leave the village?"

Juma closed her mouth and thought. If only one can go as spirit-soul, maybe the other can come on a spirit journey. That way, all of us could go without endangering anyone.

A flicker of light caught her eye, and she remembered Chunte. The princess wouldn't give up easily, and if she found three bodies lying in a trance, she would make sure there wouldn't be anything to return to. What could she do? She remembered that Selenta had talked about setting up protection for her hut after the fire. She wondered how to go about it, and asked her mother.

"I am no witch," she said. "I can watch over your bodies but although I can keep Mubuntu away, I cannot stop a determined human."

"If only I could ask Selenta. She would be able to tell me what to do." Juma frowned, then slapped her forehead. "But I can. I will go on a spirit walk. Mother, can you keep Mubuntu away from my body?" Her mother nodded, and Juma turned to Netinu and Selto. "You need to protect me and my mother from Chunte. She'll be here soon."

Wordlessly, Netinu pulled his flint knife from his belt and began to sharpen one end of the staff to a point.

Juma smiled. She handed her drum to her mother, lay down, and listened to the rhythm. Immediately she found herself hovering beside the gate. Light fell through it, illuminating her mother's features with an ethereal glow. In the shadow of a boulder, Mubuntu cowered with his eyes squeezed shut. Juma hurried up the slope, avoiding the gate. A steep incline rose behind it, and she sped higher and higher as fast as she could. After a few heartbeats, she reached the circle of fire. Beside it stood the cage with the witch's spirit.

Selenta looked terrible. Her eyes had sunk into her head. Her skin was taut over her forehead, cheekbones, and chin and extremely wrinkled on the rest of her face. Her forehead had a reddish, burned sheen to it. When she saw Juma, she frowned.

"Why are you here as spirit again? You have to use the gate." Her voice was as strong as ever. Mubuntu hadn't broken her yet, but Juma knew she'd have to hurry if she wanted to save her friend and mentor as well as her tribe. She explained about the price she would have to pay, about Monnatoba's offer, and about her plan.

"Now I need to know how to protect our bodies from Chunte and her men."

"You will need to carve totems like the ones I used in the ceremony determining your talents. And you'll have to bind Mother Earth's sprites to the wood. The problem is that it takes a lot of time and very advanced magic to create good guardians." The witch lowered her head and stared at her hands as if she had forgotten that Juma was still there.

Juma's heart sank. If Selenta couldn't help her, who could?

The witch's head shot up and she pointed to the dark sky behind Juma. "He's heading for the village again. You'd better look what he's up to. Meanwhile, I'll try to think of something else you could do."

## 21

RELIEVED SHE HADN'T BEEN FORGOTTEN, Juma did as Selenta told her. She followed Mubuntu's fiery trail back to her village, feeling her mother's unfaltering drumming vibrate in her bones. As she shot over the plain, she found that the camp of the river people was empty. With the river returned to its bed, they must have set aside their plans of war. Juma was sure they had left the Endless Well too.

She landed in the place before the Central Hall. Mubuntu's trail had dissolved, so she had to look around to find the heat dæmon. Since it was night, everybody had retreated to their huts, and Juma glided through a seemingly lifeless village. Here and there she peeked into a hut only to discover almost everybody asleep. The guest hut where her father and brothers had stayed was empty. They must have returned to the Endless Well to rebuild their home. With the river people gone, there was no need for her family to stay in the village any longer, but it hurt Juma that they had left without waiting for her return.

"We need to act as long as she's gone," a man's voice whispered in the shadow of a hut. "Either that, or you'll have to lead our tribe away from here. I didn't fight one madwoman to be ruled by another."

Juma walked closer and discovered Morva and her husband crouching behind a hut. Morva shook her head and said, "They took us in as friends. We can't leave them to cope with this problem alone."

Juma asked them what they disagreed on, but they didn't hear her. Frustrated, she slapped her hand against the hut's wall, but it went right through. A hand grabbed her shoulder and steadied her.

"Mubuntu is up to no good," her mother said. "Come with me."

Juma didn't wonder that she had come. After all, Monnatoba had chosen her to help defeat the heat dæmon. But she did wonder how she could still hear the drumming with her mother here.

"Selto took over," her mother said. "Hurry now."

Juma flew up and followed her mother past the village's thorny defense. A fire burned close to the lake. She frowned. Had Chunte left some warriors behind? She flew over to investigate, but the beach was empty except for a kikoi and a loincloth. A blue flash lit up the rushes. Immediately, Juma knew why Mubuntu had come. She hurried forward.

Kandra's laugh cut through the night's stillness like a knife. "I'm still surprised that this was all it took."

"All that was required of you." There was a definite chuckle in Mubuntu's voice.

"And now, my magic is as strong as Princess Chunte's!"

"You will be even more magnificent."

Beaming, Kandra walked from the bushes and picked up her clothing. Her eyes shone in a way Juma had never seen in her face before. She gasped. Her cousin was in love with the dæmon. Mubuntu put his remaining hand on Kandra's hip, drew her close, and kissed her with surprising tenderness.

"I am yours to command," he whispered.

"Soon." Kandra slung her arms around his neck and returned the kiss with much passion. Her face, eyes closed, looked happy.

"Seducing my niece is the last straw," Juma's mother fumed, her face twisted into a scary, pale mask. "She's been helping him before, you know. Requesting a quarter of the herd as a sacrifice was not his idea."

The words evoked the memory of the whispered conversations Juma had overheard, and she realized Kandra must have talked to Mubuntu, not Chunte.

"She chose this." Juma took her mother's arm and turned her away from the pair. "She's blinded by jealousy. There's nothing we can do at the moment."

"He is using her emotional confusion against her." Her mother's eyes bored into Juma's. "Promise you will make him pay."

Juma nodded, and her mother vanished as if she'd never been there. Slowly, Juma flew back to the village. The drumming she heard got louder, as if her mother beat the rhythm again, working out her anger. Juma sighed. Regardless of how nasty Kandra had been to her, it seemed unfair to destroy her happiness. However, there was no way she could save her tribe without hurting her cousin. She landed.

"Did you bring a knife?" Morva asked. Her husband nodded.

Without noticing, Juma had returned to the hiding couple. Grateful for the distraction, she followed them into the hut.

"You can't come in," a man said and lifted his spear. Morva's man grabbed it, pulled it out of the warrior's hands, and slammed it over his head. The man crumpled to the ground. Morva crouched and built up the fire which had been subdued for the night. Soon the inside of the hut glowed in a warm, cozy light. Surprised, Juma stared at her family. Her father, Tolobe, and Lomba had been tied to poles in an upright position. It had to be terribly uncomfortable to sit like that. Sundera lay at Tolobe's feet, curled up like a newborn. It took Juma a moment to realize she was bound too.

Morva took her husband's knife and began to cut at Sundera's ropes.

"Shall I bind the guard?" her husband asked.

Morva nodded. "Also gag him and hide him somewhere. We don't want him to wake in here."

The flint took a long time to saw through the rope's fibers. It was enough time for Morva's husband to carry the guard away and return, but finally the threads fell off Sundera's arms, and she sat up. Her eyes were swollen and red. Morva hugged her wordlessly. Juma longed to do the same but didn't try. Sundera wouldn't feel her anyway.

"Who did that to you?" she asked, but nobody heard.

Morva began picking at the knots of Tolobe's ties, her husband used his knife on Lomba's bonds, and Sundera tugged at the knots in the ropes that held Juma's father.

"Hurry up," Juma urged them on although no one could hear her.

The healer slipped in just as the last rope fell to the ground.

"You're free already. Well done." She handed a bag with provisions to Sundera. "You'd better leave now. I saw Kandra walk up from the lake. She'll be here soon."

Juma's father shook his head. "We will not flee. I owe this much to my wife and to my daughter."

"But you have to go. At sunrise Kandra's warriors will drag you out of the village to be sacrificed to Mubuntu." The healer's voice was controlled but her fear spilled into Juma. Her family about to be sacrificed by her own cousin? She felt like crying. How did that happen?

Her father smiled at the healer. "Juma said she'd be back by High Moon."

"What if she doesn't make it? Or if she's delayed?" The healer didn't give up easily.

"He's right, you know?" Sundera sat down beside her future father-in-law. "If we flee, Kandra will rule the tribe unopposed. I don't think her mother will gain consciousness again. Kandra learned too much from Chunte to allow it. Maybe Jakombe will be sacrificed in our place. Do we want to feel responsible for her death? And for our tribe's suffering?"

Tolobe reached for her hand. "I will stay with you and fight for what is right."

Lomba didn't say anything, but he picked up the guard's spear, trying to look dangerous.

Juma sank to her knees. Why did her brothers and father have to be so terribly, stubbornly honest? Was that the code of warriors her father liked to invoke?

A drum sounded from outside the hut. It woke the tribe to a ceremony. Juma assumed it was the sacrifice of her family. Was dawn so close?

The healer said, "It begins."

"You'd better leave," Sundera said. "If Kandra sees you with us and decides to sacrifice you too, the tribe will have no one to turn to; no real chieftess, no witch and no healer."

The healer frowned.

"The tribe needs you." Sundera put her hand on the healer's arm. The older woman slumped and sighed.

"I will go, but I don't approve." She slipped out of the hut.

Juma floated out to see if she got away unseen. Luckily Kandra was busy gathering everybody around her. Children leaned against their parents tiredly, and even the warriors yawned a lot. Only Kandra seemed alert and awake. By the time she turned to the hut, the healer had melted into the crowd unnoticed.

"I don't care about how early it is," she said. "Warriors, go and get them."

Reluctantly, two men grabbed their spears and walked toward the hut. Mubuntu appeared behind Kandra, and Juma realized he could burn down the hut to force her family to come out. I can keep the warriors from getting into the hut for a while, but what will I do against Mubuntu? There must be a way.

She flew up and gazed around, looking for something she could use to protect her family when she noticed that the lake glowed with a soothing green light. Was that a leftover of the power from Vanamate's tears? Without hesitation, she whizzed over, cupped her hands and dipped them into the water. The fluid remained in the lake. Juma was close to crying when she noticed that some of the glow clung to her fingers. She dipped her hands in again, and the glow intensified. As fast as she could, she gathered her hands full with the magical glow and whizzed back to the hut.

A tiny flame hissed in the thatched roof. Juma landed beside it. The green light in her hands killed the fire. She lifted her hands, gathered her magic and made it flow into her fingers to merge it with Vanamate's power. Closing her eyes, she imagined the green glow stretching and flowing out from her hands. She wanted to form a dome over the hut. With every thump of her mother's drum, she pulled at the glowing magic. It was a strange feeling. Her fingers tingled and her hair frizzed. Building the dome seemed to take ages. Finally, her magic insisted she was done. Juma opened her eyes and looked at her handiwork. To her eyes, a greenish glow encompassed the hut. The warriors had stopped at the barrier, three feet from the door. They weren't able to push through, no matter how hard they tried.

"This won't hold long." Mubuntu shook a fist at her. "As soon as the sun is high enough, I'll shatter this flimsy structure."

Juma knew he'd do just that, but didn't acknowledge his words. She only sank through the roof. The safety dome let her through without any problem. Her family had already noticed that no one could come in and was speculating on the reason, but her father cut everyone short.

"It doesn't matter why they can't come in. It doesn't matter whether it's Vanamate's blessing or a spell from Juma or Selenta. Fact is, it will buy us the time we need. Although personally I think it was Juma's doing. Somehow I've got the feeling she's with us right now."

Juma would have hugged him publicly if she had been able to. For a man, her father was unusually perceptive. She peeked through the blanket that covered the door.

Kandra had withdrawn her warriors and sent the villagers back to bed. Juma only saw a few stragglers shuffle away. It was eerie how fast they had all left. For now, her family was safe.

Of course. She slapped her forehead. I can use the same kind of magic to protect our bodies. She hurried back to the lake and filled her hands with the green glow again. When she was done, nothing of the soothing light remained. This was her only chance. As fast as she could, she sped to the mountain, and was nearly halfway there when Mubuntu's well-known firetail streaked across the sky. He seemed to be looking for her. Instinctively she accelerated, awed by the fact that she could go still faster. She had to make it back to her mother.

The summit grew nearer and the firetail's zigzagging more frantic. A howl of rage pierced the night. Juma wondered why Mubuntu hadn't discovered her yet. The light in her hands should have alerted him right away. Instead, it seemed to deflect him whenever he came closer. Thankful for the protection, Juma sped back toward the mountain, knowing she had bought them some more time. It felt good to know that she had grown more competent over the last few days.

Surprised with herself, Juma admitted that she liked using magic despite the fact that no one saw her doing it. Not even Netinu. Maybe it wasn't all that important what the others thought of her after all. With a satisfied smile, she landed beside her body. Humming a little song to herself, she lifted her hands and spread Vanamate's power with her magic, growing it into a second dome above her. This one stayed a lot smaller than the one she had built to encompass the hut, but it was big enough to protect the four people sitting inside. With her eyes closed, she could feel its smooth fabric, but when she opened them, the dome was invisible.

At that moment, her mother stopped drumming, and she woke, back in her human shell.

"Thank Vanamate, you're back safely." Netinu helped her into a sitting position.

"What's more, I have found a way to protect our bodies from Mubuntu and Chunte." Juma explained about the dome. She also told them about the pending sacrifice and the tribe's new chieftess. "Kandra has teamed up with Mubuntu. I'm loath to say it, but we will need to take care of her once we're back, or she'll turn into another Chunte."

Netinu stared at his hands and sighed. "I am feeling sorry for her. She has always been unhappy. Struggling to please a mother who clearly preferred my company, she grew bitter over the years."

"I understand her anger, but it doesn't excuse the cruelties she's planning." Juma put her hand on his shoulder. "We will have to stop her."

"Whatever you do, wherever you go, I will be yours to command." Netinu looked into her eyes and took her hands. "When I picked you as the most likely woman to annoy my sister, I never expected to fall in love with you. But that's what happened. My heart will be yours forever. I will give my life to be with you, and I will do whatever you need me to do. Without you, my world will not be complete."

Juma's jaw dropped. She had guessed as much, but the way he phrased it made her feel as if the ground had suddenly disappeared from beneath her feet. She stammered, trying to find a fitting reply. Under no circumstances would she tell him the truth, though. She couldn't admit that she was in love with him too. It would jeopardize their mission.

"We need to free Vanamate." Staring at her hands, enveloped by his, she knew she sounded flat, but she just couldn't face him.

Her mother laughed and put her hand on Juma's and Netinu's joined fingers. "Give her a little time, Netinu. She's never been very good at solving problems when her emotions take over."

Netinu nodded, something Juma only felt because his hands moved on hers. She didn't dare to look up, but she didn't pull her hands away either.

"We'll have to bring the rain back to our lands now." Gently she pried her fingers free. "Lie down on your backs and wait for me to pull you out of your bodies. That way, we can all go together but only one of us as a spirit-soul," she said to Selto and Netinu.

Netinu grinned at her. "You're brilliant." He lay back and closed his eyes.

Selto stared at the ground. "Shouldn't I stay behind to protect you from Chunte and her men?"

"The dome is taking care of that."

"What if it fails?"

"It should hold long enough."

Selto looked up at her. "Don't you understand? I don't want to leave my body. It scares me like nothing has ever scared me before. I know I owe you my life, but please spare me this ordeal."

A feeling rose in Juma that she hadn't had in a very long time. First a barely audible chuckle, it grew and grew into a full-bellied guffaw. All her bottled-up emotions, her anxiety and fear dissolved in her laughter. She doubled over. Selto looked hurt.

"Sorry." Juma clutched her sides. She spoke in bursts coupled with chortling. "I'm not laughing about you. It's just that I'm sometimes so blind. It's so funny." She crossed her legs not to wet herself. Trying to get a handle on her giggling, she forced herself to breathe deeply. When she finally calmed down, she tried to explain her outburst. "All my life I though that men, and especially warriors, didn't have to fight fear or loneliness. I should have known better. I am really sorry I laughed, Selto, but it was more about my ignorance than about your plight. Of course you can stay here. If you don't feel comfortable about coming along, I'd be as bad as Chunte if I forced you."

Selto's face relaxed and he smiled. It lit up his features considerably. "I will make sure that your bodies will be here when you return."

"Thank you." Juma stood up and walked toward the gate. The fear she had felt when she faced it before was gone. It had been washed away by her laughing fit. Juma was ready to face whatever waited for her on the other side.

Her mother followed her. Just before Juma stepped between the two stone pillars, she put a hand on her shoulder. "As a spirit-soul, you're a full person and Mubuntu can't harm you directly. But he will try to confuse you, so beware. Also, you need to take good care of Netinu, who will be vulnerable as a spirit only. Mubuntu might try to prevent him from returning to his body."

Juma didn't look at her mother when she put something into words she hadn't dared to voice before. "I'll take good care of him. I'd be devastated if he got hurt."

"A good choice. He reminds me a lot of your father." Her mother's voice was so soft, Juma knew she was smiling. Then her tone changed. "Now, remember that you don't have to hurry. A spirit-soul is not affected by time in the gods' realm. I shall see you when you return." Her mother's hand lay warm and comforting on her shoulder. Then she pushed. Hard.

Juma stumbled forward. For a fleeting moment, there was nothing but the steep cliff and air below her, then the world twisted and her feet hit the ground. She looked around. Except for an ochre tinge, it was still the same world as before. Even the bag with Mubuntu's hand still hung from her belt. The gate was still there, as were Netinu, Selto, and her mother, who had pulled Juma's lifeless body back and was laying it on the ground gently. The dome glowed in a satisfying green, and inside it the colors seemed almost normal.

Scanning the area for Mubuntu's telltale fire, Juma glanced down. The god wasn't anywhere in sight, but through the translucent ground beneath her feet she could see a head the size of the mountain. The eyes were closed, and the sleeper's body spread into the distance. She swallowed and tiptoed back to fetch Netinu. She didn't want to accidentally wake the Nameless.

She slammed into a barrier, stumbled backward and nearly fell. When she regained her composure, she reached out with her hands. The blue dome repelled her fingers.

"But this is my dome," she said. Her words floated away like silent echoes. She closed her eyes and gathered magic to push through, but the dome sucked up her magic without letting her enter. Then she remembered that she'd only been inside of the domes so far.

"In that case, I will go without Netinu." Silently relieved that he would be as safe as possible, she turned and faced the mountain. It rose steeply, and she couldn't see the summit. Not a single tree or bush was visible against the orange-brown sky. Little flames of light danced on its flanks, and somewhere to the side, a big light shone with a mild blue glow.

## 22

$\mathcal{J}$UMA TRIED TO TAKE OFF, but her spirit-soul wouldn't fly. Another disadvantage, she thought and began to slowly climb the mountain. If she remembered correctly, Vanamate was somewhere close to the summit. She had barely taken a few steps when a voice rang out behind her.

"Wait for me, Juma!"

She turned and watched Netinu run after her. Her heart contracted so painfully she clutched her chest. Past him, near the gate, she saw his body crumple to the ground. Selto picked it up and carried it over to her own body.

"Why did you come?" Her words sounded hollow as if uttered by a ghost. Strictly speaking, she was a ghost, a spirit-soul. And so was Netinu. She swallowed and shooed him away. "Go back as long as you still can."

He stopped in front of her and shook his head. "I promised to come with you wherever you go. I am not going to break my promise." He cocked his head and looked at her with his puppy-dog eyes. "Why didn't you come and get me like you said you would?"

Juma shoulders sagged. After she had explained about her inability to enter the dome, she turned and started to climb. He fell in beside her. They walked in silence for a while.

"Do you think we should investigate the small fires ahead of us?" Netinu pointed forward.

Juma shrugged. "Whatever gods or spirits they are, they might be in league with Mubuntu."

"All the more reason to see what they're up to."

She knew he was right but didn't want to admit it, so she walked on in silence. Step by step, she stomped up the mountain. Soon the first of the fires drew near. Remembering how far it had seemed to be away, she stopped and looked back. The dome had disappeared, and nothing behind her looked even vaguely familiar. Despair swallowed her heart like a black wave. Only now did she understand what loneliness really meant. Despite Netinu's proximity, she felt utterly alone. She had lost the most valuable thing in life — her body. Biting her lower lip, she turned to face ahead. She had chosen this path, and she would walk it to the bitter end, making sure that Netinu would emerge unscathed. She continued climbing toward the first fire, discovering tiny shadows that couldn't be anything but people. Suddenly it occurred to her that she wasn't exhausted despite the steep slope. She glanced sideways, but Netinu showed no sign of exhaustion either.

"You know, walking without a body is quite invigorating," he said. He must have noticed the same. Juma marveled at how often they thought along the same lines regardless of their differences in gender, upbringing, and social status. Maybe it was time to make him see how much she trusted him. She smiled at him.

"Will you spy on the people around the fire or shall I?"

A smile lit up Netinu's face — literally. It radiated a golden light that warmed her through and through. A figure with a similarly glowing face stepped away from the fire and approached them.

"Welcome." He neither seemed surprised to see them, nor did he appear to be dangerous. "We've been waiting for you. Come with me."

Reluctantly Juma followed him. Netinu, still glowing, walked beside her. Tentatively he reached for her hand, and she allowed him to take it. It just wouldn't do to let him know how much she needed his support right now. What if the strangers were Mubuntu's allies?

He squeezed her hand and turned to the stranger. "Who are you? The elders never told us about you."

The stranger smiled back at him.

"They sure did. We," he encompassed all the fires on the endless mountain slope with his gesture, "are the stars."

With a start, Juma realized why her mother had reminded her of the story she had told her before her death. Curious, she looked around.

The stranger stood with a group of men and women beside a fire that flickered with blue and white flames. Countless people sat around it. Juma blinked away her tears as best she could. A woman smiled at her. She looked very familiar.

"Don't be too harsh on yourself, darling," she said. "Only children know instinctively how to love without expecting anything in return. Come, sit with me."

Juma didn't know why, but sitting with the woman seemed the only logical thing to do. She let go of Netinu and sat. Still, her gaze followed the young warrior until he settled beside a man who looked just like him.

The woman at her side smiled. "Don't worry about Netinu. He's taking to my son, his great-grandfather on his mother's side."

"So, you're my great-great-grandmother?"

The woman nodded. "Monnatoba told us to help you if we found you worthy." She nodded at Netinu. "You've chosen well, little one. He will do great for the tribe without asking for a reward. It will be up to you to give him his heart's desire."

"I will. I promised myself before I started to climb this mountain." Juma thought she knew what her ancestor was referring to, but she was wrong.

"I'm not talking about seeing him back to his body safely. You will understand his longing when you understand his heart. Trust me." The woman patted her knee, and Juma felt comforted and loved. The time would come when the woman's words would make more sense than they did now; she was sure of it. Then she remembered their mission.

"We've got to leave now. We need to free Vanamate urgently."

"There is time still. Remember that this is the mountain of the gods. You will face some tests before you can reach the summit." The woman pointed to the fire. "Do you see the thread of gold in the blue? Fetch it for me."

Juma stared into the flames, and truly, there was a golden flame amongst the blue ones. It didn't dance quite as merrily as the others. In its graceful movement it reminded Juma of the rushes at their lake swaying in the wind. She gathered her magic to push the blue flames aside, but they didn't budge. She hadn't expected anything else. With a sigh, she accepted that she faced only two options. She could either refuse to put her hand into the fire, since it was potentially dangerous. With that reaction, she would prove good judgment, or wouldn't she? The second option would be to grab the golden flame. If this was a test of trust, her ancestor wouldn't allow her to get hurt. But what if she misinterpreted the intentions of the test? One thing seemed quite sure though: Her ancestor was not trying to trick her. She was not in league with Mubuntu.

She glanced at Netinu, but the fire flared up and obscured him. She was on her own. Breathing deeply to calm herself, she swallowed and tried to ignore the sweat on her forehead. Surely it was from the heat of the fire. She braced herself and decided to trust her ancestor. Holding her breath, she reached into the fire to grab the golden flame. Like a gentle wind, the blue fire caressed her fingers. She let out her breath and picked her target like a flower. The flame tingled in her fingers but didn't burn her either.

Smiling, she held it out to her ancestor.

"Trust doesn't come easy to you," her great-great-grandmother said with a smile. "Try to believe in your own judgment a bit more, and trust those you love."

Juma nodded, still holding out the flickering light.

"Keep it. Take it to Monnatoba. Unconditional love will always douse Mubuntu's greed."

Although she didn't know what her ancestor meant, Juma thought about stuffing the flame into the bag at her skirt that still held Mubuntu's hand. She decided against it. Carrying the fire in her hand wouldn't tire her—nothing seemed to, as long as she didn't have a body that could tire—and she needed Mubuntu's hand to stay unblemished. It was the last thing she had to keep him at bay.

Netinu put a hand on her shoulder. "We need to go now," he said.

She looked up. He carried a similar flame as she did, except that his was silver. He helped her up and they walked away from the fire.

The great-great-grandmother and her son waved after them; the others still didn't take any notice.

Hand in hand, they climbed the mountain. Juma enjoyed walking beside Netinu. It was so peaceful, especially since the steep climb didn't affect them the way it would on Earth. No hard breathing, no cramping leg muscles… she felt great.

After a while, Netinu turned to the side. She stopped.

"We need to go up, not around."

"The ancestor said we need to see Monnatoba." He looked into her eyes, and her knees grew weak. If love does that to me every time our eyes meet, I'll never be able to become good at anything. I'd be distracted all the time. She pulled herself together and followed him.

It didn't take them long to reach a rocky outcrop at the mountain's side. The soothing glow of Monnatoba drowned out the little light their flames shed. Netinu stepped around the outcrop first, but Juma stumbled into him when she followed. He'd stopped abruptly. She peeked around him, and her jaw dropped.

They stood at the rim of a gigantic circular plain that bordered on the steep slope they had just climbed. To their left, another cliff rose high into the sky. The plain was completely devoid of anything. There weren't even any rocks protruding from the ground. It was as flat as if it someone had deliberately leveled it out, and it was as semi-transparent as the rest of the mountain they had climbed. Way below, Juma could see the world she remembered. She had never seen anything like it before. The plain was bathed in the silver light of a big, round orb that hovered just out of reach. It rotated slowly, but the face it displayed was always the same.

"Welcome, travelers." Monnatoba's voice seemed to come from everywhere, but most of all from inside their own hearts. "I am so glad that you will attempt to free my sister. It will not be an easy task."

Juma caught herself faster than Netinu. She held out her flame. "My great-great-grandmother told me to take this to you."

"You have done well then. Hand it to those in the shadow."

Juma looked around. There was so much light, she couldn't make out any shadows. But when she examined the cliff more closely, she discovered the entrance to a cave in the side of the mountain. She took a tentative step toward it.

Monnatoba chuckled. "Do not worry. This cave will not lead to our father's sleeping place. Also, you will not have to go in very far. They will come when they see the light."

She was right. Juma stepped into the cave, and the brightness dimmed to a bearable semi-darkness. Interestingly enough, the walls and ground of the cave were not semi-transparent. While her eyes adjusted, Juma wondered about this until she felt Netinu step close to her. When she could see again, several women were approaching them. The foremost bowed and wordlessly held out her hands. Juma sucked in her lips. Should she really give her precious light to a stranger? Well, there was nothing else to do. No one disobeyed a goddess. Reluctantly she handed the flame over, as did Netinu.

The woman turned to her companions. In silence, they formed a circle. The woman merged the flames and kneaded them in her hands until they resembled a ball. She threw it to a woman on the opposite side of the circle. The end of a thin, glowing thread stayed in her hand. The woman on the other side passed it on to another woman, throwing it across the circle. Again and again, a woman passed the ball to someone on the other side, and threads of light began to fill the circle. The women worked silently, and Juma and Netinu watched, fascinated.

To — fro — left — right — and back again, the ball spun. It grew smaller and smaller until nothing was left. The women moved their arms up and down, and the blanket of light they had created swung like a giant wing through the air. Sparks shot in all directions, drifting deeper into the cave. When the fabric had lost most of its glow, the women deftly folded it up. The woman who had taken the flames from them carried the pile of material back to Juma.

"Use it wisely," she said. "And thank you for bringing us more light."

Confused, Juma looked up and discovered that the cave was much brighter than it had been before. When she turned back to ask what it all meant, the woman and all her companions had vanished.

"What a strange experience," she whispered.

Netinu agreed. "Shall I carry the cloth? It looks rather heavy."

"But it isn't. We can take turns, since I assume we're meant to take it to Vanamate next. Maybe it will help us to wake her."

They left the cave and looked at Monnatoba. The orb emanated a feeling of warmth and happiness. "I am looking forward to seeing my sister again."

Scared of her own daring, Juma stepped forward. "May I ask you a favor?"

Monnatoba laughed. It sounded like silver bells ringing. "If you manage to free my sister, I will grant you one wish. But it has to be something I can give or do."

"I know what I want." Juma's throat felt parched although she didn't really have a throat to dry out right now.

"Tell me, and I will grant the wish as soon as my sister's tears rain down on our mother."

Gathering all her courage, Juma said, "I want my mother to come home with us."

The big orb darkened slightly as if a black cloud had passed over it. "I am sorry, but I cannot fulfill your wish, as much as I'd like to. Your mother died in your place all those years ago. She does not have a body to return to."

Juma's heart plummeted. She longed to hug her mother again, and it would have been a pleasure to watch her take the crown back from Jakombe. And her father would have been able to smile again, something he hadn't done in a long, long while. And her brothers… they'd probably sing for joy — well, at least dance.

"Can't you create a new body for her?" She didn't dare to hope.

"Only Mother could, and she won't. She is very strict about keeping the laws." Monnatoba sounded apologetic. "All I could do is create a temporary body which will last the three days when I'm at my fullest."

A spark of hope grew in Juma's heart. "Could you create her that kind of body once a month for as long as my father lives? Having her three days a month is still better than not having her at all."

Monnatoba stayed silent.

Juma shifted the fabric onto one arm and put the freed hand on her chest. "I grew up without her, missing her every single day. I always thought she had deserted me somehow, until I learned that she saved my life. There are so many words unsaid, so many songs unsung, so many stories that need to be told. Please have mercy."

Monnatoba sighed. "It is a difficult decision because it runs against our laws. When someone dies, he or she is supposed to stay dead. I already ran a high risk when I allowed your mother to help you just now. Raising the dead can destroy Mother Earth's fragile balance."

"Mubuntu already unbalanced everything without thinking twice about the results," Netinu said quietly.

Monnatoba hesitated before she spoke. "I will have to talk to Vanamate about it."

"Thank you." Juma knew that this was the best she would get at the moment.

The ground shook slightly.

"I wish Mubuntu would stop teasing Father. With Vanamate asleep, there is no one who can calm him if he wakes." Monnatoba's voice was filled with fear.

Juma swallowed. If the goddess was scared of her father, he must be too terrible to behold for humans. She really needed to free Vanamate, before the whole world would drown in chaos and fire. She cleared her throat.

"We'd better go."

Monnatoba agreed. "And don't dawdle. Free my sister, so I can be with her again."

Juma nodded. Together with Netinu, she left the plain and walked up the slope they had traveled before. It unnerved her that the ground was semi- transparent, so she kept looking up. Way above them, the ochre sky reflected a reddish shine. That must be the place they were heading for. The ground shook again, and Juma glanced down at the Nameless. He twitched in his sleep, and his eyelids fluttered. She shivered. Netinu caught up to her.

"I don't like to admit this," he said, "but I am scared. It must be really hard to be a witch and live with this the whole time." His gesture encompassed the world around them.

Off the top of her head, Juma wanted to agree, but then paused to think first. Was being a witch really that bad? There was so much beauty in the spirit world. Facing the danger seemed worth the risk if it meant she could help people. The drawback was the need to stay a virgin, but Selenta obviously had managed it well enough. No, being a witch wasn't very hard; it just wasn't something Juma wanted to do her whole life. As a chieftess, she would have much more power and more opportunities to help her tribesmen.

The ground shook again, and Juma stumbled. When Netinu grabbed her arm and steadied her, a bolt of lightning went through her arm.

"Well, well, well! Correct me if I'm wrong, but do I detect desire?" Mubuntu's snicker made the hairs on her arms rise.

Juma straightened and glared at him. "I though we'd lost you for a while," she said. "Why the pretended friendliness all of a sudden?"

"Now that you're in my world, nothing can stop me from doing with you as I please." He stepped closer and walked around her, trailing a finger along her jawbone.

Netinu shoved his hand away, but he couldn't rid Juma of the fire that raced through her body toward her loins. She bit her lip. There was no way she would allow Mubuntu to play with her as if she were one of his pets. Apropos pets! Since he was here, Chunte would surely be close. She looked around but couldn't see the princess.

"I love desire. It's the strongest emotion of mankind. Stronger even than hunger or thirst." Mubuntu's finger glided over Netinu's loincloth, which bulged immediately. Juma forced herself not to look. Fighting her bodily reactions, she focused on the heat dæmon.

"You cannot hurt us."

"That's not true. But I prefer to fire up what's already there anyway." He grinned.

Netinu grabbed Juma's shoulders and turned her to face him. "It is true, I do desire you, but not in the way the dæmon suggests. I want you more than I ever wanted anything in my life. I long to be part of your life, treasured and loved. I would cherish you any way I can."

"I know." Juma smiled at him, forcing herself to ignore the growing longing in her loins. Heat bubbled between her thighs like molten lava. She focused on what she had to say. Finally she felt ready to face her feelings. "I want you to be part of my life. I need you like Mother Earth needs Vanamate's tears. If we survive this, I will gladly join our lives the way tradition requests. But I refuse to give in to his magic. I will not lay with you in the way of dumb animals. Desire is not the same as love, is it?"

"No, it isn't." Netinu turned to the heat dæmon. "Let us past. You have no power over us. You might be able to rouse our bodies, but you cannot…"

We don't have bodies here. We're nothing but spirit-souls. The thought flashed through Juma like lightning, and the hunger in her loins and the heat between her thighs vanished as if they had never been there. She relaxed, and Netinu looked at her in surprise. She smiled up at him. "He cannot use our bodies against us as long as we keep remembering that we are without them at the moment. Our spirits and our souls are out of his control. Mother told me, but I didn't understand."

He beamed at her. "Let's go and finish what we came for."

Hand in hand, they walked upwards toward the summit past Mubuntu. He howled in rage, and a wall of fire shot up in front of them.

## 23

"I MIGHT NOT BE ABLE to control your spirit-souls, but I can surely destroy them," he screamed.

Juma stopped when the heat slammed into her face. It hurt like a bodily beating. She turned back to the dæmon. "What do you want?"

"You have something I need, and I'm prepared to give you something you need in exchange for it."

"I won't give you your hand. There's no use in asking." Juma crossed her arms in front of her chest.

"I would set Selenta free."

Mubuntu's offer was tempting. Juma missed the old witch's wisdom, and it cut her heart that she didn't know how to free her, but they had a bigger goal. "I will only return your hand if you release Vanamate."

"You will do no such thing." Before Mubuntu could answer, Chunte showed up beside him.

To Juma, she looked strangely transparent, just like the ground. It stuck her that Chunte hadn't come as a spirit-soul. Despite the risk, she was on a spirit journey again.

"Since when does a woman have the right to order a god around?" Juma asked.

"He's a man too. His power is mine to command." Chunte glared at her.

Kandra stepped forward from the shadows of a rock. "He is much more than just a man, or the means to more power. You never understood him the way I do."

"He's mine," Chunte said.

"You can't own a god." Kandra walked closer. "You can only bind him with love."

"You know nothing of love."

"More than you ever will."

"Ladies, my heart is big enough for both of you." Mubuntu's words were drowned by Kandra's and Chunte's screeching.

Netinu tugged at Juma's hair and whispered in her ear. "Look, he's distracted. If we hurry, we can get past the wall of fire without him noticing."

Juma nodded, and they hurried onward. Glancing over her shoulder at the bitching woman for a last time, she walked around the barrier and hurried after Netinu. It wasn't much farther to the summit. They ran as fast as their spirit-souls could, and the pinpoint of red light grew with every step.

Kandra and Chunte's squabbling filled the air and bit into Juma's ears. Although individual words melted into unintelligible babbling, the women's hate was almost tangible.

The fire ahead grew to the size of a pea. Then it became the size of a normal campfire, a bonfire. When it became a blaze, the ground leveled and Juma finally could make out the fiery bars of Selenta's cage.

At that point, Mubuntu's voice rose through the woman's fighting. "They're escaping with my hand. Stop them. Right now!"

His words were followed by loud barking. Juma glanced over her shoulder. Kandra and Chunte ran after them. Their heads had turned into dogs' heads, and they snapped at each other as they rushed forward.

Juma was trying to move faster when the ground shook again. She stumbled and fell. In getting up, she looked back. Now Chunte and Kandra had fully turned into dogs.

Netinu grabbed her arm. Together they stumbled forward, coping with the shaking ground as best they could. The dogs didn't have any trouble at all. The only reason they didn't catch up with them was the fact that they kept fighting every so often, biting and clawing at each other.

Juma was very glad when they reached the top of the mountain. The ring of fire seemed like an old friend. She hurried to Selenta in her burning cage and told her what had happened.

"Put up a shield if you can," the witch said. "Then figure out a way to douse the fire so you can wake Vanamate."

"But they might attack you to cause us pain." Juma bent as far forward as she could without touching the cage's bars.

The witch smiled. "I don't think they'd dare. Mubuntu did a very good job of keeping humans on a spirit journey from destroying this cage." She lifted her arms. Blisters and burned skin covered hands and wrists. Juma had to bite her lip not to cry out.

"I'm so sorry," she said.

"If you free Vanamate, she will free me and set things right." Selenta waved her away. "Hurry!"

Although she didn't feel like singing at all, Juma hummed a song to gather her magic as she walked over to Netinu. He stood as close to the burning circle as he dared and looked at the sleeping goddess.

"You resemble her a lot," he said.

Juma blushed, but before she could answer, a ravel of arms, legs, and paws rolled onto the flat area in front of the fire. Juma threw up her shield, since Mubuntu extracted himself fairly quickly from the tangle. He kicked the dogs in the ribs.

"Stop fighting and get my hand!"

The dogs obeyed reluctantly and hurled themselves at the invisible barrier Juma had erected. She felt them bite and claw their way through, so she hummed louder.

"We don't have much time before they break through," she said. "We need to get to Vanamate now. Last time Selenta covered the ring with soil."

Netinu began to dig, while Juma concentrated on keeping up the shield.

"You!" Mubuntu stepped as close to the barrier as he could and pointed at Juma with the index finger of the hand he still had. "I will set the witch's spirit free if you give me what I want."

"You'll get the hand in exchange for Vanamate, nothing else."

"I would add your cousin's sanity to the bargain. Chunte's too far gone already, but Kandra can be saved." His voice sounded so gentle, caring, that Juma's eyelids began to droop. She stumbled, and the blanket she got from the stars slipped off her arm. Luckily her shield still held. Clasping her hands over her ears to block out the heat dæmon's voice, she hummed louder.

Netinu tugged at her loincloth. She saw his lips move, but didn't dare to take her hands down. He pointed at the blanket, and her gaze followed his finger. An edge of the delicate fabric had tumbled into the fire.

It didn't burn.

Juma couldn't believe her eyes. The fabric wasn't affected one bit by the blaze.

"Cover the fire with it," she called to Netinu. He nodded and grabbed the fabric. Juma closed her eyes and kept singing, but she felt the strength of her shield ebb away. Her heart beat faster, and she started to sweat although she didn't have a real body. The strain to keep up the shield was tiring her. She was grateful when Netinu's hand led her away from the snarling dogs. She took down her hands and opened her eyes as they walked to the bridge of material the stars had given them.

"I had to fold it several times because the fire does get through after a while," Netinu said.

The bridge was just big enough to reach from their side of the circle to its center. Side by side, they stepped through the narrow opening. Juma's shield shattered when it touched the fiery ring, so she pressed against Netinu, trying to avoid the flames that reached for her. Her throat was dry and her heart raced until a wet and cooling breeze caressed her face. They had reached Vanamate.

The goddess sat on a stone chair in the center of the ring, frowning in her sleep. Tears still ran over her face and pooled around her feet, where they evaporated. Stepping forward, Juma reached out for her. Behind her, the dogs barked angrily. They sounded so close that Juma turned instinctively. Kandra had just put both front paws on the bridge of material. Snarling, she had just stepped forward when the flames whooshed up, swallowing the star's material and the backside of her spirit. Juma screamed, jumped forward, and dragged the charred body into the circle.

Kandra lay panting. Slowly, she turned back into a human.

"It doesn't hurt," she whispered. "Why doesn't it hurt?"

Juma didn't know. Would the pain hit her when she returned to her body? Or didn't it hurt because the damage was too severe? Would Kandra's spirit survive? And what would happen to her body if it didn't?

"Why am I here?" Kandra frowned. "I want Mother."

Juma forgot about the trouble her cousin had caused. Right now, right here, Kandra was nothing but a badly wounded person, and one related to her. She wished she could do something for her cousin.

"Why is it so hot here? I want to go home." Kandra tried to sit up, but couldn't. "I'm thirsty."

Before Juma could react, Netinu stepped closer, his hands cupped and filled with Vanamate's tears. He bent down, and Juma knelt beside Kandra to help her drink. Would the tears heal her like Tolobe?

"Yuck, it's warm." Kandra pulled a face, but she didn't begin to convulse.

"It's all there is at the moment. We need to kill the flames first." Netinu crouched beside her too and took her hand. Kandra still didn't show any sign of convulsions, so Juma assumed that the healing only worked on the body she had left behind. She swallowed a tear. As nasty as her cousin had been, it didn't seem right that she should die here.

"I'm so tired." Kandra leaned against her brother. "Tell Mother I love her. I just wish she could have cared for me the way she did for you."

"I care for you." Netinu pressed her close. "You just never noticed."

Kandra smiled. Then she sighed and fell asleep. Netinu lowered her gently to the ground. Juma fought back her tears.

"You're the best, Netinu." Her voice sounded pressed and strained.

"What do you think will happen to her body if she dies up here?" He looked at Juma with burning eyes, and it hurt her to admit that she didn't know. She leaned her head against his shoulder.

For a while they sat in silence and watched Kandra breathe. It seemed to be a peaceful slumber because she smiled.

"I'm going to make Mubuntu pay for this." Juma got up and walked as close to the barrier of fire as she dared and strained to see through the flames.

On the other side, Mubuntu and Chunte seemed to be quarreling. The heat dæmon pointed to the ring of fire again and again, but the dog refused to obey regardless of the kicks and pushes.

"Why don't you come here yourself?" Juma's call drowned out the roaring of the fire. "Don't you dare to walk through your own element? Or are you scared of waking Vanamate?"

The ground shook again. Mubuntu stumbled, and the dog that used to be Chunte used her chance. Her canines dug deeply into his calf. He screamed, and the flames of the ring shot up and thickened until Juma couldn't see the other side any more. The heat increased so much she had to step back. Still, she did wonder what was going on outside the ring.

She bumped into Netinu, and he put an arm around her. Glad for his silent support, she turned to the sleeping goddess. Somehow Vanamate seemed smaller than before, barely larger than a human. Had she shrunk?

"What do we have to do to wake her?" Netinu asked.

"I don't know. I thought she'd wake as soon as we're here." Juma stepped closer to the goddess and laid a hand on her arm. It was cool to the touch but didn't resemble human skin one bit. It was more like touching a smooth stone or the surface of a lake. What were gods made of? Juma shook the arm gently.

"Please, Vanamate, wake up."

The goddess didn't react. She sat silently, slightly bent over, and the evaporating tears from the puddles on the ground filled the air with warm moisture.

"Wake up!" Juma shook harder, but nothing changed.

"Maybe we need to try something different." Netinu stepped forward and gently kissed the goddess's cheek. Nothing. He shrugged. "Sorry, but I thought it worth a try. It always seems to work in stories."

"I'm glad I fell for a man with brains." Juma smiled at him, surprised she wasn't jealous. He blushed.

"Try her mouth," she said.

Netinu pulled a face but lifted the goddess's chin nonetheless. His lips touched hers, and again nothing happened. Carefully, Netinu let the head sink back to its previous position and wiped the wetness from his face.

"What else can we try?"

Juma sat down and looked up to the sleeping, weeping goddess. She looked like a statue, sad and gray. Maybe if she cheered her up. Juma started to sing one of the funny stories her mother used to sing to her when she was still a child. Netinu sat beside her and joined in. Their voices fitted in perfect harmony. Juma began to infuse the melody with magic, filling it with merriment and happiness. Gently, she aimed her spell at Vanamate but the expression on the goddess's face didn't change.

"It doesn't seem to do much," Netinu said when their song was over. "We could try to make a racket."

"I bet she won't wake up then either. We're overlooking something." Juma stared at the goddess and pondered the situation. If only she had asked Selenta how to wake Vanamate.

Netinu touched her shoulder. "Look, the kikoi the stars gave us hasn't burned after all."

She turned. True enough. Although the flames surrounded the material, it remained intact.

"Maybe we can wake Vanamate with it." Netinu crouched low and tugged at a corner untouched by fire. Bit by bit, he pulled the fabric from the blaze. The flames died in the humid air. When he held the whole kikoi in his hands, Juma got up and helped him to drape it around the goddess's shoulders.

Vanamate shifted, and a smile spread over her cheeks. Her tears intensified and filled the pools on the ground faster, but her eyes remained closed. Juma's frustration was big enough that she wanted to scream. However, she kept her temper.

"What now?" She looked at Netinu, but he only shrugged.

Vanamate moved again, and the kikoi slipped from her shoulders. It floated to the ground and covered Kandra. The mutilated spirit sucked up the material like dry soil the rain. Juma's jaw dropped. When Kandra's spirit had absorbed the whole kikoi, her legs looked like legs again. Although they where shorter than they used to be, the crisp blackness of the burning had gone. The whole girl had changed a lot. Instead of a burnt young woman, a child, barely more than seven summers, lay curled up. She sighed and smiled in her sleep.

"Unconditional love." Netinu slapped his forehead. "That's what she needed all along."

"I don't understand." Juma looked up at him.

"Mother always loved me just the way I was. She never expected much of me. After all, I was nothing but a boy. It was different for Kandra. Mother was never pleased with anything she did. Kandra only got advice on how to improve. I think not getting praised can make a person very bitter."

"So she hated you because your mother didn't love her?"

"I'm sure Mother loves her. She just never showed it to Kandra."

Juma's heart softened when she imagined how hard it had to be for a child eager to please her mother but getting rebuffed every time.

"We need to wake Vanamate and dowse the fire so I can take her spirit home," Netinu said.

Juma nodded, but before she could come up with another idea how to wake Vanamate, something shot out of the flames toward them. The charred body of a dog landed at Juma's feet with a thud. Juma's hands flew to her mouth.

Netinu nudged the cadaver. Chunte was dead.

Juma and he looked at each other, open-mouthed. Although she felt slightly sorry for the princess, Juma was also relieved since it meant one fewer opponent to fight. She wondered what would happen to Chunte's body now that her spirit was dead.

"That will happen to you too." The voice of fire cackled and laughed. "Or something even worse. Don't you know that water can kill too?"

When Juma looked up, Mubuntu danced inside the flames and sang. He made the inferno swell. The flames at the top neared each other, forming a dome over the captured. It grew hotter inside the circle. Netinu put his arms around Juma. Her skin tingled, and she felt protected. Together they stepped closer to Vanamate. Juma noticed that the ground had dried; the increasing heat vaporized the goddess's tears faster. Soon the air around them was filled with steam.

Mubuntu shot a lance of fire toward the couple. It hissed in the wet air and died. He jumped up and down angrily, and Juma pulled Netinu back another step. Now they nearly stood on Vanamate's toes. Mubuntu attacked again and again, but his fire always died.

Netinu stepped forward, picked up his sister's spirit, and carried her back to Juma. Together, they laid her at Vanamate's feet.

"Why is he attacking us?" Netinu asked. "We can't wake Vanamate, and we can't get back out either without the star's kikoi."

Something tugged at Juma's mind, but she couldn't concentrate with Netinu so close. Perspiration ran over his body, and Juma licked her lips. His smell was intoxicating. Drops of sweat burned in her eyes, and she blinked them away. Why were things so difficult? She closed her eyes and tried to focus her thoughts.

As driven by his urges as Mubuntu was, he could well be attacking them because he was vengeful. But if there was a different reason for his attack, what did it mean? In which way could they be dangerous for him? Concentrating became harder the more the air filled with moisture. Juma tried to breathe less deeply. The hot wetness of the air burned in her chest. She tried to stop breathing at all, but found it impossible. It surprised her that she had to respire although she had left her body behind.

"The air is better here." Netinu pulled her down. He was right. It was easier to take in air sitting on the ground.

Laughing like a maniac, Mubuntu danced in the flames and reached with fiery fingers for Vanamate. If he went on doing that, it wouldn't take much longer for them to suffocate. Juma ground her teeth. If only she could wake the goddess. There had to be something they could do or Mubuntu wouldn't be so determined to kill them one way or the other.

"Didn't you forget your hand?" she called, but Mubuntu didn't answer. He kept dancing.

Breathing became harder, so Juma lay down beside Netinu. Her arm touched his, and her skin tingled, making it even more difficult to concentrate. She knew she was overlooking something vital, but her feelings interfered with her thinking. It reminded her that she only lived once. How could the stars ask her for unconditional love, when losing Netinu made her heart cramp? She had to think of a way to wake the goddess, or these would be the last conscious minutes she had with the love of her life. She shuddered.

Netinu turned and stroked her arm, sending fireworks through her body.

236

A sacrifice! Juma jolted upright. She would need a sacrifice to wake the goddess. If only Netinu's touch wasn't distracting her so much. Her brain insisted there was something they could do. The idea with the sacrifice was a good one if only they had something to sacrifice. The star's kikoi would have been the perfect gift, but they didn't have it any more. And they couldn't offer Kandra's spirit because Vanamate didn't approve of human sacrifices. They didn't bring anything they harvested or something created with their own hands either. Juma pressed her lips together. If they had some sort of material, they could make something on the spot and offer that, but there was nothing but hot air and vaporized water. They couldn't wake the goddess, and it was her fault. If only she could think of something. A tear rolled down her cheek, and her chest felt as if a giant fist squeezed it. She slung her arms around Netinu and pressed her face against his shoulder. She felt his spirit-soul react to her like his body would have. It was so unfair that she would lose him just when she had found him. A sob escaped her.

Netinu kissed her cheek and stroked her hair, trying hard to restrain his irregular breathing. His arms held her, strong and firm, but she felt him shiver. Hugging, they sank to the ground and lay side by side. The vapor surrounding them grew warmer. Soon it would be too hot to breathe down here, too. Juma wondered what would happen to their bodies when their spirit-souls were dead. She huddled closer to Netinu. His cheek pressed against hers, and their tears mingled. She kissed him to reassure him that she would stay with him to the end. Her lips tingled. He kissed her back, and the tingling spread from her lips through her whole body. Every nerve lit with a flame she hadn't known existed.

Heat surged through her spirit-soul, and every fiber of her being longed for Netinu's touch. Why shouldn't she give in to this animalistic desire? Mubuntu had won already. It didn't make much of a difference, did it?

## 24

"❝*I* LOVE YOU MORE THAN I can say," Netinu whispered in her ear.

"I love you too." She pressed her lips on his, opening them slightly. His tongue was warm and comforting in her mouth, and sparks zinged through her head, erasing her already muddled thoughts. The skin on his hands sent jolts of desire through her wherever he touched. Her desire for Netinu raged like a bushfire, swallowing all conscious thought, setting her being aflame. Sucking on Netinu's lip, she arched against him and felt his desire hot against her thigh. >From her heart, her love spread outwards. Soothing, cooling joy flooded through her spirit-soul, dousing Mubuntu's desire and changing it into something just as powerful but different. Juma opened up to Netinu, bared her spirit and her soul, and she felt him do the same. He melted into her, and as their souls touched, she shared his life. She felt his embarrassment as a teenager when Kandra had walked in to him satisfying himself. She knew his longing for his elder sister's approval, and the suffocating cocoon his mother had erected around him to keep him safe. Her knees learned about the scratches and bruises he got whenever he managed to escape her constant surveillance. And her mind shared his fear when he realized how much he loved Juma.

At the same time, she relived the highlights of her own life, revealing them to Netinu in a union more tightly bonded than twins born by the same mother. Mother... her mother... Her spirit-soul tore open at the memory. The loss of her mother had been the end of her small world, and she had erected an impenetrable wall around her pain, her longing and her love all those years ago. Those feelings were still churning inside, and now they escaped in a whirling storm of tears. The flood slammed into the wall and reduced it to rubble. Her heart was raw and bleeding tears, washing away her self defense. Losing her mother had hurt, but giving up the self-made false security of her mental wall hurt even more.

Her arms melted into Netinu's spirit-soul. Her legs and belly and throat and mind followed. They became one.

When They opened their tear-strained eyes, the ring of fire was gone. Their thoughts were clear as a crystal lake. They looked around. Mubuntu lay curled on the ground, unconscious and soaked to the skin. The old witch's cage lay broken on the ground. The bars no longer glowed, and there was no trace of the captive. They hoped Selenta had returned to her body already. Kandra's spirit had been carried away and lay close to the charred remains of the dog-princess Chunte. Vanamate reached out and touched their shoulders.

"Well done, dears." Her voice sounded like a gentle rain in spring. "Now rise."

They got to their feet. Glancing down, They discovered that They were still one.

What will we call us now — Jutinu? Nema? Awe and merriment surged through their combined spirit-souls.

"Names are not important in this realm. Neither is time. But we are aware that it is in your realm. And time in your realm is running out fast." Vanamate pointed to the plain at the foot of the holy mountain.

With surprise, the newly combined spirit-soul saw tiny humans run around, preparing a bonfire. The clarity surprised them. They could see every detail, from the stretcher with Kandra's body to the tears in Jakombe's eyes. Although awake, the chieftess was lying on a stretcher too, holding Kandra's lifeless hand.

"What are they up to?" They asked.

"They will sacrifice your family, hoping to appease Mubuntu." Vanamate cocked her head and pointed at Kandra's stiff form. "It's your sistercousin's doing. She convinced her mother of the necessity to offer human lives to Mubuntu in exchange for rain. And Jakombe believes that her daughter's spirit will return with it. She believes that High Moon is the time for miracles."

The goddess turned and waved for them to follow while the tears never ceased rolling over her cheeks. "Now, for Mubuntu."

They turned with her, but the heat dæmon was gone. The ground below Their feet shook. When They regained Their footing, the tiny humans below ran around in confusion, screaming with fear. Vanamate turned to where Juma and Netinu had come up the mountain. "The fool is trying to wake Father."

Their gaze followed the goddess's outstretched finger. The heat dæmon stood in the cave They had traveled an eternity ago, stomping and dancing on the sleeping god's forehead.

"We must stop him!" They walked over to Kandra's spirit and picked it up.

Vanamate nodded and took Their free hand. What had been supportive if semi-transparent soil just a moment ago turned into nothing. Silently They sank toward the cave. Kandra's small face rested on Their shoulder. Stars sped past and the dancing fire god grew bigger with every breath They took. Soon They landed softly beside him and saw the sleeping god's eyelids flutter. It wouldn't take much longer for him to wake.

Mubuntu laughed. "You can't stop it any more."

"Why are you doing this, brother?" Vanamate reached out for him, but he evaded her arms.

"Humans are supposed to worship us. They should do what we tell them to do." He stomped his father's skin, and waves of fire spread out like ripples in a pond. The Nameless moaned and turned his head slightly.

"They are not our slaves." Vanamate blinked and more tears ran down her cheeks, dousing the flames. "They are free to choose their own way."

"They need me."

Something occurred to the combined spirit-souls, and They spoke before Vanamate could say anything. "We need all of you. We need your passion and your drive to discover new things and question old beliefs. We need Vanamate's steadfast support, her care and unending love. We even need the beginnings and endings Monnatoba brings to give value to our lives."

"Ha!" Mubuntu's laugh didn't sound happy. He spread more flames that Vanamate doused as fast as she could. The sleeping god moved once more.

"Either of you alone is terrifying." They took a step toward Mubuntu. "We need you in balance. There has to be steadiness between life and death, despair and joy, water and fire. Without you, we won't survive. With one of you dominating the others, we won't survive. You are all important to us."

Mubuntu stopped stomping and turned to them. "Why don't you worship us then?"

"We do."

"No, you don't. Occasionally, you praise one of us or the other, but true worship is different." Mubuntu scowled. "A true worshiper gives his heart and soul for us, like Chunte did."

They thought about Chunte's dead spirit. "It didn't do her good."

"She is mine forever." Mubuntu held out his hand, and a transparent resemblance of Chunte appeared at his side. She smiled at him but didn't seem to notice anyone else, and she didn't stumble when the Nameless furrowed his brow once more.

"Worship binds you to the god you worship," Mubuntu said.

"But we don't want to be bound. We are not your slaves. We have to be free to find our own way in the world." They cocked Their head and looked at him. "Maybe you'd have to become human for a while to understand."

Mubuntu was so focused on Them, he didn't notice Vanamate stepping closer. She moved her hands from the top of his head over the contours of his body and a dome of water appeared around him. It swallowed all sound, so they saw Mubuntu scream but couldn't hear him.

"That's what he did with me. He erected a ring of fire around me when I was asleep. Had I been awake, he would never have dared." She wiped her eyes and turned to the sleeping giant. A worried frown marred her beautiful face when she noticed the rapidly moving eyes of the sleeping god. "We need to calm my father. He's very close to waking, and if he does, it will be the end of the world, maybe even our end."

They frowned and set Kandra down. The girl blinked and yawned but stood on her own. They said to Vanamate, "What are you waiting for? Sing him to sleep."

"I can't." Vanamate wrung her hands. "Not when he's this close to waking. He cannot hear me any more. He's too close to your world now, he only can hear humans."

"We are humans. We can sing your song for you."

"You're not fully human. You're spirit-souls."

"We must try. It's our only option anyway."

Vanamate nodded. A drum, a calabash rattle, and a flute appeared from nowhere. She handed the rattle to Kandra and the drum to Them. Then she told Them the words of the song, and put the flute to her lips. A melody floated through the night, filling Them with calmness and soothing Their souls. They blinked away their tiredness and began to drum. Kandra joined Them, giggling as she rattled. Together with Vanamate, They played the melody twice before They began to sing.

"Father, dearest, sleep.

I'm awake to weep.

Now, my rain so gently falls,

Listen, how your name it calls,

Sending dreams to Mother Earth

Soothing every creature's thirst

Go to sleep now, Father, dear.

I will stay with you here."

A sigh echoed through the cave. The god's features relaxed and his eyes stopped moving. For good measure, They sang the song thrice before they stopped. The furrows on the god's forehead had smoothed out and his breathing was regular and deep again. They sighed with relief.

Vanamate smiled at them. "Thank you. Now he'll hear me again. As soon as I return you to your world, I will come back and sing some more for him. He gets so lonely when I'm asleep."

She waved at them, and the caged Mubuntu, Kandra, and They floated up toward the place where the mountain of the human world had its summit. A few heartbeats later, they landed a few steps away from the gate they had used to enter the realm of the gods. With a flick of her wrist, Vanamate dropped the cocoon of water from Mubuntu's face.

"What happened to your hand?"

Mubuntu blushed but didn't answer. Lips pressed tight, he stared at the ground in front of him.

"We've got it. He lost it when he attacked our village witch," they said.

Vanamate's face became stern, and for once her tears stopped. "If you've got part of his being, why did you come all the way up here to free me? You could have ordered him to release me."

"We could?" Their eyes widened.

"Gods don't have bodies the way you do. We're a little similar to your spirit-souls. If you capture part of us, you've captured the whole. With the correct spell, you could have forced him to do anything you wanted him to do. Does none of you know that?"

Dumbstruck, They stared at Vanamate. They hadn't known.

"Not even your witch?"

They shook Their head. If Selenta had known, the drought wouldn't have lasted this long. They smiled. "She'd be interested to learn about it, though."

Vanamate's eyes went wide with surprise. "This knowledge was our most important gift when humans left our world. I wonder what else got lost. Considering your time restraints, it's been a long time since a witch conferred with us."

They swallowed and looked at Mubuntu, who stared at the ground like a sulky child.

Vanamate placed her right hand on her brother's cheek. "I'm sorry to say this, but you'll have to follow them to their world until they return your hand to you."

"I won't go."

"You'll have to." Vanamate turned to them. "Will you promise me not to maltreat him? He's my brother, after all, and I do care for him."

Before they could answer, a pale orb floated toward them, growing bigger the closer it came. Monnatoba's face radiated happiness. When she came close enough, the moon-goddess took human form and hugged her sister. "I'm so glad you're awake and free again. I was terribly worried."

Vanamate's tears returned as she hugged her sister back.

After a while, Monnatoba turned to them. "Since you did so well, I will let one of you return to your world."

Their heart dropped. They had just found each other. How could she demand They should separate again?

Vanamate put an arm on her sister's shoulder. "Don't you see there is only one spirit-soul to release?"

Monnatoba cocked her head and examined Them more closely, then turned to her sister with a frown. "It is made up of two. You merged them to cheat me."

"I did no such thing. Their merging woke me."

"But this hasn't happened since the First People left us."

"Yes, isn't it amazing?" Vanamate beamed at her. "I'm expecting great deeds from Them."

Monnatoba shrugged. "I can wait. Sooner or later, everyone returns to me." She winked at Them. "Now, children, pass through the gate, and you'll return to your bodies automatically. I already dissolved your protective dome."

"What will happen to Mubuntu?" They asked.

"As long as you hold onto his hand, he will have to follow you." Vanamate looked steadily into Their eyes, and They were touched by the sorrow within. "I don't want to see him go, but there is nothing we can do against it."

They turned to look at Mubuntu, who still frowned. "When he learns his lesson, we will let him go. What do you think?"

"I wouldn't let him get off so easily," Monnatoba said. "He's got a secret or two he could teach your people. For example, he knows how to turn select stones into tools that never splinter, withstand enormous heat, and hardly ever dull. They'd be much better than the ones you're using now." She pointed to the stone knife in the belt of Netinu's still body a few feet away on the other side of the gate.

A shiver trickled through Them. Imagine pots that don't crack when they get too hot accidentally. A warm fuzzy feeling filled Them from the stomach outward. Imagine spears that will fell prey at the first shot, knives that don't get blunt when you slice through the meat. Life would be a lot easier for our clan.

They turned back to Vanamate. "We will take him along. Aside from the things he can teach, staying with us for a while might make him see our world differently."

"It might. But don't keep him too long." The goddess blinked to force some more tears from her eyes. It pained Them to see how much she already missed her brother despite his flaming nature. "He is important for the balance of our godly powers."

"Can we go home now?" Kandra looked up at them with wide eyes. "I don't like it here."

They picked her up and looked at Vanamate. "Will her spirit remain like this?"

"It will grow with time, but this is what has to return to her body if anything is to return at all." Vanamate looked at Them with a stern expression. "Remember that water can kill too."

It took Them a moment to understand her meaning. Then They shook Their head. Kandra had been nasty to both of them, but she didn't deserve to die.

"I want my mommy!" Kandra wailed.

They squeezed her gently. "You can fly ahead. Just follow the bond to your body."

"That won't work." Monnatoba pointed to Kandra's navel. "Mubuntu's fire severed the bond. It's impossible for her spirit to find her body."

"Not if the three of us help," Vanamate said to Monnatoba. "If we squeeze her spirit into a spiritual womb, Mubuntu can burn it back into her body at High Moon."

"They won't make it back to their village in time. Also, I wonder why we should help. Kandra wasn't very friendly to her brother and his girl." Monnatoba glared at the child who hid her face in Their shoulder.

"She belongs to our family, and she suffered enough in Mubuntu's fire." They stood fast, bearing the goddess's gaze. "She has punished herself enough. There is no need to make her pay more."

"Spoken like a true leader." Monnatoba bowed a little and smiled. "Let's get to work." She took Vanamate's hand. They put Kandra down on the ground again and held her shoulders. The child-spirit trembled when the two goddesses stepped closer, reaching out with glowing hands. Warm light and water flowed over Kandra — and she shrunk. She grew so small They could hold her in one hand. The glow intensified. They blinked. When Their vision cleared, a brown nut lay on Their palm.

"Now it'll be up to Mubuntu to get it back into her body." Monnatoba shoved her brother through the gate. "Remember that he'll have to put the nut into her at High Moon or it won't work."

Gurgling, Mubuntu fell to the ground whimpering with pain. Blood flowed from the stump of his arm. He curled into a ball and hugged his arm.

"Hurry. He can't help you if he dies there. Place his hand on his arm right now, and it will attach. You can take some of his hair instead. Burn it when you decide to set him free." Vanamate shooed them away.

"By the way, I arranged a little help for your speedy return," Monnatoba said and giggled. "I'm sure you'll like it. Now, hurry."

They obeyed and ran toward the gate holding the nut in Their hand. Behind Them, They heard Monnatoba say, "Juma asked for her mother to visit. I wonder why they didn't request your permission to marry as a reward."

"I told you, humans will always surprise us," Vanamate answered. "Also, I'm sure we'll see them ag—"

## 25

BLINDING LIGHT SHOT THROUGH THEIR veins.

With a gasp, Juma sat up. She knew Netinu was doing the same. She even felt the small nut he held in his hand. Kandra's spirit. Hurriedly she pulled Mubuntu's hand from the bag on her belt and grabbed Netinu's knife. Her mother's voice blurred in her ears, and she evaded her hug as she hurried to the wounded god's side. She pressed the hand to the bleeding stump. A seam of light traveled along the cut, leaving a thin red line behind. When it was half way around the wrist, Juma let the hand go. She grabbed Mubuntu's curly red hair and cut a generous strand. He winced, but sat up soon to move his fingers. The hand had reattached without so much as a scar.

"Thank you," he said.

Juma nodded. He looked more human than he had ever before. His red hair struck up in disheveled curls, and his dark skin had wrinkles around the eyes and on his throat. He was muscular and seemed middle-aged. Juma was sure that no one would be able to guess his real origins.

Selto stepped beside her, knife at the ready, but he didn't ask where the red-haired man had come from. He just stood there, ready to protect Juma.

"You will follow us to our village," she said to Mubuntu. "We'll pretend to have met you on the way back from Vanamate." Before he could answer, she got up and turned to her mother. Wordlessly, Juma sank into her arms.

"I am so sorry I didn't manage to stop Netinu from following you." Her mother's arms formed a cocoon of love around Juma. "But I'm happy to see both of you back safely."

"So am I." Juma sighed. "Will you accompany us to the village?"

Her mother shook her head. "My work is done. I will have to return to Monnatoba, and you will have to accompany the rain to the plains." She pointed skywards, where big clouds gathered over the mountaintop. Flashes of lightning zigzagged through the turmoil, and drizzling droplets of water sprayed down on them. "Vanamate bound it to you, but you'll have to hurry, or it will turn into a thunderstorm."

Juma hugged her mother again. "Monnatoba promised you can visit us."

"If that's true, I will come as soon as I can. Now, run!" She pushed Juma gently toward the path that led down the mountain. Juma felt as if an eternity had passed since they traveled uphill. She reached out for Netinu, and he hurried to her side.

Mubuntu rose and held his face up to the spray. "There are so many sensations I've never felt before. Can I follow you at an easier rate?"

"We'll need him at High Moon, remember?" Netinu said to Juma.

Before she could answer, Selto took the god's arm, his knife still ready to strike. "I'll make sure he'll be there."

Juma and Netinu nodded. Hand in hand, they raced down the path. Mubuntu, Selto, and the clouds followed them. Glancing over her shoulder, Juma saw her mother disappear. Her heart contracted but she forced herself to remember Monnatoba's promise. She would see her mother again, soon. They ran as fast as they could through the night. The moon hung full over the horizon. It wouldn't take much longer to reach its highest point. Juma remembered the preparation of the sacrifice they had observed from above. No matter how fast they ran, they wouldn't make it before High Moon.

Netinu squeezed her hand and sped up. They flew downhill, miraculously missing holes or stumbling stones on their path. Behind them, Mubuntu laughed with delight, but they didn't turn to look back.

Soon Juma's breath became ragged, and her side hurt with stitches. Every breath burned like a lung full of fire. She also sensed

Netinu's discomfort, but her beloved didn't complain. She gazed at his features — and slammed into a gray wall.

Before she could recover, the elephant wrapped its trunk around her and lifted her off the ground. It turned and set her down on a zebra, then repeated his action with Netinu and Selto. It briefly hesitated when it smelled Mubuntu, but then put him on a zebra too. The instant they sat, the zebras raced off. They must be the help Monnatoba promised.

Juma clung to her animal's short mane, trying not to slip off, realizing that unlike humans, zebras were made for running. The rush of air on her face brought tears to her eyes. She blinked them away and realized they had already passed the valley where the river had been blocked. A little later, the zebras stopped, panting heavily. Four new zebras were waiting for them, so they dismounted and climbed onto the fresh animals. Off they flew again. Again and again, Juma glanced over her shoulder. Clouds were growing fast behind them. They rolled down the mountainside like black, billowy smoke. Slightly slower than the zebras, they followed the riders. Their mounts gave it all they had. Whenever the zebras grew tired, fresh ones were waiting. Juma would have liked to thank each single one of them, but time was running out. They didn't get a break, and playing her drum was out of the question as long as they were racing toward the village. She was too busy holding on.

The moon climbed faster than she liked, but the distance to the village shrank visibly as they traveled with the helpful zebras. As close to the village as the zebras dared, they stopped. Juma dismounted, pulled out her drum and finally thanked the pair that had taken them the last stretch. "Don't forget to pass on our thanks," she drummed.

"Monnatoba friend." Her mount rubbed its forehead against her arm. "Rain coming — thank you."

Netinu patted his zebra, gazing over the striped body at the village. "It looks deserted."

"We know where they are." Juma hung the drum back onto her belt and turned. With long strides, she ran along the way to the place where the witch had won Mubuntu's hand. Netinu ran beside her. Twice Juma looked back to see if Mubuntu was still following. Both times Selto was dragging him along, swearing and sweating. They'd probably arrive a little later than Juma and Netinu, but they'd make it before High Moon. Relieved, Juma ran faster. Although the ride on the zebras had rested her somewhat, she was still winded. More than once she stumbled, but Netinu helped her to keep her footing. Hand in hand, they neared the plain where the clan waited for High Moon.

When they reached the mountain-encased plain, Juma put her hands on her knees, breathing hard to recover. The moon was nearly overhead, but for what she had to say, she would need her breath. When she had recovered a little, they walked toward the villagers. Huddled in a tight group and staring at a figure ahead of them, no one had noticed them yet. Unfortunately, they stood with their backs to the holy mountain, so they didn't see the clouds rolling toward them. Juma and Netinu rounded the group to get their attention, but they focused too closely on the scene before their faces.

Jakombe sat on a stool in front of a big pile of timber, grass, and dried dung. Her face was ashen, her cheeks sunken. Tolobe, Sundera, Lomba, Juma's father, and Morva with her husband were tied together and stood on top of the pile. On a stretcher beside Jakombe lay Kandra.

"You do understand, don't you?" Jakombe's face looked desparate. "Netinu won't return, so she is all I have left. Please say that you understand."

None of the bound people answered her. Juma wanted to cry out, but Netinu beat her to it.

"But I did come back, Mother."

At the same time, the gathered tribe began to sing the song of High Moon, drowning out his words. Jakombe took a torch from one of the men in the front and threw it onto the pile of burning materials.

"Gods!" She raised her arms to the sky. "Please give me back my daughter. Please, Mubuntu, ease your burning and release Vanamate's tears. We beg you to accept this offering. We will…"

"That's enough." Juma walked to her side and turned to the crowd, while Netinu picked up the kikoi that covered Kandra and slapped at the flames.

"Will you pay attention to the world around you?" Juma pointed to the mass of clouds that had nearly reached them. The first gusts of wind howled over the plain, driving a steady drizzle with it. The people turned and stared with awe at the coming rain.

"We woke Vanamate like I promised." Juma spoke calmly to her tribe, knowing that Netinu was already cutting the bonds of her family. "You know full well that Vanamate would never approve of human sacrifice."

"What about Kandra? I want my daughter back." Jakombe stood up on wobbly legs, digging her fingers into Juma's arm. "She will return, won't she?" Her eyes were red, and the springy joy she usually emitted had left her.

Juma touched her cheek gently. "We brought her spirit with us, and the gods did everything in their power to reunite body, soul and spirit. But there's no guarantee."

"I never told her how much I loved her and how proud I am of her." Jakombe sniffed and looked at Netinu. "I told you, didn't I?"

"No." Netinu's face was a mask, but Juma felt the knot of anxiety in his stomach. "But you made it pretty clear that you cared about me — a bit too clear, sometimes. Kandra thought you preferred me."

Jakombe lowered her gaze wordlessly.

"Stop dawdling." Selto's angry voice carried through the night as he dragged Mubuntu toward Juma. "It is High Moon."

"Thank you for your help." Juma smiled at him, and then looked at Mubuntu. "You know what to do?"

Mubuntu nodded and crouched down beside the stretcher with Kandra's body. Sniffling, Jakombe crouched on the other side. Tears and rainwater left tracks in the dust on her face. Netinu handed the nut with Kandra's spirit to the human god. As carefully as possible, he cracked the shell with his fingers, and light spilled through the gap. He placed the cracked nut on Kandra's body where her heart thumped and placed both hands over it. The light intensified, and sweat ran over his forehead.

"You need to help," he said to Juma.

She put her hands on top of his. The spirit was struggling to get free. Juma felt the barrier Mubuntu tried to build around it and began to hum. Her magic flowed into his hands, strengthening his shield. The only direction the spirit could go now was into the body. Hopefully, it will reattach. Jakombe will go mad if Kandra stays like this for the rest of her life.

Juma closed her eyes and sang to the spirit. She told it about the beauty of life, the joy of feeling the sun on your skin and the rain on your face, the dances in the moonlight. She sang about harvesting and planting, birth and death, and joy and sorrow. With a snap, the spirit left the dome of hands. Juma opened her eyes and looked at Kandra. Had the spirit escaped or did it truly settle?

"No wonder you managed to free Vanamate." Mubuntu stared at her in awe. "Your magic is the most powerful I have encountered in quite a while."

Juma blushed at the compliment.

"Mama!" Kandra sat up, eyes sparkling. "I've slept so well. And there were these nice ladies, and they made me real tiny and put me in a golden room. And Juma was there too. And Netinu. Oh, I missed you so much." She flung her arms around her mother's neck.

Jakombe sat frozen. Her mouth stood wide open and her eyes swam with tears. Juma signaled Mubuntu and Netinu it was time to leave the two alone.

She turned back to the crowd. Taken aback by the awe on her tribe members' faces, she searched for the right words.

Netinu came to her rescue. Taking Juma's hand, he called out, "Let's celebrate High Moon like we always do. This time, we will dance Monnatoba's and Vanamate's praise together."

Of course it wasn't as easy as that. Everybody pelted them with questions until the real downpour began. It finally rained. Heavily. Like a sheet of water, the rain fell from the sky, soaking everyone and everything in mere instants. Everybody ran for cover. Jakombe barely managed to grab a couple of men to carry her daughter's stretcher. Juma let the others take the lead and followed more slowly through the rainstorm. The water ran over her body, washing away the last traces of the dirt her skin had accumulated on her travels. She lifted her face to the sky and opened her mouth to catch the water.

Netinu laughed and took her hands. "Come on. Let's dance."

Stomping, laughing and singing, they danced through the rain. The closer they danced to the village, the more people fell in. The first to join them were the children. Giggling and laughing, they reached for the rain. Soon more and more of the grown-ups joined them.

Even Selenta, the witch, left the healer's hut to sit in the rain. Frail and tired, she lifted her face. Juma wondered how much of the wetness was tears, but she was glad that the witch's spirit had returned to her body without problems. As she whirled around, the witch opened her eyes and nodded to her. A shiver of pride ran through Juma's body. So this was how it felt when you did something good for the tribe.

She reached for the sky and allowed Netinu to whirl her around. By now, everyone had come and was either dancing or sitting in the rain, enjoying it. Only Jakombe didn't show up.

They danced until the light grew brighter near dawn. Then they went back to their village. Beside the gate, Mubuntu waited for Juma and Netinu. When he saw them, he bowed stiffly.

"I decided to call myself Moboon," he said.

"The dark man? Nice choice." Netinu smiled. "Come in. I'll show you the guest hut."

Juma added, "And be at the chieftess's hut right after the midday meal. We will have to introduce you."

Mubuntu nodded. As he followed Netinu, Juma saw him look around with wide eyes. He seemed like someone in a wonderland. Shaking her head with amusement, she went to bed. She was so tired her eyes closed the minute she settled down. The other girls' babbling whirled away in her dreams.

She slept long into the day. When Sundera woke her, it was already time for the midday meal.

"I never got the chance to thank you yesterday." Her friend hugged her. "By the way, Jakombe would like to talk to you."

Juma shrugged and grinned so much it hurt. "How is Selenta?"

"A bit weak from not eating for so long, but she'll recover."

Juma decided to see the old woman as soon as possible. There were so many things they needed to talk about. She put on her spare kikoi and left the hut. It was still raining gently. During a hearty meal, she caught up on what had happened in her absence. She listened to Lomba recount the villagers' attack on the hut after the strange invisible barrier had vanished, their capture and the despair they had felt when they were prepared for sacrifice. All the while, her father sat beside her with a hand on her shoulder — stoic, silent. She felt the love and strength his grip emanated.

Tolobe kneeled in the wet sand in front of her. "Juma, since you're the last female in our family, it is up to you to tell Sundera and me how long we'll have to wait for our wedding." He bowed his head.

Juma laughed. "Anytime you want. It'll be great to have her as a brotherwife."

Tolobe got up and threw his arms around Sundera. Their eyes glowed with happiness as they hugged.

"There is one more thing I need to do." Juma kissed her brothers' and her father's cheeks before she left to meet Jakombe.

Netinu waited outside the chieftess's hut in the rain with the human Mubuntu at his side.

"Mother is disturbed. Don't be too hard on her." He rested his hand lightly on her shoulder and pushed the blanket aside that covered the door.

Juma went in and the men followed. Jakombe sat on a stool beside the fireplace, watching Kandra play with small carved animals. Whenever the girl giggled, a smile crossed the chieftess's face.

"She's happy like that." Looking up at Juma, her eyes were filled with wonder. "Why did I never see that? I should have—"

"Don't." Juma put a hand on her aunt's shoulder. "Should have, if only, and all those words will not change what happened. Be there for her now and all will be good."

Tears shot in Jakombe's eyes and she nodded wordlessly.

Juma pointed to Mubuntu's human form. "This is Moboon. We met him on our journey. He is..." she searched for the right word. "...knowledgeable. He can teach our tribe some new skills if you allow him to stay."

"He saved my daughter's life. Of course he can stay." Jakombe blinked away her tears.

Outside the hut, Moboon wiped the rain from his hair and bowed to Juma. "I am sorry I caused so much trouble. You were right. Being human changes everything. I will have a lot to tell my sisters when I return home." His longing was as clear as if he'd written it onto his face.

Juma leaned her head against Netinu's shoulder. "I'm glad you're no longer an enemy."

Moboon smiled and bowed once more. "Since I am to stay here and teach your tribe to forge better tools, I want to ask permission for courting Kandra."

Netinu frowned, and Moboon hastened to explain. "I am responsible for the state she's in. Her spirit is that of a child now, but she's in the body of a grown woman. Some people might be dangerous for her, and I want to protect her from those. She will need someone to be at her side, someone who helps her spirit grow. When she followed me, she wasn't worshiping me. Not like Chunte. She loved me. And I rewarded it in the worst possible way. Let me make amends. I promise I will never harm her. Maybe I will even begin to understand what love means to you humans."

Netinu gazed into his eyes for a while, then nodded.

Juma looked up at Netinu. "He learned a lot in this short time already, didn't he?"

He smiled at her. "Do we dare?"

Wordlessly she pulled the hair she had cut off Moboon's head from the bag on her belt and handed it to the god. "You are free to go. You do not have to teach the tribe anything, but if you really mean what you said, you're most welcome to stay."

Gingerly, Moboon took the strand. His jaw opened and closed as he searched for words. He reattached the lock of hair and bowed deeply. "I will get to know your tribe a bit better, and then you can help me set up a place where I can teach them how to melt stones and turn them into tools and weapons."

"The chieftess will see to that when she is herself again," Juma said.

Moboon bowed a last time and left. Juma and Netinu waited. After a while, Jakombe left the hut in full regalia. She hugged Netinu and Juma.

"Thank you for everything." She spoke quietly, as if her voice wasn't strong enough to carry the words she needed to say. "I don't know if your father has told you, but I have never truly been chieftess. It was your mother's office, and she never gave it up. I just got so used to being her replacement that I set my aspirations too high. I wanted to see Kandra in my office and never considered your claim seriously. I am sorry." She took off the red cloak, the crown of wheat, and the necklace of potted pearls and held them and her staff out to Juma. "You have proven to be a much better chieftess than I ever was."

Juma took a step backward, not sure what to say. She only needed to reach out and accept the cloak, the crown, the necklace, and the staff, and her dream would come true. So why did she hesitate?

"I have been informed that Selenta is recovering fast. She'll be fit enough to strip you of your magic in a few days."

"Strip me of my magic? I never thought that could be done." Juma's voice trembled, and Netinu's heart fluttered like a caged bird. Right now, it was unnerving to feel his emotions so plainly. He didn't want her to change, which fed right into her own fears.

"She did it for Kandra, when she was a baby. I wanted my daughter to become chieftess, not witch." Jakombe still held out the regalia.

"Who is going to train as village witch then?" There was an edge of panic in Juma's voice.

"Our tribe decided to merge with Chunte's since they lost their chieftess and lands, and they've got a boy who seems promising."

"A male village witch?"

"If it has to be." Jakombe shrugged.

"Why can't the chieftess be the witch too?" Juma wanted to run away from this decision.

Netinu said, "You only need to look at Chunte to understand. Too much power corrupts."

Juma looked at him, then at Jakombe. "I… I…" She couldn't make up her mind. Was her dream really worth giving up her magic? But if she didn't become chieftess, Netinu would marry someone else, and as a witch, she couldn't marry at all. The ground below her feet seemed to drop away. Netinu reached out and steadied her before her knees could buckle.

"I will always be your man. No other woman will ever take your place." His gaze bored steadily into her eyes. "No one will take that away from us."

Juma felt the warmth of his love wiping away her worry. He would be there for her whatever she chose to do. His reassurance freed her mind to evaluate the rewards and shortcomings of her choices.

As village witch, she would not have the special social status a chieftess had. She'd never wear red. But as long as she did a good job, people would treat her with respect. She could keep her magic and peek into the gods' realm again if she had to. She'd be able to help others — and she'd be good at it, as she had proven. The choice would be so easy if it weren't for Netinu.

As chieftess, she would be able to help others too, but she'd also have to organize village life. People would treat her respectfully even if she did her job poorly. And she wouldn't even have her magic to rely on. Was she really cut out to lead the whole tribe? What about Chunte's people? She remembered how lost she had felt during the attack of the river people. Sundera had known much better what needed to be done.

Her heart had decided but it hurt. It pained Netinu too, which made it even harder. With a sad smile, she turned to Jakombe. The chieftess stood beside the hut, silently waiting for an answer.

"I know how hard the last few days were for you," Juma said. "But I am not cut from the right material. As much as I wanted to, I wouldn't make a good chieftess. But I will make a very good village witch."

The two women stared at each other in silence. Juma felt Netinu's sorrow in her heart. It consoled her that the bond between them would never end.

Sundera came running. Water sprayed from the puddles with every step. Since no one spoke when she reached the group, she addressed the chieftess. "Chunte died. The men who carried her here just informed me that her body ceased to breathe. Her spirit never returned to it. Shall we prepare a funeral? I think a pyre would be most appropriate."

Jakombe opened her mouth to speak, but Juma beat her to it. "That will be your decision. Congratulations on becoming the next chieftess."

Sundera's jaw dropped, as did Jakombe's.

When Sundera regained her voice, she objected loudly. "Are you crazy? You can't give me your place. I'd never be happy."

Jakombe wiped away her arguments. "She decided to become the next village witch, and that leaves you as the next chieftess in training."

"Becoming the next witch will make me happier than anything in the world," Juma managed to lie without blushing.

"But I don't want to marry Netinu." Sundera's gaze pleaded with Juma, but again, Jakombe had the answer.

"You don't have to. Since Juma's mother never gave up her office, the true chieftess's first-born son is Tolobe."

Sundera slapped both hands over her mouth, and her eyes betrayed her.

"Of course, the Council of elders will have to agree to this solution," Jakombe said. "But I don't see why they shouldn't. Are you sure this is for the best?" She looked at Juma.

Juma nodded. "My magic is all I need. And it'll be fun to work with Selenta again. She's got so much more to teach me."

"In that case, let us get the Council together, Sundera. The earlier we can start to train you, the better." Jakombe threw the cloak back over her shoulder, took the rest of her insignia, linked arms with Sundera, and marched her toward the village center. Juma leaned against Netinu's shoulder, and he put an arm around her waist.

"I cannot and will not give you up."

"You will have my love to the end of days." Juma leaned into his embrace. She was neither going to give up hope nor Netinu. "We're one in spirit and soul already, and we've done the gods a favor. I am sure they will find a way that will allow us to marry. When things have calmed down a bit, we'll go and ask them."

Netinu's anxiety abated. Together they stood, cocooned in their hope.

"This is going to be interesting," he said. "With a god in the village, and a chieftess in training being best friends with the witch in training, no one will harm this tribe for quite a while."

"Times are changing. They might even see us all working together, regardless of gender, age, or social status." She smiled up at him. "That's all fine by me. But a male village witch? Really…?"

# World Vision®

## About Juma and World Vision

Many years ago, my husband and I decided to help a child in need. So we contacted World Vision Germany.

World Vision is an organization helping people like us find projects to support that need it the most. Aside from projects teaching people to help themselves, where sponsors like my husband and I can support a godchild with a small monthly sum, World Vision also does its best to help people, especially children, in crisis regions.

Since my parents already had a great experience with this organization, it was the one we contacted. After a very short time, they assigned little Jane Juma from Kenya to us. By now, she's quite big already, is good at school, and doesn't look hungry any more. She writes regularly, although letters to and from Kenya take quite a while.

When I started planning this story, I knew immediately how I wanted to call my main character. Of course I first asked Jane Juma if she had any objections, but she didn't mind. However, using her name doesn't mean that the Juma in my book resembles my goddaughter in any way. I took great care to create a character that is independent and stands on its own. I very much hope that our Juma will enjoy reading about her when she finally gets the book.

If you want to help children in need and their families, you can find plenty of information about World Vision on their international Homepage: www.wvi.org/

Get a free eBook of the series

TREASURES RETOLD

If you liked this book you can stay informed about new releases by Katharina Gerlach. Just leave your eMail-address at this link: http://www.katharinagerlach.com/readers

As a little thank-you-present, you'll get "The Dwarf and the Twins: Snow White and Rose Red" to your Inbox right after you confirmed your eMail address.

*Once upon a time in a world where magic and technology collide with unexpected consequences...*

When Martin helps a pregnant woman to flee from the king's men, he doesn't know that the twins she bears will change his solitary life forever.

What if the Brother's Grimm misunderstood the dwarf in the original tale of "Snow White and Rose Red"?

*The book includes a bonus story and the original fairy tale.*

## Scotland's Guardians
### with myths and legends from the Scottish Highlands

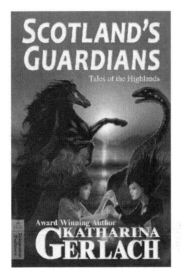

A face without a nose watches Bryanna from a window in an Edinburgh townhouse, and a hairy hand waves. A Brownie! She blinks and shakes her head. Impossible. They only exist in books. But the Brownie doesn't remain the only legendary creature she meets on her way home. Maybe I'm hallucinating, she thinks, and decides to talk to her dad.

However, he gets kidnapped by a woman whose scent seems surprisingly familiar to Bryanna. Without hesitation, she follows them and lands smack dab in the middle of the adventure of her life. The world she faces now is murderously dangerous. And if she survives the journey, she seems doomed to kill her father for his secret.

ISBN 978-3-95681-010-7

also available as eBook and – from Winter 2015 – as audiobook

# Swordplay - Gendarmerie Magique I
## Fantasy Murder Mystery

*CSI with magic but without the gore*

Despite her obvious lack of magical talent, nineteen year old Moira Bellamie apprentices with the Gendarmerie Magique, the magic police. She puts all her effort into solving a burglary at the National Museum where antique weapons have been stolen, to keep the hard won job. Falling for her partner Druidus wasn't part of the plan.

When more and more people are murdered with one of the stolen weapons, Moira must tame uncontrollable magic, or the people she cares for will die, her partner first and foremost.

ISBN 978-3-95681-016-9
also available as eBook

# URCHIN KING
## Historical Fantasy

Paul loves his surrogate family, a group of street urchins. They take him in when he is banned from the loving embrace of his foster mother at age five. During the next ten years they learn together how to blend in, how to become invisible, how to climb the steep walls of the nobles' gardens, and how to vanish in the narrow alleys behind the capital's timber frame houses.

Together, they survive.

But on Mother's Day, when the king begs the goddess for a miracle, Paul's life changes forever. Without his friends he must face new danger ... the life of a crown prince.

And if the king discovers his secret, the executioner's ax waits for him.

ISBN 978-3-95681-003-9
also available as eBook

Made in the USA
Lexington, KY
19 May 2016